# THE WITCHES' BLADE

## ALSO BY A.K. MULFORD

The Five Crowns of Okrith
*The High Mountain Court*
*The Witches' Blade*
*The Rogue Crown*

The Okrith Novellas
*The Witch of Crimson Arrows*
*The Witch Apothecary*
*The Witchslayer*

# THE WITCHES' BLADE

## THE FIVE CROWNS OF OKRITH, BOOK TWO

### A.K. MULFORD

**HARPER Voyager**
*An Imprint of* HarperCollins*Publishers*

THE WITCHES' BLADE. Copyright © 2022 by A.K. Mulford. Excerpt from *The Rogue Crown* © 2022 by A.K. Mulford. All rights reserved. Printed in the United States of America. No part of this book may be used or reproduced in any manner whatsoever without written permission except in the case of brief quotations embodied in critical articles and reviews. For information, address HarperCollins Publishers, 195 Broadway, New York, NY 10007.

HarperCollins books may be purchased for educational, business, or sales promotional use. For information, please email the Special Markets Department at SPsales@harpercollins.com.

Harper Voyager and design are trademarks of HarperCollins Publishers LLC.

Map © Kristen Timofeev

Originally published as *The Witches' Blade* in New Zealand in 2021 by A.K. Mulford

Library of Congress Cataloging-in-Publication Data has been applied for.

ISBN 978-0-06-329166-9 (paperback)
ISBN 978-0-06-329683-1 (hardcover library edition)

24 25 26 27 28  LBC  9 8 7 6 5

*To all those with stories in their hearts waiting to be told.*
*Keep going xx*

# CONTENT WARNING

This book contains themes of violence, torture, addiction, and loss, as well as some sexually explicit scenes.

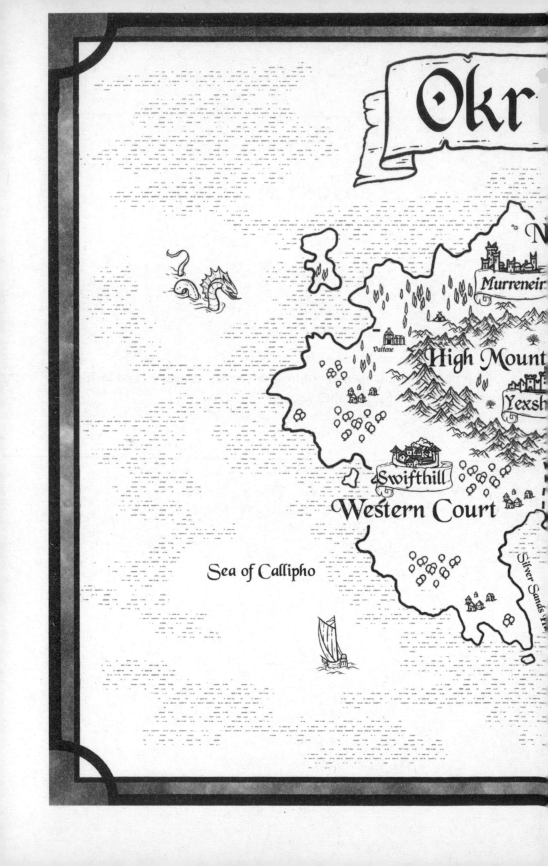

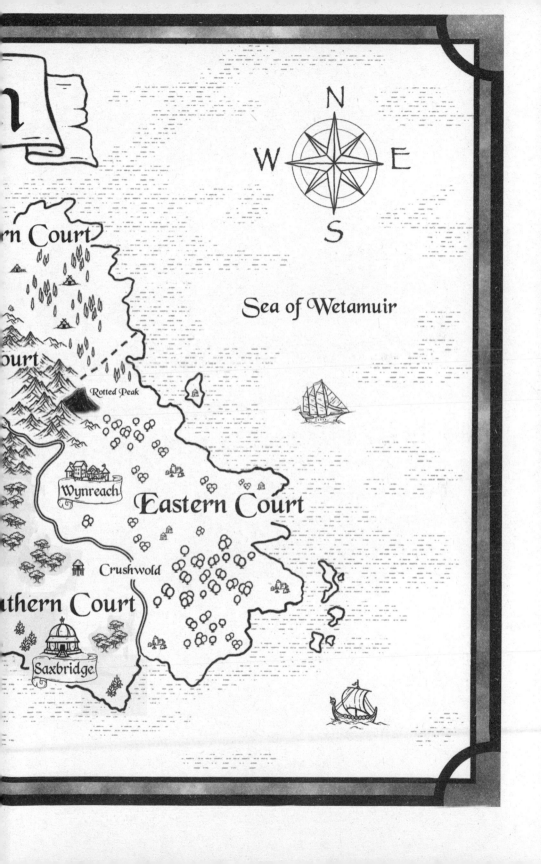

# CHAPTER ONE

**T**he song of death sang in her ears. She hacked and sliced as the coppery tang of blood sprayed through the air, the white-hot power flowing through her veins like molten gold. The screams and sobs faded away until Rua only heard the call of the Immortal Blade, begging to spill more blood. Fear and delight warred together. Joy and sorrow clashed in her mind. She could not hold it all.

Powerful arms encircled her, hauling her back against a hard chest. Hot breath pressed against her ear as a voice whispered, "Gods. Ruadora, stop."

The Witchslayer.

Of all the pleas, his was the one she should have ignored. But his deep timbre spoke down to her very gut and her grip on the blade loosened.

Warped air clearing, she peered over the throng of dead and dying. The wrath of Baba Morganna still moved the earth, the walls crumbling down from every side. Arms tightened around her, heavy breath in her hair, but it felt so distant as she scanned the carnage. Amongst the gore, her gaze snagged on him again, the reason she grabbed the ancient sword now in her hands—Raffiel. Her brother's eyes stared lifelessly toward the sky as the ground shook.

Their interactions over the years had always been awkward and stilted, but the opportunity for a stronger relationship was cruelly snuffed out. It was her fault. All of it. She should have seized the weapon sooner. She could have saved him and given herself the chance to be a better sibling . . . but she hesitated. The red witches would be so disappointed.

She was not a warrior witch—she was a fae princess frightened of what she could become with the death blade in her grasp. As she looked down to the sanguine rubies embedded in the hilt of her sword, the power in them tingled like static in the air. The fear that she had made the wrong decision doused ice on her flames.

Gasping, she yanked herself free from the Witchslayer's arms. Cold bled into her at the absence of his hold. The son of the Northern King stood stock-still behind her, surveying the slaughter. He had called her Ruadora even though she was glamoured . . . How had he known she was the High Mountain Princess?

The magic of her glamour itched, begging her to return to her fae form, as the echoes of the battle thrummed through her. Only a few quaking Northerners remained alive. The true horror was not the sea of blood, but the utter anguish on the survivors' faces. How many of those bodies were the victims of her blade? Acid burned up her throat. This was not the warrior the red witches trained her to be. She hadn't looked her enemies in the eye as she hacked them apart.

Baba Morganna halted her vengeful maelstrom of debris as she stared across the dais. The deafening rumble of rock gave way to the keening wails of those who survived. Following her line of sight, Rua spotted her sister lying limp and bloody on the white marble floor. Agonized, panicked faces gathered around her, but their eyes all clung to one person. The witch's long copper hair was tied back in a braid, a serene calm over her face as she smiled down at Remy and lifted her dagger.

Rua squeezed her eyes shut. She knew what was going to happen. The *midon brik* was the most powerful gift a witch could give, swapping her fate for another. Stomach churning, Rua's hands shook as she stared at the circle, but Remy's face was obscured. So many people gathered around her sister—people willing to exchange their life for hers. And then there was Rua, a lone beast with a sword. The battle had ended, and yet, her heartbeat ratcheted up into her throat until damning tears welled. She couldn't let them see it. Whirling, she snatched the Immortal Blade's scabbard off the table behind her. The High Mountain crowns fell to the ground in her haste, but they went unnoticed, everyone watching the *midon brik.*

Only one set of emerald green eyes tracked her as Rua fled. She hung her head as she ran, not wanting to face Baba Morganna as she surged past the High Priestess. They had trained Rua as a warrior, to stand and fight, to show no weakness, and she had always failed them. Her heart was too soft to be a red witch and too rigid to be a royal fae. Running faster, she shoved bodies and rubble aside to escape the room. She could not let them witness the tears that would betray her or watch as she retched the bile from her stomach.

She knew it made her the darkest sort of soul that she didn't turn back to see if her sister lived or died.

~

The smell of blood clung to the Immortal Blade, though its steel had never touched its victims' skin. Over the sound of her steady footsteps, Rua still heard their screams, pleas for mercy falling on deaf ears as the roar of magic had pulsed through her muscles. The whoosh of the blade striking its next casualty echoed in her mind. One day had passed, and the battle continued to rage inside her.

Her sister's guard, Bri, led Rua through open hallways filled with snow. The castle was in ruins, few rooms remaining intact. She had watched Remy's caravan trail off into the distance, frozen as she wondered if she had made the wrong choice to stay behind. Before she could yield to the mounting dread, she was called away to a council meeting.

Skirting another pile of rubble, she rubbed her hand anxiously down her thigh. Baba Morganna's destruction marked every corner of the Northern palace. The Immortal Blade tugged on her flimsy belt, a reminder of the power she now possessed. Horror bled through her pride. She had already spilled so much blood.

*Gods. Ruadora, stop.*

Rua's gaze flitted to the ground as scattered shards of glass crunched beneath her boots. Morganna practiced wrath and restraint in equal measure. She knew when to stop. Failing to master that control was what Rua feared most. Were it not for the warm whispers of an evil man, how many more heads would have rolled?

They arrived in a makeshift council chamber. Bri opened the door for Rua, allowing her to enter like a Queen, head held high. The room was little more than a closet, haphazardly arranged. By the far wall, Renwick and another elderly fae sat, another three gathering around them, as they surveyed papers and scrolls strewn across the table. They were all fae males with pale Northern complexions and aging silver hair. Watching her with cold gazes, they appraised her appearance— her dark, wavy hair, her freckled brown skin. Their eyes lingered on her attire. Bri had given her a jacket, but she looked like a child, swimming in clothes too big for her.

"You aren't wearing the Northern crown?" Rua asked, cringing at how her mouth garbled the Ific words. Of the three languages of Okrith, Ific was the one she spoke the least, even though it was the common tongue.

Renwick wore a silver circlet, a serpent coiling around the band. He sat resplendent in a velvet green jacket with golden detailing, making his eyes shine like emeralds from his pale face. Beneath the thin window, a perfect halo of light encircled him, highlighting his ash-blond hair.

The councilors stiffened, one scowling at her outright as she stared at his circlet.

Hand drifting to her hip, her fingers traced the golden letters carved around the scabbard: *Each strike a blessing or a curse.* It was written in Mhenbic, the witches' ancient language—a language Rua knew better than her own native tongue, Yexshiri. Growing up with the red witch coven gave her their sharp accent. What would her parents, the late King and Queen of the High Mountain Court, think of their youngest child: a fae princess who spoke like a witch?

"Princess Ruadora. Welcome," Renwick replied curtly, pulling her from her swirling thoughts. "I am having a new crown made."

"A new crown for a new King," the eldest councilor said with an approving nod.

It felt wrong to hear of another King Vostemur so soon. Even as the blood was being washed off the floors, Renwick had pushed for a coronation. It made his intentions all the more suspicious.

"Princess, these are my councilors." Renwick gestured around the room to introduce each of the four elderly fae. "Romberg, Berecraft, Fowler, and Barnes."

Rua noted that Fowler, the tallest and widest, did not acknowledge her other than sneering in disgust. Of course he would sneer—she was a High Mountain princess bringing the Immortal Blade into their meeting.

"There were twelve, but . . ." Renwick's eyes darted to the ruby hilt of her sword.

*But Rua had killed them.*

Bolts of golden lightning still coursed through her, beckoning her back to the blade. It was a force like no other—not the burning muscles of fae power or the buzzing dizziness of witch magic. Underneath that deceptive feeling of euphoria lurked something primordial, a promise of unfettered power. She was finally someone worthy of being feared.

"They were loyal to your father, Your Majesty," the seated councilor, Berecraft, uttered in a scratchy voice. Given his proximity and the way he spoke, Rua wondered if Berecraft was the Head Councilor.

"Indeed." Renwick frowned. He turned his sharp gaze to Rua and said, "We were just discussing plans to travel north."

Rua studied the map on the table, held open with rocks in each corner. It showed the entire continent of Okrith. The Northern, Western, Southern, and Eastern Courts circled a crown of tall mountains, the High Mountain Court, her homeland. Unceremoniously crossed out with an inky black X was the capital city of Yexshire. Rua hadn't stepped foot into Yexshire since she was five years old. She had grown up hidden in the forests northeast of the capital along with the red witches who escaped the former Northern King's grasp. They would need to draw a new map. Yexshire would rise again—her sister would make sure of it.

"With all due respect, Your Majesty, your uncle is still out there. Do you think travel northward is wise?" the smallest man, Barnes, said.

"Your uncle?" Rua asked.

Renwick clenched his jaw for a moment before he spoke. "My uncle is the real threat in the North. Killing my father has only created more enemies for your court, Princess."

A bristling, icy wind blew through the window, rustling the papers across the table.

"This is the infamous Balorn Vostemur you speak of?" Rua asked. "He was not here when your father fell?"

Renwick's eyebrows lifted. "You've heard of him?"

Despite her isolated upbringing, Rua had read stories of Balorn in the books gifted to her from the red witches. Rumors swirled through the witch camps that Balorn had gone mad when his father died and that his elder brother had indulged his bloodlust too much. Even as the whispers of him went quiet over the years, the elderly red witches remembered. They said the Siege of Yexshire was Balorn's idea, as was the torturing of blue witches for their prophecies. Rua had hoped Balorn was amongst the piles of bodies slain by the Immortal Blade.

"He was not here," Barnes stated, his hands trembling before he clutched them together. "Balorn keeps to the northern parts of the kingdom, by the late King's request."

"He wasn't much fun at a party, you see," Renwick said with a bitter smirk. He looked back to his councilors. "We need to ride north and find the Witches' Glass. It is too much power to be left in Balorn's control. We need to stop whatever he is planning before it goes any further."

"What is he planning?" Rua interjected.

"He has named himself the King of the Northern Court," the gruff one, Fowler, said. "He believes His Majesty is not fit to take the throne because he is a traitor."

A known gambler, Renwick didn't show a single emotion at that statement. Rua was sure he was hiding his tell, but staying frozen told her enough.

"We need to reclaim the blue witch fortress. The Witches' Glass will be there," Renwick said with finality.

"What is this Witches' Glass?" Rua went rigid as they all turned their pale eyes onto her again.

"So, she's heard of Balorn but not the Witches' Glass," Fowler huffed in a mocking tone.

Rua gritted her teeth. "I know nothing of the blue witches. They keep their secrets well."

"The Witches' Glass is the sacred stone of the blue witches, much like the rubies in your sword or the amulet your sister wears. It has the power to amplify blue witch magic and enact their ancient curses," Renwick murmured, his gaze locked on the map as his thumb thoughtfully stroked his bottom lip. "If Balorn is in possession of the talisman . . ." He released a slow breath. "We must reclaim it or all of Okrith will suffer."

She had not agreed to find the witches' relic. Rua had planned to wave her sword and scare off the remaining fae loyalists, but she didn't want to be around witches again.

Releasing a slow breath, she rolled her shoulders and scowled at Renwick. "Is that all?"

His lips pulled thin as he glanced at her up and down before saying, "No, while we are there, we will be building the Northern palace too."

The rest of the councilors paused. Renwick pointed to a spot on the map. Toward the top of the Northern Court, almost to the coast, were oval markings. The ice lakes, Rua presumed.

"You wish to move the capital to Murreneir?" Barnes gaped.

"Do you think that's wise, Your Majesty?" Romberg finally spoke in a high, nasally voice. "The ice lakes would be a far ride for any foreign dignitaries. What about Andover?"

"Andover is still filled with loyalists to my father. It is just as bad as Drunehan. We'll constantly be watching our backs if we remain here," Renwick said, and Berecraft's forehead crinkled. Rua was certain something like sadness flashed across his face. "We have ties to Murreneir. Rebuilding the capital there is a welcome change, and the people will follow us."

"Balorn will try to stop you," Fowler said. "He won't let you take the blue witch fortress so easily."

"It's a good thing we have the Immortal Blade coming with us, then, isn't it?" Renwick's emerald eyes darted back to Rua.

She held his stare, wondering for a moment if the flecks of green in her brown eyes matched his own. She tensed and pushed the thought away, bobbing her chin in agreement.

"We shall leave tomorrow," Renwick said, eyeing each of his councilors. "Make all the necessary preparations and assemble the guards. There's much to do before we depart."

As Renwick moved to stand, Rua stepped in his path. "What of the witches?"

The council turned to her again, their scrutiny weighing her down like a boulder.

"What of the witches?" Renwick repeated, narrowing his eyes at her.

"Have you already signed a declaration for their freedom?"

They all paused, turning to look at Renwick as she furrowed her brow at him. It was clear no one had considered the blue witches still enslaved under the Northern crown. Surely, they had made a plan for them?

"What do you suggest?" Renwick leaned back in his chair.

"All witches go free." Rua pursed her lips as if it were obvious. When none of the councilors responded, she added, "Now."

"Your Majesty," Fowler addressed Renwick and not her. "Do you think it not sensible to do things more gradually? It would probably unsettle their stability—"

"All witches go free, immediately." She cut him off with a snarl. "Those who choose to stay will receive fair pay and days of rest commensurate with your other staff; otherwise they may go."

"Go where, exactly?" Renwick watched her with the predatory eyes of a snake.

"This is a transition of power. These things take time," Barnes started, as if she should know better.

"The girl has no political prowess or leadership skills," Fowler said.

Rua's spine straightened as he called her "girl." As her hand drifted back toward the hilt of her sword, she felt its magnetic pull through her anger, the pommel heating on her palm.

"You will not speak down to me," Rua hissed. "I am not a child."

"Look at her!" Fowler erupted at Renwick, spittle flying. "She is a child, and a useless child at that!" Rua gripped her sword, amplifying the fire in her veins as the man continued his tirade. "She has no right to be on this council, other than making a foolish grab for that sword." Fowler turned, hateful eyes falling to her hand on the Immortal Blade, and he laughed. *Laughed.* "If you think you're so tough with that sword, little girl—"

Rua unsheathed the blade and sliced it through the air before he could say another word. Across the table, Fowler's eyes bugged as his hand grasped the gaping wound at his throat. Blood began pouring down his gray tunic, dyeing it crimson, as he burbled, choking on his last breaths.

With a loud, wet smack, he hit the floor. Rua knew it made her as evil as the fae around her, but she smirked at the shock on his face as he went down. Let them remember who was the master of the Immortal Blade.

"I would thank you not to kill the members of my council, Princess." Renwick looked down at Fowler as if it were a minor inconvenience. It was clear that he was used to killing people. They called him the Witchslayer after all. Rua wondered how many times he watched the life fade from someone's eyes.

"He wasn't listening to your orders, King Renwick, nor mine," Rua said, sheathing the magic sword. "I will not tolerate that level of disrespect, and neither should you if you intend to keep your crown. Now . . ." She rested her hands on the table, leaning across it with menace as she softly spoke. "The witches go free."

Renwick held her gaze for longer than she liked. He was so still, so calm, it made her want to shift under his stare. What was he thinking behind those green eyes? He did not reply, only giving a tight bob of his chin, and pulled out a sheet of parchment to begin writing the decree.

# CHAPTER TWO

Rua peered down at Drunehan. It was the capital city no longer. She could barely make out the figures navigating through the thick banks of snow below. Throughout the palace grounds, the desolation was evident. Darkened, smashed windows looked out over the snowy gardens covered in rubble. Rua was glad they would leave this place. She was certain most of the people roaming the streets would want her dead.

Bri closed the giant black chest with a loud thunk, snapping Rua out of her swirling thoughts.

She flinched at the sound and then ground her teeth together, angry that she jumped. She nearly had her head cut off only a few days ago, but she refused to reveal the effects of her near run-in with death. In the North, she couldn't afford to show that kind of weakness.

Bri plonked herself down onto the black leather lid upholstering the chest. Some called her and her brother the Twin Eagles, and it was easy to see why. With short, reddish-brown hair, a hooked nose, and golden eyes, she was otherwordly. Rua supposed it was just Eagle singular, now that Bri's twin, Talhan, had gone east to keep the peace.

"Do I really need all of that?" She eyed the chest filled to the brim with clothing and amenities secured by Bri's secret workings. "I think I'd prefer to just take a pack."

Bri squinted at the beat-up traveling pack Rua had requested from a palace servant. One rainy day from disintegrating into nothingness, the state of it told her enough about what the staff thought of her.

"Even though we are heading to a campsite on the ice lakes"—Bri turned her golden gaze back to Rua—"this is not some witch camp. You will be in the company of the King of the Northern Court."

"And?" Rua rolled her eyes. She did not care one bit how she dressed in front of Renwick. The Witchslayer was pure evil from what she could gather, or at least nearly evil. He did, after all, help her brother defeat the former Northern King. Rua was still not certain why, though. Did he really want his father dead so badly that he was willing to ally with the North's enemies? Was he that hungry for power?

"And," Bri snapped, crossing her legs and resting an elbow on her knee. "You are representing the High Mountain Court, a court many will think is weak in its infancy. You need to show strength in every way. Wearing tatty, old witch clothes does not send a powerful message to our enemies."

"Must clothes say so much?" Rua frowned at the giant chest.

"It's not ball gowns and tiaras." Bri let out a rough laugh. "It's a warm wardrobe, leathers, and weapons."

"Fine." Rua relented, eyes drifting to the Immortal Blade on her bed. "I wouldn't mind a few more daggers strapped to my belt."

"How much training do you have with a sword?" Bri asked, watching Rua's line of sight.

"Plenty." Rua stiffened. "The coven insisted on it."

"I'm beginning to like these witches." Bri smirked.

"Yes." Rua jutted her jaw to the side. "They were comprehensive in their caregiving."

Bri chuffed. "How very complimentary."

It was the nicest thing Rua could think to say. The red witches never treated her with any familiarity. She was always "other" to them. She was a symbol of all they had lost. They provided her with food, shelter, and training, but that was where it ended. She never saw a single witch cry or complain. Her fae emotions were too delicate for them. And after all they had been through, it seemed inappropriate for her to burden them with such petty things as her childhood feelings. Still, she was grateful to them for keeping her safe all of those years as they attempted to rebuild their coven in the wild woods behind the Temple of Yexshire.

Rua reached for the Immortal Blade. As she slowly unsheathed it, something in her settled, like a balm to a crazed itching she didn't know she had. She held the blade in the air, inspecting the scuffed markings down the edge.

"What does it say?" Bri's eyes scanned the scrolling Mhenbic across the scabbard.

" 'Each strike a blessing or curse,' " Rua said.

Bri chuckled. "I have bestowed many blessings over the years then."

"I am only interested in curses," Rua muttered, tracing the blade through the air, feeling its heavy weight warm the muscles in her arms.

"How do you target the magic?" Bri asked. Her wary stare held tight on the sword, as if one wrong movement and she'd be cut down too.

"The blade knows, in the same way my hand knows how to grip it. There is no conscious thought, just intention." Rua lifted the sword higher, pointing it toward the ceiling. Then added with a half-smile, "It won't hurt you."

"I'm not so sure about that." Bri hedged. "It seems to cut a lot of people down."

Rua's eyes flew to the Eagle. What was the fae warrior accusing her of? Had she seen what happened in the grand hall? Did she know of Rua's frenzied hacking, that she felt so free in that moment that she did not care who the blade's next victim would be? A sticky, hot shame lay across her skin like a mark on her soul. A small voice whispered inside her that she did not deserve the ancient sword.

"Only people who deserved it," Rua bit out.

"That is a dangerous game, friend," Bri said, standing up. "One I have played for many years now. It is a practiced muscle like anything else."

"What is?" Rua asked.

Bri's golden eyes darkened into a shade of amber. "Deciding who lives or dies."

Rua fought the urge to scowl. She lowered the Immortal Blade, resting its tip on the stone floor.

"And how do you practice other than by killing?" Rua wondered, more to herself than to Bri.

In that moment, she understood the full weight of the responsibility she bore. She would kill, possibly for the rest of her life. She was the master of a death blade. The sword had chosen her in that hour of need as much as she had chosen it. Even so, she did not snatch it fast enough. If she had grabbed it a few moments sooner, Raffiel would still be alive. That hesitation cost him his life. She knew why she hesitated. Something in her instinctively recognized that picking up that sword would change her life forever, and that inky darkness that swirled in her might rise to the surface. Now that she wielded the death blade, she feared what she would become.

"Train with me," Bri said, pulling Rua from her darkening thoughts. "I need to keep my skills sharp, too, and I don't want to practice with any of these Northern fools."

Smirking, Rua simply nodded.

"I should go contact Remy," Bri said, making her way to the door. Rua struggled to cultivate the magical flames used to communicate with other fae, not that she had anyone she wanted to speak with. "I need to tell your sister about the move north. Do you have any messages I should pass on?"

Rua shook her head, but as Bri grabbed the door handle, she added, "Don't tell her about the councilor."

Bri looked back at Rua with a thick, arched brow.

"Please," Rua gritted out, feeling slightly pathetic. She didn't want her sister to worry about the blade or to think poorly of her already. She still wasn't sure how to speak to her older sister. Older seemed silly. In another week, Rua turned nineteen. For one month, they were the same age, then Remy would turn twenty after the Winter Solstice.

"Remy is not that kind of person, you know," Bri said, as if reading Rua's thoughts. "She would not judge you like that."

"I have no idea what kind of person she is." Rua nibbled at her bottom lip with her canine tooth.

"You could try to find out," Bri challenged, cutting her down so easily.

"You may go," Rua said, as if the Eagle needed her permission. She turned back toward the window and stared out at the sea of silvery snow. Even with the roaring fire, she felt the bitter chill deep in her bones.

Bri let out a playful huff, unflustered by Rua's dismissal.

"Remy feared herself when I met her," Bri said, offering a piece of knowledge that made Rua look back over her shoulder. It was hard to believe that the same vicious fighter she saw in the grand hall was ever scared of herself. "She found her strength and confidence along the way, slowly, bit by bit. The bravery you saw was hard won."

Rua swallowed the lump in her throat. Perhaps she could find a path toward courage too. Part of her wished Baba Morganna had stayed behind to order her around. It was so much easier to be told what to do than to figure it out for herself.

"She sounds like a good person," Rua said begrudgingly.

"She is," Bri said. "As are you."

She bristled at the notion that this fae warrior could care about her. It would only be a matter of time before Bri took back that sentiment.

"You don't even know me," Rua snarled. "I could be a monster."

Bri flashed a grin, cocking her head. "It's a good thing I like to make friends with monsters then."

She knew the Eagle would not concede defeat. No matter how ornery and unpleasant Rua made herself, the fae warrior seemed determined to stick around.

She was glad it was Remy who was next in line to the High Mountain throne. The weight of the Immortal Blade was heavy, but the weight of a crown would be far heavier. Rua wouldn't see her sister again until the Winter Solstice, buying herself some time to figure out this new power. She would spend the next few weeks creating order in the North and making herself worthy of being a princess of the High Mountain Court.

"Are you going to be okay?" Bri asked. Rua's chest tightened a little. Even when Rua pushed her away, the Eagle seemed to push back. Bri might be the only person to weather her stormy moods. The Eagle and Rua were as rigid and gruff as each other. Perhaps Bri could be her friend . . . if only she didn't mess it up.

"I have it under control," Rua asserted. She knew Bri heard the lie as well as she did. She was uncertain whether she controlled the sword or the sword controlled her. Looking at the golden Mhenbic writing again, she sighed. The strike of the blade didn't worry her. It was the blade itself that would either be a blessing or curse.

~

The cold wind whipped Rua's hair across her face. She gritted her teeth as the torrent of snow bore down on them. A quick glance to her right showed Bri also bracing herself for another icy blast.

Renwick stood in front of a long line of black-and-silver carriages. No, not carriages, Rua realized as she looked closer. Where the wheels would be were giant metal skis, curling up in elegant whorls at the front.

"What in the Goddess's name is that?" Bri said, looking at the strange vehicle.

"I take it you have never ridden a sled," Rua mused, having never seen one herself apart from in her books.

"It's a sleigh, not a sled," Renwick corrected, hastily bridging the distance between them. He buried his hands deep in the pockets of his thick, gray cloak, his face sharper against the snow.

"Fine. Sleigh." Rua frowned at him. "How long is the journey?"

"Eight hours to Brufdoran," a voice came through the flurry. A soldier stepped up beside Renwick. Built like an ogre, he was tall and muscled with a mean scar trailing down from his hairline to his cheek. He did not wear the armor or crest of the Northern Court, instead favoring a heavy black cloak that made his eyes seem even darker. Golden-brown skin covered his gruff face, his mahogany hair shortly cropped.

"Your Highness." Renwick gestured toward the fae male by his side. "This is Thador Eloris, my personal guard."

"You do not trust the King's guard to protect you?" Rua's eyes darted from Thador to Renwick.

"I trust the ones I allowed to live." The muscle in Renwick's cheek popped out. "Thador is loyal to me, not the crown."

That she understood. She didn't know what it would be like—to have someone who was loyal only to her. Even Bri was a loaned guard from her sister.

The screech of a bird from overhead was the only warning before a hawk plummeted from the sky. Rua recoiled, lifting her hands to shield her face as the bird swept down and landed on Thador's shoulder.

"She won't harm you," Thador said with a deep, patronizing chuckle that made Rua scowl.

She felt Renwick's hardened gaze upon her and knew he noted how she winced. Trying to cover the embarrassment, she gestured to Bri.

"This is Briata . . ." Rua cursed herself, not knowing the Eagle's surname.

"Catullus," Bri cut in. "He knows. If it is eight hours until we break for the night, let's go," she said, though the warrior did not move from Rua's side, waiting for her instructions.

Thador's eyes roved over Bri, his lips settling into a smirk. Rua tensed, ready to berate the man for giving her guard that leering smile, but Bri beat her to it.

"I told you, if you're looking for a sparring partner, Thador," Bri said, though it was clear from her tone what kind of *sparring* she spoke of, "then I'm afraid you've got the wrong fae."

She gave Thador a wink, following on as Rua plodded toward the sleighs. Rua had forgotten that these highborn fae all knew each other. They probably grew up attending the same celebrations, balls, and masquerades.

As they reached the door, the servant sitting next to the driver leapt down from his seat and beat Bri to the handle. He opened it with a bow that made both Bri and Rua snort.

"May I take your bag?" the man asked, standing from his bow to grab the pack off of Bri's back. Bri tugged it out of his grasp on the leather strapping.

"No," she said.

"But—but there's a luggage compartment. Her Highness's luggage is already there and . . ." He spoke in a high voice as though what Bri was suggesting were sacrilege.

"I've got it. Let's go." Bri gestured with her chin to the man's seat at the front of the sleigh.

Biting her lips to keep from smiling, Rua took the servant's outstretched hand, pulling his attention away from her sawtooth guard.

She stepped into the darkness of the sleigh's belly. The insides looked much like a carriage would. Blue velvet cushions lined bench seats on either side of the doorway. Above the far window sat a shelf for hats and gloves. Cerulean curtains covered the fogged glass windows, the interior walls painted the color of midnight.

Bri clambered in after Rua, dragging the snow in with her. They had to duck their heads to stand as they navigated to the cushioned benches. Bri carelessly dropped her pack to the floor, filling the entire gap between the two seats.

Rua glowered at the bulbous pack.

"I don't like to be parted with my things," Bri said with a shrug.

"Fine." It seemed like the only word she knew how to say. Releasing a heavy sigh, she sat, resting her wet boots up on top of the luggage.

Bri unstrapped the dagger belted to her right thigh and placed it under a satin throw pillow before lying across the bench.

"You're having a nap now? It's still morning."

"Hope you brought a book." Bri chuckled over her shoulder and tucked her face into the pillow.

Rua rolled her eyes at the gruff guard.

A shout came from up ahead, and the sleigh jolted to life. Lurching forward, Rua threw out her arms to catch herself, but after the initial shake, the sleigh ran smoothly across the snow. She already heard Bri's heavy breaths coming from the satin pillow.

Rua looked out the window. The city of Drunehan was shadowy

and derelict. Braziers filled with rubbish burned a sickening scent into the air. Charcoal obscenities were scribbled over the stone walls, one claiming "Kill the witch," the other "Slay the Witchslayer." Rua shuddered. Uniting the Northern Court would not be an easy feat.

They could deal with an angry mob of humans, but the true threat lay to the North. If Renwick's uncle possessed the Witches' Glass, an avalanche of violence would follow . . . and Rua was riding right into the eye of the storm.

# CHAPTER THREE

Rua decided she preferred sleighs to carriages. They were much smoother, not bouncing and rocking on uneven terrain. She peeked out the window, wiping away the condensation building on the glass. Mostly she just saw white. Occasionally, some evergreens would stand out stark through the dead woods stretching out into the distance. As they circumvented craggy foothills, she watched their caravan lining up at narrow passes. At least thirty sleighs waited in line, loaded down with supplies, servants, and guards to take to the Ice Lakes of Murreneir.

Rua wondered if it was true that the ice was so thick that their whole caravan could camp on it. The forests of the High Mountains were laden with snow in the winter, but nothing like this. In some places, the trails carved into towering walls of ice. The snow in the High Mountains rarely fell higher than her knee. Even then, Rua and the witches would stay inside, curled around their fires throughout the long winters.

The red witch encampment had been rudimentary. They had hidden their huts in the valley of Mount Eulotrogus, half a day's ride west of the Temple of Yexshire. They positioned it so that even their smoke trails would be out of sight from looters and roving Northern soldiers. No one wanted to climb Eulotrogus or see its crumpled peak.

Rua had heard the story so many times over her childhood about how Baba Morganna had brought down the mountain on the Northern army. She had saved the red witches. The location of their camp reminded them all of what they had lost. Looking up each morning at that ruined summit prompted Rua to be quiet and grateful that she was alive. She felt the witches' bitterness toward her every time she looked at the skyline, as if it were her family that had slaughtered their coven.

The abrupt halting of the sleigh made Rua's hands shoot out to grip the edge of her seat. Had they arrived already? She heard a shout. In a split second Bri was up and on her feet, the dagger she stashed under her pillow in her grip. She opened the door and peeked out. Rua saw the flash of horror in her golden eyes before it disappeared.

Ducking back into the sleigh, Bri looked at Rua. "If I asked you to wait here, would you?"

"No," Rua replied, her hand drifting to the sword belted to her hip.

"That's what I thought," Bri groused. "Brace yourself for what you're about to see."

Rua bit her cheek. Whatever that meant, it wasn't good. She ran her fingers over the ruby hilt of the Immortal Blade, the weapon ready and waiting, eager to be unsheathed.

She climbed out of the sleigh and into the deep snow. The underbelly of the compartment was flush with the powdery white trail.

A gathering of soldiers stood at the tree line. As Rua drew closer, she saw what had startled Bri: five naked bodies nailed to trees.

Empty sockets stared out of their brutalized corpses, mottled with puckered red burns. In the snow in front of them, inked in blood, was the word TRAITOR.

The charcoal-gray cloak at the front of the gathering spun around as Rua gasped. Renwick surveyed her, clenching his jaw. She thought he might order her back to the sleigh, but he didn't.

"Who are these people?" she whispered.

"They were from the convoy of servants heading north to prepare the camp." Renwick looked to Thador and said, "Get Aneryn."

Thador gave a gruff bob of his head and headed toward the sleighs.

"This is your uncle's doing," a voice declared from the depths of a cloak. She discerned from the sound it was his elderly councilor, Berecraft.

"So it would seem." Renwick stared at the bloodied snow.

The blood had browned. It was an odd comfort that at least it was not fresh, the bodies on the trees blue and frozen solid.

"Do you think he will strike again?" Bri asked, her hand hovering closer to her dagger.

"It is only a matter of time," Berecraft said. "He may be mad, but he is not a fool. He would not attack this caravan. There are too many soldiers here."

"Unless he has gathered an army himself," Renwick said, eyeing the male.

"And that is why we are heading north," Berecraft confirmed. "We need to cut him off from the northern regions, separate him from the blue witch fortress. We cannot let him gather more support."

Thador returned with another person in an indigo cloak. She was only slightly shorter than Rua but diminutive next to Thador. Beneath her hood, her black hair was tucked behind rounded obsidian ears as she stared at them with hooded eyes. She looked young, a teenager, possibly younger than Rua.

"Who did this, Aneryn?" Renwick asked the girl, her dark eyes flickering into an eerie shade of sapphire. Brilliant blue flames licked up from her fingertips. She blinked, and her glow disappeared.

"You already know," Aneryn replied.

Rua's eyes widened. Aneryn did not look like the blue witches she had seen in the grand hall on the night of Hennen Vostemur's demise. Burns and scars had covered the elder blue witch. She had no hair, her eyes sewn shut. The girl in front of Rua seemed perfectly whole.

"Has he really released them?" Renwick's voice was a haunted whisper.

"The Forgotten Ones roam, Your Majesty, though they are not free," Aneryn said. "The Witches' Glass has been used."

"Fuck." Thador clenched his fists. "How did Balorn know how to use it?"

"Who are the Forgotten Ones?" Rua asked, pulling all their gazes to her.

"We can discuss it in Brufdoran. It's another two hours before we arrive," Renwick said.

"We shouldn't stay here," Bri agreed from beside her, the warrior's gaze scanning the trees. "In case someone stayed behind to watch us."

"You ride with Bri," Rua ordered Thador with a withering glare before turning to address Renwick. "We will discuss this now."

"As you wish, Your Highness," Renwick said with a smirk, gesturing to his sleigh.

Bri opened her mouth to interject, but Rua just gave the Eagle a stern look and her guard backed down.

"Try not to kill him," the Eagle said instead.

Two hours alone with Renwick Vostemur was sure to be unpleasant, but she needed answers, and she refused to wait for them.

~

The sleigh pulled back to life as Rua adjusted the Immortal Blade, resting its edge on the seat, the weight lifted off her belt. She would not remove the sword while she sat across from the Northern King.

Renwick's eyes rested on the scabbard.

"Start talking," Rua commanded, folding her arms across her chest.

Renwick's full lips pulled up at the sides. "For someone who grew up in the woods, you take to giving orders quite naturally."

"Who are the Forgotten Ones?" she pressed, blatantly ignoring his comment. There were more important matters at hand.

Renwick took a long, steadying breath, staring back out the fogged window as though he could still see those bodies nailed to those trees. Rua was certain she would never forget that sight. It would be added to the growing list of things that haunted her dreams.

"I'm sure you will have heard of what my father did to the blue witches," Renwick said.

23

Rua thought to the High Priestess, her sewn-shut eyes, her body covered in burns. "He tortured them."

"Emotions heighten witch magic," Renwick said. "And nothing is more potent than fear of pain."

"He'd burn their visions out of them," Rua whispered.

"Amongst other things, yes." Renwick's cold green stare lingered on her face. "The blue witch fortress beyond the Ice Lakes of Murreneir is where most of it took place. My uncle, Balorn, was the one who broke them. He took great pleasure in it."

Rua shifted uncomfortably on her plush cushion. "And the Forgotten Ones?"

"Balorn broke some of the witches *too* well," Renwick said. "They were beyond use, diminished to the husk of the souls they used to be, and so they were locked away in the bowels of the witch fortress." His gaze flitted to his hands. "It would have been kinder to kill them."

"Why didn't he?" Rua's voice was touched with malice. To drive the witches mad with pain and then hold them in their misery was more evil than she could comprehend.

"Perhaps he still saw some worth in them or wanted them to serve as a reminder. Perhaps he knew one day he would unleash them on the world." Renwick's face held so still as he looked at Rua, she wondered if he was breathing. Something haunted that face, though she did not know what. "Perhaps he just wanted to see their pain."

Renwick lifted a hand to rub across his forehead, a grimace on his face. It was there for a split second and then gone.

"What's wrong?" Rua looked at that hand massaging his temple, and he quickly dropped it.

"Nothing. It is just a headache," he snarled.

"Why not summon a brown witch?" Rua wondered.

It was uncommon for fae to have headaches. Their rapid healing powers prevented many of the ailments that befell witches and humans. Most royals moved with a team of witches, blue for Sight, red for their animation magic, green for their cooking, and brown for their healing remedies. The violet witches had conjured magical scents, powders, and incenses, but they had all gone extinct long ago. Surely Renwick had a brown witch in his convoy though.

He gnashed his teeth. "I am fine."

He did not look fine. As she looked closer, she noticed the slight purple of the half-moons under his eyes. He had a green pallor to his already pale skin. His eyes were bloodshot. He hid it well, but he looked like he hadn't slept in weeks.

Rua shrugged. His health was not her problem.

"So Balorn has released the Forgotten Ones from the witch fortress." Rua folded her arms across her chest. "And let them shred into your soldiers. Why have they not turned on him?"

"The Witches' Glass," Renwick said. "It is the only way. He has used it to curse them, and in doing so, he has gained himself an army."

"Why has his spell not worked on Aneryn?"

Renwick raised his hand as if to rub his temple again but stopped halfway. "Only weakened minds can fall under such a spell. The Forgotten Ones were broken, perfect for Balorn to control with a curse . . . perfect pawns to vanquish his enemies."

"And you are his enemy?" Rua narrowed her eyes at Renwick.

"I am now." The Northern King cocked his head to the side, the simple circlet on his head glinting in the dim light. "Believe it or not, I want to be a good ruler. I don't want my people to suffer any more than they already have, and Balorn threatens this delicate peace with his every breath."

She considered him for a moment as the sleigh gently swayed. "What are you going to do about these Forgotten Ones?"

"I am going to bestow on them the kindness that my father and uncle would not," Renwick said. "I am going to set them free—by breaking the curse or by death I do not know yet. Our goal must be to go after the spell book and the Witches' Glass. If we can reverse the spell, then his army will implode on itself and take him down with it. Breaking the curse is our priority now."

"How are you ever going to pull the blue witch coven back to your side?"

"Maybe that is something you can help with. You were, after all, raised by witches." Renwick smirked.

"I am not going to tell them to trust you." Rua shook her head. "You can try to earn it, if you are up to the task."

When he spoke, she felt his voice echo across her skin. "Then I will endeavor to do so." Renwick leaned back against his cushioned seat, stretching his legs out, his fine leather shoes resting on the seat beside Rua. She felt keenly aware of the closeness of his calves to her knees. "I hope Aneryn will begin that trust as well."

Rua thought to the beautiful, young witch. "Why is Aneryn untouched? She does not look like the other blue witches."

"Because she is mine," Renwick said, mindlessly rubbing his temples again. "My personal prophet. I acquired her many years ago after my last blue witch met an untimely end."

"And you do not torture your witches?" Rua pursed her lips.

"No." Renwick's face was hard, the muscles in his neck flexing. Something about the way he said it made Rua wonder how much he cared for Aneryn.

"Is she your lover?" Rua found herself asking before she could take it back.

"She is not." Renwick barked out a laugh.

"Don't act like it's a ridiculous notion. Many witches fill that *role* for the fae they serve." Rua's voice dripped with disdain.

"I wouldn't suppose you know much about any of that, having grown up with a bunch of old crones," Renwick said, arching his brow at her.

It was Rua's turn to guffaw. "Oh please, I am no softhearted waif. There are male witches too, you know."

"So you have had consorts then?" Renwick's cheeks dimpled as Rua's face heated.

"I don't see how that is any of your business, but yes, some," she snapped.

"Not very good ones it seems." Renwick chuckled at her sneering face, a hearty, deep laugh that had her stomach flipping even as she bared her teeth. "You've never been with a fae before."

"Nor do I want to," she hissed.

Those dimples appeared again, along with a flicker of delight. "Liar."

"You bloody fae are insufferable." Rua's hand drifted back down to the Immortal Blade, knowing exactly where the hilt would be without looking.

Renwick's discerning gaze followed the move. "You are fae too, Rua."

She hated the way he said her name—like he knew her. Pushing to the back of her seat, she looked out the window, as if it would put any distance between them. After a breath, she glanced back over her shoulder to find those emerald eyes still watching her.

"You are a monster," she sneered, thinking her words might hurt him, but Renwick's face only split into an evil grin.

"Then we are as wicked as each other, Princess."

# CHAPTER FOUR

Candles flickered in frosted windowsills as they rode through the quiet streets of Brufdoran. The beautiful town was built of log houses, icicles trailing from steep roofs, and silver bells jangling from red doorframes. A giant pine tree shot up from the center of town, decorated in glittering silver ribbons and strings of ruby-red beads. It seemed so at odds with the ruins of Drunehan and the horrors they witnessed on the road.

Rua's breath fogged the window as she craned her neck to stare up at the towering tree, its boughs heavy with festive decorations. Renwick sat silent across from her as she surveyed the town. Was this how the Northern fae lived? Nestled under a layer of fresh snow, their chimneys billowing and the smoky scent of wood fires cutting through the crisp air? The quaint merriment all around them was dwarfed by the grandeur of the castle waiting for them at the edge of town.

Stars blinked to life in the twilight as the sleighs pulled into the grounds of Brufdoran Castle. Darkness claimed the land earlier and earlier as they moved closer to the Winter Solstice. Through the frosted window sat a high black stone wall and beyond it a looming castle, the main stone structure framed by two tall turrets.

When they arrived, Rua broke away from Renwick as swiftly as possible, she and Bri hurrying after a human attendant to their rooms. She got lost for a few moments staring into the fire before Bri called her away to dinner. She splashed water on her face and left it at that.

The Lord of Brufdoran sat at the far end of the table, Renwick opposite him. Rua found herself squarely between the two silent males. Lord Omerin was a stout, aging man with graying blond hair and a thick beard. His eyes stayed permanently fixed on the plate of smoked fish and pickled vegetables in front of him.

Bri and Thador stood beside the roaring fireplace, guarding the far door as if an army might attack the dining room at any moment. Glancing over, Rua wondered when Bri would be given dinner. She wanted to invite her guard to the table but refrained. The Eagle seemed too important to be standing by the wall like a servant. Rua ate quickly, hoping to hasten the meal along.

Darting a glance between Lord Omerin's lowered head and Renwick, she raised her eyebrow at the Northern King, imploring him to start a conversation.

"Is everything quite all right?" Renwick said at last.

He had changed from his riding tunic into a green velvet jacket with belled sleeves that hinted at a silver lining, perfectly matching his green eyes and silver circlet glinting in the candlelight against his ashblond hair. Rua's cheeks heated, and she wished she had taken the time to change out of her traveling clothes.

Renwick's fork clinked onto his plate. "You seem rather quiet, Lord Omerin."

"Forgive me, Your Majesty." The Lord's eyes finally drifted up to meet Renwick's icy stare. "I was not certain whether it was appropriate to give you my condolences . . ."

Lord Omerin seemed like a gruff, formidable man. He sat rod straight, even with his stooped head, and moved in a soldierly way. Yet he seemed terrified as he quickly ate his food.

"It is a tricky thing." Renwick pursed his lips, his words allowing Lord Omerin to release a long-held breath. "I am saddened that it was necessary at all, but my father had to be stopped."

Lord Omerin's shoulders sagged in relief. "I agree, Your Majesty," he said quietly, as if he feared Hennen Vostemur might rise from the dead and strike him for it.

"My father was a cruel man, Lord Omerin. I do not blame you for fearing that I may be the same." Renwick held completely still as he spoke. That deliberate stillness told Rua enough: he feared for the type of King he would be too.

"Your father was . . . a challenge at times to host in these halls," Lord Omerin said tentatively. "But it is your uncle, Balorn, who I greatly fear."

"You have met Balorn?" Renwick's hands clenched around his silverware.

"Indeed, I grew up with them. We were young courtiers together when your grandparents reigned. The former King used to bring Prince Balorn with him everywhere," Lord Omerin said. "Everyone was terrified of Balorn, even as a boy. We could never predict what he might do. Not a single time did he visit these halls without it ending in a burial."

Rua gasped.

"Mostly servants and guards, Your Highness," Omerin said like it should comfort Rua that it was not the important fae who were killed. "But there is a sickness inside him for certain."

Rua's frown deepened. "A common sickness amongst men who were raised to believe they were owed the world."

Renwick's jaw clenched, a mirror to his fists as his gaze flicked from Rua to Omerin. "And my father did nothing to stop Balorn?"

"No, Your Majesty." Lord Omerin's eyes fell back to his plate. "The Vostemurs . . . well, your father and uncle at least," Omerin corrected quickly. "They had a bloodlust unlike any I have known. They both had wild tempers, but while Hennen's ended with a fist, Balorn's ended with a blade. Wherever they went a trail of blood followed."

"I have heard tell of those days, though I do not remember them," Renwick said.

"You were young, Your Majesty, when Hennen sent Balorn northward." Omerin took a long sip of wine from his goblet, as if trying to rid himself of the haunting images.

Renwick was wholly still to Rua's left. Something Omerin said had clearly upset him.

"I suppose you know where my father sent Balorn?" Renwick gritted out.

"To the blue witch fortress beyond the northern ice lakes," Omerin confirmed with a bob of his chin. "It is said your father tasked him with breaking the blood bond with the Immortal Blade." Omerin's eyes drifted over to Rua, and, though he couldn't see it below the table, she moved her hand to the hilt of the sword. "Hennen sent many *toys* up there for his brother to play with."

*Toys.* Rua shuddered. She knew he meant witches, possibly humans too—playthings for him to torture.

"The Kings of Okrith were not kind rulers. Apart from your father, of course," Omerin added to Rua with haste. "It is a blessing the kingdoms are changing. A new Dammacus Queen, a new Vostemur King . . . and what of the Eastern Court?"

"A council has been assembled to keep the peace." Renwick wiped the corner of his mouth with his napkin, setting it back in his lap. "Within the year, challengers from all over Okrith will compete for the throne."

Over his shoulder, Bri and Thador shuffled, clearly both eager to enter the competition. Rua pressed her lips together; she would bet all her money on Bri.

"And what does Augustus Norwood think of this plan?" Omerin asked, glancing at the fae warriors suddenly listening with rapt attention.

"The blue witches have eyes on Norwood." Renwick waved his hand, dismissing the notion that the Prince was a threat. "He and his dwindling army are barely surviving in the forests below the Rotted Peak."

"If the mountain lions don't get them, the stench will." Omerin chuckled, slapping his hand down and making the dried-flower centerpiece rattle. Petals of dried violet flowers fell onto the table.

"We have bigger concerns with B—"

An icy draft cut through the room, interrupting the warmth from the fire. The door behind Lord Omerin burst open. A young boy, no more than five, rushed into the room, followed by a harried fae woman.

"Fredrik!" she hissed, grabbing the boy's arm, but it was too late; they had been spotted.

Lord Omerin's face paled.

"And who are they?" Renwick asked as the woman gathered the boy back against her legs. The boy's eyes were wide as saucers as he looked between Rua and Renwick.

"Your Majesty, this is my daughter, Lady Mallen." Lord Omerin gestured to the beautiful blond woman, who dropped quickly into an elegant curtsy. "And my grandson, Lord Fredrik." The woman pushed her son by the shoulders down into a bow.

"A pleasure," Renwick said stiffly, turning back to Lord Omerin. "I thought you were alone in this castle, Omerin. I'm surprised your family is not dining with us. Are there any other members of your household you have been hiding?"

Lord Omerin's fingers twitched over the stem of his goblet.

"My sincerest apologies, Your Majesty, I . . . I did not know if . . ." Lord Omerin stumbled over his words.

"You did not know if I was as evil as my father and uncle," Renwick surmised. "You were afraid I might hurt your family."

"Forgive me, Your Majesty." Lord Omerin's eyes looked pleadingly at his grandson. It was the strangest thing to see such a surly man reduced to a trembling heap. That is what came of such unpredictable violence. Rua knew the feeling of bracing for a sword to swing all too well. The elder Vostemurs had killed on a whim, the blood they spilled staining every corner of the Northern Court. How could Omerin know that Hennen's son would not be the same?

"You are forgiven, Lord Omerin," Renwick said as Omerin took a deep steadying breath. Had he really thought Renwick would kill him just for that? "But I do not want any more secrets kept from me. I only ask that you trust me by my own actions and not those of my father."

"I will, Your Majesty." Omerin's shoulders dropped, his soldier's posture returning. "You already are a better leader than your father ever was."

"Are you really a princess?" A high, squeaking voice came from the corner.

Rua looked over at the boy staring at her. Lady Mallen dropped into another quick curtsy, forcing her son to bow again. She tapped Fredrik's head in a silent command to not pry, but Rua just smiled at him. What excitement it must be for him to have foreign royalty in his home.

"I am."

"You don't have a crown?" he squeaked.

"Do you think I should get one?" Rua's smile broadened.

The boy was practically bouncing with excitement. "Yes, yes!"

"I think we should let His Majesty and Her Highness finish their meal, Fredrik," Mallen said, gently steering him back to the door. "It is bedtime anyway."

"But! But ...," Fredrik whined, his bottom lip pouting out of his little, round face.

"How about we have breakfast together tomorrow, Lord Fredrik?" Rua suggested. "I think I should like your company. The conversation this evening has been terribly dull."

Omerin guffawed and Fredrik beamed as he looked up at his mother.

"Can we, Mama?" he begged.

Lady Mallen laughed, ruffling his hair. "Oh, all right."

Fredrik practically leapt with joy as he skipped back down the hall-way, Mallen shutting the door behind her.

"You don't know what you're getting yourself into, Your Highness." Omerin chuckled. "But I thank you, deeply. He will be going on about breakfasting with a princess for months."

Lord Omerin's disposition had swiftly changed from one of nervous hesitation to one of warmth. He sipped his wine again as servants brought out the next course of roasted potatoes and marinated venison.

That warmth made Rua shift in her seat. He was that happy for his grandson. It seemed so strange to her. The red witches cared for her as best as they could, but there was no love there. They did not have any joy in the wake of the Siege of Yexshire. Rua had not grown up around families such as this. She had met her elder brother, Raffiel, and his

Fated, Bern, only a handful of times over the years. Raffiel and Bern were always kind to her, but she felt wooden and awkward around them. She did not know how to speak to them, and at every parting, she wondered if she was meant to hug them. Was that how families behaved? And now Raffiel was gone, slain in the battle with the former Northern King, and she would never have the opportunity to figure it out.

She cringed, thinking of her only meeting with her sister in the snowstorm outside the ruined Northern palace. She had let Remy hug her, at least. Her elder sister had tears in her eyes when they spoke, and Rua had just frowned. Gods, she was a monster. She knew Remy was disappointed by the reunion, but Rua didn't know how to give anything more than that to a sister who was a stranger.

Rua looked back to the new Northern King as he stared at the shut doorway where Lady Mallen and Lord Fredrik had left through.

"Why are you so riled?" Rua taunted, breaking his trance. "You look like you've seen a ghost."

She couldn't imagine Renwick around children. He seemed to be as uncomfortable as she had been with her own family. But there had been many witchlings at the camps she grew up in. The youngest of the red witches seemed like the only ones willing to talk to her, so Rua volunteered most of her time to watch them while their parents worked.

Her words seemed to divert Renwick's attention back to his meal. Piercing his fork into a chunk of roasted potato, he cut it into a bite-sized piece before putting it in his mouth. Rua snorted. Such manners he had. She stabbed the chunk of potato on her plate and shoved the whole thing into her cheek. She smirked at Renwick as he rolled his eyes at her.

Omerin chuckled at the exchange. "You two make an odd pair, I must say."

Rua slanted her eyes to him, speaking through a mouthful of potato, "We are not a pair at all, Lord Omerin."

The Lord of Brufdoran merely shrugged, his cheeks rosy as he gave Renwick another look. "You are most welcome in my castle anytime you wish, Princess of the High Mountain Court."

~

Hands pushed her to the ground, knees smashing against the stone floor. The room was silent. Everyone watched them with bated breath as her red hood was yanked away from her head. *They don't know who I am. I'm going to die a witch.* She looked up into those brown eyes flecked with green, so similar to her own, her fae face looking like a feminine version of Raffiel.

Before she had a chance to study her elder sister, a spray of blood hit her face. Screaming erupted. She looked at the horror on Remy's face as a head rolled across the floor. Alana was her name. She had never liked Rua. Alana thought her presence was a bad omen, but seeing her mouth still twitching as her head rolled made bile burn up Rua's throat.

She felt the air of the sword again, another fatal blow to the witch next to her: Draigh, Alana's husband. The blade caught in Draigh's neck, and blood poured from the gushing wound until her knees were soaked.

The eyes of the Northern Court twinkled at her, so excited to see her die. How many people cheered when her parents were murdered?

Her body spasmed. She was next in line. Each wisp of wind, each movement from the corner of her eye, made her shriek. This is how her pathetic life would end.

Darkness swallowed her panting breaths as Rua jolted awake. Her hand had found the Immortal Blade, even in sleep. Not releasing the hilt, she stretched her far hand across to the lantern, twisting back the frame so the candle inside brightened the room.

Her eyes scanned the shadows, but no one was there. She was grateful for her fae vision. If she were glamoured in her human form, half of the room would still be black. She did not have to glamour often in the High Mountain forests since all the red witches knew who she was. It felt odd and irritating, like wearing a scratchy wool sweater. She couldn't imagine how Remy had kept her glamour on for thirteen years.

The foreign, stately room felt odd and grating in the post-nightmare quiet. It was so pleasantly decorated, so at odds with the horrors behind her eyelids.

Scowling at the delicate watercolor flowers painted above the mantel, she breathed in through her nose, trying to calm herself down. She was in Brufdoran, in the center of the Northern Court. That wasn't comforting.

A soft knock sounded at the door connecting her room with her guard's. Bri didn't wait for an answer and entered. "You okay?"

"Fine," Rua gritted out, hand clenching tighter on the sword. Even in the shadows, she saw Bri's golden eyes staring at the blade. "Did I wake you?"

"I was already awake. You were gasping in your sleep," Bri said through the dim room. The Eagle ambled over to Rua's trunk at the foot of her bed. She still wore her fighting leathers, her weapons still strapped to her belt and thighs. Perching upon the black leather box, she peered up at Rua.

"At least I wasn't screaming." Rua ground her teeth.

"You can put that down, you know?" Bri gestured to the blade. "You can't be harmed by any weapon now that you are in its possession, whether you are holding it or not."

"The prophecies of the Immortal Blade are all twisted and different." Rua frowned as the sword in her hand seemed to pulse. "In the red witch tomes it says: no blade can slay the wielder of the Immortal Blade . . . but what does that mean? Do arrows count? What about a rock? There are plenty of ways to kill me that don't involve a blade."

Bri considered her. "You've been thinking about this."

"I need to know what it can do." *What I can do.*

"Do you want me to shoot you with an arrow?" Bri smirked at Rua's hard expression. "The leathers I bought you will protect against far-off shooters. They would have to be close to pierce the hide, and in order to do that, they would have to go through me."

Rua held on to that golden gaze. The fae warrior was sincere. Silence stretched out between them, the rapping of branches on the window the only sound, but Bri seemed unfazed with the quiet.

"I was dreaming of that night in the Northern palace," Rua admitted as her cheeks burned.

"I figured." Bri looked down at her hands, picking at her thumbnail with nonchalance.

"Why didn't Baba Morganna do anything? She just knelt there and mumbled her Mhenbic prayers to the fucking moon." Rua looked to her sword once more, eyes gliding down its steel, before sliding it back in the sheath propped against her bed. "She was the witch that pulled down a mountain and she did nothing."

"She tore down the entire Northern palace," Bri countered, still maintaining her easy air as if they were chatting about the weather.

"Then why did she wait? Why couldn't she have brought down the palace the second we were taken? Why did she allow so many people to die?" Frazzled, Rua pushed the hair stuck with sweat off her forehead.

"She is a rare thing, that High Priestess. She had the blue witches' gift of Sight," Bri said. "It's not normal for a witch to possess the powers of another coven. Perhaps she had a blue witch ancestor . . ."

"And?"

"And maybe she Saw all the different outcomes of that battle and chose the path with the least bloodshed," Bri mused as Rua glared at her. "Would it have been worth it for her to save those two witches if all three of the Dammacus siblings fell in battle? Would saving them have been worth it if the High Mountain bloodline ended that night?"

"That is an impossible question."

"Well, it is one you'll need to start answering if you are going to be the owner of that blade." Bri's eyes darted to the ruby pommel glinting in the candlelight. Rua knew she was right. With every swing of her sword she was turning into the Goddess of Death, making the decision of which thread of life she should snip. "I wasn't there when those two witches were killed. I was waiting in the servants' passage while they moved Hale from the dungeons. I did not think Vostemur would kill anyone before . . . I would have . . ." Bri clenched her fists in her lap, looking back up to Rua. "I'm sorry."

"How could you have known?" Rua asked, though her voice was filled with bitterness. It was not the tone she had intended, her words always coming out wrong. How many surprised or angered faces had she encountered growing up when her questions were meant to be genuine? It didn't matter that she could speak all three languages of Okrith, not one could she communicate in. She shook off that pestering thought, looking back to the Eagle, who waited for her to speak as if another long silence hadn't just passed. "Raffiel seemed to assemble an army the second Remy was taken."

"The second you were taken," Bri said pointedly. "Bern said he knew the witch camps were ambushed before they even knew where Remy was. They were planning the attack to rescue *you*. When Remy was taken it only hastened their already forming plan."

Rua scowled. Her brother was coming to rescue her. Raffiel had tried to break through Rua's hard shell and be the older brother she so desperately needed, but she never let him. He struck the Northern palace before he was ready. She had forced him into actions that got him killed.

Rua thought to that moment when Renwick moved her behind him and drew his sword. He wielded his weapon against his own soldiers to protect her. Why? Because he allied with Raffiel? He had pushed her up against the thin table holding the talismans. Her parents' crowns sat on that table as a show of strength. She knew the second she got close enough to see the High Mountain crest: two mountains with a crown above them. The mountains represented the union between the red witches and the High Mountain fae. They ruled the court together. It was through their joined leadership that they became the most powerful court in Okrith. Other fae kingdoms grabbed for absolute power, even the ones that were kind to their witch covens. They never treated them as equals. It was a bitter truth that Hennen Vostemur only exploited. He wanted witches to be slaves, not equals, and when he slaughtered the High Mountain Court, their lofty tolerant ideals fell with them. He made it so. She didn't know if they would ever set the world back to what it once was. She knew Raffiel had wanted to. She didn't know if Remy could.

"I should have grabbed the Immortal Blade the second I rushed up the dais." Rua rubbed her hands together against a draft of cold wind. Bri noted the move and wandered to the darkened fireplace. Crouching, her guard placed new logs onto the blackened stones. "I was standing right there next to the sword. I felt it calling to me. The blood of my people runs through its metal, and I still refused its call."

Bri struck a piece of flint, igniting the kindling and coaxing a flame to life. "I don't blame you for not wanting to take the sword."

"You don't *blame* me?" Rua growled. "If Raffiel were here, I'm sure he would. If I had grabbed that sword a minute sooner, he would be alive. It was only when I saw him dead on the ground that I knew I needed to take it. I did it to save myself, not him."

Bri added another log into the burgeoning flames. "You nearly had your head cut off. And you're judging yourself for not thinking quickly?"

"I should have—"

"You can play that game forever, Rua," Bri said, standing back from the fire. "It changes nothing. You learn. You move forward. It is the only way and then the fear of it will lessen."

Rua noted how Bri didn't forgive her. Her guard didn't say it was all okay. She could have grabbed the sword sooner, and she didn't.

"Have you ever been so afraid you pissed yourself?" Rua's jaw hurt from biting down so tightly. She was sure that everyone smelled it on her that day. Her bladder released as the Northern soldier yanked his blade from Draigh's neck. Renwick would have known she wet herself when he pushed her behind him. She wasn't a brave warrior at all.

"Psh." Bri snorted. "Half of the most fearsome warriors I know have done it . . . more than once. Sometimes from fear, other times because you can't grab a chamber pot in the midst of war, but the battlefields are filled with everything, blood, bile, shit . . . Urine is the least of our concerns. It just smells like a night out at the taverns to me."

Rua's brows knit together. She thought the fae warrior might exaggerate to make her feel better, but that wasn't like Bri. The Eagle spoke honestly, even when the words were hard to take.

The warmth of the fire leaked through the cold air toward her. Its heat seemed to soothe the storm inside her, the haunting chill of her nightmares finally ebbing.

"Think you can sleep?"

Rua nodded, looking up into the eyes of her guard—the warrior who volunteered to protect her. "Thank you."

Bri shrugged. "It's just a fire." But it was much more than a fire. Bri had comforted her in that gruff way when she was feeling lost in the darkness of her mind.

"Are you going to get some sleep?" Rua asked.

"I can sleep on the ride tomorrow." Bri gave Rua a mischievous smirk. "Right now, there is a lonely soldier holding watch down the hall, and I think she would like some company."

~

The scent of freshly baked bread and buttery griddle cakes wafted through the room. They ate breakfast in a sunny nook, perfectly positioned to capture the low winter sun. Fredrik sat propped up on two pillows beside his mother on the bench seat. They both wore shades of soft blue, the patron color of the Northern Court. Renwick and Rua sat across from them, dressed in their dark traveling clothes, a stark juxtaposition to the pastel-colored sitting room.

Fredrik peppered them with eager questions, always right when they were about to take a bite of food.

"They call you Witchslayer?" he asked with wide-eyed eagerness.

The Northern King set down his fork—his third attempt at taking a bite of eggs. "Yes."

"How many witches have you killed?" Fredrik mumbled around a mouthful of tartlet. His mother's eyebrows shot up in horror at his side, and she shook her head in apology to the Northern King.

Renwick's eyes slid to Rua. "Too many."

His face was drawn and pale. Rua wondered if he had gotten any sleep. She saw the way his eyes looked everywhere but at Fredrik. Rua pressed her lips together to keep from smirking. He had seen so many horrors, she was certain of it, so seeing him squirm under the questions of a five-year-old was hard not to laugh at.

Lord Omerin hustled into the room and dropped into the empty chair.

"Forgive me for my tardiness," he said, taking the linen napkin out from under his silverware and draping it across his lap. "The fae fire had contact this morning, Your Highness." He looked at Rua as a servant delivered a fresh plate of fruit and spice bread, whorls of steam curling up from the tray. "The Queen of the High Mountain Court attempted to reach through earlier, but you were still asleep. I offered to wake you, but she said she'd try again mid-morning."

Rua squinted at the sun beaming through the windows, her lips pulling downward. She had thought traveling north would put some distance between her and Remy, but with the magic of fae fires, they could always be in contact. Rua had assumed it wouldn't be until the Winter Solstice that she spoke to Remy again. She thought she would have better things to share with her by then too: some accomplishments, progress in the Northern Court to make her sister proud. But there was nothing to say.

"Would you like your tea sent to the fae fire room?" Mallen offered. It was clear to Rua the blond fae had misread Rua's concerned expression for worry that she would miss her sister's call.

Sighing, Rua pushed back from the table. "Yes, please," she grumbled when she really wanted to say, "Better get this over with."

"I can join you," Renwick said, leaning forward, ready to stand.

Rua gave him a small grin and said, "No, no, I'm sure Lord Fredrik has more questions for you."

She bit her lip to keep from laughing at the glower Renwick couldn't completely hide.

When she exited the room, Bri was waiting. Her guard led her up to the third floor, where a bright green door greeted them.

They entered into a small sitting room. It seemed like a room for evening drinks, not calling fae through magic fires. The cream-colored wallpaper and burgundy floral carpet clashed with the brilliant green of the fire itself. The large hearth sat against the right wall, with eerie green flames licking up from the fire's base where it should be blue.

Rua stared at the hearth, lost in the flickering flames, until Bri approached.

"Shall I contact her for you?" Bri asked, crouching down as Rua nodded.

It took Rua several attempts each time she conjured fae fires. It was a muscle she did not know how to flex. There was no hand movement or incantation that made the magic work. It came from a part within her she struggled to access.

Bri closed her eyes for a moment, thinking of something in her mind that caused the flames to grow higher, turning a more vibrant shade of yellowy green.

"It's Bri," she said, casting her golden eyes to the flames. "I want to speak with Remy."

"We will alert Her Majesty, Lady Catallus," a voice said from the other end.

"Lady Catullus?" Rua murmured. The Eagle glanced back to her, giving her a conspiratorial eye roll, no doubt finding it as ridiculous as she did.

Remy had fae fires burning day and night now, like the rest of the fae royals and nobility. It was a strange feeling, knowing her sister had servants.

"I'm here," a warm voice said through the flames.

Rua's eyebrows shot up. Had she been close, or had she run there to respond so quickly?

"These bloody fires," Remy cursed. "Can you hear me?"

Bri snorted.

"We can hear you, Your Majesty," Rua said.

"Oh good," the voice replied. "And it's just Remy. You . . . you do prefer Rua, right?"

"Yes."

They didn't know each other's names. It was just another reminder that while they descended from the same bloodline, they were strangers to each other. Rua picked at her lips as she looked to the carpet. Gods, she had no idea what to say.

"What news, Rem?" Bri said instead, saving both sisters from the awkward silence.

"Oh, um." Remy's voice dropped an octave. "I wanted to let Rua know that we buried Raffiel today. It was a simple ceremony in the mountains. He was laid to rest next to the graves of our ancestors. We are making stones for him and our parents and Riv too."

Riv—Rivitus—was the one that people said Rua looked like.

"Good," Rua murmured, shifting uncomfortably on her feet. What else could she say?

"Sorry we couldn't be there, Rem," Bri said. "I should like to go and say my piece when we come for the solstice."

Rua pursed her lips. The Eagle made it sound easy.

"How goes the rebuild?" Bri asked.

"Well," Remy said. "It will go much faster when we return from Haastmouth Beach."

"You are going to visit Hale's mother?" Bri smiled. "Say hi to Kira for me."

"I will." Rua heard the joy in Remy's voice. Her sister was traveling to visit the mother of her Fated—another family member Remy could add to the growing community of loved ones she had.

Rua knew she should be happy for her sister . . .

"Yexshire is even more beautiful this time of year than I remembered," Remy said.

"You remembered it?" Rua mused.

"Yes, so many little things, don't you?"

"I don't remember any of it." Rua shifted again, her forefinger picking nervously at her thumb, unable to keep still. Each pause felt like a lifetime.

"Well, I am older."

"By less than a year," Rua shot back. "I should have at least some memories if you can remember so much."

Bri chuckled. "Well, now you're starting to sound like siblings."

"We should pack. We're leaving soon," Rua muttered, abruptly ending the conversation, desperate to not continue the fumbling attempts at bonding.

"Okay."

She heard the restraint in Remy's voice—her sister seemed eager to say more. She knew Remy wanted there to be a relationship between them, but she didn't know how to give it to her. They had nothing in common, apart from their parents.

"Bye, Remy." Her cheeks heated as she turned to the door.

The faint flickering of her sister's saddened voice followed her. "Bye, Rua."

# CHAPTER FIVE

The steam from her breath seemed to coat her eyelashes in a layer of frost. They had ridden through the day, Rua watching out the fogged window as Bri slept across from her. Stopping at the entrance to the winter camp, she climbed out to stretch her stiff legs and survey the ice lake. As she squinted against the wind, Rua looked down to the view below. In a crater of forested hills sat the smooth stretch of ice. She stood on a ridge looking out toward the enormous frozen lake the same color as the sky. Spiderwebs of cracked ice blanketed the lake's surface. Iron gates ringed the basin in a towering meshwork of spikes. Dotted along the hilltops were stone lookouts, the one farthest from them barely visible to Rua even with her fae vision. The vastness of the lake was like nothing she had ever seen. Unlike the lakes and ponds in the High Mountains, this was like an ocean unto itself.

A sprawling campsite was nestled along the lake's edge. Without the camp for scale, Rua wouldn't have understood the sheer size of the lake. A blanket of gravel and dead leaves lay under the campsite, sitting in a wide circle upon the lake's surface. Hundreds of tents of varying shapes and sizes took up the campground. It seemed small against the never-ending stretch of ice. Servants had already lit fires, bringing the

45

camp to life. Rua's eyes honed in on the firelight. Was it really a good idea to be lighting fires on a frozen lake?

"The ice can hold an entire legion. You don't need to worry." Silver steam whorled from Renwick's breath as he stepped up beside her.

Rua looked to her side, seeing that emerald gaze locked on her.

"It's like nothing I have ever seen before," she said, turning back to the wonder before them.

"This region has several ice lakes, though Lyrei Basin is the largest." Renwick's eyes scanned the hilltops far beyond. There was not a flat plain in sight, rippling hills and vales stretching endlessly into the distance. "The Southern Court has long bought the ice from these lakes. The people of Murreneir make good coin shipping it around the realm. But Lyrei Basin is a stronghold with the outposts all along the ridge, and the blue witches man them alongside my soldiers. Lyrei is a safe place."

Rua rolled her eyes. "Safe for you, maybe."

"I will not permit any of my people to harm you," Renwick said, watching as the sleighs disappeared toward stables built into the hillside.

"I do not think they will request your permission first," Rua snapped back.

"They are not all as monstrous as me," he murmured, more to himself than to her.

"What is over there?" Rua pointed toward the snowy slopes of a mountain beyond the basin. The trees were hacked away, the summit flattened as if sliced from the top.

"That is where the new palace will be located," Renwick said. "The hill is easily defended and the terrain around the lakes would be difficult to march an army through."

"You expect an army to be marched here?" Rua mused.

"I hope not." Renwick frowned at her. "But I also hope the castle will stand the test of time, unlike the one in Drunehan. Who knows what will be needed a hundred years from now?"

Rua looked to the flattened peak. She imagined it would be a beautiful view in every season, looking out at the lakes and evergreen forests.

"It has been less than a week since that night." She knew she didn't need to say which one. The Battle of Drunehan—the night the palace was pulled down and countless people died, many by her hand. "You already had the hillside leveled in such a short stretch of time?"

"No, that site has sat there waiting for some time." Renwick's eyes sharpened, as if he were staring further than the landscape and back into his memory. "It was meant to be the spring palace."

Rua was hesitant to speak. She did not know why his voice grew so distant, but Renwick finally spoke again.

"It was my mother's idea."

She paused as flurries of snow circled around her. She had never wondered about Renwick's mother before. Rubbing her fingertips together to combat the chill, she stared at that vacant summit. She wondered how long ago his mother had died. Rua had a mother too, though she had not one single memory of her. There was a blurry face she held in her mind, but she did not know if it was from memory or from the stories told to her about Queen Dammacus over the years. She couldn't trust any of those memories to be the truth. She was five years old when her mother died, killed by the father of the man standing next to her.

"When did she die?" Rua asked. She had not heard one word about a Queen Vostemur, not even in her books.

"I was fifteen," Renwick whispered, tucking his hands back into his pockets, arms straightening in the icy wind.

So he remembered his mother, unlike Rua. She did not know why it angered her so much that her sister could remember her family and Rua could not. How many of the people she knew had two living parents? Most of the red witches had none. The lucky ones had one. The cold steel bit into her bare hands, yet the feeling of her blade's hilt under her palm felt strangely comforting. The sword promised an unending streak of vengeance. When would the baying for blood stop ringing in her ears? Each one of her enemies seemed to hear the same call. They would all kill each other until every single one of them was an orphan.

Renwick's eyes flitted to a black spot far in the distance.

"What is that?" Rua strained to see what that black smudge was so far on the horizon.

"The blue witch fortress," Renwick said. "Murreneir is the native homeland of the blue witches. The fortress was originally built by their ancestors, a stronghold deep in the north. Though I am not sure any witches would choose to live there anymore, not after my uncle took control of it for so long."

Rua shuddered at the bleakness of that statement—where they tortured the witches for their visions.

"Are we going there?"

"Not today," Renwick murmured. "It has been a long journey already. We will settle into the camp today and go see what is left of the fortress tomorrow. My scouts say it has been abandoned, which means Balorn is on the move."

"And the witches who lived there?"

Those emerald eyes slid to her again. "They have either left with Balorn, controlled by his spell, or . . ."

"Dead." Rua grimaced. "I'm not sure which is the better outcome."

Renwick reached up and rubbed his temple as the flurries of snow blustered around them.

"More headaches?"

He dropped his hand back to his side. "The blue witches in these parts, they have had it worse than all the rest. There is a reason Balorn's curse worked on them and not the others. Their minds were already broken. They can't resist the Witches' Glass." He looked back at her. "I do not know how to talk to the blue witches who survived my father's reign. I doubt they would hear me."

"Understandable."

"Perhaps you can get through to them." Renwick huffed. "You're practically a witch."

Rua's eyebrows knit together. "My ancestors' blood was imbued with red witch magic, a gift by the ancient coven. Perhaps there was a witch far back in my ancestry, but I am no more a witch than you."

"Baba Airu has already requested to speak with you." The muscle in Renwick's jaw flickered.

Rua had seen the High Priestess of the blue witches during the Battle of Drunehan. She remembered the witch's smirk as she stood stock-still, the battle raging around her. She shuddered. *That smile.*

"Can we please go?" Thador shouted from the sleigh door to the two of them. "It's colder than a witch's tit out here."

Rua bared her teeth at the giant fae.

"What?" Thador shrugged, waving his hand at her. "As you said, you are not a witch."

Rua felt the buzz of her red magic, a happy hum that vibrated down her fingertips and out of her eyes. She lifted her free hand toward the sleigh door, and it shut with a smack, knocking the guard back inside.

Renwick let out a chuckle. "Careful," he warned. "You keep beating him up and he might fall in love with you."

Magic flickering out, Rua folded her arms. "You may think I will make a good middleman for you and the blue witches, but I will not be your messenger. I will speak to them honestly, if you wish for me to speak to them at all."

"That is all I ask." Renwick cocked his head as he considered her. "If you got to know me better, maybe you would not tell them such awful things."

Rua snorted. "I doubt that." She let out a heavy sigh, eyes looking back to the site of the spring palace.

"Thank you for helping my people," Renwick said, his eyes drifting down to the Immortal Blade.

So many kinds of power were at her fingertips. She could cut down a battalion with just a swipe of her sword. But it would be the fae who would pay for the horrors of this world, not the witches. Even the ones driven to violence had been broken by fae hands.

"I am not here for your people. I want to restore the peace so the High Mountain Court doesn't have a threat to the north anymore. Balorn is to pay for what he has done to the blue witch coven, not the witches he uses to shield himself with," Rua insisted. "I will help you break this curse and then I will go home." The word *home* rang hollow in her ears. "I will not kill any witches"—she gave Renwick a hard look—"unless they threaten me or someone I love."

"Well, Princess." Renwick's face was sharp even as a smirk played across his lips. "You better start loving me real quick."

~

The sun peeked between the heavy gray clouds as they wound through the campsite to Rua's lodgings. The small tents she assumed were for servants, the larger ones for upper military officials. Gravel crunched under her boots down the narrow pathways. At the center of the camp- site was a wide clearing, perhaps for community gatherings or soldier training. Beside it sat a large complex of interconnected tents, a pen- nant waving from the top with the Northern Court crest. The two guards stationed at the entrance told her enough: it was the King's tent.

To the right, the camp broke off into domed leather huts: the witches' quarter and to the left down winding trails were the fae tents, Rua's and Bri's accommodations sitting across from each other at the end of the alley.

As she entered her tent, Rua quickly realized it wasn't just one room, but rather, three: a sitting room, bedroom, and bathing chamber, all made from thick canvas walls. Lush furs were draped over the bed and chairs. Thick, soft carpets lay beneath her feet, everything touched with silver and gold filigree. Tea lights flickered on a silver tray. The warm scent of fresh linen, bergamot, and sandalwood floated in the air. It felt like an oasis compared to the sparse encampment she had just walked through.

The luxurious bed was dotted in burgundy velvet cushions. Side tables glowed with the light of gilded candelabras. An oakwood desk, matching wardrobe, and a full-length mirror sat beside the far fabric wall. A chair and footstool sat on the other side along with a blackened metal fireplace, a pipe rising through the hole cut in the roof in what Rua assumed was a makeshift chimney. A kettle sat on top of the fire- box, possibly for tea or water to warm the bath, for beyond it was a silk curtain to the bathing chamber.

The tent flaps tousled like waves across a pond on a windy day, the sound like a pack of cards being shuffled. The basin seemed to shelter from the worst of the wind, the high-pitched howling skimming around the ice lake.

Spongy carpet blanketed the floor, but Rua's legs still felt tense, like the ice under her feet might crack at any moment and she would plummet into its frigid depths. She crouched down and peeled back the carpet, only to find another hessian carpet underneath.

"It's perfectly safe."

Rua yanked her hand back at the sound, looking up at Aneryn. The King's blue witch stood at the threshold of her bedroom.

"What are you doing in here?" Rua asked, shooting to her feet. "What if I had been changing?"

"With the curtains wide open? You don't need the gift of Sight to figure that one out." Aneryn pointed to the open curtains that bisected the bedroom from the sitting room. "Besides, there is not exactly somewhere to knock."

Rua crossed her arms. "Then you should have bells."

Snow dusted the crown of the blue witch's head, disappearing rapidly in the warmth of the tent. "And on the windy nights when the whole camp is ringing with the sound of bells so loudly you want to pull your hair out?"

Rua gave a begrudging chuckle. "Good point." She would hate to hear bells ringing all night long. "Why are you here?"

Clasping her hands in front of her, Aneryn said, "I came to see if you would like to attend the meeting this evening?"

"We just arrived, and it is late," Rua groused.

"You don't have to come. I was simply extending the kindness."

"No, I should come." Rua sighed as she stretched her neck to the side. "If I am meant to help you and restore peace to the North, then I should be there."

"Is that what you are doing in the Northern Court?" Aneryn pressed her lips together, hiding a smirk. "I thought you just wanted to wave that sword around and cut down any fae who calls you girl."

The image of Fowler dying on the stone flashed through her mind.

She tried to summon an ounce of guilt, but she could not. The Immortal Blade resting on her bed seemed to agree. "Did you See that? Or did someone tell you?"

"Both." The blue witch's eyes twinkled. She was clearly not grieving the councilor's death either.

"Do you See a lot of my future?" Rua asked, scanning the blue witch from head to toe with a scrutinizing stare. She did not like the idea of a stranger knowing more about her life than she did.

"Not anymore," the blue witch replied.

Rua's mouth fell agape. "Because I die?"

"You fae think everything is black and white." Aneryn chortled. "It may be because you are here, surrounded by blue witches. I cannot See your future so well when it interweaves with my coven." Aneryn's eyes slid past Rua up toward the ceiling, a faint flickering of blue crossing her pupils and fading. "And I don't just See everything all the time. I have to focus on the future I want to See, not that I can See R—" Aneryn shook her head, lifting a hand to rub across her temples as the sapphire flames circled her fingertips once more. "Occasionally, if there is great danger it will just come to me, but otherwise, no."

"Like Baba Morganna Seeing the Siege of Yexshire," Rua whispered, thinking of the High Priestess who raised her.

"Exactly." Aneryn bobbed her head.

The tent flaps waved in the silence around them as Rua thought about her childhood. How strange for Baba Morganna to have the blue witch's gift of Sight.

"She kept searching for other witches over the years, but it was draining for her," Rua mused, rubbing a thumb thoughtfully across her bottom lip. "She couldn't See the witches themselves, so she had to look for fae or humans who knew of them. A lot of red witches she only Saw right before their deaths."

"I can imagine. It is very hard finding witches with Sight. Even amongst my coven, many have barely more than common intuition—a gut feeling that something bad is coming," Aneryn said, dropping her hand from her forehead.

"Do you know how to break this curse?"

"No more than any other witch's curse—it requires a spell and a witch's stone . . . though I don't know where the spell book is and I can't find the Witches' Glass in my mind's eye . . ." Aneryn let out a frustrated sigh, stepping further into the room. It was clear she had been searching her mind for the answers. "Maybe you'll be sticking around for a while."

"If you can't See me, it's more likely that I'm dead," Rua grumbled. "Hennen Vostemur was my court's enemy. And the North is filled with many I consider enemies still."

"Is Renwick one of them?" Aneryn asked, hiding her glowing blue hands back in the pockets of her thick indigo cloak.

"That has yet to be seen." Rua held the blue witch's stare. "I will stay here and use the sword of my ancestors as I see fit until I have made certain my court is safe from every Vostemur."

Aneryn's eyes guttered. It happened so fast Rua wondered if she imagined it.

"Kill Balorn, find the spell book, get the Witches' Glass, and then I will eagerly leave," Rua said, though the notion grated against her skin like itchy wool.

She didn't want to stay in Murreneir, nor did she want to go back to Yexshire. She didn't want to face the ghosts of her family or the red witches either. There was nowhere she could go where she wouldn't be known—a High Mountain princess would be spotted wherever she went. The thought left her feeling utterly trapped. She narrowed her eyes at the floor. One thing at a time. First the curse, then the rest of her life.

"If you are so eager to go, you better come to this meeting," Aneryn blustered.

The witch had clearly taken offense to Rua's fervor to leave. Rua opened her mouth to reply when Bri appeared in the doorway, cheeks wind-chapped, a swirling gust of snow following behind her through the heavy flap. She stopped short when she saw Aneryn.

"Oh," she said, darting looks between the two of them. "I was just coming to tell you about the meeting, but it seems I was beaten to it."

Aneryn just blinked at her.

Bri smirked at the blue witch, clearly not irked by her sudden silence. "Why did you come to tell Her Highness? It seems quite far from the blue witches' quarter."

"I don't reside in the blue witches' quarter." Aneryn narrowed her eyes at the Eagle, then turned back to Rua and said, "I will wait for you outside."

She sketched a quick bow and left, bustling out into the frigid evening air.

"What was that about?" Rua asked, tilting her head toward the doorway Aneryn had just exited.

"I have that effect on people," Bri said, remaining at the threshold to the tent. "Now, get dressed. I don't want to take my boots off and I don't want to tread snow into your tent. Let's go."

Rua snickered at the soldierly orders but grabbed her cloak and boots, nevertheless. As she grabbed her sword, she braced herself for another meeting like the one with the councilors in Drunehan. She silently promised herself she wouldn't cut down another angry old man. The scabbard warmed in her hand as she belted it to her hip as if speaking to her. The Immortal Blade made no such promises.

~

She followed Aneryn and Bri through the labyrinth of tents, getting more lost with each step. They arrived at a rectangular behemoth—a tent made of graying stained canvas, larger than any she had ever seen. It abutted an entire row of sleeping tents.

A screech sounded overhead and Rua flinched, covering her face as a hawk swept down from the sky. Thador turned the corner with the bird perched on his shoulder.

"You get used to it." The soldier chuckled as Rua quickly dropped her hands. "Ehiris won't harm you."

As they pushed their way into the tent, Rua watched warily while Ehiris ruffled her feathers and stared through yellow, beady eyes. It felt like being under Bri's scrutiny.

The air was only the slightest touch warmer than outside, the space too massive to heat thoroughly. Rua gaped at the rows of long wooden tables, an assortment of chairs, and long benches huddled around them. The space looked somewhere between a tavern and a grand banquet hall.

"What is this place?" she murmured.

"The dining commons," Thador said, looking up to the high tented ceiling. "It's where we take our meals. This one is for the fae who have come from Drunehan, but there's six of them around the camp."

Rua's mouth fell open, the sheer size of the encampment suddenly whirring through her mind. There must be several hundred, perhaps a thousand, of them camping on the ice lake. She squinted at the table halfway down the aisle where Renwick, Berecraft, and two other soldiers sat. A scattering of yellow papers stretched out between them even as they ate. Bristling, she stared at the peculiar scene before her: the King conducting his meeting in a shared dining space. Surely he would take his meals in his own personal tent?

"Come, let's eat." Thador led them down the row of tables.

The rest of the room was silent, the candles on most tables unlit. It was an odd hour for eating, but Rua was starved.

Renwick looked up, assessing them with his steely gaze, and gave them a curt nod. His simple circlet held his hair off his face. He had changed again—now wearing a burgundy tunic and matching satin jacket, trimmed in cream-colored fur. Attire immaculate, and without a speck of snow or wrinkle, he sat tall and rigid next to his elderly councilor. The sharp angles of his face and jaw cut through his smooth skin. Rua considered him, pondering if he had shaved before the evening meeting.

Thador sat on the other side of Berecraft, while Rua followed Aneryn around the table to face him. She swung her legs over the bench as Bri wedged herself in on the other side. This was not how she expected a King's meeting to be conducted.

Five people wearing matching forest-green aprons hustled out from a curtain strung along the tent's side. They carried plates of food and pitchers of drink, setting them down in unison in front of the new arrivals.

The enticing smell of pepper and rosemary wafted in the air as Rua watched the servants retreat back to where she assumed the kitchens were located. Noting their green aprons, she wondered if they were green witches.

Rua picked up the fork already on her plate—informal indeed. It felt like being at the witch camps, eating at leisure, no set dining times. She liked it much better than the organized dinner in Brufdoran, with its many courses and seemingly endless rows of silverware. She thanked the Gods for her little encyclopedias growing up that she had any notion of which cutlery to use. Everything she knew about being a fae, she had learned in a book.

Biting into a piece of flaky fish, she hummed her pleasure as the salty tang melted on her tongue. Renwick glanced in her direction, though he didn't break his conversation with the soldier in front of him.

"Fresh from Lyrei Basin," Aneryn said, a small smirk playing on her lips as she scooped a spoonful of pickled beans into her mouth.

"You fish on this lake?" Rua's eyes widened, looking up at the vaulted ceiling. "Do you think it is wise to be cutting holes in the ice?"

The blue witch giggled, shaking her head. "They do it at the far end of the lake. The ice is much thinner there and easier to cut into. It is half a day's walk away. We are fine."

Rua's stomach still tightened, feeling like the ice might break and swallow them whole. If they plummeted into the water now, there would be no finding the surface. The tent high above them would block any means of escape. She clenched her hands tighter around the silverware. It was the same feeling of waiting for the blade to strike her that day in Drunehan. The anticipation mounted with every breath, the panic promising to consume her as the thoughts of drowning heightened.

Bri hastily filled her goblet from the pitcher in front of her and passed it to Rua. "Here," she said, as if hearing Rua's hammering heart.

As she brought the goblet to her lips, the fruity flavor collided with the burning fire down her throat. She took another long sip. In the mountains, the witches made moonshine. It was awful and helpful in equal measure, but wine . . . she could get used to fine fae wine.

"First, we need the spell book." Berecraft's scratchy voice cut above the din. All eyes turned to him. "Going after Balorn is a death sentence. Our focus should be breaking the curse."

The group turned to Renwick, waiting for his response, but it was Thador who spoke. "We'll have to go after him eventually," the giant fae said through a mouthful of potatoes. "He has the Witches' Glass."

"It could be in the blue witch fortress still," one of the guards added.

He was a blond-haired male, muscles rippling out from under his indigo uniform. The Northern crest was painted across the fabric of his tunic, the casual soldier's attire matching the other guard next to him. It must be what they wore beneath their armor, branded with the Northern crest even under their steel.

"You think he'd leave it behind, Lachie?" Thador scoffed to the soldier.

"We should try to steal it from him, rather than engage in battle," the other soldier, with dusty brown hair, said. "We have no advantage with all the blue witches around him."

"Since blue witches cannot See the futures of other blue witches," Aneryn said, moving the beans around her plate with the tines of her fork. "Even though Balorn is fae, his future is muddied by the presence of so many blue witches."

Pursing her lips, Rua contemplated that fact. She wondered if it was the same as with the High Mountain talismans. Red witch magic couldn't levitate the Immortal Blade or the amulet of Aelusien. Rua knew Remy almost died attaining the amulet.

"How exactly do we steal from a moving target?" the blond soldier asked.

Aneryn shifted in her seat, leaning across the table to look at the guard. "The last visions I had of Balorn, he was headed west."

"There are few towns and lots of frozen tundra to the northwest." Berecraft looked down at the papers strewn about the table, tracing a crooked finger along the Northern Court. "It would deplete our resources and tire our troops to chase after him until we can pin him down."

"There will be no pinning him down until we have the spell book," Renwick finally said, his sharp eyes staring at the map.

"And where is the book?" Rua asked.

"We don't know." The lines of Berecraft's frown deepened as he glanced to the King. "It was in Drunehan. I wouldn't be surprised if Balorn had sent one of his *pets* to find the spell in the first place. Regardless, the freed blue witches took the spell book when they left."

"Since they are free to do what they wish now . . . yes, they took their sacred texts with them." Renwick looked to his councilor as if this had been an argument that had transpired many times before. "It did not seem important that they possess their own ancient scrawlings until now. How were we supposed to know Balorn had plans to enact a curse?"

"They left with it?" Bri asked, refilling her pitcher.

"A cohort of freed witches left eastward," Aneryn said. Her eyes seemed to glaze as she spoke of the blue witches. It was not the flickering glow of her Sight . . . Some other emotion plagued her. "They are taking refuge for the winter somewhere, regrouping their coven."

Rua noted the way the young blue witch said *their* and not *our.*

"But isn't Baba Airu the leader of their coven?" Bri asked.

"The witches are divided." Thador stretched his neck to the side, reaching up and feeding bits of raw meat from his plate to Ehiris. Rua gawked at the meat. The servants knew to include it on Thador's plate for his hawk. "Many do not want to follow another Vostemur King."

"Understandable," Bri said, garnering snickers from the soldiers.

"Some decided to stay. Others left." Renwick shrugged as if it were no reflection on his character what they chose to do. "We need to find them and convince them to give us their sacred book."

"We don't need the whole book," Berecraft said. "We just need the wording to the curse so that we can reverse it. Surely, they'd want to help us do that."

"I don't think they're inclined to help us at all," Aneryn gritted out. "Not after the *suraash.*"

*Suraash*, it meant Forgotten Ones in Mhenbic. It sounded so strange coming out of Aneryn's mouth, the Mhenbic name fitting better than its Ific translation. Forgotten Ones wasn't entirely accurate. It meant more that they were given up on than forgotten. The notion made Rua grind her teeth. It meant they weren't worth saving.

"But the *suraash* are their family too," Rua said, eyeing the blue witch.

"They probably think they're beyond saving," Thador said, giving voice to Rua's own thoughts.

Aneryn's eyes fell to her plate. "They would be right."

"So, where do we find these witches?" Bri asked, bringing them back to task.

"We don't know," Thador and Berecraft said in unison.

"Baba Airu does," Aneryn added. The blue witch's accent was even more clear as she spoke of her Baba. She did not pronounce the Mhenbic correctly. She spoke like a fae. "But she hasn't told us."

Bri scrubbed a hand down her face. "Why not?"

"She fears for their safety," Renwick said, green eyes falling to Aneryn. "She's tied between loyalties."

"I will keep talking to her," Aneryn said with a frustrated sigh, stabbing at her fish with her fork.

The Northern King glanced at Rua. "Maybe you can convince her to share their location."

Rua prickled as her back straightened. "I don't see why the High Priestess would trust me."

"You bridge the worlds—witch and fae," Renwick mused, his lips lingering over the rim of his goblet.

"I have a great dislike for both the worlds . . ." Rua forced away the growl in her voice, making herself add, "But I will think about it."

She was meant to be here as a show of force, but breaking this curse would be the best way to protect the new ally to the High Mountain Court. If Balorn defeated Renwick, it would mean trouble for all of Okrith. She couldn't turn a blind eye to this curse; they needed Renwick securely on his throne. Clenching her jaw, Rua forced a slow breath. It was her duty to protect the future of her homeland now . . . whatever that meant.

"So, what now?" Bri refilled her goblet for the third time.

"We need to go to the blue witch fortress tomorrow," the brown-haired soldier said, leaning far into the table to look at the Eagle.

"We need to see if there's any indication of what this curse is called," Thador added. "What book it's from, what powers it has. We will need the exact words and the witches' stone to reverse the curse. Maybe we can find some clues as to where they went."

Berecraft's crinkled eyes swept over Aneryn and settled on Rua, though she knew he spoke to his King. "Might I suggest only the soldiers attend?"

"I can come," Aneryn insisted.

"No," Renwick cut in, narrowing his eyes at his blue witch. "You stay behind." Rua furrowed her brow as the King turned his emerald gaze toward her. "Be warned, Princess. That place is a pit of darkness."

Rua leaned back as she dropped her silverware and folded her arms across her chest. "I do not fear the darkness."

"Good." Renwick nodded, pushing back from the table and standing, leaving them to finish their meal without him. "We leave at first light."

# CHAPTER SIX

The sleigh ride out to the blue witch fortress was not as smooth as the two-day journey up to Murreneir. They crammed into two sleighs, extra guards sitting on the back of the luggage compartment. Scouts had informed Renwick that the fortress was abandoned, but still they brought extra guards just in case.

Skidding to a halt, Rua climbed out of the sleigh into the snow. She looked up at the towering black fortress above her. It wasn't one building at all, but rather five, all interconnected by elaborate stone archways. The pointed spires were carved in intricate etchings and Mhenbic symbols. The musky scent of ancient magic lingered in the air. She squinted at the Mhenbic words over the highest archway: *Xeco d' Hunasht.* The Temple of Hunasht.

Rua wondered why the fae called it "the blue witch fortress." Temple of Hunasht seemed far more appropriate. But she supposed the Northern Court fae didn't care about the witches' names or their customs. They didn't learn the Mhenbic words or read their symbols. It was all beneath them.

"Don't be fooled," Thador said, looking up to the fortress built into the cliff above them. "That is just the tip of the place. It tunnels down several stories into the earth."

"Delightful," Bri said from Rua's other side. Her guard turned to Renwick as he exited his sleigh. "So what exactly is the plan?"

"I want to see if there is anything left behind that would indicate Balorn's strategy. A book of spells or scribbling of the incantation. Any sign of how to reverse the curse he made," Renwick said as his gaze drifted up along with the rest of them. "And to show you the truth of what he and my father have been doing all of these years. I must warn you, what you see inside will not be pleasant."

"I'm not turning back now," Rua gritted out. Her soul was already torn apart by the nightmares from the Northern palace and those dead bodies nailed to the trees. It all washed over her. She welcomed the horror now, let it break her into so many pieces she could never be put back together. The terror she saw all around her was like a final release from the pent-up feelings that existed deep in her belly all these years. Finally, the world around her matched the world inside her.

"Let's go then," Renwick said, taking a first step into the shin-deep snow.

Three guards took the lead, trekking up the switchback path to the fortress. Rua tried to aim her footsteps into the footprints already made, but some of the strides were too long, and she had to make her own. The snow was not a soft powder, as it had been around Lyrei Basin. Here a layer of ice sat atop the snow, not thick enough to bear their weight but enough to hold her footsteps for a second before they crashed back into the snow. The pace was grueling: step, hover, fall, step, hover, fall.

By the time they reached the gates of the Temple of Hunasht, Rua's tunic was wet with sweat. At least her fur-lined cloak would keep it from freezing against the cold wind.

Bri stopped next to Rua. "I hope this is a one-time trip."

The fae warrior didn't pant like Rua did, but her cheeks were wind-chapped and her short brown hair stuck up at the back. Rua almost smiled at Bri's grumpy expression, but the feeling in the air as they stood in front of the black iron gates stopped her. It made her want to drop her voice into a whisper. It was the feeling of death.

Renwick turned back to her. "Last chance."

"Stop treating me like some delicate flower," Rua snarled, pushing past him through the gap in the iron gates. Bri snorted behind her, boots crunching on the jagged ice.

They moved in quiet, tentative footsteps toward the large open entrance of the Temple of Hunasht. The heavy snow blew into the doorway, reaching halfway into the icy black hall.

A soldier stepped up behind Renwick and passed him a lit torch. "Your Majesty."

Lighting a candle, another soldier stepped up to Rua, bowing as he passed it to her. "Your Highness."

Rua frowned at the giant torch in Renwick's hand and then back to her little candle.

They walked into the hall, wading through drifts of snow until their feet finally found the icy black stone floor below. Light beamed in from arched windows carved into the rock walls. The cavernous hall was stripped bare. Not a single thing noted what it had looked like before.

Moving through the hall and into a narrow corridor, Rua was grateful for her candle as the light from the hall quickly fell into darkness. Her fae vision could only see so well through the dark, and even with her candle, half of the hall was shrouded in shadows. She stuck close behind the glow of Renwick's torch, too. The darkness pulled away from the walls like a living thing. The inky blackness felt thicker than normal, each shadow a gaping pit ready to swallow them whole.

They scuttled down a winding stone staircase. Rua had the urge to look back to check if Bri was behind her, but she refrained. Thador walked behind Bri along with another three Northern soldiers. As they reached the second-floor landing, the hairs on her arms stood on end. The air was charged with something, as if she could still feel the fear branded into the stone.

Pushing open a creaking door, Renwick took one step into the room. He held his torch high. In the room sat two long wooden tables, but no chairs. Something about the sight of it made Rua pause. What would they do in a room with tables and no chairs?

They moved further down the hall to the next room, another two tables. But this time, circling around the tables, were thick leather belts. The cold fireplace sat in the blackened corner of the room. A bracer filled with iron pokers sat beside it. Rua's stomach roiled. This was where they strapped witches to tables.

They kept moving to the last room in the hall. What lay inside made Rua's heart stutter. The room looked like a butchery. Chains and meat hooks hung from the ceiling above another two tables, and in the far corner . . . was a rack. Beside it was a table strewn with rusty metal instruments.

"Gods," Bri whispered from behind her. The Eagle spoke so quietly, as if the haunted walls could hear.

"There's nothing here that shows us what Balorn is planning. His office on the top floor was empty, but there are archives down in the tombs," Renwick said in a quiet but steady tone.

Bri surveyed the room. "Delightful."

"Look for papers, maps, notes," Renwick said. "Anything that could tell us where he went."

"Let's keep moving," Thador said from behind Bri. The giant warrior seemed more spooked by the room than the rest of them.

Reaching another stone stairway, they wound their way down to another floor. Rua's fingers trembled. They were so far into the earth now. It felt like the walls pressed in on her.

The third-floor hallway was lined with dozens of small doors. Renwick pushed open the first to his left. Inside sat a graying stained cot and a chamber pot, nothing else. He pushed open the next door, and it was exactly the same. All along the hall was a dormitory of bare cots and chamber pots. Rua crinkled her nose, but whatever filth remained in those chamber pots was frozen solid. There were no fireplaces, no braziers. She wondered how the witches didn't freeze to death.

She descended another staircase with mounting trepidation. When Rua's foot hit the landing, the energy shifted. A bleak and moldy stench filled the air. Renwick pushed open the door to his left. The room was bare, save for several sets of manacles bolted to the wall. Was this where they chained up the *suraash*?

He moved to the next door and pushed it open.

Rua gasped. A witch still hung from the manacles. Her blue, lifeless body was covered in only a black nightgown. Rua wasn't certain if she had frozen to death or died another way. Streaks lined the wall, looking like claw marks.

"How many times would a witch's fingers need to scrape across the stone to leave a mark?" Rua whispered.

"Thousands probably," Bri murmured back.

Renwick's breath steamed from his mouth as he turned to his lumbering guard. "We need to take her up with us."

Thador grimaced. "We'll have to find a key. Is it worth it?"

"Yes," Rua said in unison with Renwick.

The Northern King looked sideways at Rua. "She deserves a proper burial."

"Fine," Thador said. "Let's keep looking."

They opened another three doors. Rua thanked the Gods when each one was empty except for the manacles bolted into the walls. She wondered how many witches they kept in these rooms. It seemed like dozens were trapped in each one.

They reached a final door at the end of the hallway. Renwick pushed it open. The room was roughly hewn into the mountain. Craggy rocks still hung from the low ceiling. The room narrowed, the roof sloping down into the darkness. Just behind the threshold was an elegant mahogany desk, so at odds with the cavelike room. An upholstered blue velvet chair sat behind it.

"What the . . . ," Bri whispered, narrowing her eyes at the desk. Of all the things they had seen, this makeshift office was the most strange. A stack of papers sat neatly to the left-hand side of the desk and a large metal ring of keys to the right.

"Why would he leave all the doors unlocked?" Bri muttered, eyes searching the shadowed corners of the room. What she saw made her freeze. "Shit."

Rua turned her gaze in the same direction. At first she thought she was looking at a mountain of washing, a stack of clothes piled high in the corner but no . . .

There were bodies in those clothes.

Rua tiptoed over to the pile of blue witch corpses. They lay like a mound of discarded dolls stacked in a heap. Their bodies were covered in burn marks and mean scars. They each bore a matching Mhenbic symbol carved into their forehead: *suraash*. Rua trembled as she peered at the face closest to her. The witch's brown hair had been shaved close to her scalp, her long brown lashes pretty against her scarred face.

"We need to bring them all up," Rua whispered, turning back to Renwick, who pilfered through the pile of papers with one hand while holding the torch up with the other.

Renwick's eyes softened at her. "Agreed."

Rua was grateful for his acquiescence. Otherwise she would have to lug these dead witches up the winding flights of stairs herself. There was no way she could leave them here, too cold for their bodies to decay, their souls frozen along with them.

She turned back to get one more look at the brown-haired witch.

The witch's eyes were open.

~

A shriek lodged in her throat as Rua stared into those glowing blue eyes.

"Hello, Princess." The witch smiled, her wide eyes roving Rua's body.

"Run!" Rua screamed, dropping her candle as the pile of bodies animated, a dozen witches springing to life. Their screeches and growls were wilder than any animal Rua had ever heard.

They bolted back down the hallway, a horde of *suraash* at their backs. Bri pushed Rua in front of her, Thador taking up the rear as Renwick plowed ahead.

With a squealing cry, a blue witch jumped in front of Renwick. They all halted. The one that had been manacled to the wall tackled him to the ground. The torch was knocked out of his hand, still burning against the wooden door of the far room. The witch clawed at his face with glowing blue hands, screaming as he grappled for his sword.

"Witchslayer," the *suraash* hissed in Mhenbic. Her voice sounded like the scratchy yowl of a wounded wolf. Rua wondered if this cursed witch knew Renwick, if he had tortured her himself. Did he deserve this vengeance? She couldn't comprehend how he earned the name Witchslayer. For some reason, even with his cruel demeanor, she couldn't imagine him killing witches for sport, like the rumors suggested.

"Rua," Bri hissed, snapping her from her stupor.

As Bri pulled two daggers from her belt, Rua cursed herself for not thinking of the Immortal Blade sooner—too lost in her thoughts. She unsheathed the sword at her hip.

The cold metal hilt warmed instantly in her hand, the blade thanking her as she felt that white glow of power fill her body. It felt like a tugging at the center of her chest, lifting her higher into herself. In her mind, she whispered to the sword what she wanted it to do, and the sword obeyed, her hand slicing through the air. The witch's throat sliced open. Blood poured across Renwick's face as he shoved the cursed witch off him.

The door to their left was alight now. Renwick's torch sat at its base, feeding the flames. Rua coughed as smoke began to fill the corridor.

"I could use that sword over here!" Thador barked at her.

Bri and Thador battled against the blue witches behind them. Two of the other Northern guards struggled to fight the witches back. A third lay dead on the floor. A witch crouched over him, her glowing hands and mouth dripping in blood. Rua looked in terror to the guard's gashed-open throat and back to the witch. The witch was *chewing* something. Rua felt bile rising into her mouth. The witch had torn open his throat with her teeth, a magical bloodlust from Balorn's curse driving the beast.

The Immortal Blade sang to Rua, begging to be used again. She sliced hard and the witch's head went flying through the air. She swung again and again, a fire growing with each swoop of her blade, until every blue witch lay dead on the floor. She thought of the terror that had racked her body when she thought Hennen Vostemur's guards would cut off her head. These witches didn't show any fear, the spell compelling them and overriding their senses.

She stared down at their unseeing eyes, the eerie blue glow flickering out. Rua had promised herself she wouldn't slay any cursed witches and here they all were, slain by her sword. She knew that made her the worst kind of monster.

"Let's go," Thador panted. His voice sounded far away in Rua's mind, the white-hot whirring of the blade still coursing through her body.

"Rua." She heard Bri's voice and finally looked up from the bodies at her feet to those golden eyes. "Let's get out of here."

Rua released a long-held breath and turned to follow Renwick up the stairs. The fire raged behind them as they bolted, smoke chasing them into the pitch-black hallway. Rua prayed that the fire burned those witches' bodies. It would be the only burial they would receive.

"Let me go first," Thador said, pushing blindly to the front.

Rua couldn't see an inch in front of her face through the smoky darkness. Her eyes strained to make out any shapes.

She felt a hand land on her arm. She was about to snatch it back when Renwick's voice said, "It's me."

He placed her hand on his shoulder. She left it there, her other hand gripping the Immortal Blade tighter as they moved in a chain through the darkness. They hastened blindly up the stairs, pouring gratefully back out into the light of the grand hall.

Rua felt the muscle of Renwick's shoulder tighten beneath her fingertips.

"Shit."

She peered around Renwick to the bodies on the stone floor. The Northern guards who came with their convoy all lay dead, their blood staining the snow red. The far door to the hall was shut.

"Look out!"

An arrow flew through the open window.

Ducking, they rushed toward the far doorway. A tirade of arrows flew in through the windows, one striking a soldier. He crashed down to the floor as another arrow pierced his back. The giant far doors opened, revealing an army of witches. They wore flowing black dresses not fit for the cold, their smiles twisted, their eyes so wide: the *suraash*.

Rua felt a punch to her chest.

"Rua!" Renwick shouted as her eyes dropped to the location of the blow.

An arrow protruded from her sternum. Rua grabbed the arrow and yanked it free. It had pierced through her cloak and her leathers, but when she dipped a finger into the hole in her clothing, her skin was unmarked.

"I guess arrows count according to the Immortal Blade's magic." Bri looked wide-eyed at her, shaking her head in disbelief. "But I don't have a magic sword so let's get the fuck out of here."

The *suraash* surged into the hall, shrieking as they ran. Rua felt the building flames in her gut as she moved the Immortal Blade again. She hacked as quickly as her arms would allow, curving the heavy sword through the air. One witch, then another, fell to the ground. But there were too many. Each of the others were now fighting off at least three witches on their own. She spotted their impressive fighting skills from her periphery as she kept swinging her sword. Thador fought like a lumbering bear, using heavy swings of his long sword, pushing back witches with his burly free arm. Bri moved like the eagle she was, quick and predatory, holding nothing back. And Renwick . . . a strange thrill shot through Rua's body as she watched him move—his ashblond hair tousled, his normally pristine attire disheveled, his face splattered with blood. He moved with pinpoint precision, each movement exact and lethal. Rua got lost in his war dance.

A hand grabbed the back of her head, yanking her to the ground.

Rua hit the stone floor hard, eyes spotting, as a *suraash* leapt on top of her. The Immortal Blade clattered to the ground as sharpened nails clawed at her. Rua shielded her face with one hand as her other strained toward the hilt of her sword. The cursed witch traded claws for punches, raining down blows to her temple, cheek, mouth. Someone screamed her name, but the ringing in her ears was so loud she could not discern who. She felt her lip split as her fingertips finally grazed the blade. She thrust the sword straight up into the air. The witch above her seized, blood spurting from her gut as the blade's magic impaled her. Rua thrust the witch off with her forearm.

Her head throbbed as she got to her feet, swaying, spitting blood onto the cold stone. The pain seemed to ignite something within the blade. She began moving the sword faster, her mind splintering outward to several witches at once. In one swoop, three witches went down. Every shadow, every movement in her periphery was cut down before it got too close. Another swing of her sword, another two witches fell. She thought to the archers outside, not even seeing them but holding them in her mind's eye, and with another slice of her blade, she knew they all died.

*More, more,* begged the sword.

Rua's eyes filled with white lightning. A blissful feeling swept over her as her blade danced through the air. The intoxicating feeling filled her body with molten gold. She kept going, kept hacking, a smile beginning to pull up at the corners of her lips.

A hand wrapped around her torso and pulled her back against a hard chest. "Gods, Rua. Stop."

Renwick's voice sounded far away as he breathed into her hair. The Immortal Blade kept moving, demanding more, promising more ecstasy with each swing.

Rua felt the press of lips to the shell of her ear. "Control it, Rua," a hot breath whispered. The tingling sensation from that breath seemed to snap the current of energy from the blade.

Rua gasped in a breath as she lowered her sword. Her vision sharpened once more as that white whirring power ebbed and left her with the somber darkness of her own soul. She looked to the surrounding room. Bri and Thador still stood amongst a battlefield of bodies. The two guards looked at her warily as their chests heaved from the exertion of battle. The last Northern guard who had accompanied them into the bowels of the Temple of Hunasht lay dead on the floor. A clean slice gaped across his neck. That wound was not from the witches . . . it was from the Immortal Blade.

She had killed someone on their side.

Thador held his shoulder, blood weeping between his fingers as he stared at her like she was a ghost. She was certain from the look on his face that the wound was her doing. Were it not for Renwick, she probably would have killed them all.

*Gods, Rua. Stop.* The fear of Renwick's words circled her mind. He had thought she would kill them all too.

Rua swallowed, pulling out of Renwick's hold as she sheathed the blade. She did not look at anyone as she walked out of the temple and into the snow.

# CHAPTER SEVEN

Rua pushed back the heavy velvet curtains to the fae fire tent. Even in the Lyrei Basin, they kept a fae fire burning so that any fae could reach them. When they had returned from the Temple of Hunasht, Rua had gone to her tent to clean up, but Bri insisted on contacting Remy straightaway.

A giant brazier sat on a thick circle of gravel, its metal bowl filled with crackling logs. A giant green fire licked high toward the hole cut out of the roof of the tent. The room was so warm it was uncomfortable. Bri had taken off her heavy cloak and set it on one of the benches behind her that lined the walls.

"*How* many were there?" She knew that voice, though she only had the briefest conversations with the speaker. It was Remy.

"Two dozen witches from my counts," Bri said. The Eagle looked up to Rua, narrowing her eyes from where she stood across the giant fire.

Rua held a finger up to her lips and shook her head in a silent command. She did not want her elder sister to know she was listening. Sweat beaded on her brow from the fire's warmth, and she unclasped the neck of her cloak, setting the heavy, fur-trimmed garment down on the thin, wooden bench.

"And how many guards did Renwick bring?" a male voice echoed through the flames. Hale—the soon-to-be King of the High Mountain Court and her sister's Fated.

She rolled her eyes. Of course, he would be there too. Fated love was a mystery to Rua. Some people's bonds shone so brightly it existed beyond space and time. It was a magic that could be picked up by blue witch oracles. Some stories claimed blue witches prophesied a Fated love before the lovers were even born, though most were foreseen within the mates' lifetimes. It was a rare magic that Remy had been blessed with. Fated mates were not just a love match; the magic of that bond was stronger than any other. It was something ancient and inevitable.

Rua was grateful that she had no such Fated. If any match had received a Fated prophecy to her, they would have told Remy by now. Some greedy bastard would have wanted the benefit of being matched to the Princess of the High Mountain Court. There would be no reason to wait. So either Rua didn't have a Fated or her mate had died like so many others. She did not care, so long as she was left alone.

". . . blue witches can avoid the scouts." Hale was still talking, Rua realized, but she hadn't been listening. She was too wrapped up in the stupidity of Fated love. The Fates were just another trio of made-up Gods prayed to by the fae. The witches only believed in the Moon Goddess. They called Fated love Moon Blessings. Both were ridiculous.

"Renwick should have been more careful. He's been downplaying the severity of the Northern dissenters," Remy said.

"They call themselves loyalists," Bri said to the flames. The only thing that made the fire look magical was the eerie green glow at its base. It was a different color than green witch magic—that glowed a forest green. This was more yellowy, its edges glowing with white.

"Did you take any captives? Did you get any answers?" Hale asked. Bri had pledged her fealty to Hale when she joined his ranks, and because Hale and Remy were Fated, Bri's fealty went toward Rua's sister too. The fae warrior was sworn to them, not Rua. If push came to shove, Bri would follow the orders of the High Mountain Queen.

"There was no time," Bri said. "The witches were cursed, beyond questioning, and the guards . . . fell too quickly."

"I am guessing the Immortal Blade had something to do with that," he said, not mentioning Rua, the one who controlled the blade, like the fault lay with the sword and not her.

Those golden eyes flicked up to Rua, looking to her bruised forehead and split lip, as she said, "What they say is true. No blade can pierce the skin of the wielder of the Immortal Blade . . . fists on the other hand."

Rua's shoulders dropped. She was grateful Bri didn't tell her sister what havoc she wrought with the High Mountain talisman. Hale was right. The blade had the urge to kill, and Rua needed to get a better grip on that power.

After a tense silence through the flames, Remy said, "I'm sending Carys too."

"You don't need to send everyone," Bri said, rubbing the back of her neck.

"I'm sending her," Remy pushed.

"Someone needs to stay in the East," Hale's voice reminded her as Rua folded her arms tightly across her chest.

The Eastern Court was a mess all of its own. Augustus Norwood, the youngest son of the fallen King Gedwin Norwood, fled into the forests around the foothills of the Rotted Peak. He had not made any move to reclaim the Eastern capital city of Wynreach, but the day would come. Meanwhile, Remy and Hale had appointed a council of people to keep the peace until a new sovereign was chosen. Carys and Talhan both sat on that council, along with a handful of others they deemed worthy. By including witches and humans, they had already stirred up discomfort in the Eastern Court.

Rua thought to that night in the Northern palace when King Norwood revealed himself to not be Hale's true father. She would forever remember the look on Hale's face, that visceral flicker of relief and rage. King Norwood had only claimed Hale as his son because Hale was prophesied to be Fated to Remy. That was the problem with these Fates, that magical love bond was not a blessing, it was a weapon.

"Fine, just Talhan then," Remy said.

Rua cursed herself. She had not been listening again. It sounded like

Bri would be a Twin Eagle once more, that Remy was sending Bri's twin brother from the Eastern Court to join them.

"Is she okay?" Remy's voice was a murmur through the green flames.

"Oh," Bri said, looking between Rua and the fire. "Yep, she's fine."

"She's there, isn't she?" Remy asked. Rua frowned at Bri. She was a terrible liar. "You okay, Rua?"

"I am fine. Just a couple scratches," Rua called, unsure why she shouted toward the flames. "We've got the situation under control here. You do not need to send Talhan."

"I'm doing it more for him," Remy assured her. "He's bored out of his skull in all of those council meetings. He is a warrior, not a councilor."

Bri snorted. "I can't imagine him at a table covered in scrolls."

"Talhan is a good sword, and he'll help with any fights until you can reverse Balorn's curse," Remy insisted.

Rua had only spoken to her sister twice and both times her sister had done this: trying to reassure Rua that she was capable and that the things that Remy wanted were not because of Rua's weakness. It all felt like a lie. Remy seemed desperate for a relationship with Rua—not wanting to ruin their chances at a friendship by putting Rua down. But it all still felt forced and hollow.

"Fine," Rua finally gritted out.

"Talhan should be there within a week, should the snows not be too strong," Remy said.

"Is it snowing in Yexshire yet?" Bri wondered. Rua rolled her eyes. They had just been attacked by an army of bloodthirsty witches, and Bri was asking about the weather.

"It has!" Remy sounded so happy it made Rua's shoulders tighten. She sounded just like the red witches Rua grew up with—always turning toward some sort of performative joy. "We just had a beautiful, fresh snowfall this morning. Up to my ankles now."

"Sounds a lot nicer than here," Bri said, but her eyes crinkled at the flames. The Eagle was happy for Remy and Rua didn't like it.

"I'm going to bed," Rua said. She was going to stalk off and leave it at that, but she knew it would break her sister's heart, so she reluctantly added, "Good luck with the rebuild."

"Thank you." Remy's voice filled with warmth. "It is coming along so quickly. It will be ready by the time you come for the Winter Solstice."

"You've built a castle in three weeks?" Rua's eyebrows shot up.

"We have been working day and night. The other courts have sent aid too. We are clearing the roads out of Yexshire to the other courts now. The road south is already navigable. Neelo has convinced their mother to send food and clothing, Hale has sent loggers and builders, and the Western Queen has sent horses and wagons."

"Gods," Rua breathed. The other courts were sending swift aid to the High Mountain Court. Rua wondered if it was because of the talismans. Remy and Rua were formidable opponents. Were they only helping because the sisters were a potential threat? Or did they feel such relief to be taken from the grips of Hennen Vostemur that they were willing to help? Rua supposed the third option was that they were motivated from kindness, though she doubted that. She wondered if Renwick had sent any aid.

"We are building up the town as we build the castle," Remy continued. "The red witches have been using their magic to hasten things along, and now that I have the amulet of Aelusien, I can move the heaviest objects with ease."

Though she couldn't see her sister, Rua was certain that she was smiling. She sounded fulfilled, rebuilding their family's fallen home with their ancestors' magical relic.

The amulet of Aelusien was another High Mountain talisman, a gift from the ancient red witches. It could give any fae the powers of red magic, and even though Remy and Rua possessed red witch magic already, the amulet concentrated their powers. The amulet was the sister talisman to the Immortal Blade hanging from Rua's belt. The trio of talismans was completed by the *Shil-de* ring, which now encircled Hale's finger, keeping him from certain death that night in the Northern palace. Rua had thought the High Mountain Court was the only court with ancient witch relics—a naive thought—now that they hunted the Witches' Glass.

"Don't let her fool you," Hale said. "She has barely slept since we arrived back. She is so determined to have it done by the wedding."

"I'm sure the wedding will be beautiful whether you have ramparts or not," Bri said.

Rua had forgotten that the Winter Solstice celebrations would not only be about welcoming in the new light after the shortest day—it would also be her sister's wedding.

"Yes, yes, I know," Remy tutted. "And we should celebrate your birthday again when you are here too, Rua."

Rua blanched. Her birthday was in five days' time. How had Remy known? Did she have some scribe from another court look it up in their notes? The documents of Yexshire were all gone, but the births of royalty would be written down in every court. Rua knew Remy's birthday was only a few weeks ahead of hers. The red witches Rua grew up with had told her as much. Rua wasn't sure how birthdays were *celebrated*, other than lighting a candle and making a wish. It was all they had done in the witch camps.

"I should let you get some sleep," Remy said. "I will call again in a few days, but if anything happens before then . . ."

"I will let you know," Bri said.

"Good," Remy said. "Goodbye, Rua. Goodbye, Bri."

"Bye," Hale added a little too quickly, making Rua wonder what sort of mischief the two of them were about to get up to. Her cheeks heated. She knew the answer from her sister's giggle.

As the green glow ebbed from the flames, Bri turned to her. "When is your birthday?"

"In five days."

"Why didn't you tell anyone?" Bri wondered, grabbing her cloak from the bench behind her and pulling back on the heavy garment.

"When should I have mentioned it?" Rua snarled. "When we were being attacked by a bunch of crazed witches or while we were staring at naked bodies nailed to trees? Should I have just added 'Oh, by the way, my birthday is coming up'?" Rua mocked in a sickly sweet voice.

Bri grunted. "You are becoming one of my favorite people, Ru."

~

They emerged from the fae fire tent, bracing for the shock of the cold night air. At least it wasn't snowing. They wove through the narrow paths between the musty and weathered tents. Fae soldiers gathered around a fire bowl, their laughter quickly dying off as Rua walked past. Bri caught the eye of one of the female soldiers and winked.

Rua snickered.

"Let me have my fun." Bri chuckled softly as they dove deeper into the labyrinth of tents.

They passed another fire, a group of blue witches standing around it. Holding their hands out to the warming flames, they turned their wary stares to Rua and Bri. The cold reception was understandable. The blue witches had been through so much, the scent of their slain sisters still on her skin. Rua imagined even staying with the new Northern King felt wrong to them.

"Oh, it's you," a gruff voice came from behind her.

Thador stood in fresh clothing, his face mottled with bruises. The straining band of fabric around his upper arm indicated that his wound was now bandaged—the wound she inflicted. The soldier seemed to note the line of her stare. His dark eyes darted back and forth between Rua and Bri, his lips pulling up at one side.

"The King and I are going to play a hand. Care to join?" he asked, tilting his head.

Bri perked up with zeal at her side. Perhaps her guard needed a distraction from almost being killed that day too. Rua loved card games, though she rarely had anyone to play them with. She supposed the Northern King and his guard would have to do.

"All right," she said, even though her face was tight.

Bri flashed a toothy grin.

Thador led the way westward, breaking from their usual path through the campsite. They moved to the very center of the base, through a wide-open circle of gravel like an empty courtyard, but the coarse stones shifted to smaller, blue-gray pebbles.

A giant blue tent sat at the far side, ten times the size of Rua's own.

Two guards stood at the front flaps of heavy canvas embroidered in the Northern crest.

When they entered, stepping into a narrow corridor, Rua's eyes widened. The tent was like an entire house, all festooned in shades of blue, from the tent poles to the ceiling. The crunching stones underfoot changed to rough carpet, good for wiping their snowy boots on. They passed several heavy velvet curtains until they reached the second to last one.

Thador yanked apart the curtains. Rua's face was greeted by warmth as she followed him into the room. The smell of old books swirled in the air as she eyed the walls lined with towering bookshelves. A blackened steel box sat in the far corner, a pipe running up through the tent fabric: a fireplace. She wondered if every tent had these contraptions to keep warm. A large, red oak desk sat close to the far wall. Another two upholstered red velvet chairs sat tucked into the right-hand corner, a cozy nook perfectly positioned to sit and read. To the left sat a simple circular table and two wooden chairs.

Renwick turned from the bookcase and snapped the book in his hands shut.

"I've brought guests," Thador announced.

"I can see that," Renwick replied with a hint of amusement. His eyes scanned over the two of them. They snagged on the purple bruise on Rua's forehead and down to her split lip. Her fae magic was already healing her wounds, but she was certain she still looked awful.

"Shoes," Thador instructed, shucking off his heavy boots and dropping them at the threshold.

"I have not washed yet like the rest of you," Bri said, "prepare yourself."

She dropped her boots next to Thador's, and Rua followed suit.

"Please, I grew up in war camps." Thador chuckled, brushing his hand across his short, stubbled hair. "Stinky feet smell like home."

Renwick stood motionless by the bookshelf apart from his eyes tracking Bri and Thador as they dropped into the wooden seats. He looked back to his normal, elegant self. His hair was neatly combed and tied at the nape of his neck. His fawn-colored shirt was perfectly pressed. The absence of a jacket felt incredibly informal coming from him. Of course, he had not expected for the two of them to be joining him. The only sign of the events of the day were the thin trails of red scratches down the left-hand side of his face. Shallow cuts, they would be gone by the morning. His hard jawline and high cheekbones seemed warmer, softer, in the candlelight. Rua bit the inside of her cheek as she looked over his tall, lithe frame and those full pink lips. Gods, why did he have to be so damn handsome? It felt wrong for someone so cold to be so good-looking.

Rua moved to grab one of the red velvet chairs to bring over to the table, and that seemed to jolt Renwick back into motion.

"Allow me," he said, reaching for the arm of the chair.

"I can grab my own seat." Rua scoffed at his odd sense of chivalry, tipping her head to the chair's twin. "You take the other one, and let's play some cards."

Carrying the chairs over, Rua positioned hers to the opposite side of the table so that she didn't have to sit next to Renwick. After that morning in the Temple of Hunasht, she needed to set some distance between them. The memory of his hot breath in her hair made her ears tingle. That whisper had a magic all its own. It was not witch or fae, but something in it had released the Immortal Blade's grip on her.

Renwick reached into the pocket of his trousers and set a pack of playing cards on the table. They were a beautiful hand-painted deck. Without thinking, Rua reached out and turned the cards over in her hands. Each suit was meticulously painted with the crests of Okrith . . . all except the High Mountain Court. The cards must have been painted as a present to Renwick at some point in the last fourteen years, after the High Mountain Court had fallen.

The room tensed as Rua looked over the playing cards, the insult to her family evident across their detailed images. She did not care. She felt as distant to the High Mountain Court as everyone else around the table. The cards felt well used, their edges softened from several years of playing.

"What card games do you like to play?" Renwick asked, his snake eyes watching her with that stillness that told her everything. He went still when he was brimming over with emotions, not when he was absent of them as he tried so hard to bluff.

Rua cut the deck in one hand and shuffled the cards between her two palms in a perfect arch. Renwick's brows shot up, lips parting.

"I'm liking you more and more, Princess." Thador laughed, leaning his elbows on the table.

"Have you ever played witch's bluff?" Rua smirked, raising her eyebrow at Renwick.

"I am not playing your witches' game." Renwick's cheeks dimpled. "You will cheat."

Rua shrugged. He was right. She would cheat.

"I like two kings," she said, passing the deck back to Renwick. His rough fingers skimmed over hers as he took it. The feeling of that small touch sent a jolt of lightning through her body. She pulled away her hand and fisted it in her lap. The nerves of the morning had scrambled her brain. She needed to get a grip.

"Do you know the Southern rules or the High Mountain rules?" Renwick asked.

"Both." Rua's eyes twinkled as she grinned with mischief.

"Marry her, Renwick." Thador chuckled.

Bri kicked the lumbering guard under the table, and he cursed.

"You are skilled at cards? Excellent." Renwick's smile was equally delighted and predatory. In the short time Rua had been in the North, she had already heard of the Northern King's love of cards. She smiled to herself, thinking about how good it would feel to beat him.

There were not many toys in the red witch camps, but they had cards. One of the witches took pity on her and gave her a pack. Rua quickly learned every game she could play by herself. The older witches and witchlings didn't let her join in often, so Rua sat nearby and watched them play. She learned all of their tricks and techniques. It was the best she could do. As long as she didn't draw anyone's attention, they would permit her to stay and watch. When they did let her play, they realized quickly she had a knack for it.

"I am skilled," she said, "though not many were willing to play with me growing up."

"Not the favorite child of the witch camps?" Renwick taunted.

"Why would they want me?" Rua asked, making everyone at the table tense. She felt all three sets of eyes on her. "I was a reminder of all that they had lost. It was my family's fault that . . ."

"It was *my* family's fault," Renwick cut in.

Rua looked up into those blazing emerald eyes. She saw his shame, a shame that mirrored her own.

"Hear, hear," Bri said.

"Still, a red witch camp was not a welcome refuge." Rua stuck her jaw out to the side.

Bri opened her mouth to speak, but a human servant entered the room, holding a tray of food. She bowed deeply while balancing the tray.

"Put it on the desk, please, Penelope," Renwick instructed.

Rua quirked her eyebrow. He called his servants by their first names? He seemed so prim and proper, yet he treated his servants with a level of familiarity she did not expect.

"Yes, Your Majesty," Penelope murmured.

"Please, help yourself to refreshments." Renwick waved a hand over to the far desk and the tray of what looked like savory pastries and dried fruit.

Renwick shuffled the cards again. "What news from the High Mountain Queen?"

The High Mountain Queen. Remy was crowned the day they arrived in Yexshire, and Rua had not been there for the coronation, the title still sounding odd to her ears. It was barely a ceremony, according to Bri, but Remy wanted to stake her claim to the throne right away, to give the people something to unite behind following Raffiel's death. Rua wondered if Remy blamed her for Raffiel. Rua should have grabbed the Immortal Blade sooner. She was standing right next to it, and she didn't use it fast enough. She thought of Bri's warning not to play that game of "should haves," but Rua couldn't help it, not when it mattered so much.

"Remy is sending Talhan to Murreneir," Rua mumbled, looking down as Renwick dealt.

Thador laughed, leaning back in his chair. "The delightful puppy in the body of a warrior?"

"Watch it," Bri growled.

"It'll be like old times," Renwick said, rubbing his temple, thumb digging into his flesh as if he were trying to loosen a tight muscle.

Rua narrowed her eyes at the movement. "Old times?" she asked, her eyes darting to Bri.

"Oh, you don't know?" Thador began.

"Say another word and I'll cut out your tongue," Bri hissed, her voice laced with venom. Rua frowned at the Eagle. What secrets did she keep? Rua knew nothing of Bri's past.

Bri gave Rua a sympathetic look. "It's a long story."

"Yeah." Rua's frown deepened.

"The High Mountain Queen said you should have brought your own blue witches today," Bri added, pulling them out of the awkward silence. "She said that your blue witches would have been able to See the attack coming."

"I didn't want to put them through that." Renwick rubbed his temple harder. Perhaps it was the strain of this topic that was causing his pain. "Many of them were *trained* in those halls."

Trained. The word made Rua's stomach clench again. They were not trained; they were tortured. The ones deemed broken enough were then moved down to the capital to serve the former King. Rua thought to those haunted faces from that morning: the *suraash*—the Forgotten Ones. They were the ones broken too much, shattered beyond repair. It struck Rua now how young they all were. Their eerie spelled faces had distracted her from that fact. But they couldn't have been any older than her. How much of their childhoods were they tortured before they were released from that prison?

Lord Berecraft entered from behind the curtains, snapping Rua from her darkening thoughts. The rest of Renwick's lords had returned to their home counties to keep an eye out for Balorn and hints at how to break his curse, but Berecraft remained.

"Your Majesty," Berecraft said, looking shrewdly to the table. "We should be holding a council meeting through the fae fires at once after the events of the day."

Renwick let out a long-suffering sigh. "We will have one in the morning, Berecraft."

"You would meet with a foreign princess before meeting with—"

"I am *meeting* with no one. I am *playing* cards," Renwick growled.

"But—"

Renwick shoved back his chair and shot up from his seat. "Please excuse me one moment," he rumbled, pushing his way out into the corridor as his councilor followed him.

"Food time." Thador dawdled over to the tray of food on the desk.

Rua's lips twisted up as she followed, making her injured lip sting again.

Bri noted her grimace and added, "You need wine."

Shoving an entire piece of flaky pastry into her mouth, Bri grabbed another. She poured the pitcher of thick maroon liquid into a glass set next to the food tray. It smelled like wine, though Rua had never seen wine that color before.

The witch camps of her childhood were sparse, but occasionally the witches would venture to the Southern Court to replenish their stocks. There had been talk of moving to the Southern Court, where the red witches would be safer. The Southerners didn't like witch hunters coming into their court and had established vigilante justice, finding witch hunters and retaliating in kind—cutting off their heads. But Baba Morganna had insisted that the red witches stay in their native court, even if that meant camping in the woods.

Rua never understood that: only staying in the place you were from, as if every person born in the High Mountain Court was magically suited to its climate and customs. The fact it was where her ancestors were from meant nothing to her. She wanted to see the other courts and decide for herself. She'd rather stay in the frozen tundra of the ice lakes than one more day in a red witch camp.

Bri reached for a handful of dried apricots, and Rua looked sideways at the Eagle, raising her eyebrows.

"This isn't a war camp," Rua chastised. "There will be more food."

"I just eat fast." Bri's words were garbled, cheeks filled with food. "You'll have to get used to it if I'm going to be sticking around."

Rua tossed her wavy hair over her shoulder. It was growing long again, nearly past her shoulder blades. The witches used to cut it long enough to tie back but not so long it took ages to brush. She liked that no one could tell her the length she should wear her hair anymore.

"But you are not sticking around," Rua said, finally selecting a roll that looked filled with spiced nuts and cheese. She took a small bite from the corner of her mouth, careful to avoid her injured lip. Closing her eyes, she savored the taste. The buttery flavor mixed perfectly with the tangy cheese and curried walnut filling. Rua was certain then that Renwick had employed green witches. The green magic did not seem as powerful as the blue witches' Sight or the red witches' animation, but it was the magic most used by the fae, even more than the brown witches' healing. A vision was only so useful, but a tasty meal was always welcome. The green witches probably aided the Northern Court to make their short growing seasons fruitful too.

"You are pledged to serve my sister, not me," Rua said. "When all of this is over, you will go back to serving her."

"Technically, I pledged my sword to your sister's betrothed," Bri countered. "But now he is the Fated of the High Mountain Queen. So that means I serve your whole family."

Rua let out a bitter huff. "If Remy asked you to do something, and I asked you not to, which would you do?" Bri paused her chewing. "Aha, you see?"

"That is not a fair question," Bri mumbled as crumbs of pastry fell from her lips. "Your sister is the Queen, which makes her *your* Queen too. You should be following her orders."

"I am not interested in following anyone's orders but my own," Rua groused.

"I believe they call you a dissenter, Ru." Bri winked, making Rua clench her fists. These fae were infuriating. At least in the witch camps, no one talked to her. She was sick of all this fae banter. Turning from Bri, she made her way to the far bookshelf.

The shelves were lined with faded cloth-bound books. Rua's fingers skimmed across the dusty tomes. Most were history books of the Northern Court. Rua's fingers stopped on a navy-blue book called *Songs of Spring in Murreneir.* She traced the gold lettering down the book's spine. Sliding the book off the shelf, she carefully opened it. Something about this book felt special, as if its weight were more than pages.

She flicked through the worn, yellowing pages. It was a book of poetry and short stories about the town beyond Lyrei Basin. She wondered if the main city of Murreneir could be seen from the location of the new castle. Rua flicked to the title page. Inscribed in bleeding black ink was a note:

*To my darling Eadwin. One day you will read this book and know the stories of your mother's homeland. Stay well until I see you next spring, mea raga. Mama.*

Rua read it over again. *Mea raga.* It was a Mhenbic saying. It meant "my precious one" or "my little loved one," depending on how it was used. Was this a book from a witch to her child?

Eadwin? Rua did not know that name. She traced her fingers over the words as if she could garner information from the feel of the ink on the page. Perhaps Eadwin was one of Renwick's middle names? She would have to ask him. Maybe Eadwin was a grandparent . . . the book seemed old.

As she replaced the book, she heard the clink of glass. Eyes narrowing, she reached behind the row of books, her fingers skimming a line of glass vials. She pulled out one of the vials hidden behind the book. There was no label on it. Bringing the vial to her nose, she sniffed the cork: hellebore and bloodbane. Her eyes widened as she quickly put the vial back. It was the sort of elixir that should be locked away in a brown witch healer's tent, not hiding behind books. Rua had only seen it used a handful of times in her life. It had only been given to relieve the pain of those who were dying, to ease their transition to the afterlife. The witches said it was too potent to give out to others; gentler remedies should be used in other cases. Why was a vial hiding behind Renwick's bookcase? Were all the other vials filled with the same sort of noxious liquid?

The sound of thudding footsteps grew from beyond the tent wall. Taking two sideways steps, she moved further along the wall.

Rua knew she wouldn't ask about the vials as Renwick came back into the room. His face looked tight with exasperation from whatever conversation he had with his councilor, the muscle on the side of his jaw popping out.

Renwick paused for a moment when he saw Rua standing at the bookshelf. She clasped her hands in front of her.

"You may borrow any books you wish, though these are all rather boring," Renwick said as he strode over to her. "I am sure some of the others have brought more exciting reads, if you wish me to ask."

Rua narrowed her eyes at him. He was offering to find books for her?

"That's not necessary," she said. "I take it your councilor is displeased you put off the meeting?"

"Balorn will not be attacking these camps," Renwick grumbled, probably repeating the same conversation he just had with Berecraft. "The blue witches and guards on the surrounding hills would see Balorn coming from miles away. We have time to decide what we do next."

"And what do you plan to do next?"

Renwick lifted his hand to his forehead, rubbing it in that methodical way. Were his secret elixirs for his pain? She wouldn't be surprised if the powerful potion had caused his headaches, leaving a nasty aftershock.

"Not you too," Renwick jested. "I plan on asking the camp's blue witches to help us find the book of spells and Witches' Glass. It will be hard since Balorn has the Forgotten Ones with him to shield their visions . . . but with any luck they will be able to See glimpses of what Balorn and his fae soldiers are up to."

"You haven't asked them to help you yet?" Rua wondered, her tongue pressing into her wounded lip. Renwick's eyes shot to the corner of her mouth and Rua quickly stopped.

"The blue witches who remained with me were either motivated by fear or their loyalty to Baba Airu. To demand their servitude, to ask them to give over their sacred books and talismans to another

Vostemur King seemed . . . inappropriate." Renwick's eyes scanned Rua's face. She watched as he took it all in—her full lips, her freckled cheeks, her warm brown eyes with flecks of green that perfectly matched his own. "Tomorrow I'd like you to go speak to Baba Airu and ask where the faction of blue witches have taken their spell book. Aneryn will accompany you. I don't think I will be welcome in that part of the camp."

Rua gripped her hands together tighter, unsure how to speak with the same blue witch who haunted her nightmares, smiling amongst the slaughter in Drunehan. She didn't like the idea of seeing her again, let alone having to hold a conversation. Just because she grew up with the red witches didn't make her a good witch ally.

"Why did you bring the remaining witches all the way up here?"

"Murreneir is the homeland of the blue witches," Renwick said, "and if I left them in Drunehan, they would be treated . . . poorly. Here they have my protection. I did not force them to come."

"I did not accuse you of that," Rua murmured, pulling her lip between her teeth.

"But you were thinking it." Renwick watched her as if he could divine her thoughts just from looking hard enough. The intensity of his stare made her feel unsteady.

"You have no idea what I'm thinking." Rua finally looked up defiantly into those eyes, muscles tightening against the intensity she saw within them. His eyes were filled with an endless depth that she feared would ensnare her.

Renwick's cheeks dimpled. "Want to bet?"

Breaking the spell that locked their gazes, Rua looked at the card table. "I thought that's what we were doing here," Rua said. "Are you prepared to lose, King Renwick?"

Renwick flashed Rua a wicked grin as she called him by his title. "I would like to see you try."

"Come on, Rua," Bri called, waving her glass of wine at them. "I want to see Renwick's face when we beat him."

Letting out a cackling witch's laugh, Rua's whole body shook. Renwick's smile morphed from predatory to warm as Rua shook off the laugh, embarrassed. It was just another way she was unlike the fae.

Renwick reclaimed the hands he had dealt and shuffled the deck again. He went around the table, tossing each of them five cards, his practiced hands moving with a steady grace. Rua lifted her cards— three queens, a king, and a five. The crowns of the Southern, West- ern, and Northern Court sat painted on them. She hid her smirk as she looked up to Renwick, who was assessing his cards.

"Prepared to lose?" Thador taunted as he tossed a card toward Ren- wick in exchange for another.

"Never." Rua grinned, looking down at her queens. She waved her hand to show she didn't want to trade any cards, causing Renwick to narrow his eyes at her. Some people would think to trade in the five, but if the hand got too high, a low card was needed.

Bri tossed in a single card, her face dropping into a neutral expres- sion that Rua assumed meant she had a good hand. "What exactly are we playing for?"

"Loser takes off an article of clothing?" Thador suggested with a cheeky wink at Bri.

"Absolutely not," Rua said at the same time Bri bit out a decisive "No."

"Let's just play." Renwick cut a look to Thador, an apparent warning to behave. "Catullus, you're first."

They went around the table, setting out their cards into three piles laid in the center faceup. Rua's mind raced, adding up the three cards in quick succession. It took her years to become practiced in this game and now she knew almost instinctively which card to choose.

When the turn landed back on Renwick, he put down a nine and Bri cursed, tossing in the rest of her hand. Rua set down her first queen and eyed Thador. He cursed as well, tossing in his hand. Renwick chuckled, matching the Western Court suit of Rua's queen with a ten. Rua smiled, setting down her next queen and looking up to Renwick with a cocked brow.

The muscles in his cheek flickered, and Rua's stomach flipped. Bri leaned in with rapt attention, placing her elbows on the table as she watched Renwick's next move with a foxlike grin. Carefully selecting a card, Renwick set down an Eastern queen, the last in the deck. He watched Rua with such scorching intensity it made her toes curl. She pressed her lips together, setting down another queen.

Renwick assessed the table, looking between Rua and the cards laid out before him. Only two cards could win the hand without busting it now. A subtle smile played across his lips as he set down a Southern King.

"Ha!" Thador guffawed, smacking the table and making Rua jump.

Renwick stretched his arms out to his sides, already beaming with the victory in hand. Except . . . Rua produced the five and set it on top of the pile—the perfect hand.

"No way!" Bri crowed, leaping up from her chair. She hooted, pointing at Renwick, his mouth dropping open as he stared at the cards. Thador clapped Rua hard on the shoulder, belly laughing at the stunned look on Renwick's face.

Rua chucked her remaining cards onto the table, pulling Renwick's gaze back to her. "Again?"

"Lucky cards." Renwick's expression broke, showing a flicker of a smile. "I'd like to see you do that again."

Thador snorted. "I bet you would."

A fire lit in Rua's belly. If Renwick thought she'd play like a high-class fae courtier, then he was sorely mistaken. Rua was raised to be a warrior in all things, and she was determined to best the Northern King at his favorite game.

As the next hand began, Rua looked between her cards and the ones laid across the table, a smirk spreading across her face.

"That's a terrible bluff," Renwick said, watching her over his cards.

"It doesn't matter if I'm good at bluffing, so long as I beat you." Rua shrugged and smiled wider, the Northern King's face mirroring her own for a split second before he cleared his throat and looked back down at his cards.

She didn't need to bluff. She already held the winning hand.

# CHAPTER EIGHT

The pleasant hum of tiredness and a night well spent swept through her as she followed Aneryn past the maze of tents the following day. Rua had fun at that card game, delighting in the look of shock on Renwick's face when she beat him almost every single round. She held a special sort of pride from wiping that smug look off his face. Bri had cheered her on in a level of growing boisterousness until all the wine was gone. Bri taunted Thador and the Northern King as if they were at a fighting match and not a card table. Rua had loved that too—having someone on her side.

As they reached the witches' quarter, the tents turned from large box shapes to smaller round ones. They reminded Rua of the shelters the red witches built in the forest of the High Mountain Court. Witches preferred circular things, round like the moon and the Goddess they worshipped inside of it, round like a pregnant womb and the spiral of life: birth, life, death, and rebirth. The witches believed in the afterlife, like the fae did, but they also believed that parts of oneself were reborn into someone new.

Two blue witchlings eyed her suspiciously. None of them seemed to laugh or run around like the boisterous young children in the other parts of the camp.

Still, the camp was less bleak than Rua had expected. Altars of candles dotted between tents, bundles of dried herbs hung frozen from entryways, and ribbons flew on strings tied between poles high above them. There was warmth here. It smelled familiar too: a mixture of spices, herbal oils, and burning *chaewood*, a pungent shrub used in cleansing.

Rua was surprised by how many witches looked in good health. Yes, there were many who were scarred and burned, ones she was certain had spent some amount of time in the blue witch fortress, but there were many others who seemed unscathed.

As if sensing her thoughts, Aneryn said from in front of her, "Only the gifted witches were taken to the Temple of Hunasht. It was how their gifts were *heightened*. Though with any amount of training they probably could have done just as much." The witch's voice carried the bitter tone of someone later in life.

Rua noted how many male witches she saw moving around the tents, carrying firewood or baskets of food. Female witches tended to carry a stronger thread of magic. If what Aneryn said was true, then it would be mostly female witches being taken to the blue witch fortress.

"How many were left unharmed?" Rua asked.

"We have all been harmed," Aneryn said, turning to look back at Rua. She had russet-colored eyes, so large in her head they seemed almost nymphlike. "Every family has been harmed by the Vostemurs. Families have been ripped apart. So many lives have been lost . . . Some scars aren't as readily seen, Your Highness."

"Please don't call me that," Rua said. She knew the feeling so well— some scars being invisible. Rua felt them tugging on her soul, but she could not pinpoint what had caused them. She struggled to understand why she felt so twisted and wrong when there were people in front of her that were so clearly harmed. It racked her with guilt. She did not have any problems compared to them.

"You better get used to your title, Your Highness," Aneryn said again, her lips twisting. "It is who you are now. It is who you have always been."

"Right." Rua jutted her jaw to the side.

"I know what it feels like," Aneryn said, looking up to the hillside above the ice lake. Her eyes scanned the lip on the bowl that dipped down into the crater where they stood.

"What?"

"I was given over to serve His Majesty when I was just a child," Aneryn said. "The blue witches didn't like how kind he was to me, but the fae around him treated me like a dirty witch. I did not belong with the witches, and I did not belong with the fae." Aneryn cast her gaze back to Rua. "I know what it means to feel like you don't belong anywhere."

Rua's hand drifted to the hilt of the Immortal Blade. Aneryn's lips tightened as she noted the move, and Rua dropped her hand away.

"How old are you?" Rua asked.

Aneryn turned and kept moving through the labyrinth of tents.

"Seventeen," she said. Rua's eyebrows shot up. Aneryn was only a year younger than Rua . . . Well, in a few days she would be two years younger. Rua heard it clearly now—Aneryn had an Ific accent. She spoke like a fae, her words lilting and soft. Meanwhile, Rua spoke in the sharp, acerbic tone of the witches. What a strange pair they made—a fae princess who spoke like a witch, and a blue witch who spoke like the fae.

Rua felt completely turned around as they made another left. Not a single pathway kept a straight line. Some paths were wider thoroughfares, busy with people walking; others were thin trails of gravel where Rua saw the ice peeking through below their feet. They moved down one more winding path to a circular tent made out of a patchwork of thick brown-and-gray fabric.

"Here we are—Baba Airu's tent," Aneryn said, gesturing to the overlaying flaps that made up the tent's doorway. "Try not to stare," Aneryn warned.

"She can't see." Rua furrowed her brow at the witch's tent.

"But she can See," Aneryn mused.

Rua shuddered. What terrible things would the High Priestess of the blue witches See about her?

~

The scent of sage and candle wax greeted her as Rua followed Aneryn into the tent. It was more spacious than it appeared from the outside. A large bed and dresser sat against the far wall, a curtain partially obscuring it from view. A wooden table sat near the curving wall, covered in candles and silver bowls filled with dried herbs and powders. Shadows danced around the tent from the dimly lit fire, emanating heat. An ornate rug of crimson red and cerulean blue lay in front of the stove, two carved wooden chairs and a little table sat on top, and in the redwood rocking chair facing the fire sat Baba Airu.

The High Priestess wore a simple indigo dress. Its high-necked collar was trimmed in fur as well as the cuffs of the long sleeves. A fur-lined hood covered her hairless head. She wore a black pouch around her neck by a string. Rua squinted closer. It was the witch's totem bag.

Totem bags were worn around witches' necks in the days of old. After the Siege of Yexshire, the witches started keeping their bags in secret pockets hidden in their clothes. But Baba Airu wore hers around her neck like her predecessors must have done. Rua didn't remember her wearing it the night of the battle in Drunehan. Maybe this was the High Priestess's way of signifying that a changing time was coming for the witches.

"Hello, Your Highness," Baba Airu's voice sang like the deep note of a wooden lute. "Thank you, Aneryn. You may go."

Aneryn paused by her side. Rua was tempted to ask the young witch to stay behind, but she didn't. Aneryn gave her a sympathetic smirk and left.

Rua felt like when she got called into Baba Morganna's tent as a child. She wondered what she was in trouble for now.

"Please, sit." Baba Airu gestured to the chair next to her. "I would offer you food, but I do not have any in here. I take my meals in the witches' dining tent with my coven."

"It is no problem, thank you," Rua murmured, taking a seat next to the witch and bracing for a prophetic speech or lecture.

With the hood covering her head, Baba Airu's appearance wasn't as startling. Her skin pulled tightly in odd directions from the burns, and her lips were still tinted blue, but it was her eyes that had upset Rua most the first time. Looking at the High Priestess now, Rua saw that the stitches no longer held her lids closed, though the witch's eyes remained shut.

"I had them removed," Baba Airu said as if sensing Rua looking at the little dots that marked where the stitches had been.

"Will you be able to see again?" Rua asked, tentatively stooping into the chair.

"The stitches were not my doing, but I closed my eyes for good when I took the mantle of High Priestess," Baba Airu said in a slow, warm voice. "It is custom for the High Priestess to give herself over to the blessings of Sight. It is the only vision I choose to have now. The stitches . . . were Hennen's doing. He thought I would cheat," the High Priestess said with a hint of disgust, like the implication that she would be opening her eyes in secret was the worst kind of disrespect.

"The Vostemurs thought they understood our powers and customs, but they didn't," the blue witch said. "They thought they could make our powers stronger while making us more subservient to them . . . A whole generation of witches has been lost to their cruelty, dead or worse."

Worse. Rua thought to the *suraash* lying dead in the Temple of Hunasht, the ones she had killed. She did not know how much of their hollow, haunted eyes was from Balorn's curse and how much from being broken so badly before the curse was ever placed upon them. The marks upon their foreheads were the most upsetting of all: *suraash*, not worthy of being remembered, not worth saving. And she hadn't saved them; she had destroyed them.

"It was a better end for them, Your Highness," Baba Airu murmured. Rua's eyes darted up to the High Priestess's face. Had she Seen what Rua was thinking about? "You will kill many more before this war is done."

"So, it is a war?"

"Balorn wants to be King, not just of the Northern Court, but all of Okrith. He pushed Hennen to take the realm, and once he had, Balorn was going to take it from him . . . but the Fates wove another thread

95

the night you picked up that sword." Baba Airu gestured perfectly toward the Immortal Blade.

Rua knew Fates changed. There were an infinite number of outcomes to anyone's future. The blue witches tapped into the most likely ones, but they could always be shifted, some threads more delicate than others. Had Rua truly shifted the future of Okrith by picking up the sword?

"Yes," Baba Airu said with a soft smile. "You did."

Rua rubbed her hands together against a chill she did not feel in her body, but in her soul. The High Priestess was in her mind.

"This is a lot," Rua whispered, looking to the rubies on her sword's hilt.

"It depends on what you choose to do with the power you have been given," Baba Airu said.

"What am I meant to do?"

"I cannot See if you will defeat Balorn." Baba Airu pursed her lips. "But you will help break his spell, of that I am certain. You will save the blue witches."

Her chest seized. "How?"

"The path forward is not clear. Blue witches cannot divine the Fates of each other. Balorn has encircled himself with blue witches to protect him from our Sight." Baba Airu's hairless brows dropped heavy over her eyes. "I can only catch glimpses from the other fae in his retinue, but I can feel that you are a key player in this battle."

"How do I break the curse?"

"You need to unite the blue witches." Baba Airu's fingers traced the outline of the totems in the bag on her chest.

"Unite the witches?" Rua scoffed. Surely that was a job for the High Priestess. "I am not a witch."

"Nor are you fond of them." Baba Airu chuckled.

"I—"

"It is understandable, based on your upbringing. The world was cruel to the red witches, and they didn't have any more to give to you than their protection."

Rua's ears burned. "Shouldn't that be enough?" The red witches had fed her, clothed her, and hidden her from the many fae who wanted the High Mountain royals dead.

"Did it feel like enough?" Baba Airu's lips pulled up to one side. Rua looked again at the witch's blue lips. Once again, Baba Airu spoke as if reading her mind. "It is from a special tea. It is a secret of the High Priestesses who came before me. Their spirits now fill mine and whisper to me these secrets. It is the tea that stains my lips blue."

Rua chewed on the inside of her cheek. She thought the blue lips were another symbol of their torture. She realized now how little she knew about the blue witch customs. So much of what she had assumed about them had been wrong. The closed eyes and blue lips that filled her with dread were probably symbols of honor and beauty to the blue witches. It was just another way she was too selfish—never thinking to look beyond her own nose and consider the people around her.

Rua rubbed her hands together again. "The witches who left Drunehan . . . where did they go?"

"I am not prepared to say."

"Why not?"

The blue witch began rocking as she spoke. "The blue witches hear me, but they do not always believe. They do not trust that the Northern King is any different from his father . . . but they do trust the High Mountain fae." Rua felt the High Priestess's focus on her. "Your people believed the witches were equal to them, Your Highness. They let the High Priestess of the red witches rule alongside them. It was that bond that made their kingdom once powerful."

"It did not protect them from Hennen Vostemur," Rua said bitterly.

"No. But that does not mean all of that suffering has to be in vain. The world has already been torn down, but perhaps you can build a better one," Baba Airu insisted.

Rua huffed. The High Priestess sounded just like the red witches, full of wishy-washy hope. "Do those witches, the ones who left, do they possess the book of spells?"

"Yes."

"But you won't tell me where they are?" Rua clenched her jaw, already knowing the answer.

"No."

A groan sounded from her snarling mouth. "How am I supposed to *build a better world* and all of that nonsense if you won't tell me how to break this curse?"

"The spell book is only half of the curse," Baba Airu said, lifting her chin and glancing up toward the roof. "You need the talisman—a stone forged from witch magic—for the spell to work."

"So where is the Witches' Glass?"

"With Balorn."

Rua pressed her palm into the socket of her eye, exasperated. "And where is Balorn?"

"I do not know."

She was ready to burst out of her chair, using every bit of strength not to scream at the High Priestess. "Then why in the Gods' names am I here?"

"The blue witches trust you, Ruadora," the witch said with a patient smirk. "I still am not certain that they should. Your Fate is murky, even to my Sight. Show me that you are worthy of that trust, and I will tell you everything you want to know."

"Of course, I have a murky fate," Rua muttered. She couldn't get one step forward without meeting another dead end.

Baba Airu gestured to the doorway to her tent, granting permission to leave. "Perchance your stay in Murreneir will make it clearer."

Rua scowled at the High Priestess and left without so much as a parting word. She was ready to take her magic sword and murky fate and run away . . . but the only place she wanted to be even less than Murreneir was her homeland.

～

The steam rose off their bodies as Bri and Rua stood in the ankle-deep snow. They had found a clearing in the forest to spar. Bri said she needed to practice with a harder opponent. Rua knew it was just flattery, but she had relented. After her failed conversation with Baba Airu, she was ready to hit something. Her only condition was that she wouldn't go to the training rings by the soldier's quarters, so they trekked into the woods circling the frozen lake. A guard post sat on the hill high above them, and she could barely make out the guards looking toward the frozen tundra.

"I'm impressed," Bri panted.

Rua gave her a satisfied smirk. The red witches mostly ignored Rua at their camp. There was only one thing they were sure to educate her on: fighting. The red witches were a strange combination of calm and deadly. They valued that ability to protect themselves above all else, especially after the Siege of Yexshire.

"Feels good to hit something, eh?" Bri's short brown hair clung to her forehead with sweat. In the bright winter sun, Bri's hair had streaks of auburn, just like a golden eagle's feathers. She looked a lot like the Eastern Court's fisher hawk, too. Rua wondered why her people had chosen to nickname her based on an animal native to the Western Court and not her homeland. Rua had seen a golden eagle only once. It had somehow flown over the High Mountains, possibly lost in a storm. It was bigger than any bird she had ever seen, far bigger than what the little drawing in her books depicted. Rua wondered what happened to her little encyclopedia of Okrithian animals. She pored over those tomes as a child. There was one for wildlife, one for the native plants of each court, and one for the royal castles and customs. They were beautifully illustrated, and she was the only one who had treasured them. They were probably rotting away in the woods now.

"Ready for round two?" Bri asked, shaking out her hands. The steam rising from their bodies had lessened, and the cold was creeping into Rua's sweaty fighting leathers. They had shucked off their cloaks, abandoned on a tree branch, and now stood in their tight-fitting gear. It was good to move in, but not insulated against the cold. "Let's add in some magic."

"I don't think you want me using this sword on you." Rua dipped her chin down toward the sword on her hip. She had insisted on keeping it on while they sparred with their fists. She needed to learn to fight with its weight tugging down her left-hand side.

"We haven't really tested what it can do." Bri cocked her head at the Immortal Blade—an Eagle indeed. "What will it strike down for you and how?"

"It feels a lot like witch magic," Rua said, looking to a pine cone on the freshly fallen snow. She summoned the witch magic in her blood, the buzzing spooling out into her fingertips. The pine cone levitated into the air. Rua released her mental hold on the pine cone, and it dropped back into the snow. "You have to hold the intention in your mind."

"So you think of who you want the blade to strike and it does?" Bri mused.

"Not just who," Rua corrected. "I think of how far away they are from me. I think of where on their body I want the sword to pierce. I think of how hard and fast the blow will be. I imagine it exactly as if I were doing it myself."

"Then how did you kill those archers outside the blue witch fortress?" Bri picked up the pine cone out of the snow and then reached for another.

"I knew they were out there. I could imagine what their faces might look like, what clothes they might be wearing," Rua said, remembering that white light swirling around her body, the sensation like floating. "It was enough for the blade to know what to do."

"It seems to follow your orders well, better than any soldier could." Bri chuckled.

"I'd rather command this sword than an army." Rua bounced up on her toes to keep her muscles warm.

"Does it only cut down living beings?" Bri asked, lobbing a pine cone at Rua. The pine cone bounced off Rua's chest as she gaped at Bri.

"I guess pine cones don't count as blades, then." Bri laughed, picking up another pine cone from the base of the towering tree.

"You didn't throw it hard enough to break my skin anyway," Rua heckled. She lifted a finger to the hole in her leathers where the arrow had struck her in the Temple of Hunasht. She still hadn't mended it. It was a long thin slice, right at the center of her chest. "I can't believe that arrow stopped when it touched my skin."

"And yet, you wield a magic sword that cuts down soldiers from twenty paces away. Can you believe that?" Bri smirked. "That sword wants to protect you. It was made for your people, the blood of the High Mountain fae, the gift of the red witches. You carry all the High Mountain Court within you. The blade recognizes that."

Rua turned away from Bri's pointed words. Her eyes drifted above the lip of the Lyrei Basin. The bare hilltop where the Palace of Murreneir was going to be built was bare no longer. Small dots moved across the hillside. Sleds filled with rocks were pulled by shaggy-looking oxen. Rua knew from her encyclopedia that those were Northern oxen, bred to withstand the Northern snow. The hillside had seemed large before, but now that she saw people atop it, she realized it was humongous. They were digging the palace's foundations deep into the earth. She wondered if there would be dungeons below the palace. Would they look like the ones they kept her in before the Battle of Drunehan? It all flashed through her again. The screams still rang in her ears, the tang of blood on her lips, the keen awareness of a guard who was moments away from slicing off her head.

Rua shook away the thought as the hairs on her neck prickled.

"I am not as important as all of you claim," she whispered.

It all felt like too much. Baba Airu told her that the blue witches would trust her and that she would break Balorn's curse. Bri told her she held the power of the High Mountain Court . . . She couldn't carry all that.

"Only bad things come from hiding from your destiny, Ru," Bri said, toeing the snow with her boot. Her voice dropped an octave. "Trust me on that one."

Rua turned back to ask what the fae warrior had meant, but another pine cone hit her in the face. Bri held an armful of them now.

"Hey!" Rua barked.

"Try to stop them with the sword," Bri said, lobbing another at her.

Rua ducked out of the way with an indignant guffaw, unsheathing the Immortal Blade. The sword seemed to sing a different song through her body then. The white-hot buzzing didn't feel lethal; it felt playful, like it wanted to join in their game.

Rua swung the sword as Bri tossed another pine cone, but nothing happened. She couldn't hold the cones in her mind the same way she could a person.

"This is ridiculous," Rua groused as she tried and failed again.

"You may have many attackers coming at you," Bri said. "You need to be prepared to stop them."

"I would," Rua hissed as another rough pine cone bounced off the top of her head.

"How?"

"Like this." Rua splayed out her left hand, her red magic flowing with years of practice. She knew how to test the boundaries of her witch magic better than her fae. The fae's magic was tied into their bodies. It made them fast and strong. They healed quickly and heard things from far away. But the witch's magic was more external. It was used to impact the world around them. The red witches moved objects, the brown witches made potions, the green witches grew and cooked their magic, and the blue witches divined others' futures. It was something that happened outside of themselves.

With just the splaying of her fingers, Rua's red magic was able to halt the pine cone's trajectory in midair. She curled her fingers, flicking them to the right, and the pine cone flew off into the snow. She lifted her palm to the sky and crooked her fingers. The pine cones in Bri's arms lifted all at once into the sky, and when Rua straightened her fingers again, they all flew off into the woods as well.

"That's cheating but . . . wow." Bri's teeth glinted as she grinned. "I didn't see Remy use her hands like that to cast her magic."

Rua narrowed her eyes at the Eagle. "Remy was not trained in how to use her magic properly. I'm sure the red witches will be instructing her, especially now that she wears the amulet of Aelusien."

"How long until you can wield your magic again?" Bri asked.

Rua gave Bri a quizzical look. "It would take a lot more than some flying pine cones to drain my stores of magic. It is a muscle like any other. The more you flex it, the stronger it gets."

Bri's eyes swept over Rua: her hands, her sword, and back to her face. "For someone who has a lot of bad things to say about witches, you sure make a good one."

Rua clenched her fists at that. She wasn't a witch; the coven who raised her made that abundantly clear. She didn't feel much like a fae either. She didn't want to be anything.

"Can you try with just the sword?" Bri asked, picking up another pine cone.

"No," Rua said. She sheathed the Immortal Blade back in its scabbard. She swore she felt its disappointment at being put away. "I have the Immortal Blade and I have red witch magic. Whichever I use to be successful in battle is of no consequence."

"Training helps you become better at choosing the right magic to use," Bri countered. "It helps you make better choices in the field of battle in a lot of ways."

"I know what I did, Bri," Rua growled.

"We were ambushed, it was . . ."

"Don't make excuses for me. You're better than that," Rua snapped. "Don't tell me it was their life or mine. I could have chosen to spare some. We could have taken captives. I kept swinging even when the last witch fell. I kept hacking at them, even after the fatal blows, just to watch them bleed. I am no less of a monster than those Forgotten Ones."

"Rua—"

"No, listen," she hissed, her voice getting choked up as she spoke. The thought of doing it again filled her with horror. The bloodlust pulled her under until everyone was her enemy. The sword would make her kill them all if given half a chance. "If it ever gets too much, you have to stop me, Bri. No blade can pierce my skin, but I know you will find a way."

Bri's wide eyes drifted up past Rua, looking over her shoulder. Rua cursed herself. She already knew who would be standing there by the look on the Eagle's face.

She turned to find Renwick in a midnight-blue cloak, watching them. He leaned against a tree trunk, arms folded. His sharp face watched her from the shadows of his hood.

"Mistakes are made in battle all the time, talisman or not," Renwick said as he pushed off the tree trunk and strode toward her. Rua froze as he approached, suddenly aware of her curves being exposed in her fitted clothes. "You would not be the first soldier to cut down an ally by mistake."

Rua shook her head. "What was his name? The guard I killed?"

"Don't—"

"Tell me," she insisted.

"His name was Lachlan," Renwick said, his green eyes piercing into her.

"Were you close with him?" she breathed, steam swirling around her face.

Renwick swallowed, his lips parted, but he waited to speak. Finally, he said, "Yes."

Rua hung her head. She looked down at her booted feet. She had killed one of Renwick's trusted guards because the siren song of the blade grew too powerful. She was not strong enough for this. "Did he have a family?"

"No." Renwick reached out with his finger and lifted her chin so that she would meet his gaze. She braced herself as she lifted her lashes to meet those brilliant eyes, as if she were falling every time she looked into them. "I never thanked you for saving my life that day." His voice was a soft whisper on her cheek. "We would all have been dead were it not for you."

She thought about that witch who attacked Renwick in the Temple of Hunasht. She would have clawed out his eyes. The thin lines down his cheek were already gone. His alabaster skin was smooth as porcelain.

Rua wanted to tear her gaze away, but Renwick's hand slid to her neck, his thumb under her jaw. He held her so gently, making her maintain their stare.

She saw emotions warring in his eyes, emotions she couldn't name, but they were so unlike his normal sharp countenance. Who was this fae King? She suddenly felt like she didn't know him at all.

"I did not come here to watch you train," Renwick murmured. "There's something I want to show you."

He dropped his hand, Rua's skin cooling in the absence of his touch. As she followed after the King, she grimaced at herself. She wished that hand were back on her cheek and she hated herself for it. That yearning would be nothing but a problem.

# CHAPTER NINE

R enwick led them to the edge of the campsite, where a host of sleighs was parked downhill from the stables. Ice gave way to frozen earth as they moved away from the lake and up the hillside. The sheer size of their camp hit Rua once more. It was a city, and come spring, it would all have to be moved.

Aneryn waited for them by an open sleigh. It was a simple contraption, barely more than a bench affixed to skis and harnessed to two large black horses. Another sleigh sat in front, slightly more detailed with black and gold paint.

"Where are we going?" Rua asked, pulling her cloak tighter around her, the sweat on her body now chilling her.

"Up to see the progress on the spring palace," Renwick said to her with a smirk.

"I've been wanting to get a closer look," Aneryn called to them.

"Pestering me about it, really." Renwick's cheeks dimpled at the witch's excitement.

Rua stared at those dimples. Renwick was as sharp as ever, but he seemed steadier than normal. He usually held himself so tightly, like she did, as if they were waiting for an invisible blow to strike. She did not know what she was bracing for anymore, just knew that it would come. When the world would batter her down again, it wouldn't be a surprise. If she lay in a pool of her own blood by tomorrow, her only thought would be "of course."

Renwick's brows dropped heavy over his eyes as he watched Rua, as if he saw the swirling of her thoughts. She stared vacantly up at the hilltop beyond them.

"Ride with me?" Renwick's voice was low and razor-edged, cutting through the air and straight into her mind.

"I think Aneryn is eager to ride in your sleigh." Rua took an icy breath. "I'll ride with Bri."

That muscle on Renwick's cheek popped out as he bit down, but he did not argue with her. Rua did not want to spend a whole sleigh ride talking about the things that haunted her. She would rather plummet through the ice lake than talk about what had happened while training with Bri.

Rua climbed up into the second sleigh, while Renwick and Aneryn climbed into the first.

Bri looked at Rua incredulously. "I don't know how to drive one of these things."

"Move over," Thador said, pushing his way through the line of sleighs to join them.

Bri climbed in next to Rua, and Thador after, grabbing the reins. The fae soldier was so large, he took up most of the sleigh. Bri and Rua squashed themselves onto the side of the wooden armrest.

"Is this really better than riding with the King?" Bri growled, her body so folded inward her shoulders were practically touching. The pommel of the Immortal Blade dug into Rua's hip. "All because you're scared of talking to him."

"I am not scared of talking to the Witchslayer," Rua snarled as the sleigh in front of them lurched to life. She and Bri were thrown back as their sleigh followed.

She couldn't tell for certain with their hoods up, but it looked like Renwick and Aneryn were talking. They had so much room on that sleigh. She did not know why it bothered her, the two of them laughing together, but it did.

They crested up and over the bowl of the Lyrei Basin and back into the valley below. The snow was deeper, their feet nearly skimming the powdery surface as they rode.

It was a short trip up to the building platform as the giant horses made quick work of mounting the summit. Tents had been set up, covering building materials and tools, and red-hot forges burned, the clink of metal being hammered accompanied by the hefty thwack of stones being piled. A line of three Northern oxen pulled sleds of earth and rock across the site. Dozens of builders bustled about, only stopping to hastily bow to Renwick as they went. They worked with an eagerness Rua couldn't understand.

"This way," Renwick said, leading them through the swarming workers and into a long green tent. Rolls of parchment were tucked into baskets along the walls. A wooden table sat in the middle of the room and behind it a human man stood surveying papers.

The man's bushy gray eyebrows bunched. "Your Majesty," he said, dropping into a deep bow, and then added, "Your Highness," bending slightly toward Rua.

"Lawrence," Renwick replied with a bob of his head.

She didn't think she would ever get used to the bowing. It didn't feel genuine; if anything, it felt like mocking. She was no more royalty than the man standing in front of her. Most of the workers they had passed were fae. They were stronger and faster than humans, able to erect a castle quicker, but the foreman was a human. Rua's eyes ran over Lawrence's rounded ears once more. It was a rare sight to see fae working for a human. She couldn't help but wonder if Renwick brought her there to demonstrate his willingness to change.

"Hello, Lawrence. I've come to show Her Highness the plans for the castle. Would you be so kind as to get them out for us?" Renwick spoke with a level of decorum that made Rua want to gag.

"Of course, Your Majesty," Lawrence said, hustling over to a dresser stacked with thin drawers and opening one. He selected out three different papers and brought them carefully to the table.

The first two pieces had sketches of the aerial layouts of the palace, and the third was a drawing of the exterior. Rua's mouth dropped open.

It was the most beautiful castle she had ever seen. She had combed through the book of castles and palaces so many times as a child that she could see each page with her eyes closed. She had imagined what it would be like to live in one of those palaces. But the drawing in front of her now was better than any one she had seen before.

It had seven spires twisting toward the heavens, flags blowing from each of their peaks. An intricately carved archway led to covered corridors through twining gardens. Octagonal windows framed either side of a giant doorway. The exterior looked like a beautiful maze, bridges and pathways zigzagging throughout the drawing. The palace bore the signs of spring from the rambling roses climbing up the facade to the whorls of flowers carved into the stone. The gardens had always been Rua's favorite part of castle drawings. Some of the castles had dedicated maps and seasonal sketches of their gardens. They had vegetable patches and herb gardens at the witch camps, but nothing ornamental or so grand. She loved the idea of planting flowers just for their beauty and for no other reason, that everything didn't need to have a purpose to be worthwhile.

"You like it then?" Renwick's voice cut through the haze, and Rua looked up with him, taking a breath she did not realize she had been holding.

"It's beautiful," she said.

Renwick's gaze softened, that calm warmth so at odds with his normally stony features. In that moment, looking in his eyes, something shook inside her, thoughts begging to be freed, but she wouldn't allow it.

Rua looked back to the layouts. "Seven stories?"

"Plus the spires," Lawrence said. He spoke in Ific, the common tongue, but his Northern accent fizzled out at the end of each sentence, making her strain to listen. "Two of them will be underground ... do you think it's not enough, Your Highness?"

Rua snorted, looking up to Lawrence, when she realized he was serious. "I don't really think it's appropriate for me to have an opinion on the Northern King's palace."

Renwick stiffened by her side. She looked over the layouts again.

Everything from ballrooms to libraries, kitchens to servants' quarters, was allotted for. The entire sixth floor was allocated for the King and Queen. Rua wasn't sure why she bristled at the scrawling letters of "Queen's sitting room" and "nursery."

She crossed her arms and looked back to the first drawing of the palace's exterior. This was a dream in the form of ink and paper. She couldn't imagine any of them living in such a place. They did not fit these happy plans. Marriages and children and flowers—what nonsense.

"Thank you, Lawrence," Rua said to the man in a clipped voice. She turned and walked back out of the tent, Bri on her heels.

They walked across the building site, watching fae soldiers heft colossal slabs of granite. Masons were already in the pit, laying out the basement flooring. It was moving along at an incredible pace, though not at the speed of the castle in Yexshire. If they had red witch magic, Rua estimated they would have the whole thing built within a month.

She considered for a moment offering to help as she peered at the straining arms of the workers hauling stones. Her magic could move that stone with a flick of her fingers. No, she would not help build someone else's dream. Clenching her fingers at her side, she turned away.

Bri hung back as Rua walked to the far edge of the hillside. From there she spotted the village far below. She assumed it was the town of Murreneir, the center of the Northern county bearing the same name.

Without looking, she felt him standing behind her. It was hard to pick up his scent, so similar to the world around them, like freshly fallen snow with a hint of evergreen trees and cloves. He smelled like winter. Only that slight hint of musky earth separated him from the world around them.

"Is it abandoned?" Rua asked, looking down at Murreneir. Not a single pillar of smoke billowed into the sky. It looked like an avalanche had buried the town, only the rooftops discernible above the blanket of white.

"In the winter, yes," Renwick said, stepping up beside her. "The town is part of the Lyrei Basin encampment. The snow falls too heavy in the valley of Murreneir; the houses are nearly swallowed by it. But the ice lakes are protected in the craters from the heaviest of the snow. The whole town migrates there every winter."

Rua's eyebrows raised. It shouldn't have been a surprise. She thought to those bookshelves in Renwick's office. Even with their large caravan of sleighs, there was not enough room for that kind of furniture. It must have been brought over for him from the town of Murreneir.

Her eyes scanned the horizon for the Temple of Hunasht, but the view of it was obscured from this vantage point. Renwick followed her line of sight out toward the West.

"Why do they call you Witchslayer?" Rua whispered. She supposed the answer was obvious, but the thought of Renwick going on witch-killing rampages . . . something about it didn't add up.

"It was a nickname given to me," Renwick said, his gaze holding tight on the horizon.

"By whom?" Rua asked, though she already suspected she knew.

"My uncle," Renwick confirmed. "I spent winters in Murreneir. My father sent me here to work for Balorn."

Rua swallowed, her chest constricting. "Work for him how?"

"I suspect you already know." Renwick's eyes flitted back to her.

"You tortured witches for your uncle." It wasn't a question.

"I did what I had to in order to survive." Renwick's voice was sharper than a knife. "I have more blood on my hands than I can ever wash away."

"In that, we are the same." Rua finally looked at Renwick. The power of staring into his eyes made her rock back like the force of a sleigh springing to life. He had done terrible things but moved so easily through the world. He still seemed so put together. Rua's heart clenched. She wished she could do that, be that strong. "How do you not let it break you?"

Renwick's eyes darkened as he looked over her face.

"You think I am still whole?" His shoulders tensed. "I am not a good person, Rua." The low timbre of her name on his lips echoed through her mind. "The only good left in me is in little, fragmented pieces."

Her eyes guttered. In that they were the same too. She was sure there were some shreds of goodness buried at the bottom of her soul, but they were so far down, more buried than the town of Murreneir in cold, hard ice.

"It will be a beautiful home for you," Rua said, looking back at the pit carved into the frozen earth. She couldn't imagine Renwick in a castle covered in roses.

"One day, maybe," Renwick said, looking toward the mountains of stone. Rua tossed those words around in her mind. Maybe Renwick was too far from happiness to feel it either. Maybe there were too many broken pieces of each of them to ever be put back together.

As the dappled sunlight strained behind the heavy clouds, she wondered if, even between the two of them, there might be enough to make one whole.

~

The shrieking screams echoed off the charred walls. A witch flew out of the darkness, colliding into the body in front of her. She was wild and deranged and completely free. It wasn't just horror that filled her— no, there was envy too. How good would it feel to claw out the eyes of your enemies? The blade shouted at her hip, "Use me," like a too-eager child. The blurry face under the scrambling witch morphed, and she saw the likeness more clearly: sharp cheekbones, ash-blond hair, and piercing green eyes. The blade screamed to her louder, "Use me, save him." But she resisted saving the Witchslayer. The Fates had brought their reckoning—it was time he paid for his crimes. She would not touch its hilt.

She held in a scream as that witch lifted a dagger high above the Witchslayer. His green eyes widened, shooting to her, his hand reaching out to her as the witch drove the knife into his chest. The shrieking was deafening.

Rua sucked in a whoosh of cold air as her eyes flew open, as her heart punched into her ribs. The screaming wind matched the screaming in her mind, making her reach up and plug her ears. It was just the wind. The ruby pommel of the Immortal Blade seemed to flicker at her in the darkness, as if it knew her dreams as well as she did. The blade taunted her. She should have used it, but she couldn't. She was paralyzed in her dream, frozen with fear. She could feel her soul being corrupted with every swing of that blade, and so she had refused to touch it. And Renwick had died. She still felt his haunted eyes staring at her as if she had betrayed him.

The screaming wind grated against her nerves, making her heartbeat pound into her eardrums. The air in the room felt as thick as soup. She clawed at the neckline of her chemise, yanking it past her collarbone, as she took another drag of thick air. She needed to get outside.

She didn't grab the Immortal Blade or her boots, only the fur blanket that covered the back of her chair. She wrapped it loosely around her shoulders as she pushed open the flaps to her tent.

Icy air stung her face as her heartbeat surrendered, beginning to slow. Rua stared across to the tent flap ahead of her. The moon was high in the sky. She wondered if Bri would be awake.

Tiptoeing toward Bri's tent, she heard a voice. She crept a little closer and leaned her frostbit ear toward the tent's fabric. A feminine breathy moan whispered into the cold night. It was not Bri's voice. Her guard was not alone.

Rua's bare feet crunched on the rough gravel as she retreated, moving down a narrow back alley, away from the burning fires of the guard posts. Faint voices whispered around her. She heard a masculine chuckle and another feminine giggle. It sounded like the whole camp was in each other's beds. Her cheeks burned. Was she the only one who was not secreting away to a lover in the night?

The tents grew closer together as she reached the outer ring of the campsite. She had to turn sideways so as not to push herself against the thick fabric. Finally, she reached the edge of the camp. The ring of gravel upon which the campsite sat gave way to the thick ice. Rua looked out in either direction. She thought she had turned toward the shores of the lake, but she was now standing in the middle of it. It would take her ages to find her way back to her tent.

She stepped one bare foot out onto the slick ice, then another. A slippery layer of water formed under her feet. Feet wobbling, she took another careful step, and she strained to keep upright. She slid her feet along rather than lifting them as she scooted herself toward the shoreline, following the outer edge of the camp.

The darkness yawned around her. Only the light of the moon lit her path as she glided her way along toward the snowy banks. The water below the ice was utter blackness. She felt like something was staring up at her from its depths. The thought of eyes upon her made her heartbeat stutter again. The witches' screams still whistled on the wind. The powerful Northern gales blew above the bowl of the Lyrei Basin, not dipping down into the camp, but the torrents yowled high above. It was the same screams that radiated from the walls at the Temple of Hunasht. They were burned into the stone. How many of those echoes of pain had come at the end of Renwick's own knife? The biting of Rua's fingernails into her palms was the only thing that kept her moving. She thought of that knife driving into his chest. Her muscles were so tight she thought they might snap.

Perhaps he deserved that end. Perhaps she deserved it too.

When she reached the shoreline, her tight fists unclenched. She found a rock sitting above the deep line of snow and perched on it. The cold sliced into her as she wrapped the fur tighter. She tucked her raw, red feet under her, warming them as she sat cross-legged on the smooth lake rock. Looking back at the camp, she wasn't sure which alleyway dumped her out into the middle of the lake.

Great. Now she would have to wind her way through guard posts and fae sneaking into the beds of their lovers. She growled at the night. She was so pathetic. She had never had a lover. Who would have accepted her offer in the red witch camps? There had been one girl when she was sixteen that she had been infatuated with, but she had left for the Southern Court before Rua could ever confess her affections. News came a year later of her death at the end of a witch hunter's blade.

No one would dare touch her now, not as a princess of the High

Mountain Court, not even if she wanted them to. She could only think of one person who had the power, who might be willing. She shook away the vision of his wide green eyes as a blade drove into his heart. That would be a more dangerous game than any of the others, luring that snake into her bed. Perhaps she should just say she swore herself to the Maiden Goddess and refuse all advances . . . but she knew that wasn't what she wanted.

"Are you all right?" a soft, feminine voice sounded behind her.

Rua whirled, dragging up from the pit of red magic in her gut. She was about to cast out her power when she saw the familiar pair of nymphlike brown eyes.

Aneryn.

"You wield so many forms of magic. I'm glad to see you don't always travel with that sword," she said, scanning Rua's body.

Rua released her grip on her red magic, and the buzzing warmth in her fingertips relented back to the cold.

"Why are you here?" Rua's voice came out with more bite than she intended.

"I'm here to show you the way back to your tent," Aneryn said.

Rua considered the witch. "How did you know I would be here?"

As Aneryn smirked, her braids fell, loosely framing her face around the halo of her indigo hood. "How do you think?" She raised her eyebrow in a mocking mirror of Rua's own.

"You had a vision of me?"

"I have many visions of you, Your Highness." Aneryn looked up toward the hills in the direction of Murreneir. Rua wondered how far the blue witch could See through the darkness.

"What did you See?" Rua looked off in the same direction as Aneryn but saw nothing there.

"Tonight, I Saw you bumbling through the campsite, trying to find your way back to your tent. You sheepishly asked a guard to point you in the right direction. I felt your cheeks burning as you heard their laughter behind you."

Rua's eyes widened at the witch. "You Saw all of that?"

"Some witches' visions are foggy. They get only feelings and brief glimpses into the future. Others are stronger, their Sight more clear."

"Like you," Rua guessed, and Aneryn gave a pithy nod. "You must be very powerful."

"I come from a long line of witches with a strong gift of Sight." Her voice was slow and controlled in a way that told Rua there was a lot of pain behind her story.

"They didn't take you to the witch fortress?"

"They wanted to," Aneryn whispered. "My mother was tortured by the Vostemurs. She gave me to Renwick as a birthday present when I was five years old."

Rua gasped. "Why would she do that?"

"Her visions were clear," Aneryn said, her boots trudging through the snow toward Rua until she came to sit beside her. "She knew that if she gave me to Renwick, he would protect me. She knew he would spare me from the same fate as hers."

"What happened to her? Is she . . ."

"She died in the battles of Falhampton on the Eastern border," Aneryn lamented.

Rua shifted the furs around her. "I am sorry for your loss."

"As I am sorry for yours," Aneryn said. "Not many of us come from whole families anymore. That is the brutality of war. It will be another generation or more before the thought of family doesn't bring such heartbreak to the minds of people."

"Have you Seen it? Have you Seen that far into the future?" Rua wondered.

"It is too far ahead for me to See clearly. But one of the many possible threads feels warm. It feels . . . hopeful." Aneryn's large brown eyes slid to Rua. "I feel you there in that future."

Rua peered at the blue witch beside her. "How can you possibly say that?" Rua gritted her teeth, thinking of the bodies strewn across the floor in the Temple of Hunasht. "I am not made of light and hope."

"I didn't say that you were," Aneryn countered. "But you will be the bringer of it for others, of that I am certain."

Irritated, Rua shook her head. "I don't know what that means."

Aneryn let out a soft laugh. "Neither do I." She looked back out over the frozen lake. "And no amount of pain would make that vision clearer."

That's what the Northern fae had done. They had tried to get clearer visions, desperate for more answers, incensed by the half-spoken truths of the blue witches' visions. Rua knew that desperation to know what the future held. It scared her to think she understood why they did it, even if she could never do it herself. That desperate addiction to know the future would drive anyone to madness.

"Are you ready to head back?" Aneryn asked, rubbing her arms to keep warm.

Rua's lips pulled to the side. "I don't know, you tell me."

"I can't read your mind." Aneryn's body vibrated with laughter as whorls of steam rose up toward the night sky. "That's not how it works."

Rua let out a long sigh, sinking her bare feet back into the snow with a wince. She had not felt the bite of the ice in her agitation before. But now the chill stung her raw feet.

"The cold helps with the panic," Aneryn said, eyes dropping to the snow. "Winter is a good time to shed yourself of such things. There is always snow to stick your feet into."

Rua rolled her eyes. "I don't think I will be shedding myself of such feelings for a very long time."

"Then you will have to order your servants to bring down ice from the mountains, I suppose." Aneryn grinned, her smile making her seem younger. "Princesses are allowed to demand such things."

Standing, Rua chuckled. "Ready."

"Let's go." Aneryn looped her arm through Rua's as the pair stepped onto the ice. They wobbled for a moment with a laugh. Aneryn's boots slid wildly across the slick surface, but Rua held her up.

They made their way to a thin gap in the maze of tents. Aneryn gestured to it with her free hand. They stepped back onto the gravel path. Wincing as she walked, the tingling cold seemed to make every rock feel sharper, the sting more acute. She followed Aneryn through the back alleys until they turned down a wider path, stopping at her tent.

"Thank you," Rua said to the blue witch as she reached the entrance.

"You're welcome," Aneryn replied with a wink, "and happy birthday."

Rua tried to hide her surprise as she examined the stars peeking through the haze of clouds. It was past midnight. She was nineteen years old.

# CHAPTER TEN

The sun streamed in through the gaps in her tent as Bri arrived.
Shielding her eyes from the light, Rua groaned. Why did it
have to be morning?

"Right, I wanted to let you have a good sleep, seeing as it's your
birthday, *Princess*," Bri quipped in her dry tone. "But you have to get up
now or you will miss your birthday party."

Rua sat up, rubbing her eyes as sleep clung to her. She didn't have
any more nightmares after she returned to her tent. Exhausted, her
body had surrendered to a deep, dreamless sleep. She wanted to rest for
another several days to recover from that haunted nightmare and the
cold walk across the ice.

"What?" Rua grumbled, not having listened to Bri. Throwing herself down on the sumptuous pillows, she pulled the plush duvet over
her head again. She had a terrible headache, and all she wanted to do
was sleep.

"You have to get ready for your birthday party," Bri commanded,
yanking the duvet down and forcing Rua to sit up again.

"A what?"

"Your party? For your birthday?" Bri's lips twisted to the side, her
brow rising. "You know, your ... birthday ... party?" Bri cringed at

her explanation, casting her golden eyes to the ceiling. "Did they not celebrate birthdays in the witch camps?"

"They lit a candle," Rua said. "You would force me out of bed to watch someone light a candle?" Bri's wry expression made Rua hiss, "Do not mock me."

"I am not mocking you," Bri said, keeping that hint of a smirk. She walked over to the wardrobe and selected a green dress. "I think you're going to have fun. There will be food, music, and gifts."

"I don't want any of those things. I don't want anything from anyone." Rua folded her arms, scrutinizing the low-cut dress. "And I am definitely not wearing that."

"I knew you'd say that." Bri put the dress back and pulled out a forest-green jacket dress. It had broad shoulders and a trail of golden embroidering down either side, held together by golden clasps. It had a thick black belt that circled the waist. A golden buckle was etched with a crown over mountains: the crest of the High Mountain Court.

It was a stunning jacket. It looked both beautiful and commanding, hints of royalty and military in its styling. Rua was itching to put it on.

"You picked that garment just to get me out of bed," Rua said, pouting.

"Is it working?" Bri grinned.

"Yes." Rua relented, rubbing her eyes again. "Okay, fine."

Bri lifted her chin, victorious. "Good, I would never forgive you for keeping me from those little cheese rolls that I saw the kitchen witches making."

Rua held in a chuckle as she rolled out of bed. Perhaps it wouldn't be that bad.

~

Ignoring the roving eyes of passersby, Rua followed Bri toward the center of camp. For once, she was not wearing her baggy gray tunic over her fighting leathers. She had traded her usual worn brown boots for knee-high black ones. The small heels of the boots made her stand a little straighter. Her hair was braided back from her temples, the rest of her brunette locks draping down her back.

They turned into the large open space in front of the King's tent, but now it was filled with tables and people. Paper garlands twisted high above their heads, twining their way onto a center pole. Strings of beads were tied to the pole too, stretching out like a beaming sun to the rooftop of each surrounding tent. The little glass beads shimmered in the wintery sunlight, casting spectrums of light on the people below.

Little tables of food and drinks dotted the corners of the crowd. In the center, surrounding the pole that held up the decorations, was a string quartet and two tables. The table next to them was mounded high with presents, making Rua's mouth drop open. Were those gifts for her?

On the other side of the musicians was a table stacked with small porcelain plates, and beside it . . . a giant pink-and-white cake. Thin unlit candles circled its white-frosted top, while curls of chocolate wrapped around the base of the cake. Rua had heard of birthday cakes, but she had never tasted one before.

The conversations around her faltered as she walked into the space. Bri stepped up next to Rua as one by one the gathering turned toward her. All at once the crowd bowed, and when they rose again, they were all smiling. She couldn't understand it. Why would these people be smiling at her? Their happiness made her feel uneasy.

"Smile," Bri muttered through her teeth.

Rua realized she was scowling at them. They were mostly fae, but there were witches and humans in the crowd too and not just the servants. Renwick really was earnest in his efforts to make a change in his court then, if he had invited humans and witches to this party.

Rua's lips pulled up at the sides in an awkward smirk as she bowed her head slightly to the crowd in thanks. That seemed to release them from the spell, and they all went back to chatting.

Aneryn broke through the faces in the crowd. Her hair was twisted up on top of her head, and she wore a blue wool dress.

"Happy birthday again, Your Highness," she said with a conspiratorial grin.

"Again?" Bri questioned, stepping between them into a triangular conversation.

"You didn't tell her about your midnight stroll across the lake?" Aneryn's brazen brown eyes looked between them.

"Your what?" Bri blustered, turning squarely on Rua. Partygoers gave her a wide berth as they moved toward the tables of refreshments.

Aneryn only smirked. She really was a meddlesome little witch.

Pinching the bridge of her nose, Rua let out a frustrated sigh. "I just needed some fresh air."

"You left the campsite? Without me?" Bri's harsh face was so like a bird of prey now. "You could have told me. I would have come with you."

"You were . . . preoccupied," Rua said with a sideways glance.

Bri's golden eyes widened for a moment. That swaggering smirk of hers settled back into place as she seemed to remember what had transpired in her tent the night before. "I would have un-preoccupied myself," Bri protested as Rua huffed. "Just don't go anywhere without me again, okay?"

Rua gave her guard a brief nod that they both knew was meaningless.

"What do you think of the party?" Aneryn asked, waving to the canopy of garlands above them.

"It's beautiful. Where did all of these decorations come from?" Rua wondered, regarding the strings of beads and white paper garlands.

"The people of Murreneir brought them. They hang them up for the Winter Solstice celebrations," Aneryn said, beholding the delicate ornaments, "but Renwick had them dig them out of their storage boxes for today."

Rua's hand rested on the pommel of the Immortal Blade. "It would benefit him to stay on my good side, I suppose," Rua mused, scanning the event with wary eyes.

"Yes, I'm sure that's why he did it." Bri snorted. Her eyes lifted to over Rua's shoulder, growing wide, her face bursting with light as she exclaimed, "Son of a bitch!"

"I heard there was a party," a male voice called from behind her.

Bri barreled past and grabbed him into a tight hug. Rua knew instantly who it was—the same auburn hair, sharp features, and golden eyes. His hair was longer, tied up into a short knot on top of his head. He stood only a couple inches taller than his twin, his shoulders a bit broader. But the likeness was striking: Talhan, the other half of the Twin Eagles.

"Only you would battle a blizzard for the promise of cake." Bri laughed as she clapped him hard on the shoulder.

"Oh please." Talhan chuckled, elbowing her. "You would absolutely do that too."

His eyes lifted over Bri's head to Rua, and he smirked at her. He dropped his head into a small bow as he said, "Your Highness, thank you for saving me from the eternal boredom of council meetings."

Rua couldn't help but give a begrudging smile. He was a charming one. All the nearby fae seemed to be drawn in. Between the two of them, Rua was certain the Twin Eagles could woo every courtier on the ice lake.

"You smell like a horse's ass," Bri said, looking her brother up and down.

He wore his riding clothes and thick wool cloak. He must have just arrived.

"I will bathe after I eat the cake," Talhan said, nudging his twin with his shoulder.

Feeling people jostling behind her, Rua turned. Three young witches, two boys and a girl, waited. They wore blue cloaks, their totem bags hung proudly around their necks. They didn't seem afraid to advertise to everyone here that they were witches. They couldn't have been more than thirteen. The one in the middle with copper skin and a thick mane of straight black hair held a gift in her hands. She lifted it up with trembling fingers.

"Happy birthday, Your Highness," she said, gawking at Rua as she held out their gift.

The witches on either side of her seemed equally nervous. The girl chewed her lip, and the boys held their hands tightly behind their backs. They were nervous to speak to her? She was no one.

Rua took the thin square present, turning it over in her hands. It was wrapped in scrap fabric with a cerulean ribbon tied in a bow.

"Have you come from Drunehan?" Rua wondered, eyeing the three of them.

"No, Your Highness," the middle one said. "We are from Murreneir."

Rua pulled the ribbon's edge, untying it and carefully opening the wrapping. Three pieces of square canvas were stretched over thin frames. It was artwork of Lyrei Basin—one in winter, summer, and autumn.

She flicked through each painting, the colors of each season more beautiful than the last.

"I did that one," the boy to the right said, pointing to the autumn painting.

"I did the summer one," the girl said, her voice an octave too high and shaky.

Glancing up from the paintings, Rua met their anxious eyes. "These are beautiful," she said. The trio sagged with relief. "I will treasure them, thank you."

"Thank you," the girl replied. "Thank you for helping our people."

The words punched into Rua's gut. She hadn't helped anyone. What did these young witches expect her to do? They bowed and scampered off before she could ask.

"I'll take those and put them with the others," Aneryn offered, taking the paintings from Rua's hands.

"Here, open this one next," Bri said, holding out a golden box.

Rua eyed her guard suspiciously but took it. Sounds of laughter and light string music danced around them. They were the sounds of luxury—tittering laughter and string quartets.

Rua took the heavy box. She lifted the rectangular lid and gasped. Inside was a dagger. It had a silver scabbard engraved in spirals of detailing and golden suspension rings. The gilded pommel had a circle of rubies that matched the Immortal Blade.

Rua gaped at Bri, and her guard's grin widened.

"I thought your blade might get lonely." She smirked.

"Thank you," Rua whispered, lifting it out of the box. She immediately unbuckled her belt and clipped it through the rings so the dagger sat on her right hip. It was not as heavy as the Immortal Blade, but its weight helped her straighten. The muscles down Rua's right side had been barking at her ever since she first obtained the Immortal Blade. She was always pulling herself to the right to keep from leaning under the sword's weight. The heavy dagger seemed to pull her back into alignment. She wondered if her guard chose a heavier dagger for that very reason.

"Another dagger, really?" Talhan jested, peeking over his sister's shoulder. "Is that the only thing you can think to give the Dammacus sisters?"

"Shut it," Bri ordered, shoving her brother.

"That is from both of us, by the way," Talhan said, pointing to the dagger.

Stepping in front of him, Bri snarled, "No, it is not."

Rua couldn't help but laugh. They must have been like this their whole lives. She wondered what it must feel like to have a sibling like that. She didn't think she would ever have a relationship like that with Remy. She didn't need one, anyway.

Bri indicated behind Rua with a lift of her chin. Another well-wisher must be standing behind her. Rua braced herself for another doting smile and turned.

Renwick stood there waiting. He was dressed in a matching forest-green coat, the same golden patterning down the front, though the shoulders were wider. It made his eyes look darker. Rua was ready to stab her new dagger into Bri for what her guard had done. She had dressed her to match the Northern King.

Renwick's eyes looked Rua up and down, taking his time as he noted everything from the braids in her hair to her new black boots.

"Happy birthday," he said, his voice a rolling whisper that sent tingles down her spine. The sound felt like a hook in her chest, dragging her closer to him.

Renwick held out his hand toward the center of the clearing, and Rua followed through the parting crowd. People whispered in excitement as she stepped up to the giant cake. The marbled pink-and-white frosting swirled up five layers on frozen waves of sugar. Rua reached absently for a chocolate shaving and popped it in her mouth.

She heard a couple titters behind her and looked to Renwick, who was smirking down at her.

"What?" She squinted at him.

"It is customary to sing to you before you eat the cake," he said.

Rua glared at the people watching her before muttering to Renwick, "I am meant to eat this whole cake?"

He chuckled. "No, no, just we sing and you make a wish on candles . . . and then everyone eats the cake." His eyes drifted down her face, his voice softening. "Did you not celebrate birthdays in the witch camps?"

"Do *not* pity me," Rua snarled.

"Oh, I'm not." Renwick's cheeks dimpled. "It is awful to be sung to. I never know where to look."

She tucked a stray lock of hair behind her ear as a servant holding a candle exited Renwick's tent. The rest of the conversations dropped to whispers. The servant lit each of the small nineteen candles on top of the cake, and as they stepped back, the crowd began to sing.

Jolting, Rua twirled to look at them. The crowd sang a tune in Ific, a song about well wishes and the light of life in the snow? It did not make much sense. Rua was used to the Mhenbic prayers the witches would chant, just a lone solemn prayer for protection one more year, and then she would blow out a candle. But this . . . so many eyes watched her. Their cheeks and noses were rosy from the cold, and their smiles were too wide as they sang. It felt like a scourer scratching down her arm. Rua looked up to Renwick standing beside her. His eyes twinkled with mischief, like he knew all too well how uncomfortable she was, but his voice was a beautiful, smooth baritone.

The singing abruptly finished, and everyone watched Rua in bated silence. Was she meant to say something?

"Make a wish," Renwick murmured, tipping his head toward the cake.

Rua stared at the nineteen candles glowing before her. Feeling the weight of the many eyes, she made the first wish that came to her mind. The crowd cheered. If only they knew what she wished for.

As she watched the little streams of smoke circle skyward from the candles, she felt the shame of her wish. She could have wished for health, for peace or prosperity for her home court ... but she only wished for Balorn's head—a bloody death by her hand.

The cake was whisked off to be cut for the crowd. Renwick still stood tightly beside her, a wrapped gift in his hands.

"I wanted to thank you for being here," Renwick said, looking over the pile of presents. "For helping my people."

"I am here to keep you and your people in line, not to help you," Rua said stiffly.

Renwick bobbed his chin. He wasn't going to argue with her today it seemed.

"Happy birthday," he said, offering her the present.

The small rectangular gift was wrapped in blue fabric, folded and tied together in a neat bow. As soon as her fingers touched it, she could tell it was a book.

She unknotted the bow, unfolding the fabric as she felt Renwick's rapt eyes watching her. When she saw the cover of the book, she gasped. She knew the inlaid golden writing, the coarse gray fabric, the symbol of the High Mountain crest on the front cover and the words: *Encyclopedier dun' Yexshire.*

It looked just like one of the encyclopedias she grew up reading, but this one was different. It wasn't about castles or animals; it was about the capital city of the High Mountain Court. Rua flicked through the first pages. They were written in Yexshiri, the language of the High Mountain people. Rua had taught herself to read it through these books, though she had seldom tried to speak it.

"How did you find this?" she whispered.

Inside the book were elegantly inked descriptions and illustrations. Each drawing and notation was filled right to the edges of the page: town maps, customs, holidays, even little histories of special events. She skimmed to a landscape showing the sprawling city of Yexshire, the High Mountain palace watching over the city like a sentinel on the mountain beyond. She wondered if Remy would rebuild it to look the same.

"I found it in a dusty box of books brought over from Murreneir." Renwick's hot breath skimmed across her cheek as he leaned in to look at the page.

"Hmm. I don't think it would have survived in your father's palace," Rua whispered, flipping through the book with stunned reverence.

"Your parents commissioned a new one to be made as an announcement of your birth. Look," he said, gently taking the gift and flicking toward the middle. He passed the opened book back to her.

Six sets of eyes stared at Rua: two adults and four children. The adults sat on lavish thrones, spired crowns atop their heads. She remembered those crowns from the palace in Drunehan, sitting beside the Immortal Blade. The Queen, her mother, looked so much like Remy. Even in the simple sketch, they had the same faces, same curly, dark hair. The fae male had a dark beard, his tight wavy hair similar to Rua's own. Names were written under each of the children: Raffiel, Rivitus, Remini, and Ruadora.

Her fingers traced Raffiel's face. He looked the same as he had as an adult, already broad shouldered with a charming grin even as a child, a reflection of the soldierly prince he would become. Little one-year-old Remini sat beside him, holding her elder brother's hand. But her eyes snagged on the little spectacled boy standing beside her mother. Rivitus had been seven years old, the only one of her siblings to be slayed during the Siege of Yexshire. Rua's fingers stilled. It was true, she looked like him. They had the same large eyes, more round than their siblings'. Their hair was wavy instead of their mother's loose curls. They had the same button noses and oval faces too. People said they looked like their father, but between his beard and his crown it was hard for Rua to tell. She looked at the swaddled baby in her mother's arms. She felt her soul reaching out in every direction, as if perhaps if she could focus on that sensation enough, she would still be able to remember the feeling of her mother's arms around her. They seemed so happy. However briefly, she had been loved.

Rua shut the book and swallowed. So many people watched her. Forcing a stillness into her limbs, she spotted two elderly fae speaking at the edge of the crowd, laughing and eating cake. The same people who had sneered at her and called her a *girl* now delighted in her festivities. They all wanted something from her. She thought about those hopeful young witches and their painted gifts. She didn't want to be needed by any of them.

"Thank you," she said, steeling her gaze as she looked at Renwick. "I'd like to leave now."

Renwick's eyes guttered, those damned jaw muscles popping out again. She knew she had surprised him, even as he willed his body into that telltale stillness.

"If I offended you . . ."

"No." Rua put her arm on the sleeve of his forest-green jacket, the one that matched her own. He looked down at where her hand rested on his arm. "This . . ." She held up the book, gesturing out toward the party. "Thank you, for doing all of this for me."

"I thought you might like to have a proper celebration, seeing as it is your nineteenth birthday and all," Renwick said, placing his warm hand over the top of hers, making her heart leap into her throat. It was such a small gesture, but it felt like a hot brand on her skin. "I promise I will do something smaller next time."

Rua pulled her hand away, brow furrowing. "There won't be a next time." She looked back to the spot where her cake once sat. "I will help you defeat Balorn, and then I am going . . ."

"Home?" Renwick offered.

The word stuck in her throat. She did not remember living in Yexshire. She had seen it through the forest a few times, and one time she had gotten so close . . . and it had ended terribly for her. She pushed that memory away. Yexshire was as foreign to her as Murreneir was.

"Yes," Rua said, though her words felt hollow.

Renwick cocked his head at her. The light made his ash-blond hair glint with streaks of silvery white. "You must remind your sister that you don't like to be doted on when you return then," he said in a clipped voice. Gone were his dimples and that hint of warmth in those cold green eyes.

Rua shifted on her feet, looking back toward the path from which they came.

"Go," he said with a sigh. "I will make excuses for you. I have hidden from many a party in my honor as well. It is something you never grow used to, Princess."

"Thank you," Rua muttered. It felt like the only thing to say.

She didn't look Renwick in the eyes again before she turned and moved back through the lively crowd. Bri and Talhan broke off behind her as she pushed her way through the narrow alleys.

"Give me some space," Rua snapped at them when they reached a quiet enough path.

"Remind you of someone?" Talhan murmured to his sister, but they continued to follow.

Renwick had thrown her a party with gifts and cake and well-wishes . . . and all she wanted to do was cry. But the red witches taught her that tears were a sign of weakness, that she hadn't tried hard enough to turn toward brighter feelings. She felt that thick choking knot in her throat as she looked up into the bright sky. She knew if she looked up into the sun, the knot would push its way back down her neck into her chest. It was a trick she had learned as a child. She had swallowed enough rocks in her throat over the years that her chest was now a hard boulder.

"Forgive me, Your Highness?" a mousy voice came from behind her.

"What now?" Rua turned with a frown to see a young witch in a blue cloak waiting.

"Baba Airu wishes to speak with you," she said.

"Of course she does." Rua sighed, looking up toward the sun once more. "Lead the way." She clenched the book in her hands tighter until its edges cut into her palms.

# CHAPTER ELEVEN

They twined their way through the witches' quarter. Rua was beginning to understand the layout of the place. It did not seem like such a mishmash of tents anymore. Few witches moved through the tents this day. She wondered how many were back at her party.

It felt wrong to be celebrating, to be eating cake and singing songs when Balorn was still out there. They should be spending every waking second trying to find him. Once he was killed and the curse broken, Rua would be free. She needed to be the one to save the North, to prove herself to her sister, to take her place in the High Mountain Court. This was her opportunity to prove her worth.

The young witch stopped at the flap of Baba Airu's tent. She gave Rua a brief bow and turned to leave. Rua looked back at the Eagles, who waited at the doorway beside her.

"You really don't need to be here," she grumbled, looking at Talhan. "Why don't you go clean up? Your sister is right, you stink."

Talhan grunted out a rough laugh. "Fine." He hugged his sister one more time and left. Bri's face still held that stoic look, but Rua knew her guard well enough by now to know that she was buzzing from her brother's arrival. She thought about the way Bri had barreled into him and then to the way Remy had tried to hug her in Drunehan. It was not the same. Remy was a stranger. She didn't think they would ever greet each other that way.

Rua bit the inside of her cheek and pushed her way into the tent, leaving Bri out in the cold.

Baba Airu sat in her rocking chair, facing the wood-burning fire. Wandering over, Rua took the seat next to the High Priestess and waited for her to speak.

"Happy birthday," Baba Airu said in Mhenbic. The furs from her hood blew back and forth as she rocked herself.

"Thank you." Rua slipped easily back into the witch's language. It was a relief after speaking with so many fae. She knew Yexshiri and spoke Ific, but Mhenbic was the language she had used for most of her life, taking no energy to summon the right words. She folded her hands over the book of Yexshire. "You did not wish to come?"

Baba Airu's cheeks lifted. "I have Seen it already," she said. "My presence can be . . . upsetting for some."

Rua observed the witch's scarred face. She had been one of those people frightened by the High Priestess. The burns, the closed eyes, the blue lips . . . and most of all the way Baba Airu smiled amongst the slaughter in the palace at Drunehan was unsettling. It was not the witch's face that frightened her anymore, Rua realized, it was her power.

"I'm sorry," Rua said, shame roiling in her gut.

"I do not mind sitting here quietly in my tent, Princess," Baba Airu said. "It allows me time to See finally. Hennen Vostemur was constantly pulling me out of my visions, trying to show me off as the weapon he thought I was. I am enjoying the freedom to be quiet now."

"I am sorry I misjudged you before," Rua said, worrying her lip. "I thought the blue lips and closed eyes were Hennen's doing."

"They are strange customs if you do not know them," Baba Airu said simply. "We are all strangers to each other until we try to look deeper."

"I don't know how much deeper I want anyone to look at me," Rua muttered, toying with the corners of her book.

"I am sorry that the book in your hands upsets you," Baba Airu said. "The High Mountain Court was a shining light in Okrith once."

"Lot of good it did them." Rua thumbed the spine of the thick book.

"The peace that Okrith knew for hundreds of years was led by the example of the High Mountain Court," Baba Airu answered. "Is all of that time worth nothing just because it ended?"

"My parents were the weak link in that chain then, if they did not see their fall coming," Rua gritted out. She had questioned it many times. Did they become too confident? Were they too blind to the world? Did they think it would always carry on that way?

"Your parents were good people," Baba Airu insisted. "They saw witches as their equals."

"I am not my parents," Rua warned. The heat of the room was beginning to make her skin swelter through her thick jacket dress.

"You grew up with witches," Baba Airu said, touching the totem pouch on her chest. "You wield the Immortal Blade forged by them. You have sworn to cut down Balorn and keep the Witchslayer in place . . ."

"You still call him Witchslayer?" Rua whispered. So the witches did not trust Renwick, after all. To follow a King nicknamed the Witchslayer . . . must be terrible for them.

"My people want to trust *you*." Baba Airu cocked her head in Rua's direction.

"Well, they shouldn't," she grumbled. The most warm feeling Rua could summon for the red witches was a begrudging gratitude for keeping her safe. The witches did not feel the way the fae did. She had always felt like her emotions were too big for them. They made her feel different, weak. And now their sister coven to the north was treating her with trust?

"Whether it has been earned or not, it is there," Baba Airu said. "It is up to you what you do with that trust. You could bring on the dawn of a new world."

"I don't think you will like that dawn," Rua cautioned, looking over the aging witch's face. What did Baba Airu See in Rua's future? All Rua saw was the Immortal Blade cutting across the lands. The power would consume her. The dawn of the new world would be one of blood and death.

"You sould like your sister now." Baba Airu's lips twisted up.

Rua stiffened. "I am nothing like my sister."

"I have had visions of you two your whole lives," Baba Airu said. Her voice became softer, as though she were fading away from the room. "I can See her future wedding in my mind's eye even now."

"You have been spying on us our whole lives, you mean." Rua gripped the book tighter. She had the urge to throw it into the fire, but she held herself back.

"I may be able to focus on some more than others, but the visions are given to me by the Fates themselves," Baba Airu mused.

Rua rolled her eyes. The Fates were as fake as the Moon Goddess the blue witches prayed to. The other witch covens simply called her Mother Moon, but it was the same magic, the same life force that they prayed to, though it had different faces. The fae prayed to the Fates too, along with a pantheon of other Gods. The idea that it was the Fates that were showing Baba Airu her future was laughable.

"I do not believe in the Fates," Rua retorted. "It is just simple magic in us. There is nothing divine about it."

"And what of Fated love?" Baba Airu asked. "Do you think that is a lie as well?"

Rua thought about her sister and Hale. The magic was a thick rope between them. Even when Remy hugged her, Rua felt that connection back to Hale. Something about that bond was real. Stories said that the Fates had conjured up a tapestry of power that was stronger than all others. They wove those threads through the world, a power so mighty that it was felt long before the couple even met. Before the Siege of Yexshire, many blue witches made their livings feeling for those Fated bonds and professing them to rich fae.

"The Fated bonds are real," Rua said, "but they are random. I do not believe that the Goddesses in the sky pick who receives them."

"It feels easier if it were random, doesn't it?" Baba Airu contemplated. "If it were all meaningless, it would be easier to accept it. Knowing that you are important is not easy. I know what it is to See into your future and fear if you will be able to survive it." Baba Airu slid her totem bag off her neck and opened the pouch. She took out a silver ring and slid it onto her finger. Rua stared at the simple ring with a dulled blue stone embedded in the band.

Rua waited for Baba Airu to explain her totem, but the High Priestess simply said, "I have Seen your life for a reason, Ruadora. Only those who have important destinies are shown to me."

"So you don't have a lot of visions of people squatting over chamber pots then?" Rua growled.

Baba Airu's face split in two, and she let out a cackling laugh, placing her hand on the center of her chest as it shook. "You are definitely a Dammacus, child." The witch crowed. "Your sister was too cautious, and you are too reckless, but you are two sides of the same coin."

The Battle of Drunehan flashed in her mind. She saw her brother's bloodied body discarded on the floor, his Fated, Bern, forced to drop him and carry on the fight. No one was near enough to save him. No healers or witches sacrificed their lives for him the way that brown witch had for her sister. She remembered the horrified looks as that brown witch pulled out her dagger and performed the *midon brik*. The witch had swapped her life for her sister's, and Rua had fled before even seeing if her sister survived it.

"Her name was Heather Doledir," Baba Airu said. Rua gritted her teeth. How did the High Priestess do that? Could she See memories as well as the future? "She loved your sister. That sacrifice she made was a gift."

"I never want anyone to give me that gift." Rua dropped her head. "I don't want anyone dying for me."

"You are a princess of the High Mountain Court," Baba Airu said. "People will willingly die to keep you safe. That is a truth you must come to grips with."

"I don't want this." Rua shook her head. With pleading eyes, she looked to Baba Airu, as if the High Priestess could take it all back. "You keep telling me I will help your people, but I am not that person. What am I supposed to do?"

Baba Airu's rocking paused. "I Saw what happened in that council room in Drunehan."

Rua thought about the councilor whose throat she had sliced with the Immortal Blade. The adrenaline of the battle had still coursed through her veins, and she had taken his life without hesitation.

"Fowler would have plotted against you," Baba Airu said. "He would have betrayed the Witchslayer too. It was wise that you killed him."

"It did not feel wise," Rua muttered, picking at the edges of her book.

"Renwick was unsure of what to do with the witches that day," Baba Airu said. "And you demanded us to be freed . . . and paid."

Rua's eyes drifted across the room. It was a modest but elegant tent. The bed was new, not a scratch on the carved headboard. The intricately detailed wood was clearly made in the Eastern Court. The rugs were expensive ones from the Southern Court. Everything looked freshly purchased.

"How many stayed after they were freed?" Rua asked, peering at Baba Airu's neck. A thin line, a shade lighter than her tan skin, still circled her throat where her witch's collar had been.

"More than you would think," Baba Airu said. "Renwick is paying them one thousand *druni* a month to stay."

"Gods," Rua gasped.

*One thousand.* No wonder Baba Airu had purchased all new pieces of furniture. The witches' currency of silver pieces, *druni*, were stamped with the phases of the moon. They mixed amongst the rest of the currency of Okrith, each of the classes preferring different precious metals. The fae used mostly gold, the witches silver, and the humans copper. But no currency was turned away.

"He offered ten thousand to anyone who chose to leave too." Baba Airu twisted the silver ring around her index finger. "Some took the money and left for the countryside, but most stayed. Not out of loyalty to Renwick, but for fear of Balorn and his many loyalists. Witches may be free, but the shadows of our collars prevail."

Hennen and Balorn Vostemur may have brought about the enslavement of blue witches, but their people had allowed it. There might have been quiet dissent in the Northern Court, like with the Lord of

Brufdoran, but Rua imagined that many of the Northern Court fae agreed with them. Blue witches still had to fear the Northern fae. Rua wasn't sure if that would ever change.

"I can't believe he offered that much," Rua whispered to herself. The pockets of the Northern Court were deeper than she knew. The world after the Siege of Yexshire had fallen apart for the rest of Okrith, while the Northern Court consolidated its wealth.

"He did not do it for us . . . ," Baba Airu said. Rua felt the witch's focus on her, even through her shut eyes. "He did it for you."

"No," Rua interjected.

Baba Airu gave a knowing smile. "He was unsure of what path to take until you demanded it. You made him see things more clearly," she insisted.

"I will not always be around to whisper in the King's ear for you," Rua hissed.

"Then help us now." Baba Airu tilted her face down to the book in Rua's hands. "Help Renwick see his path forward. Help the witches to trust him. Then you can go wherever feels most like home."

Standing, Rua swallowed the lump in her throat. *Wherever feels most like home.*

"Will you tell me where they are gathered now?" Rua shifted on her feet. "Where is the book of spells?"

"Raevenport," Baba Airu said with a faint nod of her head. "Enjoy your birthday, Your Highness."

Rua's mouth fell open, not expecting to get a real answer from the High Priestess. She clenched the book tightly between her hands—the book about her supposed homeland and the strangers that were meant to be her family. She shook her head as she blustered out of the tent.

"What was all of that about?" Bri asked as Rua stormed down the cold pathway.

"We're heading to Raevenport," Rua gritted out. "She also told me I'm supposed to unite her people and save their kingdom."

Bri snorted. "So, nothing too big then?"

# CHAPTER TWELVE

They had departed for Raevenport at once upon hearing of the spell book's location. From the looks of it, Raevenport was a half-forgotten town built for scoundrels. Rua scrutinized the run-down taverns and brothels teeming with drunk patrons. Outdoor crowds gathered around barrels burning foul-smelling refuse. Every person she spotted had a bottle in their hand. Sordid-looking fae, armed to the teeth, merrily stumbled their way down the icy stone lanes. This was a thief's paradise. The way they tracked the royal sleighs as they rode into town made Rua shudder. Greedy eyes scanned them for coin purses, jewels, and expensive weapons as they disembarked and continued on foot. Her companions seemed to silently agree to get out of Raevenport as quickly as possible, taking the steep ice trail eastward with haste. Finding her footing on the slick ice, Rua wondered if their sleighs would even be there when they returned.

A thin trail carved its way through the ledge of the ice cliff. They carefully switchbacked higher and higher, navigating across cracks and crevices in the undulating ice. The seedy little village quickly disappeared out of sight as they climbed into the clouds.

Her teeth ached more with every jagged breath. The bitter gales sliced across the exposed landscape. Ice encrusted the hood of her cloak as plumes of breath clouded the frozen air.

"There better be a bloody feast for us when we arrive," Talhan groused, hugging tightly to the ice wall as they moved at a grueling pace toward the witches' forge.

"And mulled wine," Bri added, her face pinched against the cold.

Thador's hawk, Ehiris, soared through the thick gray skies, circling far ahead.

"Nearly there," Thador called back to them from his lead position.

"Raevenport was filled with thieves," Talhan said, glancing to his right, where dunes of powdery snow gave way to a steep drop and a forest far below.

"And?" Bri gritted out.

"Are we sure we'll have sleighs when we return to the village?" Talhan pulled his cloak tighter around him, the charcoal gray turning white with snow. They'd be bleached of color in another hour, exposed on the cliff's side.

"They won't steal from their King," Renwick called from up ahead. His words were clipped. She was surprised he had breath for them at all.

Rua remained silent, saving her energy as she put one foot in front of the other. The forest far below seemed like a painting of miniature pine trees, stretching out on the rippling horizon. A turquoise, frozen river wove its way up through the forest, wide enough to be seen even from their dizzying heights. They were in the clouds, so high the billowing shroud of mist blew through them with each gust. She kept her gaze downcast to keep the icy gales from assaulting her eyes.

The blustering wind came in sudden bursts, impossible to anticipate or lean into. Each step was a battle. Leaning too far into the wind, Rua stumbled forward as it ebbed, only to be shoved backward by its force again.

"Halt," Thador shouted.

Rua squinted up into the wind, icy tears being forced from the corners of her eyes as she steeled herself against the rush of snow.

A figure stood in a cerulean-blue cloak. He was nearly the height of

Thador, his beard dusted in snow. Staring daggers at Renwick, he lifted a beckoning hand and veered off the trail around the corner.

Following him, they descended the hairpin slope sculpted into the ice, its appearance blending into the whiteout. They probably would have missed the path entirely were it not for the cloaked man in front of them. Perhaps the blue witches Saw their convoy lost in the blizzard and had sent him to find them.

As they cut down toward the tree line, a fortress came into view. It was made of iron and ice, cutting into the mountainside. Large open gates mirrored those at the Temple of Hunasht, but the forge was nothing like the intricately constructed temple. The wind eased as they followed the path toward the wall of solid stone, not a single window carved into it. A lone doorway cut through the rock, carved Mhenbic symbols warding the entryway.

A looming sense of dread filled Rua as they filed through the narrow doorway. Ehiris called from a perch on a nearby tree, sheltering while her master entered the forge.

They spilled into a cavernous, dark entryway. Two torches mounted to the walls provided the only light. Beyond the roughly hewn room was a wooden doorway, painted with more Mhenbic protection spells.

The delicate tips of Rua's ears burned along with her cheeks. Her raw lips and the tip of her nose tingled. She was certain they were bright red like her companions, feeling the effects of the trek now that the assaulting wind was gone.

The man pulled back his hood and stared at them with glowing blue eyes, waiting for them to talk.

"We need to speak with your leader," Renwick declared.

Apparently, it was the wrong thing to say.

Scowling, the witch boomed, "You should not have come here, Witchslayer."

Renwick stilled, eyes hardening, though he did not seem surprised.

"We are not with the Northern Court," Bri said, pushing to the front of them. "We are emissaries from the High Mountain Court, and we need to speak to the witches for the safety of all."

The witch chuckled, a gruff, mocking laugh. "Do you know what this says?" He waved his hand to the Mhenbic painted on the door.

"It says only witches may enter," Rua said in Mhenbic, drawing the witch's gaze to her.

"It does." He bobbed his head, eyeing the Immortal Blade.

The rest of the fae watched them cautiously, not understanding what they were saying.

"May I enter?" Rua pursed her lips.

He looked at her with a confused expression, probably bemused by her perfect Mhenbic. Scratching his beard, he muttered, "You are a fae."

"I am a fae with witch magic and a witch talisman." Rua glanced at the door. "Do you think your wardings will recognize me as friend or foe?"

"What are they saying?" Talhan grumbled to his sister. Bri just cut him a look.

"You can try," the witch said, bowing slightly and gesturing to the shut door.

Rua turned back to the rest of the fae. "I'm going to talk to the witches. I will be back," she said in Ific.

They each spoke over the other, voicing their discontent all at once. The idea of her going into the witches' forge without them was unpleasant, but necessary. Somehow, she knew the witches wouldn't hurt her.

"It will be fine," she assured Bri. "We need this book."

"We can find another way to get the book," Bri snarled.

Rua glanced to Renwick. "We've come all this way. At least let me try."

Renwick clenched his jaw but nodded reluctantly.

"Fine, we'll just sit here freezing our asses off." Thador pouted, perching himself on an outcropping of rock.

"I don't suppose we could trouble you for some wine?" Talhan asked the witch with a hopeful grin. The witch only narrowed his eyes in response. The fae would find no hospitality here.

Rua didn't look back as she reached out for the door with her red witch magic. It opened under the invisible force of her power.

"Mother Moon," the witch cursed in Mhenbic.

A small smirk pulled up on her lips as she walked through the threshold. The rubies on the hilt of the Immortal Blade began to glow as if speaking to the Mhenbic wardings she passed through.

"Wow." Bri gaped at her as she carried on down the hallway, the crimson glow of her sword lighting her way through the shadowed hallway.

"Try and bring back some wine, Ru," Talhan called after her, the Eagle's voice echoing all around her as she tunneled into the mountain. The door shut behind her, and she was left alone in the flickering red darkness.

A thin strip of orange light flashed up ahead as Rua's eyes strained to see the outline of a doorway. The sound of her footsteps and her quiet breaths echoed across the gloom. The darkness pulled tighter as the rubies on her sword flickered out.

"No," she cursed down at the Immortal Blade. She grabbed the hilt as if her hand would turn the glow back on, but the sword did not respond. Her footsteps faltered as she focused on that thin strip of light. She wondered if she passed doorways, if more hallways spider-webbed off this main one, but she saw nothing.

A mounting trepidation that she was not alone filled her as the thick blackness swam around her eyes. She swallowed the tight knot in her throat and kept moving toward the doorway. The feeling of unseen eyes crawled across her skin. Her stomach tightened as she finally reached the far door, relief washing over her as the door pushed open and she stepped back into the light.

The warmth of the fires did not soothe the chill she felt down her spine as she walked into the great hall. A crowd of witches stood on either side of the room, making a thin aisle for Rua to walk down. Hushed voices skittered across the vast stone forge. There were no decorations, no grandeur to the bare walls and jagged ceiling.

Behind a large oak table at the far end of the room sat five witches. The two men and three women were all unmarked, unlike so many in the crowd.

"You have come for our book of spells, Princess?" the middle witch, a midnight-haired matronly woman, asked.

"I have." Rua watched cautiously as she took a few more steps, feeling the eyes of the crowd upon her.

"You dare bring the Witchslayer to this sanctuary and ask for our sacred book?" snarled a witch at the far end of the table.

A few gruff murmurs of agreement sounded behind Rua.

"Onyx," the middle witch scolded.

Rua assessed the witch to her far right, Onyx. She seemed as young as Rua despite her silver hair. She had sharp brown eyes and thin, scowling lips. The flickering light of the torches high on the walls made her features even more severe.

"Why should we trust you?" Onyx asked.

One of the male witch's eyes dipped to the Immortal Blade. "She wields the ancient blade, forged by the red witches. She is *Mhenissa*."

*Mhenissa*. The word was whispered all around her a dozen more times.

Rua narrowed her eyes at the lean man, questioning how much of her life the witches had Seen.

"Baba Airu sent me here for the book," Rua said, hoping invoking the name of the High Priestess might help her curry favor with the witches. Instead, their faces turned to stone.

"She works with the Witchslayer," Onyx growled.

The second male witch folded his arms across his barrel chest. "Not all of us are so willing to follow another Vostemur King as eagerly as Baba."

"Can't she See it? She must have her reasons for doing so?" Rua protested.

The gruff witch put his hands on the table, leaning in and staring at her under thick brows. "Do not lecture me about the gift of Sight," he muttered. "The Baba may well See a future worth fighting for, but that does not mean it will come to pass. It does not mean it is the future the rest of us See either. Maybe we will fade away like the violet witches."

Narrowing her eyes, Rua looked down at the line of witches. She wondered what future they all Saw. Did they really See an end to the blue witch coven like the violet witches of the East? How different could this vision be from the Baba's own?

"I am not asking you to follow Renwick," Rua argued. Several barks of discontentment sounded as she used the Northern King's first name.

"The princess was the one to demand our freedom," the midnight-haired witch pondered. "She is the reason we no longer wear the collars."

The crowd shifted behind her.

"I cannot take credit for your freedom. I'm sure you would have claimed it regardless," Rua said, watching as the witches gave her looks of begrudging agreement. She hoped that meant the tides of the conversation were turning. "I understand you wanting to break away from the Northern King." She huffed, hoping she was winning them over. "I look forward to breaking this curse and ridding myself of him too."

"Oh, I doubt that very much." Onyx's lip curled, the prickly, silver-haired witch determined to shove her back down.

"We want to break the curse on your sisters!" Rua barked in exasperation. "What have you done for them?"

She braced for the backlash of those words but instead was met with five sets of wide eyes. They darted looks to each other as if this were a conversation they had before.

"They are as good as dead," Onyx murmured to her hands.

A somber feeling blanketed the room as Rua spoke into the quiet. "Would you want to be left to suffer, if it were you?"

"It nearly was." Onyx's eyes lifted, letting Rua see the haunted memories churning in her gaze.

She knew that feeling all too well—the horror of nearly dying and of nearly losing yourself to a fate worse than death. She bet Onyx had nightmares each night too. They were all haunted. The weight of the trauma thickened the air, so potent Rua felt it pressing down on her. She was the least tormented out of them all, but she felt like she was falling apart even worse than these tortured witches.

"This is not about Nave, Onyx," the stout, blond-haired witch beside her whispered.

"Is it not?" Onyx spat back as Rua's heart lurched into her throat. "Should we tell her who killed my sister and why she had to die?"

"Enough." The witch silenced Onyx with her raised hand as she glared at Rua. "It is the fae who should break this curse." Mutters of agreement rang out around her. "This is the Witchslayer's problem, not ours. It has been only a few weeks since we were freed." Her brilliant blue eyes shone through the shadowed room. "The phantom collars still choke us."

Rolling her shoulders, Rua tried to stretch away the growing tension. "Will you not even let us try?"

"This is not our fight," the middle witch said.

"I am not asking you to fight!" Rua's fingers twitched to grab the Immortal Blade, but this was not a battle she could win with her sword. She tried to cool her tone. "I don't need the whole book, just the one spell. Go find it and I will leave you in peace."

"The book is not here," the middle witch proclaimed, standing from her chair as the rest of the coven whirled to look at her.

Rua's mouth fell open. "Say that again?"

"The North is not a safe place right now, Princess. Balorn is as likely to show up on our doorstep as you. Now that he has the Witches' Glass, he could do all sorts of terrible things with that book."

"Where is the book?" Rua clenched her fists, already thinking to how she was going to break the news to her freezing companions waiting outside.

"It was given to the High Mountain witches for safekeeping. It resides in the Temple of Yexshire now."

Rua's heart sank even as rage coursed through her tightening muscles.

"You seem disappointed, Princess? Surely you should be pleased the spell book is with the witches who raised you?" Onyx's voice dripped with sarcasm. The young blue witch seemed to know more about her than Rua liked. "You could contact your sister through fae fire and ask for her aid, but you won't, will you? You need to do it all on your own."

The blond witch beside Onyx squeezed her arm. "Stop."

Onyx ignored the command, wrenching her elbow free. Her words were more cutting than any blade as she said, "The broken fae princess who talks like a witch."

The Immortal Blade couldn't protect Rua from the stabbing pain in her chest. Everything the hateful witch said was true.

"Go to Yexshire," the middle witch instructed, trying to pull Rua back into the conversation.

Rua's pulse pounded in her ears and the urge to unsheathe the blade at her hip escalated with each breath. Rage roiled in her chest. She did not want to go to Yexshire.

"Thank you for telling me where it is, at least," Rua gritted out, turning without any parting words and striding back up the aisle of witches.

"Have a nice walk home, Princess," Onyx's voice sang after her.

Rua gripped the hilt of the Immortal Blade tightly, taking a steadying breath as she pushed through the heavy wood doors. She braced herself to share the bad news—just another in her long list of failures.

～

She didn't feel the biting cold as the wind whipped her cheeks. A far bigger storm churned inside her. She couldn't go to the Temple of Yexshire. She never wanted to see those red witches again. Baba Morganna's serene face as blood splattered across the room flashed into her mind. Baba Airu had been the same. Did all High Priestesses smile in the face of death? Rua's limbs still trembled, the hairs still prickling on the back of her neck as she waited for the sword to strike her.

Baba Morganna had not lifted a finger to save her during the Battle of Drunehan. But it was not because of those horrible memories that she feared returning to Yexshire. She feared the red witches would see it—that gaping hole inside of her where all the pain and terror still gnawed away at her. She had always been a failure to the witches. She hadn't tried hard enough to push away that darkness. The witches viewed it as a shortcoming, as if sheer determination could shove the pain away . . . but the harder she tried to deny it, the wider that pit stretched. She teetered at that precipice, waking each day, wondering if it would be the day she finally plummeted into its darkness.

Renwick's voice muffled on the icy wind. "Stay on the path."

Rua squinted against the bright glare, continuing her trudge through the ankle-deep snow beside the path. The Eagles plodded along in grim silence, snow clinging to their clothes and faces dispirited. The mood of the convoy had grown colder than the ice cliffs surrounding them. They had come all this way for nothing.

"The edge is right there," Renwick called with urgency, pointing to the drift of snow beyond her. "The rest is just powder and ice. It is closer than it seems."

"I am fine," Rua hissed, the cold air painfully numbing her teeth.

Renwick stomped over to her, muttering curses, until he was right in front of her. "Stop straying to the cliff's edge." His voice was a low growl.

"You're telling me how to walk now?" She scowled up at him, moving to push past, arcing further toward the edge, but he easily positioned himself in front of her again.

He could have grabbed her and pulled her into line, but he didn't. He just stood there frowning at her, his voice deep and hoarse as he said, "I know you are angry about the book, but we can handle it later. Now, please, before my heart stops beating, get back to the path."

Rua narrowed her eyes at him. "I don't serve you, Witchslayer."

His face tightened as he opened his mouth to say something, but a groaning crack boomed through the cold air.

Before Rua realized what was happening, the ground dropped out from below her. Those wide, fearful eyes were the last thing she saw before plunging downward. The roaring of moving snow and whining crackles of ice was deafening. Bri screamed her name as the violent force of the avalanche took her.

Every time she thought she had reached the end, the cresting wave of snow collided with her and pushed her further down. She tumbled like she was being rolled in a barrel, head over heels against the coarse, burning snow. Branches snapped, the scent of crushed pine needles lashed through the powder above her. She remembered a forest lay beyond the ice cliffs. If the rush of snow smashed her into a tree, it would kill her. Throwing out her red magic wildly, she pushed in every direction, trying to keep the wall of snow from crashing into her. She pushed and pushed, struggling to animate a red orb of protective air around her, but she couldn't hold the image in her mind; the whirling of her vision was too great. Weighed down by her sword, the avalanche dragged her under.

The roaring in her ears ebbed, leaving the sudden high-pitched ringing of silence in its wake. She wasn't sure if she was still moving. Her eyes only saw white, uncertain which way was up, after being flung like a limp doll. The numbing snow was so strong she did not know if she was injured. All her limbs might be broken, she did not know. She was buried in the snow but still could see, so she knew she must be close to the surface. Panting, a droplet of blood fell from her nose sideways. That must be down. She pushed a disoriented hand up toward the fissures of light, unearthing herself as snow slid beneath her clothes, watery trickles of frost melting against her raw skin.

She gasped as her face breached the surface, sunlight beaming down on her as she surveyed the devastation. She was in the forest. Gaping up at the trees above her, a hawk screeched. Ehiris circled them, and she waved up to the bird as if it could fly off and tell Thador that she lived. Glancing toward the ice cliffs high on the ridge, she was barely able to make out the black dots on the trail. She had been pushed so far.

She screamed out to the three dots on the horizon, but her voice was lost on the wind. They probably couldn't see her. The whole ice shelf was split in two. The path to Raevenport was blocked now. The blue witches would have to find another way out of their forge.

Hauling herself to her feet, she narrowed her eyes at those three dots again. Only three.

Shit.

Renwick had fallen with her.

Her breath caught in her throat as she began scanning wildly around her. Sticks, pine needles, and stones dotted through the muddied snow, but she did not see anything else. Her heartbeat hammered in her ears.

No, no, no.

Frozen, she didn't know which way to run. She walked in wild zig-zags, searching with a growing panic, looking for that midnight-blue cloak and that ash-blond hair. Horrible visions speared through her mind of Renwick impaled on a pine branch or his neck snapped under the force of the avalanche. Acid climbed up her throat as her hands shook.

Ehiris screeched again, landing on a low branch. She flapped her wings in irritation, drawing Rua's stare. The hawk was trying to tell her something.

She rushed to the large trunk of the pine tree and spotted it: a triangle of blue wool peeking above the snow. Her chest seized and her lungs strained against her rib cage as she dropped to her knees.

She clawed through the snow, scrambling more wildly than any *suraash*. She unearthed more of the cloak, then a pale blue hand. Cursing again, she shredded her raw fingertips, scooping snow with a ferocity that made a groan rumble through her chest. Reaching his shoulder, she tugged, pulling Renwick's limp body up.

She got to her feet. Wrapping her arms under his armpits, she squatted, thighs straining as she yanked him out of the snow. The churned snow gave way, and they both toppled backward.

Rua touched her hand to Renwick's blue, lifeless face as burning hot tears sprung to her eyes. Gods, she had killed him.

# CHAPTER THIRTEEN

Her body spasmed violently, her mind no longer in control of her limbs. Another screech of the bird above them pierced the frozen air, making her jump.

Renwick gasped, eyes flying open, jolting to life at the sound.

"Oh, thank the fucking Gods," Rua gasped, voice trembling. Her shaking hands skirted over Renwick's body as his emerald eyes found hers. "Are you injured?"

"I don't know," he breathed, his chest rising and falling in heavy pants. He lifted an icy hand to her face, sweeping his thumb across her cheek.

"We have to find shelter and get warm now," she snapped, heart jittering as she jerked out of his touch. "We need to dry our clothes if we're ever going to survive the walk back to the others."

Rua's teeth clacked together as the handfuls of snow shoved into her clothes melted. Her tunic was as soaked as if she had jumped into the ocean. Renwick would be the same.

"Downhill." Renwick trembled through shivering blue lips. "There are caves by the river. Thieves and looters use them. If we find one of their hideouts, there will be supplies."

"Can you stand?" Rua asked, groaning as she pushed up on her sore legs. She extended her hand, and Renwick took it but was unable to bend his frozen fingers around her grip. Reaching down, she grabbed him by the collar and hoisted him to his knees, helping him stand. Pins and needles shot through her hands as she strained to touch her thumb to her fingertips. They needed to get warm as fast as possible.

Looking up to Ehiris, Renwick called, "Here."

The bird flew down and landed on his outstretched arm, talons digging into the wool of his cloak. He popped the lid of the minuscule canister strapped to the hawk's leg, producing a tiny scroll and needle-like stick of lead. With shaking, clunky hands he lifted the stick to his lips, clenching it between his teeth, as he scribbled something onto the paper. Fumbling to put it back in the tube, Renwick finally closed the lid and lifted his arm. Ehiris took flight, soaring off into the gray skies.

"What did you say?" Rua watched the hawk disappear into the low clouds.

"That we survived and we are taking shelter," Renwick said, wrapping his arms tightly around himself, tucking his stiff fingers into his armpits. "That we will meet them in the village tomorrow."

"Tomorrow?"

"We have fallen far off the path. The trek through the woods will be twice as long. We need to take shelter and survive this night," he said despondently, looking up to the darkening skies. They had spent the better part of a day getting to Raevenport. The winter night was already looming. "If you would like to plod through the night in frozen clothing, be my guest. I will collect your corpse in the morning."

He didn't wait for her as he turned and trudged downhill. She deserved his anger after what she had done. It was a miracle they were alive, let alone able to walk.

Snow melted into her wet boots as she slogged through the forest. Her muscles strained to keep her upright through the uneven terrain, flipping between lightning bolts of aching pain and sweet numbness. She hoped the challenging walk would warm her body. A whimper escaped her lips of its own volition. She was so desperate for warmth.

Renwick paused up ahead, as if waiting to hear if she followed. When she nearly reached him, he took off again. Their steaming breaths floated like mist through the graying twilight.

The frozen turquoise river appeared through the valley, and beyond that a tapering cave mouth. Rua fought with her sleepy mind, willing a few more minutes of focus, pulling up on every reserve to keep her wits and not succumb to the cold.

Sleep. It was all her weary mind wanted.

Narrowing her eyes, she searched for footprints in the powdery snow, but she saw none. The cave was abandoned.

Placing her feet carefully across the ice, she shuffled after Renwick. A creak sounded, and her boot pierced the ice. Rua gulped a breath as she tried to yank her boot free. Icy water filled her shoe, but she didn't feel its sting. Her feet were already wet with melted snow. The toe of her boot had dived through the ice, and now she couldn't get it out the same way it entered. Her frozen foot would not obey.

She bent to punch a wider hole in the ice as Renwick shouted, "Don't." He slid back over to her. "You'll make the ice unstable." Stooping, he grabbed her calf. Bending her ankle, he guided her boot out of the hole she had made. "I'm not going to jump into the freezing water after you."

It would be the perfect end—surviving an avalanche only to drown in the icy river.

As she limped across the slush and into the cave, the urgency of a fire began to mount. If she didn't get her wet boot off, she wouldn't have toes in the morning.

The cave had clearly been inhabited: dusty bedrolls and blankets scattered the floor. Charred rocks sat in a circle toward the back of the cave, where fissures in the rock opened to the sky above. It was the perfect place for a fire, where the smoke would be sucked up into the air. Scraps of chicken bone and stalks of foraged herbs lay strewn around the forgotten campsite. A large branch had been dragged in, some of the smaller limbs already hacked away. There would be no food, but at least they wouldn't have to forage for dry firewood. Rua thanked the moon for thieves and looters.

She braced against the limb as she snapped the branch from the main stem with her boot. She broke it again over her knee and chucked the sticks into the fire pit. She did it again and again as Renwick's trembling hands fumbled with a piece of flint over the pine kindling. The sight of the first spark made Rua release a long-held breath. They might survive her latest mistake after all.

Her body shook in aching spasms now that they had relief from the glacial wind. Reviving herself from the cold would not be pleasant. If she were a witch, she didn't think she would have survived the fall. It was the first time she ever felt a begrudging gratitude for being fae. It had probably saved her life.

When she had stacked enough logs on the fire, she shucked off her wet boots. Grabbing the clasp of her cloak, she looked to Renwick and said, "Take off your clothes."

His lips twisted up at the insistence in her voice as she yanked her tunic over her head. "I never thought I'd hear you say that." He grinned as he hung his cloak up on an outcropping of rock.

"The fact you are teasing me right now means you are far less cold than I am," Rua growled, hooking her thumbs into her trousers.

Renwick's eyes skimmed down her half-naked body, lust filling them even as he trembled. He crouched, grabbing a blanket off the floor and shaking it out. Stepping over to her, he wrapped it around Rua's shoulders.

Tilting his head to the fire, he said, "Get warm."

The threadbare blanket grated against her raw skin. "Take your clothes off and come get warm with me or you will die. Now," she commanded. She was not willing to let them both die from his false sense of modesty. His lips were still blue. His hands still shook, though they seemed more dexterous. He would fade into the cold by nightfall.

Renwick chuckled and bowed his head in acquiescence as Rua lay down on the thin bedroll beside the fire. The heat of the flames scoured her skin, feeling like a million tiny needles pricked into her. She gritted her teeth against it, closing her eyes as the warmth touched her face. She yielded to the exhaustion, her limbs sagging in relief after their panicked spasms.

She was half-asleep when she felt the cool body press up against her back, pulling another blanket on top of them both. Renwick's muscled arm circled her waist and pulled her back against him, his nose and lips burying into the hair at the back of her neck. He took a deep, sleepy breath. She felt his muscles sigh just as hers had, her warmth reviving him. Her mind was too far away to register what it meant, every ounce of her energy being funneled into getting warm and staying alive.

"I'm sorry I almost killed you," she whispered into the darkness. For a moment she wasn't sure if her lips formed the words or if it was merely a thought in her mind.

A warm breath skittered across her neck. "Why do I have the feeling this won't be the last time you make that apology to me?"

She nestled back further against that warming body, finally relenting to the heavy undertow of sleep.

～

Knees soaked with blood, she knelt on the floor in Drunehan. She looked in horror at the crowd, scanning their faces for someone to save her. But instead of Hennen Vostemur's host of Northern fae, it was the crowd from her birthday party. They stood holding gifts and smiling at her as she trembled in anticipation of the sword behind her, about to cut off her head. They didn't care that she was about to die. They just smiled and stared as she felt the whooshing of the blade behind her.

"Rua," a warm voice muttered as arms coiled around her stomach.

Her chest heaved, her throat raw.

"It was a dream," Renwick whispered, lips skimming the shell of her ear as his thumb lazily circled her navel.

Morning light peeked through the cracks in the rock. Blinking again, she regained her wits. They had slept for so long, but it felt like only minutes. She was suddenly aware of the naked form behind her—the hot muscles, the warm, sleep-addled voice, and the hardness of him pressed against her backside.

Rua jolted up, wrapping the blanket around her as she clambered to a stand. Renwick draped the other blanket around his waist, rapidly coming to his senses from his sleepy stupor. The fire still burned. He must have fed it all night while Rua slept. The cave was sweltering, the rock floor warm beneath her bare feet. Her lips were cracked, her throat scratchy and dry as she put distance between them. Her head pounding, she grabbed her discarded clothing, all laid out to dry.

Rua blanched as she picked up her undergarments. Renwick had moved them too. She was so desperate for warmth that she hadn't thought to dry her wet pile of clothes. He had. Tucking the blanket under her armpits, she stepped into her underpants and then her trousers, jumping to shimmy them up over her thighs. Renwick moved to do the same as Rua's eyes snagged on his pale, rippling abdomen. Had he always been that muscled? In his tailored court attire Rua had thought he was more lean, but this . . . this was distracting. She had not anticipated that corded muscle under his refined clothing. He was built like a warrior, not like a King.

Closing her gaping mouth, she turned her back to him as she pulled her dry tunic over her head. When she turned around, Renwick was the Northern King once more, in his elegant embroidered jacket, surprisingly uncrumpled, hair tied back, expression severe.

"We should make haste," Rua said, pulling her woolen socks on. She thanked the Gods that they were dry. "It will be a long slog to the village."

"Yes," Renwick said, belting his sword to his hip.

Rua picked up the Immortal Blade, shoulders tightening under its weight. The magical sword did not save her from the avalanche or from the bitter cold. It was a powerful talisman, but it was not her savior. Still, she was glad she had not lost it buried under the snow.

She laced her boots and wrapped her cloak tightly around her. Rua's mind raced thinking about Renwick's body pressed against hers. The air was charged in a way that made her shift uncomfortably. She couldn't be thinking like this. Not about the Witchslayer.

The moniker still smashed against her senses. She did not understand it. They seemed like two different people—Renwick and the Witchslayer, the fae who dried her clothes and gave her thoughtful gifts versus the monster who tortured witches. She couldn't comprehend the stark contrast of those two beings. It muddied her opinions of him. Her sleepy mind was now scrambling. So many unanswered questions assaulted her as Renwick stomped out the dwindling fire.

She needed the fresh air. Not waiting for him to put on his cloak, she sped toward the cave mouth. She scanned for footprints again, but apart from a few rabbit tracks, there were none. Her brisk pace pushed her legs into a near run.

"Rua, this is a long trek; you'll burn out going that fast," Renwick said from right behind her, easily keeping pace.

She kept moving like she was fleeing him, that shared moment in the cave chasing after her. She rushed as if she could outrun the smiling faces of her nightmare too.

"Your stubbornness will be the death of all of us," Renwick grumbled.

It was the truth. She couldn't handle any of it. All she did was mess things up, her escalating list of mistakes accumulating every day. She clenched her jaw, moving faster, needing to put some space between the next mistake following her.

Renwick moved to her side. "Talk to me."

Her footsteps faltered as she whirled at him. "Why did you pull me behind you in Drunehan?"

Renwick blanched. It was clearly not the question he was expecting, but she had to know. He had protected her, jumping between her and his own soldiers, killing them to keep her safe.

"I . . ." He shook his head, eyes pleading as he looked at her.

"Why?" she pushed, her words cutting sharper than a blade.

Renwick's eyes fell to his feet as he rubbed his forehead. He pressed his eyes shut as if bracing against an unseen pain. When he opened his eyes, they were steeled once more.

"You were the sister of my ally," he said.

Her lips parted. That was all. He was protecting his secret alliance. It would have looked poorly on him to have let her die.

"How chivalrous," she snarled, moving through the dense trees.

"I'm sorry," he called, hustling back to her side. "I don't . . . I don't know how to do this. Everything I say makes you push me away."

Her eyes darted to him again. "And I'm trying to figure out *why* you don't want to be pushed away."

He pulled up short. Even if he was an ally to her court now, she was there as a symbol of High Mountain power. He shouldn't want to welcome her. She had anticipated reluctant respect, if not total indifference, but this . . . this was different, and she needed to know why. But he didn't say anything. He stared at her hard, as if his eyes could explain all the thoughts swirling behind them.

Rua clenched her fists. She was sick of these games that everyone seemed to play. Pointing an accusing finger toward Raevenport, she said, "You're as bad as those bloody blue witches."

She stormed off, leaving Renwick to trail behind her at a greater distance. She hoped he felt ashamed for not responding, wanting him to feel as vexed as she did herself. What was wrong with these people? He said "talk to me" and then he said he didn't know how. Her legs already burned, her breathing ragged as she poured her rage into thundering back toward the village. Each step was a punishment for another foolish mistake. She doubled down on her promise to herself—she would find the Witches' Glass and break the curse on the blue witches. Then she would get as far from the Northern Court and its King as she could think to go.

# CHAPTER FOURTEEN

A mountain of opened gifts sat on Rua's desk. She stared at the stack of blank papers before her, the ink from her quill already bleeding into her fingertips. The morning sun still hadn't lifted the chill from the frosty air. Her head felt squeezed under an invisible vise, her skin still raw from the burning frost. Muscles she didn't know she had ached. Even with a fire burning, she breathed whorls of steam into the cool air. She pulled the fur mantle sitting on her shoulders tighter around her neck.

"Do I really need to write a thank-you note to every single person?" Rua groused.

"Yes," Bri and Talhan said simultaneously from behind her.

Bri sat in the armchair beside her desk, back to the wall, and Talhan stretched out leisurely on the bed. Bri busied herself sharpening her sword while Talhan ate some sort of dried meat from his pocket as if the war camp rations were the only food available to him. Rua stared at the blank paper again. She still had dozens more letters to write.

"They gave me these presents of their own free will." She frowned at her ink-stained fingers.

"And you will thank them of your own free will," Bri said, the sharpening stone screeching down her sword's edge.

Rua cursed the Gods. The Eagles had remained stiflingly close to her since her near-death experience on the ice cliffs. They hovered over her as if another avalanche might sweep through her tent at any moment.

"The life of a royal is not all cake and parties, hey?" Talhan smirked, the right side of his cheek bulging with food.

"We shouldn't be having parties at all," Rua snapped. "That is not why we came here."

"Agreed," Bri said, stretching her neck. "We should be finding that spell book in Yexshire and getting out of the bloody North." The Eagle looked back at Rua. "Now write the damned letters and then we can go train."

Rua sighed, her fingers tightening around the quill. She looked back to the stack of presents: jewelry, clothing, fine furs and silks. The wealth of the North was astounding. But there were simpler gifts too—little notes and hand-drawn pictures. There was a basket of dried herbs and potions from the brown witches in the camp. A platter of spiced muffins was gifted to her by a green witch who worked in the dining tent. The Twin Eagles had already eaten half the platter.

Rua's fingers shook slightly as she looked back at the two words she had written on the page: *"Dear Renwick."*

She had managed to write ten notes already. She had another two dozen to go, but this one she couldn't write. Starting to write the word "I," she paused and scratched it out.

"Can't I just say thank you and sign my name?" Rua griped, crumpling up the letter and chucking it to the floor. What could she possibly say? I'm sorry I nearly killed you? She had already said that.

"No," Talhan tutted. "At least thank them for the specific gift and then one more sentence like you really appreciate it or you're grateful to get to know the Northern Court more or something . . ."

Rua narrowed her eyes at him. "Why don't you write it for me?"

"Not a chance." He grinned. "I've written too many of those over the years. If I were ever a royal, I'd demand no gifts just to spare me."

"How do you learn all of this stuff?" Rua murmured. Is this what they taught the fae—not only how to fight with swords but also how to craft finely worded thank-you notes?

"We grew up in Wynreach along with the other highborn fae of the Eastern Court," Bri said.

"You don't look like an Eastern fae." Rua looked at their light copper skin and reddish-brown hair. Those golden eyes threw her too. They were fairer than the Western and Southern fae and didn't look like the High Mountain fae either. But they were darker than the Eastern and Northerners. Rua couldn't place them at all.

"We aren't Eastern fae by blood," Bri said, as if that were all the answer Rua needed.

"The Courts are melting pots nowadays anyway," Talhan said. "Carys is Northern by blood, but she grew up in the Southern Court and now she resides in the East. It doesn't mean anything."

Rua jutted her jaw to the side. It was the same with the humans and witches. It was impossible to tell their coven just by looking at them. The only real way to tell was when their magic glowed. The color would show what kind of witch they were.

Rua turned back to the parchment and wrote, *"Dear Renwick,"* again. The Eagles could have their secrets. That was fine. She didn't need to be brought into their lives, and they didn't ask her any more about hers. They were her guards and nothing more.

Rua stared at the spine of the *Encyclopedier dun' Yexshire.* She had opened it only once more since her birthday. She had gotten as far as the title page. Renwick had written a note in Ific to her below the title: *"Rua, I thought one day you may want to know more about your family and the High Mountain Court. Happy birthday. Renwick."*

Something about that note made her shut the book and leave it. *"One day."* Why had he said "one day"? Did he think she was not ready to open that book now?

She looked at the gold lettering of the Yexshiri words down the book's spine. A raw ache radiated from the pit of her stomach. There was a word for it in Yexshiri: *aviavere.* It meant nostalgia for something that never was. She missed a world she didn't remember. She couldn't close her eyes and see the castle of Yexshire or hear her mother's voice.

She wasn't fluent in Yexshiri. If Rua met her mother in the afterlife, she wouldn't be able to speak to her in her native tongue. They would be strangers even then. Occasionally, the old red witches would slip into some Yexshiri at the witch camps, but Rua was far from conversational. She could read the words but hadn't heard them spoken in years.

*Aviavere.* She longed for a home that never was. It was a homesickness for somewhere she knew she could never return.

"You think that quill is going to magically write the notes for you?" Talhan jeered from the bed.

"Shut up and stop watching me," Rua growled, eyeing the Immortal Blade leaning against the desk. "Or I will turn that blade on you."

"You can be as grim and threatening as you like, Princess." Talhan smiled, hooking his thumb at Bri. "I grew up with that one, so it just makes you feel like family to me."

"Shut it," Bri snarled.

"You see?" Talhan grinned.

Rua pushed up from her chair, grabbing the Immortal Blade and fixing it to her wide belt.

"I'm taking a break," she announced, picking up the stack of finished notes. "I'll go find a squire to send these and then come finish the rest."

Bri and Talhan were on their feet in the blink of an eye. Bri sheathed her sword as Talhan pulled on his heavy cloak. Rua rolled her eyes at them. They were soldiers through and through.

She adjusted the buckle that held the gray fur mantle over her shoulders. Her wavy brown hair covered her delicate fae ears, keeping them warm as she ventured out into the cold. A fresh layer of snow marked the pathways. The gravel shifted beneath her boots, but she couldn't see it through the layer of snow. She wondered what they did with all this gravel when the ice lakes thawed over summer. Did they let it sink to the bottom of the lake? Or did they clear it off when they moved back to Murreneir to use for the following year?

The logistics of living this far north confused Rua. She liked the ritualistic rhythms of the seasons, though she found winter irksome. The winding down over winter, finding warm clothes and huddling around fires, seemed quaint, but the winter demanded slowness. It forced even the busiest person to pause and take stock of their lives. Rua just wanted to keep her head down and keep moving through her life. She knew if she lifted her head up, she might never take a step forward again.

Two Northern guards pushed past her. They hastened their way toward the center of the camp, toward the King's tent. They were not running, but they moved with an urgency that bade Rua to follow. She tucked the letters into the deep pocket of her jacket and veered off course to follow them. Bri and Talhan were right on her heels. They must have felt that something was amiss as well.

No one stopped Rua as she entered the King's tent. The two guards standing watch barely even looked her way. She supposed her status granted her permanent permission to visit the King.

She moved her way down the corridor inside the main tent and turned into the last archway on the right. Renwick, Aneryn, and Thador stood at the front of a crowd gathered around a table, maps and papers strewn about its surface.

Renwick looked up from where he stood, pointing at the map.

"Good, you're here," he said. "We were just about to send for you."

Another handful of guards stood ringed around the table behind them. No one had bothered taking off their boots, so Rua entered, hand perched on the pommel of the Immortal Blade.

She looked down at the intricate map of the Northern Court. "What's going on?"

"There has been a sighting of Balorn in Vurstyn," Berecraft said from his chair beside the table. He pointed his knobby fingers at a town between the Lyrei Basin and the border of the Western Court.

"How far is it to get there?" Even as she spoke, Rua felt her muscles readying for battle.

"A day's ride," Berecraft replied, tracing a curving line toward the village of Vurstyn.

Thador rolled his shoulders, shifting beside Renwick. He was ready-ing for battle too. "It's a trap."

"Of course it's a trap," Renwick said in a steely tone.

"I can See it," Aneryn murmured, her large eyes clouded over into shining sapphire blue as she stared down at the map. Her gaze seemed to stare straight through the paper. "He thinks the blue witches surrounding him will protect him from our Sight, but there are too many fae in Vurstyn. I can See them."

"Good," Renwick said. "How many of them are loyal to Balorn?"

"Some are truly loyal." Aneryn's fingers twitched as if she were feeling the air. "Those closest to him will fight for his side. But most of the town is afraid. I can taste their fear. They would not fight you if you were to rid the town of him."

"That is a terrible idea," Berecraft countered. "You cannot battle Balorn in the middle of a town. There will be too many casualties."

"Balorn plans to trap you between the high road and the hills into Vurstyn," Aneryn said. "He thinks you will ride your troops through the gully there."

"What else do you See, girl?" a soldier butted in. Rua cut the taciturn fae a sharp glance, and he blanched. Maybe he had heard what happened when Fowler called her *girl*. His eyes widened at the Immortal Blade as he bobbed his head to Rua in apology.

Aneryn smirked. "Balorn has been talking to too many fae. He either doesn't see the carelessness of those actions or he doesn't care that we know his plans." She looked at Renwick. "He knows you will come to save Vurstyn."

"What has he done to the town so far?" Renwick asked tightly.

"He unleashed the *suraash* on the town," Aneryn said in a haunted whisper. "He reined them back in, but at least a dozen are dead. He wanted Vurstyn to know what would happen if they didn't obey him."

Renwick curled his fingers into fists and rested his knuckles on the table as he peered at the map. "It is only a matter of time before the Forgotten Ones spill more blood."

Aneryn dipped her chin in agreement. "A few in my coven wish to come with you."

Renwick's eyes darted to the blue witch's face. He gave a nearly imperceptible shake of his head.

"They know you are not asking them to come. They are offering their magic to you of their own free will. They want to end this too," Aneryn said with a hint of pleading.

Rua was certain this was a conversation they had before.

"The blue witches are our strength in battle," Berecraft agreed.

"Fine," Renwick gritted out. "Only those who volunteer."

Aneryn dipped her head again. "I will go ready them."

Renwick turned behind him to Thador. "I want fifty soldiers ready to ride within the hour," he ordered.

"Only fifty, Your Majesty? Is that wise?" Berecraft cautioned, the lines in his face deepening.

"I will not leave Lyrei Basin unprotected. We leave enough soldiers here to easily fight back any strike against the ice lakes," Renwick said. "Balorn is drawing our gaze to Vurstyn. It would be a perfect time to strike."

"But we have hundreds more who could come," the councilor questioned, his bushy gray eyebrows lifting into his hairline.

"Moving hundreds of soldiers will slow us down. Balorn has a dozen Forgotten Ones with him and some Vurstyn fae on his side . . ." Renwick's emerald gaze looked up to Rua. "But we have her."

Rua's heart pounded. It was time to show Balorn the power of the Immortal Blade.

～

They arrived at the stables, where the crest of the Lyrei Basin met the forest slopes below. Six black-and-gray horses were saddled and waiting for them. Rua stared at the giant beasts. They were twice the size of the ponies they rode in the witch camps. The witches only had three ponies for everyone to share. They were too hard to care for in the depths of the forest to keep any more. Rua was occasionally allowed to ride them around the campsite but nothing else.

"You can't ride, can you?" Aneryn asked, stepping up next to Rua.

Her hair was twisted back into two thick braids. She wore a full chest plate of armor. Metal cuisses covered her thighs to the knee. It was not the full suit of armor that the guards mounting the horses up on the hill wore, but from up on a horse she would be well protected.

"I can ride a horse just fine," Rua grumbled. She wore her thick leathers and a simple half-moon breastplate that Bri had forced her into wearing. She braided her hair back into a singular rope that hung halfway down her back.

"You should ride with me." Renwick's voice cut through the air.

"No," Rua countered before she even turned.

Looking over her shoulder, she nearly stumbled backward at the sight of Renwick. Gone were his fine clothes with delicate embroidery. He was dressed for war. Rua gaped at the black leathers he wore, at the daggers belted to his muscled thighs. Thin layers of silver covered his arms and torso like scales of a fish. He wore a simple chest plate without the etchings of the Northern Court crest that the guards wore. A sword strapped to his left hip and a dagger to his right mirrored Rua's own.

Renwick's lips pulled to the side, the only indication he gave that he knew Rua was staring.

"Gods, look at you!" Talhan exclaimed, looking Renwick up and down.

The Twin Eagles trudged up through the snow. Thick clouds of hot breath circled them like halos.

Bri elbowed her twin. "Cut it, Tal, you're practically drooling."

"Who knew he was hiding all of that under those posh clothes?" Talhan guffawed, gesturing toward the Northern King.

Rua couldn't help the blush creeping up her neck. She turned back to the horses, focusing too hard on their thick black hooves.

"Can you ride?" Bri asked, echoing Aneryn's earlier thoughts.

"Yes," Rua said, eyeing the horses warily.

The Northern steeds had long shaggy manes and hair around their ankles. Their coats seemed thicker, bred to protect against the winter's chill.

Talhan gave her an easy grin. "Maybe you should ride with someone—"

"I do not need anyone's help." Rua's voice was a lethal warning.

"Fine," Bri said. "Let's go. It's a long ride to Vurstyn."

Nodding, Rua approached the mare in front of her, trying to hide her trepidation. She was certain if she could just get on the creature that she would be fine.

She grabbed the horse's saddle and hoisted herself up by her foot in the stirrup. Gods, it was giant. Her heart hammered in her chest, not from the exertion of the mount but from the height she now sat. At least it would be easier to use the blade from the protection of a horse . . . hopefully.

Renwick came up to her mare, stroking his hand down the horse's muzzle. Nostrils flaring, the horse sniffed him and settled. The tension in the horse's body ebbed from beneath her thighs.

"Is this your horse?" she asked, watching the way Renwick seemed to soften as he rubbed a hand across the mare's cheek.

"Technically, they are all my horses," Renwick said. He nodded to the horse beside the one Rua sat atop. It looked much the same as her own, though its mane was slightly darker, and its body was more charcoal gray. "I normally ride Zeffem."

*Zeffem.* It was a Mhenbic word. It meant "strength." Why a fae King would give his horses Mhenbic names, she did not know.

"Does she have a name?" Rua asked, patting a hand against her horse's neck.

"Her name is Raga . . . It's Mhenbic for—"

"I know what it means," Rua cut in, "though I don't know why you'd name a warhorse that."

*Raga.* It meant "precious to me." It was a name witches gave to things special to them, a nickname used for children and special small belongings. It was not the name for a giant Northern horse.

"It's a long story," Renwick muttered, turning to Aneryn and helping her up onto the horse in front of Rua. The little blue witch looked like a child sitting atop such a colossal steed. Renwick moved to Zeffem, and Rua found her eyes snagging on those thighs once more as he hoisted himself into the saddle.

Talhan and Bri navigated their horses up in line with Rua. The Twin Eagles looked easy on their mounts. They wore coordinating bronze-tinted armor that perfectly matched the color of their hair and made their eyes even more golden. Rua saw, peeking out from their thick cloaks, that they wore only a light amount of armor like Renwick, the styling very similar to his own. It must be what the high-class fae wore while ruling the courts of Okrith. Rua kept forgetting that Bri and Talhan had grown up in the Eastern Court, around royals and courtiers. They had known the children of the Kings and Queens of Okrith. They might not have been *friends* with Renwick, but they knew him well enough. It made Rua feel even more like an outsider. They all had decades of relationships between them, and she was a stranger to them all.

Bri's eagle eyes watched the moving convoy of horses on the horizon. Two dozen soldiers moved out toward the southwest. Another two dozen moved northwest. They would circle either side of Vurstyn while Renwick and the others moved straight through the gully. Two blue witches volunteered to accompany each faction. Rua prayed their presence would be enough to obscure their plan from the *suraash's* vision.

"This is a terrible idea," Bri nagged, looking up to the soldiers on the hills. "We shouldn't be using you two as the bait."

"Scared?" Rua smirked at the female Eagle. Bri rolled her eyes.

"Only the reasonable amount." Talhan huffed out a laugh as he pulled his cloak tighter around himself with a shiver. "If I am to die, I'd prefer it to be in a more tropical climate."

"It will be fine," Rua said, though the words felt hollow.

"Says the female with the magical sword that protects her from harm," Thador scoffed, giving his horse a kick and coaxing it forward.

Renwick gave Zeffem a tap with his calf, and then he was moving too. No more talking. They had to get to Vurstyn and intercept Balorn before he realized their plan. Balorn was betting on Renwick not bringing any blue witches with him, and they had to use that advantage while they still had it.

Raga began to move of her own volition, following behind Zeffem. Rua gripped the horse's reins so tightly that Raga shook her head and pulled against them.

"Sorry," Rua whispered to her horse, loosening her grip.

Raga didn't require much directing, following Zeffem like a packhorse. They trotted in a single line through the thin trail that Thador's lead mare was carving through the snow. Rua stared at the midnight-blue hood of the King in front of her. She imagined what it would have been like to ride with him, to feel those muscled thighs framing her own, his hot breath in her hair. Rua cursed herself.

They were about to meet Balorn face-to-face. Riding themselves into the center of an ambush, they were putting themselves in the most vulnerable position for attack to draw Balorn out. It would be too tempting for him to resist. But if the other soldiers didn't arrive at precisely the right time, they would be sitting ducks against a horde of *suraash*. Rua only hoped that in his eagerness to fight them, Balorn would lose focus on the Witches' Glass and she would be able to seize it.

She was meant to be thinking about battle, not about the surprising muscles of the Northern King. She bit down, stifling her frustrated groan. This was going to be a long ride.

# CHAPTER FIFTEEN

The trail dipped down into the hillside. The ride had been a bitter trek through belting frozen winds. Rua was grateful for the heat radiating off Raga. She wished she had taken Renwick up on his offer to ride together, longing for the same warmth she felt in that cave.

The walls of snow piled higher around them as they moved downhill toward the town of Vurstyn. A windmill on the far hillside spun with life as the village popped in and out of sight behind the high walls of snow. The houses were clustered close together, painted in every shade of blue like an ocean against the snowfall, but from what Rua could see the town looked intact. Whatever Balorn had planned, it hadn't ended in the razing of Vurstyn at least.

Cattle lowed in the distance as their horses trudged downward deeper into the ravine.

"Helmets on," Thador called from the front as he lifted the helmet on his lap.

One by one, Aneryn and Renwick put theirs on too as the walls of ice around them grew above their line of sight. All it would take was a couple of archers to stand above them now, and they would be completely trapped. Rua knew that was the point. They were intending to trap themselves to draw Balorn out of town, but Gods, she did not like this feeling.

"I can't see in that thing," she groaned, looking to the dented metal circle in Bri's outstretched hand. The helmet was not made for her. It was too big, the metal falling into her eyes and the sides obscuring her periphery. The narrow trail was suffocating enough. She did not need her face encased in metal as well.

"Put it on," Renwick commanded in that sharp tone, swiveling back toward her, face severe under his silver-crested helmet. The shadows of his nose guard made his green eyes shine through the darkness.

"I won't get hurt anyway," Rua groused. They could fire a dozen arrows down on her and not one would break her skin, not while she possessed the Immortal Blade.

"They might start throwing pine cones," Bri quipped as her twin snorted.

"Ugh, fine," Rua snarled, grabbing the helmet from Bri. They might throw rocks at her for all she knew.

The cold metal bit into her fingertips. The icy frost of the cheek guards made her shudder as she slid the helmet on. It bobbled on the crown of her head, making her feel like a child playing dress-up. Aneryn's helmet fit her fine. How come Rua couldn't get a smaller one?

Her eyes scanned her surroundings more rapidly now that her vision was constrained by the helmet.

"Soon." Aneryn's voice was a quiet warning. "Get ready."

The Eagles unsheathed their weapons. Renwick's hand drifted to the hilt of his dagger. The path was too narrow for swinging large swords.

If she were going to use the Immortal Blade here, she would have to make short, sharp movements. There would be no sweeping of the blade in this tight space.

A shriek rent the air. The *suraash* were coming.

Rua's eyes darted to the top right as a witch leapt into the ravine, colliding with Thador. She impaled herself on his dagger as he threw her to the ground.

Rua's heart punched into her rib cage.

The witch lay bleeding on the ice, writhing with wide eyes. This one wore proper clothes, unlike the ones in thin slips of fabric at the Temple of Hunasht. But the look of a *suraash* was clear, not only from the Mhenbic symbol carved into her forehead but from her matted hair, scars, and wild, cursed eyes. She looked like the rabid dogs who started attacking people for food in the witch camps. One look in those eyes and it was clear that sickness had poisoned their brains.

Rua felt that white-hot buzz of the Immortal Blade now. The magic warped the air, an invisible zephyr spiraling around her. The rest of her companions were stock-still, listening. But Rua's eyes fixed on the dying witch whose eyes were bulging, blindly looking skyward. With a swift stab of the Immortal Blade into the bending air, she pierced the witch's heart, and the *suraash* went limp.

There was no time to take a steadying breath as another two *suraash* clawed down the side walls, skittering across the cold surface like spiders. One scrambled toward Bri, and with a sharp slice of her guard's sword, the *suraash* fell to the ground. There was no defensive maneuvering from the witches. They simply attacked and fell, spurred on by the curse. Implements of chaos, they moved without thought or free will. The only thing they seemed to know was: attack.

The *suraash* in front of her crawled toward Aneryn. "Traitor," it screeched. The voice was like the sound of metal grinding on a blacksmith's wheel.

Aneryn screamed as the *suraash* scratched, trying to pull her out of the saddle. Renwick moved with incredible speed. His dagger flew through the air, striking the Forgotten One in the center of her chest. She tumbled to the ground.

Raga bucked, forcing Rua to grab the horse's crest to keep from falling. As more shrieks echoed above them, the other horses began shifting on their feet, readying to bolt but having nowhere to go.

"Steady," Rua whispered to the spooked horse. She wasn't sure if she said it more to herself or to Raga.

Renwick dismounted Zeffem and moved to the witch he had struck.

171

He yanked his dagger free and sliced across the witch's neck. Her eyes rolled to the back of her head, the blood dyeing the snow scarlet. The path filled with bodies scattered down the tight ravine.

Renwick looked up at Aneryn, breath steaming along with the swift rise and fall of his chest. "You okay?"

Rua watched as Aneryn's helmet nodded. Renwick dipped his chin, patting her horse's flank before walking back to his horse.

Where were the other soldiers from Lyrei Basin? Were they drawing the rest of the *suraash* away? Where was Balorn? Rua needed to get above the high snow walls to find a better vantage point. She needed to know what was going on.

But before she could speak, three more *suraash* appeared at the lip of the ravine, and this time, they were not alone.

Two fae archers stood with them.

Shit.

The *suraash* leapt, each targeting a different rider. Rua was able to shove hers to the ground, the witch not jumping far enough to gain purchase on the saddle. Raga bucked again, one hoof landing back down on the witch's side as she shrieked. There was no space. The witches were getting trampled.

An arrow flew across her vision, landing just wide of Renwick, stuck into the leather of his saddle. She felt the punch to her bicep as an arrow embedded in her leathers. But just as in the Temple of Hunasht, it didn't pierce her skin.

Rua focused on the archers as the other warriors dealt with the Forgotten Ones. Twisting the blade, one archer dropped his bow as he clenched his chest and fell backward into the snow. Rua tried to move to the next one, but an arrow whizzed past her, this one nicking Raga's flank. The horse screamed, stomping violently.

Rua's rage grew hotter than the hilt of the Immortal Blade under her palm.

Enough of this.

She grabbed her helmet off her head and hurled it up at the other archer. It did not hit him but pulled his focus as Rua made a brutal slash from one wall of the ravine to the other and his head tumbled from his body.

Fresh air filled Rua's lungs. Now that she was free of that stuffy helmet, she could get her bearings more clearly. More *suraash* came pouring down the icy walls. They were like a never-ending horde of insects, scrabbling at them. Thador frantically hacked and kicked to keep them off him. Another witch jumped, colliding into the giant guard as he tumbled out of his saddle to the ground. He rolled quickly to avoid his horse's hooves as Rua focused the force of her blade on the witches at the front, slicing through them in quick succession. If more came, they would soon be buried under the pile of bodies.

They needed to get to higher ground. She wanted to see how many more were coming and cut them down before they were right on top of them.

Rua shakily moved her feet out of the stirrups.

"Steady," she whispered to Raga again. She crouched up on her horse's saddle.

"Rua!" Bri shouted as the warrior booted another witch in the face. Blood sprayed across the snow. "Don't."

Renwick spun to see what was happening, but it was too late. Rua was already jumping. She leapt to the lip of the ravine and pulled herself on top of the slick surface.

"Rua!" Renwick's voice boomed from behind her.

She rolled into the thin layer of powdery snow and sprang to her feet. Past the short stretch of open snow lay a thicket of dense woods, the town of Vurstyn beyond. But it was who was standing in the clearing that made Rua gasp.

She knew him straightaway. He looked so much like Hennen but leaner, younger, and surprisingly handsome.

Balorn Vostemur.

His hair was more auburn than Hennen's flaming red. He had sharp cheekbones, a short, trimmed beard, and forest-green eyes, perfect for the snake embroidered across his black jacket. He wore no armor.

Behind him stood a dozen fae soldiers dressed in full suits of armor, emblazoned with the Northern crest. They looked like the same guards that marched her to her death in Drunehan. Some of the palace guards were still loyal to Balorn, it seemed. She did not spy their own retinue of soldiers from Lyrei Basin sweeping in from the South yet, but they wore the same armor. When they arrived, it would be chaos trying to figure out who was on which side.

It was the three guards standing next to Balorn, or rather who stood in front of each of them, that made Rua freeze.

Three human children, one in front of each guard, stood shaking and wide-eyed in the snow. The littlest one couldn't have been more than six. Rua gaped at them and then back to Balorn. He would use children as a shield?

"It's a pleasure to finally meet you, Ruadora." Balorn spoke with a charming warmth that felt so at odds with the shrieking screams of dying witches around them.

She had expected a gruff, drunk male like Hennen, but Balorn was none of those things. Fae lifespans were longer but not in a linear way, they grew and faded as rapidly as the witches and humans but the middle of their lives stretched out, doubling, sometimes even tripling, that of the witches and humans depending on how well they took care of themselves. Clearly Balorn took better care of his health than his elder brother—his handsomeness a mockery of the cruelty that lay below the surface.

He flashed a charming grin from his full pink lips. "I'd like you to lay down your sword, please."

Rua's brow dropped heavy over her eyes as she glowered at him. He spoke to her as if they were enjoying tea together.

"Put down the Immortal Blade," Balorn insisted, cocking his head at her.

Dumbfounded at his request, Rua panted thick steam into the cold air.

"All right." Balorn shrugged, signaling to the guards beside him.

"No!" Rua screamed as one guard lifted his dagger to the first child's neck. She remembered how quickly the guards started killing the red witches in Drunehan. She couldn't risk a split second of hesitation. It would cost a child their life.

Balorn lifted a hand, and the guard halted. Bile rose in Rua's throat as she threw the Immortal Blade into the snow. Its absence felt like a cold trickle of ice down her spine.

"Good, now we can talk." Balorn smiled at her, flashing his perfect white teeth.

"You would kill children just to speak with me?" Rua shouted.

Balorn's grin widened. "Yes, and you would too if it gave you a chance to speak to the wielder of the Immortal Blade."

"Where is the Witches' Glass, Balorn?" she seethed, shouting over the wind.

"So you know my name?" He smirked, eyes twinkling. "Good."

Strands of freed hair swept across her forehead as Rua spat at him.

"Oh my." Balorn chuckled, delighting in the insult. "You are better than I even imagined." His forest-green eyes scanned her curves hungrily. "I don't want to kill you, Ruadora. I want you." His voice was a deep purr that made Rua's gut clench. No one had ever wanted her before. "Your power is incredible. You would be the mightiest force in Okrith if you were at my side. I am offering this chance. Come with me. I can show you so many pleasures you have never known."

"Never," Rua snarled even as her cheeks heated at Balorn's devilish grin. She knew what *pleasures* he offered. Revulsion and excitement warred between her, making her grind her teeth.

"You think you are so different from me?" Balorn raised an eyebrow. "You are just as power-hungry as I. I know what you did at the blue witch fortress. Tell me. How good did it feel to sing that death song?"

Rua gaped as Balorn's lips pulled up knowingly.

"I would never try to stop you from being what you are," Balorn vowed. The honesty in his stare made Rua's brows knit together. "With me, you wouldn't have to hold that power all alone."

His words cut into her, calling to the dark pit in her gut. She wanted to protest . . . but she couldn't. Somehow she knew the words would ring hollow. She felt shackled by the responsibility to her court, the blue witches, and her newfound family. They didn't want her. They wanted something *from* her, and she knew she would fail them.

"Rua," Renwick's voice panted behind her as he clambered up the side of the ravine. Blood splattered his face and clothes. The sounds of screaming from behind them were quiet now. Had all the *suraash* been killed?

Renwick pulled up short when he saw the three human children being held captive. "Balorn," he growled.

"My little Witchslayer." Balorn smiled at his nephew, but his snake eyes were cold and lethal. "What a pathetic thing you have become."

"Let those children go. Now." Renwick promised violence as his grip tightened around his dagger. Muscles coiled, he was ready to spring into action.

Snickering, Balorn gestured to the first human boy, the smallest. He had blond hair and rosy cheeks, trembling as the guard gripped him by the shoulder.

"Does he remind you of someone?" Balorn's teeth glinted against the beams of sunlight breaking through the heavy clouds.

"Do *not* speak of him," Renwick hissed.

"You are as weak as Eadwin was . . . ," Balorn began when a witch burst through the line of trees.

She wore a sapphire cloak, her eyes and hands glowing a matching blue. She dashed up to Balorn, whispering in his ear. His jaw tightened, the only sign he gave of displeasure as his eyes darted back to Renwick.

"You still have some cunning in you, Witchslayer." Balorn grimaced. He turned back to Rua, that charismatic smirk returning. He spoke in a soft lover's voice as he said, "Think on my offer, Princess. I can give you all of Okrith. I can give you the world."

Renwick stiffened at Rua's side.

Balorn turned to the three guards. "Wait until we reach the tree line . . . then release the children. If anyone moves, kill them." He eyed Rua, giving her a brief bow. "Goodbye for now, Your Highness."

His blue witch rushed after him as they made for the thicket, the fae soldiers parting for them to pass. His warriors followed, hastening into the forest. As the last soldier disappeared into the line of trees, the three guards holding the children released them. The children fled, running downhill through the snow.

As soon as the smallest one was out of their grasp, Rua dove for the

Immortal Blade, somersaulting over the powdery snow. The second her hand gripped the hilt she slashed it through the air. One by one, the three remaining soldiers fell to the ground. Their armor wouldn't protect them from the wrath of her magical sword. Pools of crimson blood dyed the ice beneath them.

Rua bolted toward the woods in front of her. She threw out her senses, trying to feel for the other guards though she couldn't see them. Balorn's smug face burned into her mind. The urge to slice into that arrogant smile rose in her like a cresting wave.

With lightning speed, Renwick appeared in front of her. Rua threw out her arms, almost crashing into him as those emerald eyes ensnared her with a magic all their own.

"Not everyone has to die today, Rua," he whispered. "Their time will come."

His words threw ice on the fire building in her. Rua took a steadying breath and sheathed her blade. The horror of what had just happened, of Balorn's smiles and smooth words, bled into her worse than any wound. Her pulse ratcheted as she thought about his offer.

She needed to get out of this place.

# CHAPTER SIXTEEN

Each minute of the ride back, Rua's throat had constricted further as Balorn's face flashed through her mind. Those gilded promises. He hadn't lied. Rua could be as powerful as she wished. All she needed to do was let go. Her heart hammered so loud, it pulsed up to the tips of her pointed ears.

Aneryn was wounded in the attack and so they had not delayed. They would have camped in Vurstyn but they needed to return to Lyrei Basin and its brown witch healers. Rua had watched Aneryn's pinched face as she rode with Thador, cradling her wounded shoulder. The horse's jostling gait made Aneryn grimace, but she did not cry out. Thador whispered hushed words to her the entire ride. The pain must have been excruciating.

They didn't converse on the ride back, leaving Balorn's words to haunt her every heartbeat. The intensifying dread gripped her to the point of near suffocation. She needed to get as far away from this place and these people as possible. She had to get out of the Northern Court.

Rua shoved the flaps of her tent open, trudging snow across the sumptuous rug.

Bri lingered behind her. "Are you okay?"

"Go away, Bri," Rua snapped, fishing for her empty satchel at the bottom of the oak wardrobe.

"Where are you going?" her guard asked from the threshold of her tent.

"Anywhere else," Rua said, grabbing a handful of woolen stockings and shoving them to the bottom of her bag. She didn't need much; just a change of clothes would do.

"Rua—"

"Get out," Rua commanded without looking back at Bri. "Now."

Bri let out a sigh and left.

The tent was dark and cold but she didn't light a fire. She would be gone before it warmed her room anyway. Pulling garments off hangers, she unceremoniously bundled them into a wad of fabric and shoved them into her satchel. She'd leave the trunk and the glamorous garments behind. She just needed a spare pair of leathers.

Though not a speck had touched her skin, the coppery tang of blood assaulted her senses. Her sword shone in pristine condition at her side, but the mark of death was upon it. She had killed those *suraash* and those fae guards. How many more marks were there against her soul now?

And Balorn was the worst of all. He looked at her like she was a goddess, like every killing blow was a thing of beauty and not of evil. The allure of his words made her shudder. It would be so easy to unleash herself on the world. She felt if one more string were cut loose to her grip on her power, she would drift away into the chaos of her own mind. Shame clawed in her gut. It would feel so good to free herself of that searing pain, to not hurt anymore. She was so close to agreeing with him.

She needed to get away. From Balorn. From all of them.

The tent flap rustled behind her again.

"I told you to leave me—"

She twisted toward Bri, but it wasn't Bri standing there.

Renwick's presence seemed to take up the whole room. He still wore his armored leathers, his face still splattered with blood. His countenance was completely still, other than the heavy rise and fall of his chest as though he had been running.

Rua couldn't bear to meet that razor-sharp look in his eyes as she said, "I suppose Bri fetched you . . ."

"What did Balorn say to you?" Renwick asked in a deep, slow timbre.

"Nothing I didn't already know," Rua said. The thought of Balorn's knowing smile felt like beetles crawling across her skin. She wanted to scratch her eyes out to rid herself of that image.

"You're leaving," Renwick muttered, his voice a barely controlled calm.

"I don't need any of this," Rua hissed. "I don't need anyone."

She moved to grab another cloak from the wardrobe. Renwick was there in the blink of an eye, his hand resting on her elbow, halting her movement.

"You know what really broke Balorn?" Those green eyes pierced into her. "He didn't need anyone. Not even my father could reach him." He took a ragged breath. "Needing people doesn't make you weak, Rua, it keeps you sane."

Rua shook her head at him as she pulled her arm from his grasp. "I . . ."

"I need you," Renwick whispered, "to keep me from being a monster." His eyes dropped to the Immortal Blade at her hip. "And I'll keep you from becoming one too."

Rua's eyes flared. She didn't know how or why, but Renwick always stopped her. His voice pulled her back, though one day it might not. She felt herself slipping further with every kill.

"If I start to fade," Rua murmured down to her feet. "If I start to lose myself in that power . . ."

"I'll hold on to you," Renwick vowed, moving his fingers to her chin. Rough with gore, they did not seem elegant anymore. He was not a King in that moment, he was a warrior. Not hiding behind his refined clothing, he finally felt real, and his promises to her felt real too.

She lifted her eyes to meet his. Something raw and pleading was there in them.

"Stay."

Rua held his stare as she revealed the horror in her own. "I could kill all of you . . ."

She could do it—kill them all with her sword. Razing the entire Northern Court for vengeance. No one could stop her. The thought alone stole the breath from her lungs. She wished it felt impossible to imagine herself doing it, but it felt only one step away. And standing in between her and that last step was Renwick.

He dropped his fingers from her chin. "You won't. I know that bloodlust, and I don't see it in you."

"You don't know me, Witchslayer," Rua sneered, knowing it would hurt him. His body froze for a moment, his telltale sign, but he shook it off quickly. He had been called that for long enough now that it didn't seem to hit him so hard.

"I do," Renwick said, "and believe me when I tell you, you can make the whole world bleed and it will never make you feel safe."

"And what will make me feel safe?" Rua snarled, moving to push past him.

He grabbed the crook of her arm, his face mere inches from hers. "Me."

The world stopped moving at that word. She couldn't hear the whipping wind or far-off voices or the sound of horses; she only heard the pounding of her heart and the echo of his voice. *Me.*

She shoved him against the wardrobe, his eyes flaring as her lips crashed against his. She pinned her soft chest against his hard body, enveloping him in a scalding kiss. Renwick's hands froze for a moment before circling around her and pulling her tighter to him, his lips meeting hers with equal frenzy.

*Me.* It was true. He stopped her again that day. Simply stepping in front of her had pulled her back to the world. He kept her anchored. This time she had more control of it, yes, but he had also sensed that she needed his intervention. He stopped the spiral before it began.

Renwick's tongue brushed the seam of her lips, and she moaned as his tongue slid into her mouth. She threaded her hands into his hair, pressing against him as if she could fuse their bodies.

"Rua," he murmured onto her lips, the sound of her name breaking the spell.

Her stomach dropped as she lurched away from him. He panted as he stared at her, wide-eyed.

What had she done?

Her lungs squeezed to the point of pain as she gritted out the word, "Leave."

Renwick's chest still heaved, lips parted as his gaze dropped to the floor. He swallowed, pushing off the wardrobe and past her out the doorway.

She dragged a rough hand down her face, releasing a string of curses as she grabbed her satchel and threw it against her tent's wall. The fabric bowed to the weight, the whole room swaying in response.

With a long, ragged breath, the icy air filled her lungs. She glanced at her desk, and to the book of her home court, her family. Balling her hands into fists, she swallowed back the tears pricking her eyes. Her fingers were so cold they felt numb. If she had a fire going, she'd throw that bloody book into it. All it did was remind her of everything she could never be.

She thought to what Renwick had said, and a new layer of ice chilled her. Of all the foolish things she had done, this was the most reckless—more than jumping in front of arrows or falling off ice cliffs. Kissing the Northern King was the most dangerous gamble of all.

～

Rua walked beside the head healer down the long aisle. Sick beds lined the brown witch tent, partitioned by white curtains. The brown witch's hood was pulled so low over her face that her eyes were shadowed in darkness.

Bri and Talhan waited outside the main entrance. The Twin Eagles were more subdued today. Rua had not apologized for kicking Bri out of her tent the night before, and she didn't like the strangeness between them now.

A large metal bowl sat in the center of the room. Echinacea and *chaewood* burned inside it, the smoke cleansing the air. The beds were empty, apart from the last one where Aneryn lay.

Rua had forgotten about the blue witch in her own panic. Bri woke her up the following morning and mentioned Aneryn was healing in the apothecary tent. Rua had been so consumed by her own panic that she hadn't bothered to check on her.

Aneryn had saved her that night before her birthday. Rua would have probably died in the snow out of sheer stubbornness if the blue witch hadn't found her. Shame filled her as they reached the bed at the far end of the long rectangular tent.

Aneryn's head shot up. She sat propped up against her pillows, grinning. "I knew you would come."

Rua rolled her eyes. *Blue witches and their bloody Sight.* "Of course you did."

She perched on the edge of Aneryn's bed. The brown witch healer gave them a succinct nod and carried on.

"Are you okay?" Aneryn asked.

"Shouldn't I be asking you that?" Rua examined the bandage around Aneryn's shoulder. A small spot of dried blood seeped through the fabric. The bitter scent of healing poultices lingered in the air.

"I have never been shot with an arrow before," Aneryn said, feigning a weak smile. "It went straight through me. I didn't think they did that. It will make a good story at least."

Rua chuckled. Even though the blue witch's face was pallid and heavy bags sat under her eyes, her spirit was in perfect condition.

"I'm sorry," Rua confessed.

Aneryn cocked her head. "Why are you sorry?"

Searching for an answer, Rua settled her hand on the Immortal Blade. Aneryn's eyes tracked the movement.

"That blade was forged with witch's magic," Aneryn said. "The red witches of old made it as a gift to the High Mountain fae. It is linked to your blood, but it was made by my kind." The blue witch seemed so much older than her, and yet, she was a year younger.

Rua arched her eyebrow. "What is your point?"

"You use it like its fae magic, like if you push it harder it will work better," Aneryn observed, as if it were obvious. "But like all witch magic, that blade responds to heightened emotions. The reason you fear it is because you use it in panic and anger. Those are rapid emotions. They burn bright but fast. You need to find more enduring ones to wield that blade properly."

Baffled, Rua blinked at her. She hadn't considered that before. It was easier to use her red magic when she was happy and erratic than to cast when she was angry. It made sense that the blade would be the same.

"Which emotions?" Rua asked.

"Like love, joy, courage." Aneryn gave her a half-smile.

"Then the blade is useless to me." Rua laughed bitterly. Those were not emotions she knew how to use.

"Hmm." Aneryn pursed her lips. "You don't really believe that."

"You have Seen into the future," Rua griped. "Why don't you just tell me what to do and I'll do it?"

"I could tell you all of your Fate, *Princess*." Aneryn chuckled. "But it wouldn't make the path you walk any easier. There are still many things you must choose for yourself. Otherwise, the future would turn into something else."

"Do you tell Renwick his future?"

"No," Aneryn said, wincing as she leaned against the headboard, her pillow having slipped down to her back.

Rua snatched another pillow off the empty bed beside them and propped it behind Aneryn's head. "We shouldn't be talking about this. You should be resting."

"You two are not so different, you know," Aneryn said with a heavy breath. "He has done terrible things, but he has suffered them too. You wear as much armor as each other."

"I don't wear any armor." Rua frowned. "I don't need it."

"I've felt that darkness as clear as any Sight. I know you fear us Seeing it." Aneryn reached a shaky hand toward the glass of water on her bedside table. Rua grabbed it and passed it to her before the witch could move any further. "I know what that darkness whispers, and how the lies begin to sound like truth. We wear those lies like armor, thinking they will protect us. Do not expect Renwick to take off his armor without proving you will not cut him down for it."

Rua's cheeks burned. "I do not care—"

Tittering laughter came from the far end of the tent, silencing her. Rua looked up to see four young witches hovering by the doorway. As soon as her eyes landed on the gaggle of witches, they scattered.

"They are excited to see you," Aneryn said, passing her water back to Rua.

"I have not earned that admiration." Rua thought to the stacks of bodies in the snow of Vurstyn.

Wincing, Aneryn closed her eyes and took a breath, clearly trying to focus past her discomfort. "You wield the sword made by our kind. You will use it to save our kind."

"I've used it to *kill* your kind," Rua countered.

"What you did to the *suraash* was a blessing, not a curse," Aneryn murmured, opening her eyes again.

Rua thought to the Mhenbic etched around the scabbard of the Immortal Blade: *Each strike a blessing or curse.* Rua shook her head, but Aneryn continued, placing a gentle hand on her forearm.

"The blue magic can be a curse to those who can't control it too. Balorn pushed the *suraash* too far and their magic destroyed them. His curse keeps them going, rabid and wild. They are trapped in those visions. They are trapped in pain." Aneryn's voice wobbled. "If it were me, I would want you to kill me."

Rua gripped the edge of the bed so tightly she was sure her fingers would turn white. It was all too much.

"Tell me my future," she pleaded. "Tell me how I'm supposed to fix this."

"If I tell you your future, it will change," Aneryn said softly, folding her hands in her lap. "And I wouldn't dare risk what I have Seen."

Rua bit the corner of her lip. "You cryptic witches are going to be the death of me."

"You love us." Aneryn smirked.

Rua glared at the blue witch but didn't push her any harder. She was healing from her wounds. A question begged to be asked at the tip of her tongue, but she refused to ask it. She wouldn't be another fae begging a blue witch for her prophecies. Besides, somewhere deep in her gut, she already knew the answer.

# CHAPTER SEVENTEEN

Rua whirled toward the sound of the scream, knowing it was Raffiel before her eyes landed on him. He stood stunned, gaping down at his belly. A sword impaled straight through him. Behind him, the sword twisted. His killer looked up at Rua with dark green eyes, a smile twisting his face upward.

Balorn.

"Hello, Princess," he purred.

Rua shuddered, but her feet kept walking toward him. She felt her lips pulling up into a smile. Inside her mind, she screamed at her treacherous body.

She watched as Balorn tugged his bloody sword free. Raffiel collapsed to the ground as Balorn gazed at Rua, reaching his hand out to her.

*Gods, no*, she screamed at herself, but she had no voice. She stretched out and took Balorn's smooth hand. He pulled her tight against him as her hands roved his hard, muscular physique. He eyed her up and down with a wicked, adoring smile.

Rua's heart pounded in her throat as he lowered those soft lips to hers. He claimed her mouth, pulling her in like he was trying to swallow her soul. She moaned against him, threading her fingers through his auburn hair, pulling his head closer. She wanted him just as badly, her core pulsing with desire. He dropped the bloody sword to the ground, his free hand pulling her hips tighter to his. They kissed as they stood in the pool of her brother's blood.

Rua bolted upright.

Her breathing came in ragged gasps. Bile burned its way up her throat as the darkness of the tent devoured her. Her stomach wrenched as her mouth filled with saliva and she spasmed, trying to keep from vomiting onto her sheets. She needed to get out of this room and get her feet in the snow. The ice below the carpet wouldn't be enough. She needed the fresh night air. Snatching the fur blanket off her chair, she plunged out into the cold.

Rua swallowed large gulps of icy air while her pulse still pounded in her throat. The harder she pushed away the haunted thoughts of her dream, the more they assaulted her. She didn't want Balorn, she told herself over and over. It was a nightmare, she swore, and yet, she was equally terrified and aroused. Groaning, she tried to pull herself free of the horrifying vision. Her brain spun so rapidly she thought she might topple over.

Stomach roiling again, she moved barefoot through the alleyways of the campsite. Her mind was so full of whirring thoughts she didn't acknowledge the few humans and fae still moving about camp. The moon was high in the sky. The following day would be the Harvest Moon. The witches believed that it was a day for communing with their ancestors and loved ones who had passed into the afterlife.

Rua made a note to herself to not go anywhere near a candle tomorrow. Gods, did her family know what she had become? How many ways had she failed them? She couldn't imagine speaking to Raffiel.

Her hands trembled as she plodded across the gravel. The bellyfuls of air didn't slow her racing heart. She debated for a second moving toward Renwick's tent. She knew he could calm her down. But her feet steered toward the outer reaches of the camp instead. She couldn't bear to look him in the eyes. She had just dreamed of kissing his uncle. She still felt that hot yearning in her core. It made her eyes well with tears. She couldn't let him see how broken she was.

She hoped the spirits of her ancestors wouldn't find her. They would curse her name if they knew. They were a reminder that she was undeserving of the life she had been given.

She heard voices on the screaming wind calling her name. They were the screams of every soul her sword had slain. She rushed to the edge of the camp, finding her way this time onto the snowy banks near where she and Bri had trained days before. She trekked through the snow, deep enough to circle her calves. The cold burned into her flesh. Good. Let it all burn away.

She turned toward the tree line and kept trudging through the snow. Her skin would be raw in the morning, but her fae healing would make it go away fast enough. Even if it didn't, she didn't care. She didn't care if her toes fell off, not when her soul was exploding out of her chest. She fled into the trees.

She stood there, gasping up at the nearly full moon. Her heartbeat dipped for a brief second and then ratcheted up again as the image of Balorn's lips flashed into her mind. The tightness in her chest wouldn't release. She felt it rising in her like a fiery wave. She wanted to scream into the night and ram her fist through her own chest just to take away that tight knot of panic. Anything. Anything to make it go away.

She would keep walking all night if she had to. She would keep circling the ice lake until she found a moment's peace.

~

Rua stared hatefully up at the swollen blue moon. Fuck the moon and the Mother Goddess who created it.

At least there were no witches to drag her out in the middle of the night to pray to it anymore. She had never kept a totem bag. Why pretend to be like them when they reminded her at every moment that she was not?

She stumbled through the snow, having only enough sense to wrap her fur stole around her shoulders to keep her thin nightdress company. Even with the shadows of the forest, the moon on the snow made it bright enough to see. When she was far enough into the woods, she released a final shuddering breath.

*Breathe, breathe,* she willed herself.

The echoes of screams and metallic smell of blood finally ebbed from her system as the cool air pulled her back toward the earth. The sound of footsteps trudging through the snow made her spin.

Renwick swayed to a halt when he saw her. "What are you doing here?"

Something sounded odd about his voice. He was probably drunk.

"I couldn't sleep," she snapped at him. "What are you doing out here?"

"Nothing," he said. Gone was his normal rigid posture, his limbs loose as he shifted on his feet.

Rua walked over to him, and he retreated a step. "Very convincing."

"Go back to your tent, Rua," he warned as she stepped close enough to get a good look at him in the moonlight.

He did not look like the pristine King she knew. His hair was disheveled, his tunic unbuttoned at the neck. But it was his eyes that made Rua stifle a gasp. His pupils were so dilated only the faintest rim of green hugged the edges. She got a whiff of his scent, not the usual evergreen and cloves. He stunk of hellebore and bloodbane. It was the potent pain elixir she had found hiding behind his books.

"You're hurt?" Rua murmured, more to herself.

"I am fine." He retreated another step, as if he stood far enough away she would not be able to smell the poison. "Go back to your tent."

"You do not give orders to me," she hissed.

"I am the King of these lands, and you would do well to obey me." His voice dropped an octave, but his words were hollow.

"*I* am the only reason you are permitted to be the King of these lands, and you will not forget it." Rua threw his words back at him.

Renwick took a step closer to her, his black eyes gleaming in the moonlight as he sneered. "Oh yes, I forgot. You are the savior of the North, *Mhenissa.*"

"Do not condescend to me," she growled.

"Or what? You will cut me down with your magical sword?" Renwick smirked, his eyes trailing down her body, noting no blade hung there, but his eyes snagged on her bare feet in the snow. "Gods, you are even more reckless than me."

Another flash of her nightmare bolted through her like lightning. She winced against the memory. Renwick's brow furrowed. She couldn't tell him, refused to tell him how muddled up her mind was, how deep in that black tar she had descended.

Rua didn't think as her hand lashed out and grabbed the back of Renwick's neck. She lifted on her toes and planted a hateful kiss on his lips. She lowered back down to her feet as Renwick's blackened eyes bored into her, his body frozen. She was about to lower her hand when he reached out, grabbing both sides of her face and pulling her lips back to his.

His mouth slid over hers in a crazed rhythm. Her fingers gripped the back of his neck, holding him as tightly as he held her. Their mouths battled against each other. Renwick pushed her hard against a pine tree, caging her in with his arms. Rua let out a snarl as she pulled his hips against hers so that she could feel all the places where they met.

Renwick's fingers slid up her bare thigh and under her nightgown. He hissed as his fingers trailed over her bare backside.

Mindlessly, Rua's fingers drifted down and began unbuckling his belt. She didn't want to think anymore.

"I want you," she growled against his mouth as she freed him. She gripped his satin, hard length, positioning him between her legs. "Do you want me?"

"Yes," he gritted out as she moved him to her entrance.

"Then have me," she demanded, pulling his lips back to hers.

Her vicious command unleashed him, and he slammed into her in one hard thrust. She tried to hide her cry of pain, but she couldn't, not as she felt her sensitive flesh throb from his huge size.

Every muscle in Renwick froze at the sound. He broke their kiss. His pupils had narrowed, and she saw that emerald green once more, like the sound of her pain brought him back into his body.

"Are you okay?" A look of horror filled his face as it all at once dawned on him. "Gods, please—please tell me this is not your first time."

She tried to keep that shield of armor even as he was motionless, buried inside of her. "Maybe."

"Gods damn it, Rua, why didn't you tell me?" he shouted, eyes darting back and forth between her own. "Are you hurt?"

"I'm fine." She lied, her breath steaming out of her as the pain between her legs grew.

"Rua."

"Don't stop." She tried to move herself along him, even as it made her insides sting. She didn't care if she couldn't walk tomorrow, not as those visions of her dead brother haunted her eyelids again. She didn't care if it broke her. She was already broken; she was just making herself feel it.

"Rua," Renwick whispered again, stilling her.

The scent of it hit them both then: blood. Renwick's nostrils flared as he pulled out of her and looked down at the evidence of what they had done.

"Fucking Gods," he panted as he buttoned his trousers.

"I am fine." Rua gritted her teeth at the look of torture on his face. "Everyone says it hurts the first time . . ."

"It doesn't have to!" he shouted.

She pushed off the tree trunk and balled her fists at her sides, using every ounce of restraint not to throttle him. "Stop making this a big deal."

"It *is* a big deal." He bared his teeth as he yelled at her.

"No, it's not!" she screamed back. She didn't care if she woke the whole camp. "I wanted this. You wanted this. There doesn't need to be a bigger reason."

She turned and began to stomp through the forest.

"Rua, wait, please." Renwick tried to grab the crook of her arm, but she snatched it away from him.

"Don't follow me," she snarled. And he didn't.

∾

When she broke through the flaps of her tent, the tears began to fall. She waited, like always, until she was alone so no one would see her weakness. She crumpled at the foot of her bed, head falling into her hands as she sat on the cold rug.

Heaving sobs racked through her as she cursed herself for what she had done.

She wasn't sure if it was hate or lust or desperation or exhaustion. Something about her just wanted him. She thought it would get the horrible images out of her head.

Such a stupid, foolish thought.

Every choice she made seemed even more damning than the last. She would never be able to look him in the eyes again. Maybe that was a good thing.

Gods, she was so embarrassed. The pain between her legs ached as the salt from her tears stung her chapped lips. She had done it all wrong. There was nothing gentle or pleasurable about that experience. She had demanded it, and all it did was get herself injured.

As she thought of the horrified look on Renwick's face, the tears fell heavier. She heard the tent flap opening and looked up through bleary eyes to see Bri standing there. The fae warrior didn't look at Rua, just walked over and sat down beside her. Rua dropped her face back in her hands as Bri sat with her.

Her guard didn't say anything for a long time, just sat there listening to the sounds of her crying. But Rua was glad for it, glad she wasn't alone. She had never cried in front of anyone else. Only once before when she thought her head was about to be chopped off. The red witches didn't allow it—it was a sign of a weak mind, of a lack of determination to choose better feelings, so Rua had hidden in her room when she couldn't stop the tears from falling. Having Bri with her—so unworried about her tears—it felt good.

After a long stretch of time, Rua's tears abated. Bri reached into her pocket and passed Rua a glass vial. Pulling out the stopper, she smelled the mixture of arnica, chamomile, and witch root. It was a healing remedy. Unlike the toxic one Rua smelled on Renwick, this was mild, but it would expedite her healing.

Nibbling her lip, she wondered if Bri had followed her into the woods. She didn't care. For some reason, she wasn't as embarrassed in front of the Eagle.

"I really fucked up my first time," Rua sniffed, drinking the bitter tonic.

Bri snorted, and Rua scowled at the warrior.

"I'm sorry." Bri grinned. "It's just that there is no one first time. You will have lots more first times. Let that be the first and only of your shitty experiences barefoot in the snow."

Rua let out a rough laugh. She never wanted to replicate that experience. That was true.

"I'm not sure there will be a next time." Rua chucked the empty vial across the room. "I'm not interested in anyone . . . not after that." Rua shifted backward, taking the weight off from between her legs. She couldn't find a way to move that didn't feel sore.

"That was not sex, Rua," Bri said, golden eyes flitting to the wall of the tent. "That was anger."

So Bri had followed her into the night. The warrior had listened from the woods as she had bungled up her first ever interaction with a partner.

Rua rubbed her hands over her face, shaking her head. "I'm so embarrassed."

"Well, welcome to the legion of fae who had embarrassing starts." Bri gave her a mocking clap on her shoulder, and Rua rolled her eyes. "Next time you will wait until the outcome seems more exciting than embarrassing."

No one had ever spoken to her like this. She had known about sex. She had learned what it was about. But she never had anyone to talk to—no one to give her advice.

It felt a lot like having a big sister at that moment. It's what she had hoped she might have had with Remy, if they had grown up together.

"You should light a fae fire. Talk to Remy," Bri said, as if sensing her thoughts.

"She is a Queen now and far too busy to burden herself with these things." Rua clenched her jaw.

"You know that's not true," Bri said.

Rua did. Her sister was more than eager to support her. "I don't want her to know. I don't want her to think of me that way . . . like I'm a failure."

"You are not a failure, Ru," Bri said. "You just made a mistake."

"All I do is make mistakes."

"Remy knows what it's like to have her choices held against her. She would understand."

"I don't want her to know," Rua repeated, looking up from her wet eyelashes to meet Bri's golden stare. "I don't want you to tell her either."

Bri pressed her lips together but bowed her head. "It's not my story to tell."

"Thank you," Rua muttered.

"No problem."

Rua swallowed the hard knot in her throat. "How am I going to face him tomorrow?"

"You face him exactly as who you are: a royal warrior from the most powerful court with the most fearsome talisman in all the realm." Bri smirked. "You face him like if he says one wrong word you will slice his throat."

"You know, that's terrible advice." Rua laughed.

"I know." Bri shrugged, smiling at the sound of Rua's laughter. "But I'd love to see the look on his face."

They both chuckled softly to themselves in the darkness.

"Will you be able to sleep?" Bri asked.

Rua knew if she lay down, her mind would play over and over what had just happened in the woods. She knew she would be haunted all night by the embarrassment of her mistake.

"No," she confessed.

"Good," Bri said, producing a pack of playing cards from her pocket. "Want to play a game?"

# CHAPTER EIGHTEEN

Rua slept most of the day. Bri had left as the predawn sky began to lighten. It was evening when Talhan brought her a tray of food. He gave her a half-smile and left. She didn't think Bri had told him, but his twin must have warned him not to push her today.

Rua ate only a few bites of food. Her body ached. Her feet were bright red still, burned from the snow. But it was nothing compared to the pain when she sat up. There was no comfortable position. She cursed herself again for what she had done. Did everyone hurt like this? Bri seemed to think not. They had gone too fast, Rua pushing him too far, and she had hurt them both in the process. Her face still burned with shame. She would never be able to look Renwick in the eyes again. She thought about leaving. She could flee in the night, but the Eagles would go with her. She could say she was going to Yexshire to find the spell book, but the only place she'd rather be less than Murreneir was Yexshire. Besides, the thought of riding a horse with the pain between her legs made her wince. She would need another day to heal.

The sound of revelry picked up as the Harvest Moon celebrations were kicking off. The faint sound of music and people cheering found its way from the center of the camp all the way to her tent. Rua set her glass of water back down on her tray. She needed a real drink. And to stop sitting in this tent thinking about all the ways she had messed up.

She pushed the tray to the side. She didn't want more dried fruit.

Moving to the wardrobe, she picked a pale blue dress. It was made of thick wool with long, belled sleeves. It was beautiful, but plain. Perfect. She did not want to draw attention tonight. She layered her silk chemise under the dress, protecting her skin from the itchy wool. Then she donned her gray fur mantle over her shoulders. She slipped on her black leather boots. They were not appropriate for a celebration, but they were more comfortable than her slippers and her feet still ached. Her long skirt would hide her boots, anyway.

She left her hair unbraided, flowing in long dark waves down her back. When she pushed her way out of her tent, she found the Twin Eagles standing there.

"See?" Talhan smirked at his sister, holding out his hand. "I told you she'd want to go."

Bri rolled her eyes and passed her brother a gold coin.

"I take it you two want to go to the Harvest Moon celebration?" Rua asked, feeling a lightness finally starting to lift from that hard rock in her chest.

Bri shrugged. "They will have mead."

"Right, well, let's go then." Rua gestured down the path.

"Yes!" Talhan whispered excitedly to himself. Rua couldn't help but chuckle at his excitement.

"You could have gone without me." Rua raised an eyebrow to him as they walked toward the larger pathways leading to the center of camp.

"We wanted to wait for you," was all Bri said.

Rua wasn't sure what that meant. She didn't want their pity.

The sounds of music and chatter grew louder as they ambled into the open space. The area had been transformed. Three times as many people crammed themselves in front of the King's tent as they had for Rua's birthday party. The music was more lively. A circle had been carved out in the crowd where people jigged about.

It smelled of greasy food and mulled wine. Tables of long tapered candles dotted the periphery of the space, white wax pouring over their sides. Many of the candles remained unlit, waiting for another person to step up and light one. Others crowded around the tables, whispering into the candles and saying their prayers to their ancestors while the revels carried on.

Relief coursed through her when she didn't spy Renwick. The crowd was a tight press, but Rua didn't mind. No one seemed to notice her in the business of the throng.

Bri passed her a goblet of mead with a smirk. The sweet wine lit up her tongue, much more pleasant than the shock of moonshine they drank at the witch camps. Many of the witches lost themselves to moonshine. It seemed the only way to rid themselves of the horrors of what had happened after the Siege of Yexshire. But this . . . she took another long sip of the mead. A warm, pleasant buzzing blanketed her skin. The knot in her chest loosened a bit more. The weight of it was still there, but it felt farther away. A smile stretched across her face as she gave herself over to the sound of music and laughter.

Talhan tapped her on the shoulder as he drank his ale. "Let's go revel," he said to Rua with a wink, pulling her toward the circle of dancers.

Rua cackled. "I don't know how to dance."

"Does anyone here look like they know how to dance?" Talhan grinned.

Sure enough, the witches and fae all bounced and gyrated to their own rhythms. This was no formal ballroom. They just moved to the music, each in their own way. Talhan lifted his ale higher in the air as he began to sway along. Rua grinned, swishing her hips along to the sounds. She took another long sip of mead. Closing her eyes, she let the buzzing of the drink and the sounds of the drums wrap around her. Her fingers tingled as her body yielded to the surrounding sounds.

They danced like that until the moon was high in the sky. More and more people joined into the movements until the clearing was crammed with dancers. The revels were like nothing she had ever known. The fae were partial to these sorts of parties, usually favoring the solstices and equinoxes. The witches celebrated the moon, and their festivities were usually much more subdued. Here it was a mixture of both, a celebration unique to the people of Murreneir. The revelry of the fae and the rituals of the witches coalesced into one celebration. Even humans were there.

This was the world her parents had wanted. A world where everyone celebrated together. She knew Remy's court would be the same. There would be fae, witches, and humans at every level.

Rua sang and swayed her way through several glasses of mead before Bri swapped her goblet for a chunk of fresh bread. Rua smirked at her protector and ate it. But no amount of wine would spare her from her sore feet and aching body. Finally, she relented.

"I'm heading back to my tent," she shouted into Bri's ear to be heard over the crescendo of sounds.

"I'll come with you," Bri shouted back.

Talhan had drifted toward the middle of the ring of dancers. He now danced about with two young blue witches and a fae guard. They all laughed to each other like they were lifelong friends. Talhan made it look so easy.

"No, you stay," Rua insisted. "I'm just going back to my tent. You have fun."

Bri paused for a moment, but Rua gave her a look and her guard shrugged, moving back into the throng.

Rua was still smiling absently to herself as she ducked and looped out of the dense crowd. Pushing through the hordes that had spilled into the pathways, she made her way back toward her tent.

The sound of a shout pulled her to a halt. Looking over her shoulder, she peered through the tent gaps as a group of soldiers gathered around an outdoor fire. Two guards stood there, one of them gripping a young witch by the arm.

Rua moved without thinking, storming up to the fire pit. The two guards' eyes grew wide as they saw her.

"What is going on here?" she demanded, staring pointedly at the guard's hand on the witch.

He immediately released the girl, who scrambled to Rua's side.

"Nothing, Your Highness," the soldier replied. "We were just chatting."

Rua turned to the young witch and ordered, "Go."

"Thank you, *Mhenissa*," she said, bowing her head to Rua and skittering off into the night.

Rua blanched at the title, quickly recovering as she turned back to the fae guards.

"Do you always grab people when you are chatting with them?" Her voice filled with ice.

The guards looked down to her waist, noting that she didn't have the Immortal Blade. But the dagger Bri had given her was attached to her thin belt. She didn't need the dagger either. They were fools if they thought she was powerless without her weapons. This is how they saw her without the blade: a weak girl.

"Give us a break, will you? It was just a bit of fun," the other guard snickered.

Rua's eyes darted to him. Maybe some fae were learning to respect witches, but these two surely weren't. A flicker of panic flashed in the guards' eyes as they drifted up and over her shoulder. Grimacing, she knew who stood behind her without even turning.

"I will give you one chance to apologize to the Princess of the High Mountain Court." His voice was a lethal rumble at her back. "Or I will not lift a finger to help you when she starts to flay the skin from your bones."

Rua couldn't help but smirk at that. Renwick knew she could do it. He didn't underestimate her.

Both guards immediately dropped into deep bows.

"Forgive me, Your Highness."

"My sincerest apologies," the other said.

"Good," Renwick said from behind her. She didn't turn to look at him. "You two are dismissed from your post this night. Go reflect on whether you would still like a job come the dawn."

Their faces blanched. One swallowed a lump in his throat as they bowed again to their King and ran off.

Rua stared at the fire in front of her. Panic began to claw at her now that the guards were gone.

Renwick stepped in front of her. "I need to speak with you."

"I am tired," Rua said, turning to go back toward her tent, but Renwick moved in front of her again.

She felt those sharp green eyes assessing her. She wanted to shrivel up against his stare.

"Are you drunk?" He sounded amused.

"I had a couple glasses of mead." Rua rolled her eyes. She braced for his reprimand, but it didn't come.

"Murreneir's finest." Renwick smiled. His casual tone felt like a deliberate calculation. "I was hoping you could come help me with a decision I am struggling with. I need an answer by tomorrow and . . . I'm not sure which one to choose."

Her eyebrows rose in interest, but she didn't look up into those green eyes. The smell of cloves and snow wafted off him. She still tasted him on her lips from the night before. His stare felt weighted with lead. There were so many unspoken words between them.

He had once promised to make her feel safe. Gods, she still wanted it to be true.

"Fine," she said to her hands. This was the exact thing she didn't want: to be alone with the King again.

～

The office was cast in shadow. Only two candles flickered on Renwick's desk. He went to the stove fire and opened the window to the hearth, casting a gold-and-red glow across the room.

Rua's heart thrummed in her chest. It was too quiet. All she could see when she closed her eyes was the look of horror on Renwick's face when he smelled her blood. The same scent of hellebore and bloodbane wafted through the room. She was certain if she looked at him, his pupils would be dilated just the same. Perhaps he poisoned himself every night.

"What do you think?" he asked, passing her a piece of paper.

Rua looked down at three drawings of different court crests.

"You are changing your crest?" she murmured, looking over the paper.

"The snake was my father's symbol. The guards who defected with Balorn wear the same crest on their armor," Renwick said. "It is time for a change."

Rua traced her finger over each of the drawings. "Yes, it would have been disastrous if your soldiers clashed with his."

"Which one do you like?" Renwick asked, making her hands still. It did not matter which one she liked. Rua was certain his councilors would have opinions. She supposed he was asking because she was royalty like him. What would she pick if she chose a crest for herself?

"This one," she said at last, pointing to the one with a sword piercing down through a crown with a smattering of stars behind it. "It shows strength and isn't too cluttered."

"I like that one too," Renwick said, stepping closer to her.

Rua passed the paper back to him and wandered to the bookshelf. She needed to put some distance between them. The smell of him overwhelmed her, and she couldn't tell how far gone he was to the witch's poison without looking into his eyes—and she was determined not to do that.

She ran her hands over the spines of the books, her fingers snagging over the book she had picked up before: *Songs of Spring in Murreneir.* The note inside had been inscribed to Eadwin. It was an unusual name. She tossed it around in her mind.

Like a punch to the chest, she remembered where she had heard it before: Balorn had said to Renwick that he was as weak as Eadwin that day in Vurstyn.

Renwick approached as Rua whispered, "Who is Eadwin?"

The full intensity of Renwick's stare weighed heavier than a boulder. She was certain his eyes bored into her as she pressed her lips together.

Renwick took a long, steadying breath. "He was my younger brother."

*Was.*

Rua had suspected, but the truth of it still made her ache.

The firelight flickered, the silence stretching out between them before Renwick said, "He was six years old when he died. I was fifteen."

Rua swallowed the lump in her throat. "How did he die?"

"Balorn killed him and my mother," Renwick said as Rua took a jagged breath. "They were trying to run away from my father. Balorn . . . stopped them."

"And you weren't running with them?" Rua murmured to keep her voice from wobbling.

"I was already called the Witchslayer by then," Renwick said. "I don't think they would have wanted me to come."

Tears threatened to spring from Rua's eyes at that admission. His own mother had left him behind. He knew what it felt like to be unwanted. She knew that pain herself, but she felt it so much keener coming from him.

"We both know what it means to lose a brother." She kept her gaze fixed on her trembling finger, tracing the letters down the book's spine.

Renwick reached out his warm hand and gently wrapped it around hers. The contact made her jolt. Rua snatched her hand away at his tender touch. She couldn't take it. That tenderness. She was certain accepting it would create a yawning pit of sorrow below her feet that she would plummet into.

"Rua, look at me," Renwick whispered.

Rua shoved down that sadness that threatened to devour her and steeled her heart with fire instead.

"I'm tired; I'm going," she said, turning to leave.

"Wait, please." Renwick's hand reached out to cup her cheek.

The feeling of his hand on her face had her moving without thought. Her hand snatched the dagger on her hip, and she whirled, stilling the tip of her sharp blade against the flesh of his neck.

"I am not in the mood for more commands today, *King*." Rua's voice was not her own. It was a rasping, wicked sound. Her eyes lifted to meet his. This is how she would look at him—only like this—when he was at the end of her dagger.

She expected his eyes to be wide with shock, but they were sharper than the tip of her blade. His chest rose and fell in heavy pants as he stared straight into her soul.

"If I hurt you . . . ," he began.

"Stop," Rua said, pushing the blade in a little more, threatening to pierce his skin.

Renwick's eyes hardened as he pushed his head forward, letting the dagger bite into him until a trickle of scarlet blood ran down his neck.

"I didn't think I could hate myself any more than I already did," he said, his eyes never leaving hers. His pupils were so wide she could barely see the green.

"I don't want to talk about this." Rua's hand shook, her breathing as frantic as his own.

"Don't pull away from me," Renwick pleaded with hooded eyes, pushing further into the blade.

More blood streamed down his neck and Rua finally relented, pulling her dagger away and sheathing it.

She walked to his desk and looked down at the empty vial sitting atop it. He couldn't feel the pain of the steel, not while he was drugged on dangerous potions. He was destroying himself even more than she was. It made her more angry than she ever felt for herself. His life had been filled with so much more pain than her own, but she had been the weak one. She refused to be weak anymore.

Furious, she smashed her hand down on the empty vial, shattering the glass under her bare palm.

"Rua!" Renwick barked, darting to her.

Rua held up her palm, pulling a shard of glass out of her flesh. Blood pooled in the wound and then trickled over the side. Droplets fell like raindrops onto the surface of his desk.

"I can feel this." She held up her bleeding palm to him.

Renwick's eyes narrowed, the smell of her blood pulling him back in on himself just as it had the night before.

He reached out and grabbed her hand, pressing down on her cut and lifting her hand in the air to stop the bleeding.

"Why would you do that?" he snarled, his eyes scanning her face.

"In my tent, after that day in Vurstyn . . . you asked me to stay," Rua reminded him. "Do you remember what you said?"

Renwick's eyes cleared even more, brilliant rings of emerald visible now. Just as he pulled the compulsion of the blade out of her, she pulled the poison out of him.

"I told you I'd hold on to you," he whispered, keeping his thumb pressed to her hand.

Rua held those vivid green eyes as she said, "I'm not the only one fading away."

Renwick's gaze fell from the shame of those words. He knew how bad it was, what he was doing to himself, though she was certain he would say he had it under control.

"Why do you do this?" Rua's voice was edged with despair.

Renwick shook his head, moving her hand back down between them. He lifted his thumb to check the bleeding had stopped, and dropped her hand.

"If you were drowning and someone threw you a rope, wouldn't you grab it?" he murmured, reaching a hand to the drying blood on his neck. "It's only once you start pulling yourself in that you realize that rope is attached to nothing."

"It doesn't really take your pain away," Rua lamented.

"It helps," Renwick snapped.

"It doesn't help!" Rua shouted at him, drawing his eyes back to her. "You can change your crest a hundred times over and carve as many bloody roses on that castle as you want, but poisoning yourself will never bring you peace."

"Why do you care, Rua?" Renwick growled at her.

"Because I do," she yelled.

"Why?" His shouting rose to match her own.

"Because I care about you, Renwick, damn it!" she hissed. "That's what you wanted to tell me that day in Raevenport, isn't it? That you care about me too?"

Nodding, he reached out to her, and she pulled away from him again, moving that space back between them. Her eyes flitted back to the bookshelf. To the book his mother gave to his little brother. So many books they had of families long gone. So many people they loved lay forever in the ground.

"I shouldn't care about you." She choked on her words as she turned to leave.

Renwick didn't follow.

The sounds of shattering and crashing echoed after her down the hallway. It sounded like a beast tearing apart his office. Part of her yearned to comfort that beast. The same one she knew lived inside of her, but she did not pause or turn back. He needed to remember what it was to feel something. They both did.

# CHAPTER NINETEEN

Weeks passed in glum silence until the day arrived that they had to leave for the High Mountain Court. The gentle swinging of the sleigh finally brought Aneryn's bobbing head down on Rua's shoulder. The soft sounds of the blue witch's breathing mixed with the muted snores of the Twin Eagles across from her.

Aneryn had crammed into the sleigh with Rua and the Twin Eagles for the journey southward. The blue witch insisted she didn't want to waste a sleigh, but Rua knew her friend didn't want to be alone, especially not after the attack in Vurstyn. Aneryn's wounds had healed over. Though, as a witch, it took much longer. No one would get near her when she was sitting beside the Immortal Blade and across from the Twin Eagles. So the four of them rode together.

They were headed to Yexshire for the Winter Solstice celebrations. It was the first time Rua was going home.

Home. It still felt like a hollow word. She had conjured an image in her mind of what she would see when she arrived, but she knew it would not look the same.

Rua peered out the fogged window while everyone slept. She had to lift her hand every minute to wipe away the buildup of condensation.

They had taken their cloaks off instantly, the heat of four bodies in that small space keeping them warm.

They passed through evergreen forests and small villages nearly buried under snow. She kept a watchful eye on the tree line, thinking that at any moment she might see a *suraash* run out and attack them. Every hour she wondered if they would see more bodies nailed to trees.

"You will see nothing out there," Aneryn murmured, keeping her head on Rua's shoulder.

Rua glanced down at her drowsy friend. The blue witch looked healthy and vibrant once more. She wore a cream dress jacket with silver embroidery down the front, her hair in twists that hung down to her shoulders.

Rua had stayed away from Renwick since the night of the Harvest Moon. It was too much, far too much. Instead, Rua poured herself into caring for Aneryn and spending time in the witches' quarter.

The rest of the camp was either boring or filled with soldiers and pompous fae, and she wanted to be around neither . . . especially one pompous fae in particular. She found her feet walking the winding paths most days toward the other side of camp. The Twin Eagles had left her to her own devices. They often went off as a pair, sparring, readying themselves for the next opportunity to attack Balorn. Rua still shuddered to think of him.

"I still think us leaving the Lyrei Basin unprotected is a bad idea," Rua whispered to Aneryn, even though she knew she wouldn't wake the Eagles.

"We left most of the guards and witches with them. The basin is one of the most protected places in the Northern Court," Aneryn reassured her, voice distant as if sleep were pulling her under again.

"Balorn has not been defeated yet . . ."

"I have Seen nothing, Rua. Neither has Baba Airu," Aneryn confirmed, tucking her head further into the crook of Rua's neck. "In my last vision, Balorn was outside of Valtene."

Rua thought to the disputed territory on the Western border. He was moving that far west? Was he going to leave the Northern Court? Was he fleeing?

"D—"

"Yes, the Western Court knows he is there," Aneryn murmured with a heavy sigh.

Rua clenched her teeth together. She hated how Aneryn could do that: guess her questions before they came out of her mouth. She wasn't sure if the blue witch had visions of her asking them or if she just knew her that well by now.

"And Queen Thorne is not sending soldiers to Valtene?" Rua questioned.

The Western Court Queen had always been too lenient with the Vostemurs. She had let the witch hunters run rampant through the Western Court. No wonder Rua's sister had to stay so firmly hidden in backcountry taverns in the West.

"The Queen ceded Valtene to Vostemur during the Autumnal Equinox," Aneryn said.

Yes, Bri had told Rua about that, about the severed heads they dropped in the middle of the ballroom in the Eastern Court that night: a warning to King Norwood of the East to not be as foolish as Queen Thorne or his people too would die. Remy had been there that night, glamoured in her human form . . . though everyone had thought she was a witch. Witches and humans looked the same; they only felt different to those who sensed magic. Since Remy and Rua possessed both fae and red witch magic, it would have been easy enough to assume she was a witch.

What a terrible disguise, Rua thought, to be glamoured as a person that was being actively hunted. The only worse thing was to be what they really were: the heirs to the High Mountain Court. It was a terrible choice: hide as a witch or hide as a High Mountain fae. Rua didn't need to glamour herself in hiding in the mountains near Yexshire. She could barely hold on to her glamour when they were captured by the Northern soldiers and brought to Drunehan. Baba Morganna had implored her to hold her glamour, a fat lot of good it did her. She was seconds away from having her head cut off as a nameless red witch instead of the Princess of the High Mountain Court. It didn't matter. Death didn't care what title she had. It would come to claim her all the same.

That had only been a couple months ago. It felt like a lifetime since she first picked up the Immortal Blade.

"Renwick should stay here with his people," Rua said, unsure if Aneryn would respond.

"He was invited to the royal wedding of his new allies," Aneryn murmured groggily, still awake after all.

Rua had nearly forgotten about the wedding again. Remy and her Fated were going to be married on the Winter Solstice. The ball afterward would not only celebrate the return of the sun, but also the two of them, the sovereigns of their court. Dignitaries from all the courts would be going. It would be the first time Rua had to play the part of princess. She knew she would be under the scrutiny of many eyes. She would need to prove to them that she was worthy of the Immortal Blade.

Stepping into that world, she would not be able to hide from who she was in Yexshire. The red witches she grew up with would be there. Her stomach dropped at the thought. She didn't want to face them, nor did she want to face Remy. She thought about their first and last interaction. The hug had been so awkward. It never got easier with Raffiel either. She didn't know how to talk to them like they were family. They were strangers. How were families even supposed to talk to each other?

The sleigh slowed to a stop, and Aneryn's head lifted off Rua's shoulder.

The blue witch yawned. "We're here."

The light was already fading as they neared the shortest day of the year. They had left that morning in darkness and were arriving in darkness as well. The Northern Court had weeks without the briefest peek of sunlight bursting through the clouds. She had not appreciated how different that was from Yexshire, where the sun shone every day, even in the depths of winter. Rua preferred the darkness of the North.

The Twin Eagles opened their eyes at the same time. Sitting up, Talhan cracked his neck, Bri rolled her shoulders, and that was it. They were ready for whatever came next. Rua pursed her lips at them. How did they do that? How did they fall asleep so quickly but were instantly ready for battle the second they opened their eyes? She wasn't sure it could all be chalked up to training. The Twin Eagles were built this way. They were natural-born predators. Not in the evil snakelike way of Hennen and Balorn, but in the stealthy way of a bird of prey like Ehiris. Bri had been striking enough on her own, but now with Talhan there, Rua found her eyes snagging on their otherworldly features.

She heard the voice of Lord Omerin from outside the sleigh. "Your Majesty."

Rua opened the sleigh door and stepped out into the powdery snow. Aneryn followed, the fresh snow coming up and over her boots. As the Eagles clambered out the opposite door, they stood staring up at the Castle of Brufdoran. It had felt like a lifetime since their last visit. Rua remembered the panicked nightmare she had while sleeping in that castle. She prayed the nightmares wouldn't find her again that night.

Renwick and Thador lingered around the arched entryway. Lord Omerin was not alone in greeting them this time. His daughter and grandson stood with him in matching fur-trimmed cloaks. The young boy's eyes scanned the gathering travelers until they landed on Rua.

"Your Highness!" Lord Fredrik shouted with excitement.

"Lord Fredrik," Rua said with a grin. "You have grown three whole inches since last I saw you."

Fredrik puffed out his chest. His mother, Lady Mallen, gave his shoulder a gentle squeeze.

"Will you be dining with us this time?" Rua asked, arching a conspiratorial brow at him.

The little boy looked up at his grandfather. "Can I, Granpapa?"

Lord Omerin smiled warmly at his grandson. "That is a question for the King."

Rua's eyes flitted briefly to Renwick. She had not been near him in weeks, and he looked terrible. His face was pale with dark circles under his eyes, and his normally pristine attire was crumpled. She pondered if he had been trying to stop drinking the sleeping poisons. It was clearly a bigger battle than he had expected. Even a lifetime practicing hiding his pain had not prevented it from seeping into his appearance this time.

Renwick's eyes stayed glued to the waiting boy's face. To anyone else it would look like he was frozen in thought, but Rua knew, knew it was pain on his face, and this time she knew what he saw when he looked at Fredrik: Eadwin.

Gods, Rua had teased him for it before. She had taunted him about being afraid of children. But really, the little Northern boy probably looked like his brother. A hot pain twisted in Rua's gut. She had poured salt into those wounds without even knowing.

"We have already discussed it," Rua said, rescuing Renwick from the lingering silence. "We would love for you to join us." Rua looped a hand through Aneryn's arm. "And make a seat for Aneryn and the Eagles too."

Lady Mallen gawked at Aneryn. "A witch?"

As Aneryn's eyes dropped to her feet, Rua pulled her friend closer.

"Yes, a witch," Rua snapped. "Do you not have witches dine with you often?"

"Gods, no." Lady Mallen started to laugh, but the glare in Rua's eyes cut her off. "I mean—"

"The times are changing quickly, Your Highness," Omerin cut in, "for the better of course. We are rushing to keep up."

Sneering, Rua looked Mallen up and down. "See that you do." She glanced at Fredrik, face softening, and gave him a quick wink. "See you at dinner." She prayed that the world would change fast enough that he wouldn't be infected by the prejudices of his elders. Looking into his beaming face, Rua hoped he never felt the way she did inside.

Not waiting for Omerin to invite them in, Rua and Aneryn stepped up the frosty staircase toward the main door.

As the Eagles ascended the stairs behind them, Omerin chuckled, saying to Renwick, "I bet you have your hands full with that one."

"Indeed." Renwick's voice was low and hollow, no mirth in his reply.

Aneryn nudged Rua with her shoulder, whispering, "That was amazing."

"I didn't like the way she looked at you." Rua shrugged, eyes skimming over the opulent room, from the oil paintings to the golden chandeliers. These fae had probably never felt discomfort or hunger or fear.

"I'm used to those looks," Aneryn murmured, "but Mother Moon was it fun to see you tear down Lady Mallen like that."

Rua smirked at her friend as they headed up the winding steps of the Castle of Brufdoran to the second floor. "I suppose I haven't fully explored the perks of being royalty." Rua grinned. She did not care about gilded decor and fine clothing, but being able to speak her mind with impunity was a true luxury.

They were about to take the final step up the stairwell when Aneryn gasped. Rua's eyes darted over to the blue witch. Her hands and eyes were glowing a faint sapphire. A vision was taking over her mind.

"What is it?" Rua whispered as the glow faded from Aneryn's eyes.

"I couldn't see. It looked like a haze of violet clouds. But it felt like . . ." Aneryn didn't have time to continue before a fae guard appeared in the doorway above.

"My Lord!" he called down the steps to Lord Omerin. "A voice is calling from the fae fire."

Rua straightened. The look on the guard's face told Rua this was not a social call.

"Who is it?" Rua asked.

It was Aneryn who answered. "Balorn."

❦

Lord Omerin led them through the halls of his castle to the green door on the third floor, the same room where Rua had spoken to Remy so many weeks ago. No one spoke as Omerin gestured to the door with a bow, and Renwick charged inside. Aneryn and Thador remained at the threshold, as if it were common to wait for their King while he communicated through fae fire. The Twin Eagles had no such qualms, darting in after Rua.

No one sat on the elegantly upholstered chairs surrounding the fireplace. They all braced themselves, looking into the flames, as if a beast might emerge from them.

"What do you want, Balorn?" Renwick gritted out.

"I don't want anything from you, Witchslayer. You are a traitor to the crown," Balorn's smooth voice echoed out from the flames. Just the sound of it made Rua's arm hairs stand on end. "I wish to speak to the true power in the North. Is she there?"

Renwick held up a hand, signaling Rua not to speak. She rolled her eyes at him. It was the most interaction they had in weeks.

"Your silence is deafening." Balorn guffawed. "How are you this evening, my dear Ruadora?"

Her whole body went rigid at his soft, flirting tone. She wanted to ask Balorn what he wanted from her, but she knew she wouldn't like his answer. The nightmare from weeks ago flashed unwelcome through her mind. She still felt his lips on hers and the thrill that had raced through her body. Even though it was a dream, it had felt so real.

She changed tack. "What are you doing in the Western Court?"

"Those witches of yours are good," Balorn said, "though not as good as mine. We are doing nothing to concern you, my dear, just visiting some old friends."

The Eagles exchanged quick glances, a whole conversation happening between their golden eyes. Renwick was watching the Eagles too. Did they have some connection to the West that Rua didn't know about?

"Who is this friend?" Rua asked. "Do they have the Witches' Glass?"

"I will tell you once I see you in person, love. You know where to find me now." His voice was a soft lover's whisper. "Come see me and we can talk."

Renwick's fists balled at his sides, but he didn't turn to Rua.

"I would very much like to never see you again, Balorn, though I fear it might be inevitable," Rua snarled, forcing more strength into her voice. "Someone has to put a blade in your chest."

"Keep that fire in you, Rua." Balorn chuckled in amusement, as if she were an oddity to delight in. "You are going to need it when we are together."

"We will never be together," Rua bit out.

"Who else could handle you, hmm?" Balorn's smugness could be heard all the way from the Western Court border. "Who could take on all that darkness inside of you?"

The words punched into her, stealing the breath from her lungs. The sticky tar of shame burned across her neck and cheeks. She wished the floor would open up and swallow her whole. At least the Eagles and Renwick had the good sense not to look at her. But she felt their attention on her still. She knew they sensed it, too, that darkness Balorn spoke of. But to hear it said out loud . . . To have her flaws laid so bare in front of them . . . it made her want to shatter, but exploding would confirm everything Balorn had accused her of. She would not unleash that darkness now; no, she would push it down deeper in that gaping hole in her gut. She did not know where that pit had come from. Everyone around her had suffered terrible things, worse things, but they all seemed to cope. Even Renwick's dependency on pain potions was nothing compared to her. He managed to talk to his uncle with some semblance of logic, even though Balorn had killed his mother and brother. How could he possibly stay so even-keeled?

Rua clenched her jaw so tightly she was sure to crack a tooth. She needed to get out of this room. The air was too hot. She needed to get into the snow.

When Renwick spoke, her panic ebbed, the sound of his voice soothing the torrent inside of her. "The North no longer belongs to you, Balorn. Witches are free here now. A new day is dawning."

"Listen to you trying to sound like a King," Balorn tutted. "You are too weak to rule the North, nephew. You will rue the day you let the blue witches off their leashes. There will be nothing stopping them from tearing your court apart."

"It is you they want retribution from, not me," Renwick said, his words decisive and cutting.

"Are you not a Vostemur? Are you not a fae?" Balorn asked. "You believe they will be satisfied with anything other than a witch as their ruler?"

Renwick's body braced as if something Balorn said had spooked him.

"Who rules the North is no longer your concern, Balorn. Yield to Renwick while you still have the chance," Bri finally spoke.

"Ah, Briata Catullus, the greatest disappointment in the Western Court," Balorn said. "Is that fool of a brother there with you?"

Rua furrowed her brow at the Eagles. What disappointment was he speaking of? Bri looked at Rua and shook her head.

"Later," she mouthed to Rua.

"I'm here," Talhan said.

"Aren't you an odd little bunch?" Balorn laughed gruffly. "A Northern traitor, two displaced warriors, and a High Mountain princess with a magic sword. Gods, it's the start of a tavern ballad, I'm sure of it."

"If the West welcomes you, Balorn, then fine," Renwick seethed, growing louder with each sentence. "I will not hunt you past our borders, but stay out of the North."

"You are nothing more than children," Balorn sneered. "All of you tied to the High Mountain Court think you are so special, don't you? That you all can bring a new order to Okrith, but you know nothing. Wait another few decades and all that hopefulness will disappear, and you will realize that this is the way the world needs to be."

"You think we are filled with hopefulness?" Rua asked incredulously. The Eagles let out matching chuckles as the muscle on Renwick's cheek ticked. "You are not in a position to get to decide what the world needs to be anymore, Balorn."

It struck her then that she was. It was what Baba Airu had been trying to tell her—that she had been granted a seat at the table, whether she liked it or not. She could balk from that responsibility, or view it as a burden, but the people who scrambled for that power were not the ones who should be wielding it. She thought about Remy. Her sister didn't want her crown at first, but she had accepted it. Better that she had to battle with that decision than to step into it eagerly. That hesitancy would make her evaluate her choices better. She wouldn't take her power for granted in the same way people like Balorn did. Balorn was born into every sort of privilege, and now he'd come to expect it.

"You are not owed anything," Rua said, drawing Renwick's gaze. "The world has moved on without you."

"You speak with such confidence for someone so young," Balorn said. "You will make the perfect Queen by my side, Ruadora. You belong with me."

Renwick let out a low growl.

"I belong to no one." Rua met Renwick's stare, her words from that moment in his tent flooding her mind. *I can't care about you.*

"Think about it, Princess," Balorn said, interrupting the storm brewing between their eyes. "Think about what we could be together."

Turning to the hearth, Rua shuddered as she watched the green bleed out of the flames and return to a normal fire once more.

The room stayed frozen in silence until she heard Talhan whisper to Bri, "He called here just to seduce her?"

Bri elbowed her twin. "He called to sow the seeds of distrust in everyone's minds."

"Like how you've never told me why you're *the greatest disappointment of the Western Court?*" Rua asked, folding her arms across her chest. "What was that about?"

Bri grimaced, looking up at the delicate flower painting on the wall. "Not here." She shook her head. "Wait until we're in Yexshire, and then I'll explain. I promise."

"What did he mean by friends?" Renwick asked the Eagles in a clipped tone. "Who are these friends he is meeting up with?"

"I have no idea, but I know who might," Bri said, glancing at her twin. "Delta Thorne will be at the wedding in Yexshire."

Renwick seemed to know who that was, but Rua had no idea. Thorne was the name of the Western Queen, but she had never heard the name Delta. She was reminded again of how these three had known each other all their lives. They knew all the important fae in all the courts.

"Who is that?" Rua's voice carried a hint of exasperation.

"The Western Queen's niece. The Western Princess's royal guard," Bri said, fixing Rua with her golden stare. "She is going as a representative of the West to the wedding."

"Abalina isn't coming?" Renwick pursed his lips. Rua had heard of Abalina Thorne before, the only child of the Western Court Queen. "Are they pulling away from their ties to the High Mountain Court?"

"I don't know," Bri said. "But we need to find out. If Queen Thorne is letting Balorn through her borders with immunity, that is going to be a problem for us all."

"She did nothing about your father's witch hunters," Talhan said to Renwick. "What's to say she would put her foot down now?"

"We will find out when we get to Yexshire." Renwick inclined his head. "There will be emissaries from every court there."

Talhan looked skyward, releasing a whine. "Why can't a royal wedding ever just be a wedding? Why does there always have to be politics involved?"

Bri punched her brother on the arm. "You've got to earn that ale and music, Tal."

Rua knew this was what would happen when she went to the Winter Solstice celebration in Yexshire. The diplomacy of her newborn court was too important for her to mess it up. Balorn was still on the loose. They needed allies from the established courts, the ones that had resources and armies. Rua's shoulders deflated as she thought of the many duties she was bound to have when she reached Yexshire, and Bri chuckled.

"You two, honestly." Bri rolled her eyes. "It will be fine. You just need to talk to a few people."

Talhan looked at the sword on Rua's hip. "Who knew wielding a magic sword would be the easy part, hey?" He winked at Rua. "Talking to rich, highborn fae is what we really should have been training you for."

She groaned, releasing her arms from across her chest.

"Come on, dinner," Bri said, herding Talhan to the door.

Rua glanced to Renwick. The Northern King stood staring into the flames. For a brief moment, Rua had forgotten the ominous things that Balorn had said. She got distracted with court planning.

"Give me a minute?" Rua murmured to Bri. The Twin Eagles exchanged knowing glances and left.

Rua stared at Renwick's shadowed silhouette. They stood in a long stretch of silence until Renwick's fists unclenched.

"Are you okay?" Her voice felt too loud in the silence.

He didn't turn. "I'm trying to be."

She looked down to her palm, where she had smashed her hand against his empty vial of poison. There was no scar. Her fae magic had healed the wound completely within a week. She had told Renwick she had cared about him and then immediately said she wished she didn't.

The more distance she tried to put between them, the more she felt pulled in. Maybe Yexshire would be the perfect distraction for her. They would be too busy to be together much. She would have some time to figure out what was going on between them.

She thought of what Balorn had said about her darkness. Maybe she was too broken, even for the Northern King. Maybe her darkness was that much greater than his. Who was she to suggest he quit the one thing keeping him from drowning along with her? She shook her head and left.

~

The former capital city of Drunehan had fallen from its former glory. It wasn't just the palace in ruins anymore, the entire city looking more derelict than when they left. Stepping out into the courtyard beside the city stables, she surveyed the chaotic scene. The streets were littered with filth. The shops around the castle were looted, broken glass strewn across the dirty snow. Rubbish piles sat stacked with the ash remnants of books, paper, and wood.

Talhan and Bri stumbled out of the sleigh and instantly began stretching out their weary limbs as stable hands raced around them, unhitching the horses. Aneryn and Rua walked along the far stone wall, looking at the charcoal images drawn into the gray slate.

"Don't stray too far," Thador called from the front sleigh as they wandered down the alley between the buildings. Aneryn waved a hand back to him as if he gave her such warnings all the time.

They would switch to wheeled carriages for the rest of their journey. Servants hastily lugged their trunks into the awaiting carriages. Drunehan would not be a long stopover.

"What happened to this place?" Rua murmured, looking at the scrawling words of "traitor" and unflattering caricatures of Renwick with pig noses and goat horns.

"Drunehan was populated by loyalists to Hennen Vostemur. They benefitted the most from his reign," Aneryn said, face puckering at the image of Renwick in a lewd act with an unknown figure.

Rua blanched when she saw the mountain and crown crest above the cartoon. Was that meant to be her? Stomach roiling, she pulled them further into the alley.

"What happened to all of them?"

"Most of them died during the battle of Drunehan," Aneryn hedged.

Rua rested her hand on the Immortal Blade. "You mean I killed most of them."

"Yes." Aneryn pressed her lips together. "But not everyone would have been in the castle that night. There are probably family members and lower-class fae who didn't get an invitation." Aneryn eyed the wall. "They won't be happy with you or Renwick."

"Clearly." Rua snorted, looking to an image of her severed head.

Aneryn forced out a chuckle. "It is the curse of being a ruler," she said. "Some people will always hate you." She steered Rua to another sketch. "But some will love you too."

They stopped in front of a charcoal likeness of Rua. In the image, she pointed the Immortal Blade toward the sky, a crown atop her head. The word scrawled below it read: *Mhenissa*.

They reached the end of the alley where another scrawling graffiti read: The free witches follow *Mhenissa*.

Chewing on her cheek, Rua grimaced at the words. It made her wary—this adoration. It felt like the blue witches knew something she did not.

Talhan turned the corner, still buttoning back up his trousers from wherever he went to relieve himself.

"There is some pretty interesting art on the walls around here." He chuckled, giving Rua a wink. She rolled her eyes at him, praying it was no worse than the images they had seen.

She guided Aneryn up to Renwick, using the blue witch to buffer the anxiety to speak with him.

"What are you doing about Drunehan?" she asked with an accusatory glare.

"What do you mean?" Renwick narrowed his eyes back at her.

"Look around!" She gestured to the graffitied walls and broken doorways. "Does it look like this city is under control?"

Renwick cocked his head. "The people who live here loved my father. They practically worshipped him. The fact they are allowed to live is a mercy."

"Are there only fae in this city?" Rua hissed, already knowing the answer. The lines of Renwick's frown deepened. "What of the witches? What of the humans? Do they not deserve their King's aid either?"

"They were welcome to join us in Murreneir," Renwick said. "They have chosen to stay behind."

"Not everyone has the gold to just up and leave." Rua laughed mockingly, knowing it would infuriate him. "You think the chaos you have left them in will bring them to your side?"

"What would you suggest I do?" Renwick growled.

"You need representatives in Drunehan just like your councilors in other counties. You need someone here who can enforce your rule and pull this city back together. Drunehan requires new governance, and whoever is currently running this place needs to go." Rua shook her head, absently eyeing the vacant streets. "I can stay behind. With the blade, I can keep them in line—"

"Nope." Bri snickered, sidling up beside them and slinging her arm over Rua's shoulders. "Nice try, Ru. You're going to your sister's wedding."

Rua silently cursed the Eagle for sensing her eagerness to stay behind.

Renwick and Thador exchanged glances, a soundless conversation happening between them, before the King's guard nodded.

"Thador will stay behind with a few of my guards," Renwick announced.

Rua gaped as Thador ambled to the carriage and removed his pack, signaling two soldiers to do the same. Just like that, they were diverting from their trip to Yexshire.

The ogre of a fae put his hand on Renwick's shoulder, the Northern King mirroring the movement, saying farewell in actions rather than words. Thador seemed like Renwick's only confidante, and Rua noted by the look on the King's face, it pained him to say goodbye. He still had done it, as if it were nothing, all at Rua's behest.

The Eagles climbed back into the new carriage, Renwick moving to the front one alone now that Thador was gone. Looking back and forth between the two carriages, Rua hesitated. They would reach Yexshire today. She would be going to her homeland and seeing the new castle and greeting the people, *her* people. Her chest seized up at the thought, clenching tighter with each breath. She thought for a moment of darting back down the alley and out into the city of Drunehan.

"It'll be fine." Aneryn chortled, tugging Rua toward the carriage with the Eagles.

She looked back toward Renwick's lone carriage, her stomach dropping. She doubted it would be fine.

# CHAPTER TWENTY

Their carriages wobbled down the slick, icy roads. The path to Yexshire was not maintained from the north. Rua wondered if that was a pointed jab at the Northern Court, if the rest of the roads to the other courts had been cleared. They had switched to wheeled carriages in Drunehan, and the ride had become more unpleasant and jerky after that. She was ready to get out of the carriage, but she also dreaded what awaited her up ahead.

"Gods, do you see this?" Talhan wiped a hand down the fogged window. Rua mirrored the action on her side.

Buildings appeared in the distance. The first few looked dilapidated—the roofs caving in and giant drifts of snow covering their stoops. But further along she saw a line of smoke billowing skyward from a chimney. Then another. As they pulled closer, she spotted freshly thatched roofs, painted doors, and patched windows. Signs of people. Yexshire was alive.

The roads through the city were shoveled and clean. The sun shone out over the rooftops, dusted in a fresh powder of snow. People gathered in windows and stoops, peeking out to see their carriage pull past. A few brave souls gathered in the town square, waving at her from their bundled cloaks.

A kick to her shin snapped Rua's head back to Bri.

"What?"

"Wave," Bri said, raising her eyebrows as if it were obvious.

Talhan and Aneryn were already waving from the other side of the carriage.

"They don't even know you." Rua forced a smile as she waved at the well-wishers.

"People love to be waved at," Aneryn said. "The Northerners loved it when I waved to them, even though they knew I was just a witch."

"You're not *just* anything." Rua frowned, but she kept waving.

The main road of shops was freshly revived. Painted signs hung from papered-over windows. Merchants and traders had populated the city. She read the titles as she waved to the people in the streets. The surnames were native to every court, matching the patchwork of faces that greeted her.

There were witches in the crowd, though she did not recognize them. They wore their totem bags around their necks like Baba Airu. Witches weren't afraid to advertise their magic anymore. Rua wasn't surprised witches had left their home courts to come to Yexshire. The past fourteen years had not been kind to witches of any coven. The red witches were slaughtered, the Northern Court witches enslaved, but the rest of the covens lived in fear as well. Many were trafficked and sold to the North over the years. Even more were killed in an attempt to claim the bounty on the red witch heads. It made sense after all those years that they would want to move to a city whose sovereigns valued witches.

Yexshire was a true melting pot. There were shops from all over Okrith: eateries and foodstuffs from the far reaches of the Southern Court, the fine carpentry of the Eastern Court, the pottery and brown witch apothecaries of the West. Yexshire would be the city that had it all. She swallowed back the tears welling in her eyes as a knot tightened in her chest. This was something special.

The crowd grew larger as they drew closer to the castle. More people rushed with zeal into Main Street, waving at her.

"My arm is tired," Rua groused.

Bri cocked her head at Rua. "You train with that heavy sword for hours a day, but waving your dainty wrist is too much?"

"The castle!" Aneryn gasped.

Rua pushed her face closer to the glass, looking up the winding road into the mountains. Sitting on a ledge hewn from the mountain-side was the Castle of Yexshire. Her mouth fell open. It was gigantic.

"How in the Gods' names did they build that so quickly?" She gaped at the looming monstrosity.

It wasn't an exact match of the previous castle that Rua had seen in her little book, but it had many nods to the original design. Some of the black rocks used around the foundations looked original, but this castle was far grander. Her parents' castle looked more like a fortress, but this looked like something straight out of a fairy tale.

Twelve huge square towers surrounded the castle, reaching twice the height of the walls, connected by high bridges made of dark stone. Towering, ornate windows looked out over the city below. The warm glow of firelight shone through them.

A mighty gate with broad metal doors bisected the road. Beyond, a trail of flaming torches led up to a pavilion in front of the towering wooden doorway.

Rua squinted against the brilliant beams of sunlight. She saw hints of each of the courts in its design. The crenellations of the battlements emulated the Western Court defenses. Looking at the trellised archways, she knew come spring they would be covered in climbing flowers—a nod to the Northern Court. The intricately carved wood of the main doorway paid homage to the Eastern Court, and the golden-framed windows were done in the Southern Court style.

But the symbols and colors of the High Mountain Court were the prominent features, from the carved mountain landscapes on the outer walls to the red pennants blowing in the wind. She wondered if the twelve towers symbolized the twelve highest summits of the High Mountains.

She wanted to freeze time and take it all in. The castle so perfectly reflected its citizens in the city below, a beautiful amalgamation of the different identities of Okrith. It was stunning, and Rua felt like even more of a foreigner than she had in the North.

The carriage jostled its way up the steep road, Bri and Talhan having to brace themselves to keep from sliding off their seats. A crowd gathered in front of the castle, and standing at the front was a woman with flowing black curls, a golden, ruby-studded crown atop her head.

Remy.

Aneryn's warm hand settled on Rua's forearm. "It's going to be okay," her friend murmured.

"Have you Seen that or are you just saying that to make me feel better?" Rua arched her eyebrow at Aneryn.

The blue witch grinned. "Does it matter?"

"Yes."

Aneryn pressed her lips together to keep from laughing. Rua knew the blue witch wouldn't tell her either way.

"Hale!" Talhan shouted, leaping from the still-moving carriage.

Her sister's fiancé was a tall, muscular fae with wavy hair a shade lighter than Rua's own. He had warm golden skin, even in the depths of winter. He looked older than the last time she had seen him. His stubbled face had grown longer, and he wore formal attire instead of battle leathers.

Hale braced for the impact with a smile as Talhan barreled into him. Their joyous embrace made Rua pause. She didn't know how to do that.

Rua recognized only a few faces in the crowd. The rest were strangers. They all watched her carriage with eager excitement that made her stomach cramp. She wondered for a moment if they could turn the carriage around, but it was too late.

"Go on." Bri nudged her with her boot.

Rua whirled on her and seethed. "Stop. Kicking. Me."

"Just go say hi to your sister." Bri's lips twisted up at her as she added, "Please."

Gritting her teeth, Rua rolled her shoulders back and puffed out her chest. It was time to be a princess.

Remy's face split into a warm smile as Rua stepped out of the carriage. All eyes turned toward her. Aneryn had tried to convince her to change into more formal clothing, but Rua still wore her woolen jacket dress and riding trousers with boots that came up to her knees. If Remy was displeased, she didn't show it.

Rua crossed the distance to Remy, careful not to slip on the icy paving stones. Her breath billowed out of her into the cold air. When she reached Remy, she dropped into a bow.

"Your Majesty," she greeted her sister formally.

Remy's hand shot out to her shoulder and pulled her up from the bow into an embrace. A collective sigh rang out from the crowd, a few even clapping. Rua woodenly moved her arms around her sister and gave her a quick pat on the back.

"It is so good to see you," Remy said, not releasing Rua from the hug.

"Okay, my turn." Bri's voice came from behind her.

Rua thanked the Gods for the Eagle in that moment as she cut off their awkward hug. Remy shifted to the fae warrior, wrapping her in a tight embrace. The two of them acted like old friends. It was a stark reminder once more that Bri was her sister's guard, not hers. Bri's allegiance was to Remy. She swallowed the bitter taste in her mouth. They all had each other.

"How was the ride?" Remy asked, beaming at her friend.

"Long," Bri said.

Remy looked back at her. Rua had no idea what to add to that statement.

"And cold," Rua replied, cringing at the monosyllabic conversation.

"Well, come inside and get warm then." Remy smiled with ease, gesturing to the castle behind her.

The crowds parted for their Queen as she led the way through the massive wooden doors. Rua walked a pace behind her. Remy made it look easy, summoning that calm confidence. How had she transformed into a ruler so quickly? Rua wondered if any of it was a show or if Remy really did take to sovereignty so gracefully. She thanked the Gods again that she was the younger sister, and it was not her leading the rebuilding of their court.

The scent of winter citrus and fresh paint greeted her as she stepped over the snowy threshold into the grand hall. The room echoed as they moved inside. It was barely furnished but still elegant from the few details that had been added. Slender braziers sat at the bottoms of each of the twelve travertine columns, and the coffered ceilings danced with flickering yellow light.

They crossed toward the dais at the far end of the room. Two redwood thrones were bathed in glowing light from a stained glass window high above, perfectly positioned to shine directly on the dais. Rua noted that the thrones were of equal size and stature, unusual for the reigning sovereign to give their consort an equally grand throne. Both seats were carved with the crest of the High Mountain Court. The wood was inlaid with golden detailing, each of the armrests ending in a constellation of rubies that matched the hilt of the Immortal Blade.

She was a part of this, she realized. The blade that sang to her blood was a part of this court.

She stepped onto the crimson rug that ran down from the thrones to the base of the stairs. Another ornate chair with scarlet upholstery sat to the left of the thrones. She blanched. Was that chair meant for her?

She felt Remy move to her side. Her sister was looking down at the gold-and-white marble that covered the steps to the dais. Rua's face heated. Her sister had reclaimed the marble from the castle at Drunehan. Rua stared harder at the gleaming marble, as if she could still see the bloodstains. Her parents had died on that marble, so had Renwick's father, Remy's guardian, and so many more.

"There wasn't enough to salvage the whole thing," Remy said. "Just the stairs. The Southern Court has donated the rest."

Rua's eyes followed the line of marble. It was only noticeable if one was looking for it, but the marble was a shade lighter off the stairs, the gold sparkling more. New marble for a new Queen.

It was such an eerie feeling to know she had stood in that exact spot before, though she had no memory of it. She felt like she should say something to her sister, but she had no idea what. Her words had to be emotive and meaningful. She had no idea how sisters were meant to behave. Did they just sit around and talk about their feelings?

Looking over to Remy, Rua found her sister staring at the throne, worrying her lip in the exact same way. Rua released her lip from her teeth.

"Greetings, Your Highness," a voice came from behind her.

Rua turned to see a silver-haired fae with icy blue eyes and golden-brown skin bowing to her.

"Hello, Bern."

Bern, her elder brother's Fated, would have been a King if Raffiel still lived. He looked much the same as he had last time, but his eyes looked hollow as the light in them had dimmed and the cheeky smile that normally played across his face was missing. Rua couldn't imagine what it must feel like to have lost his Fated.

"How have you been?" Bern asked, eyes dropping to her sword.

"Oh, you know, ridding the North of evil," Rua said, the muscle in her cheek twitching.

Bern snorted. "You've been spending too much time with Bri."

"How have you been?" Rua asked in a stilted voice, looking beyond him as the crowd filtered into the grand hall.

"Keeping busy." Bern gestured around the room.

Rua glanced up to the high ceilings. "I can't believe you've managed to do all this in such a short span of time."

"It was in large part to Her Majesty," Bern said, pulling Remy back into their conversation.

This courtier business was a dance. Conversation seemed like an art form harder than any other. Remy's hand lifted to the faintly glowing red stone around her neck: the amulet of Aelusien. Rua knew Remy and Hale had summited the Rotted Peak to acquire the High Mountain talisman, but she still hadn't heard the whole story. She knew if she asked, her sister would gladly share it, but she refrained.

"Yes, I can imagine the red witch magic helps a great deal," Rua said, rubbing her hands together to occupy them.

Remy toyed with the pendant hung along its golden chain. "It certainly helps, yes, but it's been the efforts of all the people who have made this dream into reality."

It was a very diplomatic answer. Her sister didn't seem to want to give too much credit to her talisman any more than Rua did the Immortal Blade.

Rua looked over Bern's shoulder and found Aneryn talking with an impossibly tall blond man. She furrowed her brow at him.

"You remember Fenrin?" Remy followed Rua's line of sight. "He is now the head brown witch for the High Mountain Court and one of my councilors."

"Your council?" Rua's eyes darted briefly back to Remy before looking at Aneryn. The blue witch smiled down at her hands, as if whatever Fenrin said had been deeply flattering. The brown witch had filled out since the last time Rua had seen him. He was still long and lithe, but not as gangly as before.

She didn't like that blushing grin on Aneryn's face. What were the two witches talking about?

"I have humans on my council too," Remy said, pulling Rua's focus back to her.

Rua forced herself to refrain from rolling her eyes. Wasn't her sister so considerate. Remy really was living up to their parents' legacy and more. She included all of Okrith in her city, her castle, and even her council. It made Rua nauseous, how perfect her sister seemed now. It made her feel even more unworthy to be a part of it.

A buzzing sensation lifted her eyes to the threshold of the throne room. Her heart stuttered. Silhouetted in golden sunlight stood Renwick, his green eyes hooked on Rua. She felt it like a living thread of power, that connection between their eyes. The rest of the room seemed to fade as she looked at him. He wore shined black leather boots and tucked-in trousers with silver embroidery up the outer seams, matching the crown atop his head. Rua's mouth fell open. It was not the simple circlet he usually wore, no—he was wearing a breathtaking crown. As the sapphires sparkled around its base, it was the first time Rua truly felt it: he was a King.

"I better go greet him," Remy murmured beside her. The voice of her sister snapped that thread. Yes, Remy would need to go speak with him. They were the crowns of two courts of Okrith.

She fought the urge to follow her sister. That undeniable pull was nothing but trouble. Instead, she found herself steering toward Aneryn.

She injected herself into the middle of the friendly conversation between the two witches.

Fenrin's blue eyes flitted to her, and his face split into a wide grin.

"Your Highness, it is so nice to finally meet you," he said, his blue eyes beaming at her. "I'm—"

"Fenrin, yes," Rua cut him off. She glanced at Aneryn in a look that promised they would be discussing this interaction later.

"What do you think of the palace?" Fenrin asked, then looking back to Aneryn, he added, "I helped with the design."

"Really? What parts did you design?" Aneryn's voice was an octave too high.

Rua shook her head. The two witches delved back into conversation, but at least Rua had subdued their enthusiasm slightly.

A tap on her shoulder had her turning. Bri stood behind her with a piece of white paper in her hands, passing it to Rua.

Elegant calligraphy scrolled down the page. It was written in Yexshiri. Rua could read it but still found herself grumbling, "What in the Gods' names is this?"

"It's your itinerary." Bri's voice dripped with sarcasm.

Eyes bulging at the list, Rua's mouth moved along with the words she read: temple visit, birthday, prayers, rehearsal, wedding, ball, dinner, council meeting. They had planned for the next two weeks down to the very minute. Her stomach dropped to her feet.

Bri nudged her shoulder. "Let's go see if they've stocked their wine cellar yet."

Rua looked back to her sister and Renwick as they spoke in tense conversation. She knew by Renwick's stillness that the words they exchanged were not pleasant, though they both wore fake smiles, their golden crowns glinting through the dappled sunlight.

"Don't you want to stay with your friends?" Rua didn't mean for her voice to come out as a snarl.

Bri's eyes were molten gold. "You're my friend too," she said, making Rua shift uncomfortably from foot to foot. "But wine and spirits are my best friends, so let's go find them."

She chuckled, tucking the itinerary into her pocket, and followed the Eagle into the belly of the castle.

# CHAPTER TWENTY-ONE

B ri had an uncanny ability to find the wine cellar, but they couldn't hide long before they were whisked away to another activity. They had a schedule to keep up with. Remy and Rua were to visit the Temple of Yexshire in the afternoon before dinner. It was the activity Rua was least looking forward to, and it was happening on the day they arrived.

Aneryn hooked her arm through Rua's as they waited for the entourage to assemble. The warm buzz of the wine in her veins evaporated against the cold air.

"At least you're coming with me," Rua muttered.

"I think they believe all witches can't wait to meet each other," Aneryn said with a chuckle. "I think they might be trying too hard."

Rua snorted. "They see you as equals, but they know nothing about you. How would they even know what that means?"

"I mean, I think your sister is trying too hard to impress you," Aneryn said. "She wants you to like it here."

The giant wood doors behind them opened again and Remy walked out, flanked by guards. Hale and Renwick walked, deep in conversation, behind her.

Rua's muscles tensed as she looked at Renwick, still in his finery, wearing his crown. Her entire body felt weightless when she looked at him, as if she might topple over. Was it the crown or the way he carried himself around the others? He seemed different in this light. It was strange to see the others engaging him, even if it was begrudgingly.

"Have fun with the witches," Hale said, giving Remy a kiss on her cheek. Rua's eyes tracked the movement. It was such an easy action, like he had done it a million times before.

"Fun?" Renwick cocked an eyebrow at Hale. His gaze slid to Rua, and she almost felt knocked over by it as his lips twisted into a smirk. "They don't know what your childhood was like then?"

"What?" Remy's eyes darted between Rua and Renwick.

"It's nothing," Rua said, shaking her head in reassurance. She had the urge to ram Renwick through with her dagger right then and there, muddling in their family's business.

"If you think it won't be a pleasant trip," Remy asked the Northern King, "then why did you request for your blue witch to accompany us?"

Rua's mouth dropped open for a split second. Renwick stood stiffly, staring at her sister, but Rua felt his attention on her. He was the one who requested for Aneryn to come with them? He seemed to know how much she disliked the red witches and how strained her relationship was with her sister. Did he know she'd feel better with Aneryn by her side?

"I requested it," Aneryn chimed in, rescuing Renwick from revealing his real intentions. "Shall we walk? It's beautiful and sunny today."

Rua wanted to kiss her. "Yes, I'd prefer walking to jostling in another carriage again," she added.

Remy furrowed her brow at the awaiting carriage. Polished and showy, it seemed hardly used. "I suppose so . . . We will have to cut the trip shorter in order to account for the time. Dinner will be just after sunset."

Rua leaned her shoulder into Aneryn. Thank the Gods for the blue witch.

Looking out over the forested valley and the white monolith of the Temple of Yexshire, Rua said, "Shall we then?"

"Well, you ladies have fun," Renwick farewelled. His voice was even, but Rua knew the sarcasm under that statement. Renwick looked at Hale as the two males turned back toward the grand entryway. "Care for a game of cards?"

"Don't even think about it," Remy cut in, raising her eyebrows at Hale. Remy looked at Rua with a shrug. "He's a terrible cardplayer."

Hale crossed the distance to Remy, arms encircling her waist and pulling her against him. "Is that an order from my Queen?" His lips skimmed across hers as he spoke.

Rua looked down at her hands. They were about to be married. She didn't know why she was so surprised. But to see them kissing while Renwick was there made her want to bury her head in the sand.

"Yes, it is an order." Remy gave Hale one last kiss and pushed on his chest. "Now, go find something useful to do. We have many more preparations before *our* wedding."

Hale cupped Remy's cheeks and pulled her back into a kiss, the promise of their wedding loosening his grip on control.

"Gods, you two are just as bad as that night in Ruttmore," Renwick jeered. "Not much of an act then, was it?"

What happened in Ruttmore? Her hands clenched at her sides. Even her sister had stories with these people before Rua knew them. Rua was the only one who didn't have a story, no shared memories.

Remy and Hale broke their kiss, and the two fae walked back inside. The guards waiting behind Remy stepped forward as she joined Aneryn and Rua. The soldiers weren't as heavily armored as they were in the Northern Court. They were probably much warmer for it, too, preferring fur-lined leathers over the cold bite of metal. Still, they looked lethal. It felt strange to Rua that Bri and Talhan weren't there. They weren't officially her guards, but they had acted like them during their time in the North. She wondered if they would want to stay in the High Mountain Court now that they had reunited with Hale.

Remy followed Rua's gaze to the shut doors of the grand hall.

"They'll be fine," Remy said. "They will probably go to the study and commiserate over whisky about their rotten fathers."

Rua finally met Remy's eyes, grinning. Gedwin Norwood, the former Eastern King, was not truly Hale's father, but he had claimed Hale as a son, hoping Hale's Fated bond with Remy would boost their king-dom's standing in Okrith. When Norwood presumed Remy was dead, he was eager to get rid of his would-be son too.

"Yes, I would say the two of them are tied for the most rotten fathers in all of Okrith." Rua chuckled.

She looked up into her sister's warm brown eyes, flecked with green. They were the same eyes Rua saw in the mirror every morning. It was a strange feeling. Her hair and skin were a shade lighter. She did not have Remy's perfect curls. Some of her brunette hair was wavy, others stubbornly straight. Rua didn't have Remy's physique and was several inches shorter. But their eyes were the same. Their mother's eyes.

Rua remembered what Gedwin Norwood had said about Remy that night in Drunehan: she was the spitting image of Rellia, their mother. A knot seized in Rua's throat as she looked at Remy. Part of her wanted to throw her arms around her sister, but she abstained, instead swal-lowing that lump and heading down the steep, icy hill to the Temple of Yexshire.

~

Even in the depths of winter, the beaming sun made Rua sweat in her fur-trimmed cloak. Her fine leathers and detailed tunic made her look more like a Queen's guard than a princess. She knew she would have to relent for Remy's wedding, but wearing a dress to see the witches was the last thing she wanted to do. The witches needed to see how fierce she had become. She was the wielder of the Immortal Blade now, not their ward.

Rua cursed the sunny weather and the thinning snow as they climbed the foothills of Mount Lyconides. The snowdrifts were small compared to the Northern Court, but they were crusted over with ice and dangerously slippery. Rays of warm sun melted the snow, only to be frozen over again as the nighttime temperatures plummeted. The wildness of the North was better, the snow fresh and deep, the sky a dark gray that matched the melancholy season.

The sunshine of Yexshire seemed to mock her as they reached the clearing through the forest. The base of the looming white temple appeared.

"Wow," Aneryn whispered by Rua's side.

They craned their necks up to the spire rising high above them. Blowing in the gentle breeze, red ribbons waved from its tallest peak. Rua clenched her jaw as she stared up at those ribbons silhouetted against the sun. Even in their camp in the hills, the witches had used red ribbons in their prayers. She had lost count of how many times she was forced to tie ribbons to the makeshift prayer pole in the center of their camp.

A voice jarred her from the memory.

"Greetings." Baba Morganna stood at the threshold of the white temple.

"Baba!" Remy called, happily. "How are you?"

"I am well, Little Sparrow." The High Priestess cast her arms out wide, beckoning them closer, as she slid her gaze to Rua. "Little Starling."

Rua's fingernails dug into her palms as she forced a smile at her nickname. She hadn't realized Remy had such a nickname too. She wondered if Baba Morganna had once given nicknames to her elder brothers.

"I called Raffiel, Little Hawk, and Rivitus, Little Rook," Morganna said, scanning Rua's face with a smile.

"Moon's tit, that is bizarre," Aneryn muttered. "A red witch with the gift of Sight."

Rua snorted as they followed Remy up the stairs. Rua realized they were all speaking Mhenbic. The witches' language flowed the easiest off her tongue. Remy, too, seemed the most fluent in Mhenbic. That notion grated against Rua. Their native language should be Yexshiri, yet here she and her sister were, speaking a language that wasn't of their people.

Her sister embraced Morganna in a warm hug, but Rua simply greeted the High Priestess of the red witches with a bob of her head.

Remy didn't know Morganna like Rua did. She probably still found Morganna's prophetic nonsense alluring. That warm, calm countenance probably seemed appealing to a newcomer, but Rua knew it was empty. Trying to find real emotions behind it was like trying to grab a handful of fog.

The High Priestess looked exactly the same. She had eyes like bronze medallions and light brown skin the same shade as Rua. Her hair carried the same wave as Rua's too, though the High Priestess's hair had aged to white. Deep smile lines denoted a happy visage that did not match the childhood that Rua had known. Smiles meant nothing if there wasn't anyone to hear her cries. The red witches only had tolerance for warmth and ferocity. Sadness reflected a lack of self-control and was ignored. Rua still carried the shame that she couldn't control her feelings as well as the others. Red witches were stern, wise, brave, and even lethal when it came to it, but they never showed sadness. She thought to the night in Drunehan when Baba Morganna was tossing armored Northern soldiers across the room like rag dolls. The High Priestess had been mighty, but her countenance had been even. Rua had wondered many times if the witches didn't feel things as deeply as she did, if there was something broken in her that made her feel more acutely. Regardless, Rua was only ever allowed to be happy, and if she couldn't be happy, then at least be silent. So Rua kept to herself most of her childhood.

Flowery aromas greeted them as they stepped onto the first floor of the Temple of Yexshire. The guards who had accompanied them on their hike waited at the footsteps of the temple. This was a witch sanctuary, not meant for fae soldiers. Rua placed her hand on the hilt of the Immortal Blade as she stepped into the foyer.

As they followed the round walls to the right, a prayer room appeared. Bouquets of dried flowers were spread across long, curving tables, edging the outer walls. An aisle bisected the room, stretching up to a blue glass window depicting the phases of the moon. Rows of wooden benches sat on either side of the aisle, completing the simple room.

Rua heard the voices waiting as they followed Morganna up a second set of stairs. Chunky white candles peppered the steps, casting light across the white stone. A crowd of red witches greeted them. The second floor seemed to be an informal assembly hall. Chairs and tables had been pushed to the far walls to accommodate the flock of witches.

The entire room froze for a moment, all eyes darting to Rua. Not to her face, but to the magical sword on her hip, its magic pulsing like a beacon to them. One by one the spell broke, and they began to move again, but Rua knew they marked her.

Her eyes scanned the throng, recognizing many of the faces. But there were many more now, too, ones that did not grow up in the witch camps. Were they red witches who had fled outside Yexshire? Every few months in their camps, another red witch would find them. Baba Morganna knew she couldn't use her Sight to find the witches directly, but she could search for any fae who may have encountered one. The High Priestess made Rua communicate through fae fire with Bern for many years, even before she knew he was Raffiel's Fated. Bern had been working to ferry red witches into their camp for as long as she could remember. The numbers of witches being found dwindled as the years passed. By the time Rua was a teenager, she thought there were no more left. But here, standing before her, was a crowd of red witches double the size of their camp. However they managed to stay so well hidden for fourteen years, Rua admired them for it.

Remy seemed prepared to absorb the witches' admiring stares, but to Rua they felt irritating. Remy broke off from Rua and Aneryn to mingle in the crowd. Two female witches, a few years older than Rua, approached.

Brigetta and Thalia were their names. They had always sneered at Rua, snickering about her behind her back, but now advanced with the same fake, wizened smiles that were so praised growing up.

"Rua!" They bounced over to her as she felt Aneryn step an inch closer.

"I mean, Your Highness," Thalia added, dropping into a quick bow, her mousy-brown hair falling into her eyes. "How are you?"

"I am well," Rua said in a clipped tone, frowning back at them. "And you?"

"We are splendid!" Brigetta giggled. Rua lifted her chin to peer up into Brigetta's stony blue eyes. Whatever smile played across the red witch's face, her eyes were still as cold as Rua had remembered. "The temple is so grand, isn't it? We each have our own room! It feels so strange not to be in a tent in the woods anymore."

Brigetta had been at the camps with her father. Thalia, an orphan, arrived with the help of Bern when Rua was ten. Both of them had lived most of their lives outdoors. She imagined a stone temple would feel strange.

Thalia's eyes drifted down to the Immortal Blade. Her voice was an awed whisper as she said, "The sword of power."

"I can feel its magic from here. My whole body is shaking," Brigetta said. "It feels much like your sister's amulet."

Rua found Remy standing in a circle of elder witches, wearing a wide grin as she gossiped to them. Her sister toyed with the amulet around her neck.

"Can we touch it?" Thalia asked.

"No," Rua and Aneryn said in unison.

The red witches skimmed their eyes over Aneryn. Ah, there it was, that same disgust they used to look at Rua with.

"So you're a blue witch?" Brigetta cocked her head at Aneryn. "You don't look like the other blue witches."

Thalia snickered. "You've got hair and eyes for starters."

They said it like Aneryn should laugh, *laugh*, at the memory of her coven being tortured.

"I can't believe you grew up with these people. They're awful," Aneryn said to Rua without blinking.

Rua chuckled as Brigetta and Thalia paled.

"Girls," the voice of Baba Morganna said behind them, "why don't you go get some drinks? I'd like to speak to Her Highness for a moment."

The red witches' faces blanketed back over into that practiced mask, and they bobbed in hasty bows to Rua before they left.

Rua's eyes dropped to the linen satchel Baba Morganna held in her hands. She instantly recognized the bag as her own.

"I thought you might like this, Little Starling," Baba Morganna said, handing her the bag. "I brought it from the witch camps with us when we moved into the temple."

Rua rubbed her fingers over the fabric, feeling the weight of her books inside.

"Thank you," she murmured.

"You are on a better journey now," Baba Morganna said, dropping her gaze to the Immortal Blade.

Remy came back to join the conversation, seeming even more buoyant. "Shall we take a tour around the temple?"

"Delightful," Rua said through gritted teeth.

Aneryn leaned against her in a silent command to behave. "Sounds fun."

Smile faltering, Remy looked between Rua and Aneryn. Rua could tell her sister was trying to decide if they were being genuine or sarcastic.

"Whispers travel farther on ice than water," Baba Morganna mused.

"What does that even mean?" Aneryn muttered to Rua.

Rua bit her lip to keep from laughing. The things the High Priestess said only meant something to good people . . . people like Remy. Rua had no such hope. What good did all that blind optimism do for them, anyway? It wasn't really optimism. It was stifled bitterness, repressed feelings hiding behind neutral faces. She couldn't believe Remy couldn't see it.

When Rua was really hurting, when she really needed comfort, they had turned a blind eye to her or would give her meaningless mottos about bubbles on the water or wind in the trees. Fuck their water and wind. They would all realize that their foundation was built on nothing but denial and wishy-washy proverbs.

Aneryn pressed harder into Rua's side. She stowed away all the ridiculousness of the trip so that they could blather about it later. She thanked the Gods again that Aneryn had accompanied her. The trip would have been unbearable without her there. She gave silent, begrudging thanks to the Northern King, who had requested it. She thought back to Renwick standing before the High Mountain palace in his gleaming silver crown. The power that radiated off him had made Rua gape. It shifted something in her to see him that way, to see him the way the rest of the world saw him, with fear and awe. He had let her peek beyond that elegant finery. She might be one of the only people who he let see him for all he truly was.

Rua followed Morganna stiffly through the tour of the temple, but her mind stayed fixed on one person alone. With each step up the white stone stairs, her mind flashed images of emerald eyes and ash-blond hair.

～

Her legs ached from the climb up the tower steps. They ascended to the very top of the temple, past numerous floors of dormitories and dwellings. The library was not just a room, but the entire floor, filled with dusty shelves and leather-bound books. In the center was a modest wood table and a mishmash of chairs assembled on a threadbare rug.

Rua peered out the window. Across the valley, on the mountain parallel to them, was the Castle of Yexshire. The palace glowed with warmth, the sun glinting off the gilded windows. Past the valley of trees, the city of Yexshire sprawled through the foothills of the High Mountains, thin trails of smoke rising from the city.

Aneryn clutched Rua's forearm as she peered down the open window to the ground far below.

Her hands trembled. "We shouldn't be this high."

Rua chuckled as Aneryn gripped her arm harder, like the talons of a hawk. "This temple has been here for hundreds of years, Aneryn. You're safe."

"Then why do I feel like I might fling myself over the edge?" she muttered.

"You're in a temple full of witches with the power to animate objects," Rua reassured her. "I'm sure someone would slow your fall."

"Great, thanks," Aneryn gritted out.

"It's a beautiful view, is it not?" Baba Morganna's voice carried across the library. "To see your home court rebuilt?"

"Yes," Rua said tightly.

She turned toward the High Priestess. Remy had broken off from the tour to visit with a few of the witchlings, her Queenly duties coming to her with ease. A thought flashed through Rua's mind: perhaps she didn't do it because she was the Queen; perhaps she genuinely cared. Rua's frown deepened as she moved down the stacks.

Her eyes skimmed the spines up and down. "I'm looking for a book."

"An encyclopedia?" Baba Morganna said warmly, making Rua cringe.

"No." Rua's fingers traced across the shelf. "I am looking for the spell book the blue witches gave you."

Baba Morganna's brow crinkled. "I know of no such book."

Aneryn whirled to the High Priestess as Rua's mouth dropped open. "What?"

"We have some ancient red witch spell books that survived the Siege of Yexshire . . . I don't think the looters knew what they were—"

"The blue witches said they gave you the book," Rua cut in, anger burning up her neck.

"I have only spoken to Baba Airu once through candlelight," Morganna said, looking up as if trying to remember another conversation. "She did not tell me about a book."

Clenching her fists to keep herself from attacking the bookshelf, Rua hissed, "They lied to me."

The High Priestess folded her hands together. "I am sorry they did not trust you, Little Starling." She took a step closer. "They have suffered terrible things. To put their sacred book in the hands of a fae must be terrifying to them."

"I need that book to break a curse," Rua said, trying to breathe away her simmering rage. "I am trying to help."

Aneryn stepped to her side. "Can we look at your spell books?" she asked Baba Morganna. Her Mhenbic was too flowing, her words rolling into each other the way they spoke in Ific, the witch sounding more like a fae. "Maybe the spells are similar enough."

"Of course." The High Priestess pulled three heavy tomes from the shelves and laid them on the table. "But the spells of each coven are unique. You will need the exact words used in casting the curse to break it."

Rua was about to shout more curses when Aneryn said, "It is still worth a look." She took a seat in front of the books and opened the first one, glancing up to the High Priestess. "Thank you for your help, Baba. Would it be all right if we looked these over for a bit?"

"Of course," Baba Morganna said. "That concludes the tour, anyway." Her eyes flitted to Rua. "I hope you enjoyed seeing how well the coven is doing here."

"It's lovely," Rua said in a clipped tone.

Baba Morganna's eyes saddened even as she smiled. "We tried to be a home for you, Little Starling." Rua's eyes snapped up, staring at the High Priestess. "I'm sorry we failed you. We were foxes trying to raise a wolf." Her eyes crinkled. "I hope with time it won't feel so painful to visit here."

Rua stooped into her chair, pressing her lips together as she nodded at the High Priestess. The knot in her throat thickened. The Baba had Seen it all. She had known how hard it was for Rua to grow up with them. They had tried, and they had failed . . . and Rua didn't know what to do with that. Guilt churned in her gut. They did the best they could for her, and it wasn't enough. She knew she should feel gratitude to the woman who raised her, instead of spite.

As Baba Morganna left, Rua stared at the book in front of her with unseeing eyes, the memories of her childhood flashing through her mind. More than any image, she felt the constant sting of loneliness, of otherness—the bud of that darkness that bloomed within her now. She was a wolf raised by foxes.

Aneryn reached over and opened the book in front of her. "I would ask if you are okay, but I know you're not."

"I should be, though," Rua muttered.

"When I was given to Renwick," Aneryn said, drawing Rua's eyes to her. "The other witches hated me for it—that I could grow my powers through my own determination and not under knives and flames. I was spared, and they detested me." She flipped through the yellowing pages. "The fae treated me like a dog. Were it not for Renwick, I'm sure it would have been worse. Still, they spit on me and shoved me when he wasn't looking. I feared being alone with any one of them. I feared everything."

"I'm sorry," Rua whispered, heat filling her face as the pressure grew behind her eyes. She took a deep breath, forcing away the tears.

"It doesn't make the anger any easier to bear," she said.

"What doesn't?"

The blue witch looked up at her, eyes filling with a shared pain. "Having no one to direct it toward."

"I can direct it toward Balorn," Rua hissed, flipping through the spell book. She couldn't see any curses. They were simple protection spells, wardings, and cleansing rituals, but nothing about a curse that controlled a witch's mind.

"Balorn isn't the cause of your pain, Ru," Aneryn said, shutting the heavy book and grabbing the next one.

"I know," Rua muttered, slamming the book closed and pinching the bridge of her nose. "But it will still feel good to kill him."

Aneryn smirked, tracing her finger down the browning pages. "I've never seen a violet witch book before."

Rua leaned over, examining the page. Drawings of flowers and herbs were etched in the margins along with scribbled notes. The Mhenbic words at the top read: Drowning on Land. "A suffocation spell."

"Gods, I thought they just made perfumes and candles," Aneryn whispered, flipping through the pages of curses and hexes, all sorts of ailments written below her fingertips. "They were rather vicious for people who like drawing purple flowers on everything." She chuckled, shutting the book. "But it won't help us break the curse. We need the blue witches' spell book."

"The path to Raevenport is blocked now." Rua thought about the avalanche she triggered, that thick guilt roiling inside her. "It will take days to trek back there."

"I will go with you," Aneryn offered. "Not that they will listen to me, either. I think they dislike me even more than you."

Rua leaned against her friend. "Abhorred by witches and fae alike." She grinned conspiratorially to Aneryn.

"We should make badges," Aneryn said as she chuckled.

What an odd pair they were. The pain of the memories didn't ease, but at least she wasn't alone in them anymore.

# CHAPTER TWENTY-TWO

The red witches watched as Rua knelt before them. The sun beamed pleasantly through the windows, lighting the Temple of Yexshire's white stones. Body shaking so violently she thought she might topple over, she choked on her heartbeat as it slammed up her throat. She braced for the impact of the sword, waiting for the metal to bite into her neck. She knew it would be any second. Warm liquid streamed down her legs as her bladder released. Praying it would be swift, Rua peered up at the witches with watery eyes. They wore tranquil smiles as they waited for her execution.

Rua bolted upright, heaving drags of air. Her heartbeat thrummed along every nerve like a war drum. She stared into the darkness of the room, her fae eyes making out the shapes of the furniture by the moonlight peeping through the heavy curtains.

She was in the Castle of Yexshire.

It should have brought her comfort, this location. Below the new stone and hasty decorations, lay the ruins of her once home. She was born here. All her ancestors before her were born here too. The shadows crept in on her. This was where her parents and Rivitus were killed, along with all the royal members of their court.

Of course, she should find no comfort from her haunted dreams here.

Remembering her nightmare, she pulled back the blankets, sensing the warm liquid between her thighs. Sighing, she saw the telltale sign of blood on the sheets. She had lost track of her cycles in the travel to Yexshire. Quickly doing the math, she nodded. Right on time.

Rolling out of bed to avoid smudging the white sheets further, she waddled to the bathing chamber to wash herself. The room was well appointed for her arrival. She found a rag and began washing the scarlet rivulets down her legs.

She didn't know how the humans did this every month. She thanked the Gods that fae bled only once a season. Pushing away the images of those serene witch faces, Rua hunted through the cabinets for something to wear.

Hands snagging on soft black satin, she pulled out a stack of undergarments.

"What in the name of the Fates . . . ," she muttered, flipping the items over in her hands.

They appeared like any other undergarment from the outside, but the inside had a thick lining sewn in. It reminded her of the fabric strips the witches affixed to their briefs. But these were a fine material, the lining not as bulky.

An unburdened thought swept into her mind: Did they know she was going to be cycling during her visit? Or did they always leave menstrual undergarments stashed in the cupboards for their guests?

It was a question she knew would go unanswered. Mother Moon would fall from the sky before Rua asked Remy about it.

She donned the garment, regardless. It was surprisingly comfortable, far better than the rags and strips of fabric she normally used. She hunted through the wardrobe for another nightdress. Glancing over to the bloodstained sheets, she wondered if she should call for some new ones. It was what a princess would do . . . Rua debated climbing back in bed on the other side and just avoiding the stains until morning, but she couldn't bring herself to let the stain set and ruin the expensive sheets.

Her shoulders slumped as she stripped the bed and brought the bundle of fabric to the elegant marble tub. Her body felt more weary with every step. It was still evening, judging by the moon. She must have only just fallen asleep.

By the time the sheets were soaking in the ice-cold water of the tub, Rua was wide awake and hungry. She grabbed a tunic and trousers, hastily dressing and leaving the room.

As she ambled into the hallway, the torchlight revealed she had chosen a lavender tunic and cream-colored trousers. Rua fumed—the absolute worst color to wear during her cycle. The lavender annoyed her too. She would have never selected the color for herself, but she also couldn't be bothered lighting her candles so she only had herself to blame. She prayed she would not run into anyone as she went hunting for the kitchens.

As her bare feet slapped against the cool stone, she plunged deeper into the palace. The hallways seemed ancient, as if the stones were placed over many years and not weeks, the everlasting quality so at odds with the newness of the freshly painted portraits and newly woven tapestries that lined the halls. It was a true feat, one of many, Rua hoped, that showed what the High Mountain Court could achieve.

A figure turned the corner, nearly colliding into her. Rua jolted backward as Aneryn laughed.

"I didn't mean to scare you," the blue witch said, steadying Rua with her hands on her forearms. "I thought I'd spare you getting lost on the way to the kitchens." Aneryn paused, looking over Rua's attire. "Though I did not spare you from selecting that outfit."

"I didn't think I would run into anyone," Rua groused. She had planned to snag a loaf of bread and hurry back to her room, sleeping on the elegant couch until the maids arrived in the morning.

Aneryn looped her arm with Rua's. "I couldn't sleep. Spending days in those bloody carriages has made me restless." She looked up to Rua as she steered her down a hallway to the left. Rua wouldn't have thought to turn that way, the opposite direction to the wine cellar she had found with Bri. She was thankful the blue witch had saved her once again from getting lost. "I like this palace; its warmer than the others."

They descended a spiraling set of stone steps. "You've been to the others?"

"Now that we've come here, I can say I've been to every court in Okrith." Aneryn puffed up her chest at the accomplishment. "The Southern Court has the best food, and the Western Court has the most detailed decor, but this place feels like something entirely new," she said, surveying the tall mirrors hanging from the walls.

Rua could feel it too—an excitement in the air. The castle looked much like what one would expect but the place was charged with possibilities, a blank canvas ready to paint a new world onto it.

"What do you think the palace in Murreneir will look like?" Rua found herself wondering out loud. She knew, just like Renwick, it would be beautiful and immaculate, detailed down to the last painted ceiling and bronzed door handle. Cheeks heating, she quickly added, "It doesn't matter."

It was silent as they tiptoed down the halls, sinking into the belly of the castle. The smell of dried herbs and yeast guided them.

Candlelight flickered through the open doorway up ahead, and the two of them halted. Two feminine voices chattered. One of them she recognized as Bri.

"Does she spend every night wooing ladies?" Rua whispered to Aneryn as her friend grinned. "Who is with her?"

"I don't know," Aneryn muttered back. "I can See through the future, not through walls."

The scuffle of footsteps sounded behind them, and, with a giggle, they ducked into the nearest doorway. Eyes adjusting to the dimness, she peered into the root cellar. Crates of covered potatoes lined the floors. The shelves were stocked with pickled vegetables, and braided strands of onions hung from the ceilings.

As they moved deeper into the cold cellar, the door behind them opened and a wide figure holding a candle silhouetted the threshold. She clearly hadn't shut the door quietly enough.

Talhan.

"What are you two doing in here?" He smiled, lifting his candle to survey the room.

"Oh, we, um . . . were hungry," Rua said, making Aneryn titter.

"For onions?"

Talhan stepped into the room. Before he could shut the door behind him, a hand pushed it back open. Bri stood with another female fae. Rua recognized her long blond braid from the melee at Drunehan. This must be Carys. So Bri wasn't wooing females after all. The Eagles had been incessantly pestering Remy for updates of Carys's arrival from the East.

Bri held a bottle of wine in each hand, Carys holding a tray of breads and cheeses, as they stepped into the room.

"Is this where we're gathering tonight?" Bri asked, sitting on the cold stone floor. She bobbed her head in greeting to Aneryn and Rua as if it weren't odd to find them amongst the crates of potatoes. Carys joined Bri with a shrug, leaning her back against the opposite shelves as she placed the tray of food between them.

The blond warrior extended a hand out to Rua. "I'm Carys, Your Highness."

"Just Rua," she replied, shaking her hand and tentatively sitting down beside her.

Carys reached over to Aneryn and shook her hand as well.

"I did not See this," Aneryn murmured beside Rua as she wedged herself up against the shelf of pickled vegetables.

Rua chuckled. Hunger made her stomach rumble and the three fae blocked her exit down the narrow aisle, so she decided to stay. Bri's eyes swept over Rua's attire, quirking her brow.

Rua scowled. "I got dressed in the dark."

"Clearly." Bri took a sip from one bottle of wine while passing the other to Rua.

The cool maroon liquid burned down her throat as Rua took a long swig. She felt the warmth spreading down her arms and up her neck.

"What have you been talking about?" Talhan asked his twin.

"Carys has been regaling me with the ministrations of the Eastern Court," Bri said.

"You are just like your brother." Carys huffed. "I'm sorry you find council meetings so boring. Maybe you shouldn't compete for the crown if you find them so tedious."

Talhan flashed a foxlike grin. "You're just trying to get rid of the competition."

"Hardly." Carys snatched the bottle of wine from Bri. "With you two there, it'll prove, without a doubt, that I am the best candidate."

Rua noted the strange lilt to Carys's voice as they all laughed. She didn't have an Eastern Court accent. Her words rose up at the end like they did in the South, and yet, she was as fair as any Northern fae she could think of. Rua narrowed her eyes at the warrior, as if she could discern her heritage from squinting alone.

"You're all competing in the Eastern games?" Rua asked, looking at the three friends, who all nodded in unison.

She had only heard murmurings about the competition for the crown of the Eastern Court. It made sense that the Eagles would want to participate, but Rua felt the sting of their future departure all the same. She knew it would be fleeting, whatever this sort of friendship was.

"What will this competition entail?" Rua passed Talhan the bottle of wine. These three were friends and Rua felt like an intruder.

"Fighting and feats of strength." Bri's teeth gleamed.

Carys rolled her eyes. "Not just that. There will also be written examinations, interviews, public speaking ... They want to know what plans the candidate has for the Eastern Court and why they think they would be the best to fulfill them." She glanced between the Eagles. "That is the most important part."

Talhan shrugged. "But there *will* be sparring."

"Are you designing these tests?" Rua's eyes scanned the beautiful blond.

"No. I can't, if I want to compete. I'm just helping organize the council," Carys said. "The council will select the tasks, and ultimately, the people of the Eastern Court will vote."

Rua's hands stilled as she reached for a piece of cheese. She had never heard of such a thing. It stood to reason that the people would choose their ruler. The humans elected their local officials. The High Priestesses of the witch covens selected their successors ... but the fae only concerned themselves with blood bonds and birthrights.

"Have you Seen who wins?" Talhan asked Aneryn.

"Perhaps." Aneryn grinned, accepting the handful of dried fruit Rua passed her.

"Ooh, so mysterious." Talhan waggled his fingers at her. "I bet you wouldn't tell us, even if you knew."

Aneryn lifted her chin, clearly used to fielding these questions. "You are correct."

The shadow of footsteps passed from under the cellar door, pausing at the doorframe. The door squeaked open again, and Remy peeked in.

"What in the Gods' names are you doing in the cellar?" Her eyebrows shot up.

"We're drinking." Talhan gestured to the others. "What are *you* doing down here?"

Remy pushed back her tousled black curls. "I was hungry."

"I bet you were." Carys chortled.

Rua's eyes scanned Remy's bare feet, thick robe, and flushed cheeks. The musk of Hale was still on her sister. She was certain the other fae could scent it, too, judging by their mocking grins.

With a shake of her head, Remy sat next to Talhan and grabbed the bottle of wine from his hands.

"I'm so glad I busted my hide making those Godsdamned sitting rooms, only for you all to be sitting in the cellar," she muttered around the opening of the bottle.

"Oh, come on," Talhan said, leaning into her. "It's just like old times in Lavender Hall."

Rua frowned—yet another reference she didn't understand.

"We have my birthday party tomorrow. We can't get rip-roaring drunk tonight," Remy warned them. They all laughed like she was telling a joke.

"You have to receive your guests, but we have to do no such thing," Carys said, eyes twinkling. "The woes of being regent."

Bri winked at Remy. "You know we can hold our liquor."

"Don't worry, we can always prop her up and put a floppy hat on her so she can sleep in the corner." Talhan tilted his head to Rua.

"Please." Rua snorted, taking another long swig. This was water compared to the witches' moonshine. "I could drink you all under the table."

The Eagle's golden eyes lit up. "Challenge accepted."

Rua took another long swig of wine, wiping her mouth with the back of her hand as Talhan snickered.

"What will you do if you don't win the crown?" Rua asked.

"Come back here where they belong," Remy said, nudging Carys with her elbow. Carys seemed to know that nudge meant to pass the food, and Remy snatched up a giant handful of crackers and cheese, plopping them in the bunched fabric of her lap.

As if the last hold on decorum was broken, everyone launched themselves at the food platter, grabbing handfuls of charcuterie.

Remy leaned back to speak to Rua and said, "They're a pack of wolves, this lot." She chuckled as she shoved another cracker into her cheek. "You better grab some now."

Narrowing her eyes at her sister, Rua didn't move. Gone was the Queenly perfection that she had seen that morning. With mouthfuls of cheese and an oversized robe, Remy seemed far less intimidating than the regal persona that came to her so naturally.

"How do you ever eat with them around?" Rua asked, making Remy cover her mouth to laugh.

"Quickly," Remy replied, biting into another cracker.

"We're going to need more food," Talhan said.

"And more wine," Bri added, snatching the bottle back from her brother.

"Your wish is my command." A deep laugh sounded from the door-frame and Rua looked up past the others to spot Hale, the necks of two more bottles clenched in one hand and a tray of food in the other. His clothes were disheveled, trousers wrinkled, and shirt unbuttoned to the navel as if he had hastily dressed.

"You're a bloodhound for debauchery," Carys said, reaching up to take the tray from him.

He squeezed in beside Remy, wrapping his arm around her and pulling her into his lap. His lips lingered against her skin as he kissed her temple. It was such nonchalant affection, making Rua's stomach clench.

"You mentioned drinking under the table?" Bri asked, passing Rua a fresh bottle of wine and pulling her from staring at her sister.

"I'd be careful," Aneryn said, wiping the cocky grin off Bri's face. "I have Seen what she can do."

"You two are a scary pair," Talhan slurred, already succumbing to the potency of the wine.

"You have no idea." Rua laughed, wrapping her arm around her friend. She lifted the bottle back to her lips, gulping back the burning liquid to the last drop and wiping her mouth on her shoulder. Bri began slow-clapping as Talhan gawked.

Carys touched her boot to Remy's as she tipped her head to Rua. "She's definitely one of us, Rem."

~

Colorful beads hung from the windows, casting rainbows of light across the bright room. Rua glowered up at a string of paper snowflakes. Who had cut these all out? Remy's birthday party was held in a small reception room, one of the few rooms in the castle that seemed fully furnished. A long table bisected the room laden with food and presents. Seating areas of burgundy, satin furniture were arranged on the right side, the bright sun beaming down on the seated guests. To the left ran a bookshelf along the entire wall. An assembly of well-wishers stood, drinks in hand, nattering away. The voices in the echoing room made Rua's head throb, an invisible force squeezing her temples. She had too much to drink the night before. They all did. Now it was just a competition to see who could hide it the best. Smoothing her hands down her flint-gray dress, she absconded to the darkest corner.

It seemed so strange for everyone to be dressed in light pastels in the depths of winter. The person she found sitting in the shadows, tucked between two bookshelves, seemed to agree. They wore a black velvet jacket and charcoal-gray trousers; their thick black lashes under hooded eyes peered down at a thick book in their hands. They had dark umber skin, thick black eyebrows framing their face. Wearing delicate golden rings on their fingers and golden cuffs at the top of their ears, they had an androgynous mixture of attire.

This must be Neelo Emberspear, Heir of Saxbridge, and future ruler of the Southern Court.

Rua slumped into the chair beside Neelo, her body aching. Resting her chin grumpily in her hand, she wished she were back in her chambers. She just wanted to lie in bed all day in nothing but the underwear that she now was convinced was made with some kind of witch magic. She didn't know if she was meant to keep them or not . . . but they would be going back north with her, regardless.

Morosely staring across the room, her eyes flitted to Remy and Hale, standing beside the table. His arm was firmly fixed around her waist as they greeted their guests. It was as if he couldn't bear to not be touching her, even as they navigated around the room. Her sister looked stunning in a mint-colored gown, her black hair flowing over her shoulders, her gold-and-ruby crown making her posture even more straight. Her radiance made bile rise up Rua's throat.

The Eagles and Carys crowded around the finger food, chuckling in conversation, concealing the effects of the many bottles of drink they had consumed in that root cellar. Rua's eyes landed at last to the far corner of the room. The spectrums of light glinted off the silver crown atop ash-blond hair. Renwick was deep in conversation with three elderly fae. Heavy brows fell over his eyes, his expression as sharp as a dagger, and yet, he still blended in perfectly in the crowd. He was meant to be there, confidently interacting with the highest tier of society, as he had done since birth. Rua's gut tightened. She didn't belong there. She had the manners of a tavern wench, the accent of a country witch, and the temper of a street fighter. She was no Yexshiri princess.

A heavy book thudded into Rua's lap. She looked down at the blue dragon breathing flames across the cover.

"You don't have to read it," Neelo said, looking up from their book. "But sitting with your face in your hands like that is going to invite people over to cheer you up."

Rua quirked her eyebrow at the heir. It was a good point. Opening the book to the middle, she rested it on her lap, praying no one would come over to speak with her.

Neelo didn't say another word, equally welcoming of the silence.

Many minutes stretched by as Rua and Neelo shut out the world around them. The bright colors, boisterous sounds, and honeyed smells all assaulted her senses. Crowd quieting, Hale raised a glass to his fiancée, Fated, and Queen. His words were beautiful drivel that had Remy's eyes welling with tears. The crowd cheered as the two kissed. Neelo and Rua rolled their eyes in unison. The heir snorted and smirked at Rua, a begrudging compliment, though it did not meet their eyes. Rua was glad she wasn't the only one who thought this whole thing was ridiculous.

Remy accepted the songs and praise with grace, looking ever the Queen as she blew out her birthday candles. She was one year older than Rua once more. Only one year. Yet she was so accomplished—the ruler of a kingdom, the future hope of their people, and she made it all look easy. Rua gritted her teeth as she watched her sister thread her fingers through her Fated's hand. Rua knew she should be happy for her sister, she wanted to be happy for her . . . she just wanted to be happy from far away in the North, not confronted with all this merriment.

Realizing someone loomed over her, Rua looked up to see the back of Bri's pewter jacket. The warrior was turned from her, speaking in a low voice to another fae. The female Bri spoke with was equal parts handsome and beautiful, with dark copper skin and short coils of onyx hair.

"I am serious, Delta, you need to speak with Abalina, make her confront the Queen," Bri hissed.

So this was Delta Thorne, niece of the Queen and one of Princess Abalina's personal guards.

"I have tried," Delta snarled in a low Western accent, her words a biting staccato. "They won't listen to me. It is *you* who should be the one convincing them."

"I am not going back to the West."

"You returned west to find your *Queen*," Delta growled as she eyed Remy.

"I was glamoured as a human for most of the time," Bri retorted. "We stuck to the backcountry and left as quickly as we came. I am not going to Swifthill."

"Your people need you."

"They are not my people," Bri snapped. "They never were."

Delta's eyes went wide, her thick muscular frame coiled as if she might lash out at Bri. These two were formidable warriors, sparring like two mountain cats. Rua wasn't sure which one would win in a fight. They appeared equally lethal.

Delta's bronze eyes, the same shade as Bri's jacket, narrowed. "I see."

"Delta—" Bri started, but Delta was already walking away.

"You're a Westerner?" Rua asked, startling Bri, who spun that violent golden gaze to her.

"It's complicated." She cracked her knuckles.

Neelo huffed, sliding a bookmark into their thick book and glancing at Bri. "It is not that complicated. There was a prophecy that you would take the Western Court throne, and so the Western Queen exiled your parents when you and Tal were newborns."

Bri scowled. "When you say it like that . . ."

"What?" Rua's mouth fell open, eyes darting to the Eagle. "When were you going to tell me this?"

"It's an old story." Bri rubbed the back of her neck. "And the prophecy was: The Eagles are born—Briata will seize the crown from its sovereign. Whatever that means. It was a prophecy told to the Queen by her blue witch oracles on the day of our birth."

"How will you steal the crown from her?"

"I won't," Bri said, picking at her thumbnail. "The Queen changed that prophecy the moment she kicked my parents out of her kingdom."

"Mm-hmm," Neelo hummed.

"Don't start with me too, Neelo," Bri grumbled as if the monosyllabic heir would suddenly launch into a tirade.

Rua swept her eyes over the Eagle, tracing over her golden-brown skin. "You don't look Western."

Bri pinched the bridge of her nose and let out a long-suffering sigh. "That's because I'm no more Western than Carys is Southern."

"She *is* Southern," Neelo interjected, eyes drifting to the blond warrior talking to Talhan around a food tray. "She was raised in the South. We claim her."

Bri kept her stare fixed on Rua. "My father was Eastern, my mother was Yexshiri."

Rua's eyebrows shot up. "You are part Yexshiri? Why didn't you tell me?"

Neelo crossed their legs and leaned forward, as if waiting for the best part of the story.

An apologetic look crossed Bri's face. "I haven't told Remy, either," she said. "Your sister knows about the prophecy, but not that Tal and I are part Yexshiri . . . When my parents were banished from the West, they tried to flee to Yexshire . . . and your parents refused to grant them asylum."

A hammering pulsed in Rua's ears. "Why?"

"They didn't want trouble with the West. They feared the prophecy might refer to another crown—their crown."

Rua fisted her hands together in her lap. All the stories she had heard of Rellia and Vigo Dammacus were painted as them being fair and generous sovereigns. Of course, all the stories she had ever heard were from people who resided in the High Mountain Court. Rua's thoughts spiraled. Were her parents not the people she once thought?

Another even more troubling thought crossed her mind: "My parents wouldn't take your family in, but Gedwin Norwood did?"

"The Eastern King wasn't troubled by the prophecy. He didn't believe it pertained to him. My parents folded into his slimy court with ease." Bri clearly had a similar feeling toward her parents as Rua did her own at that moment. "Gedwin Norwood thought that I might fulfill the prophecy, ruling the West."

"How convenient for him," Neelo said, glancing sideways at Bri, "that he embraced your parents so warmly, the parents of a future Queen."

"His plotting was endless." Bri shifted her shoulders as if stretching a muscle. "Lot of good it did him."

Remy stepped up to the three of them, abruptly cutting off their whispered conversation.

"Your Highness," Remy said with a slight curtsy to Neelo.

"Your Majesty." Neelo dipped their head.

"Goddess of Death, strike me down, can we stop with the titles?" Bri snarled, clearly still frustrated with the previous conversation. At the look on Remy's face, Bri added, "I mean, we've known each other forever."

"I haven't," Rua said, drawing the eyes of the other three. She stretched up, rising off her chair. "I think I need some refreshments."

Her sister opened her mouth as if to say something more, but Rua pushed past her.

"Pleasure," Neelo called after her.

"Same," Rua said, matching that dry tone.

Rua wanted to know what that conversation between Bri and Delta was about. She wanted to know what her parents were truly like too. But she had no idea how to ask those questions.

Beaming sunlight attacked her as she ambled to the drinks table. Stomach threatening to rebel, she squinted against the glare. Her pulse had ratcheted up into her throat. Blackness clouded the periphery of her vision, a flush of heat blanketing her skin. She needed to get out of this place. She needed to take off her shoes and plant her bare feet in the snow before she collapsed in front of this whole crowd.

She imagined the gossip scattering to every corner of Okrith, of the hungover princess who fainted in the middle of her sister's party. Fae from every kingdom were here. Too many eyes watched her. She dove deep into that pit of darkness swirling in her gut and forced herself not to tremble as she made her way through the crowd. She grabbed a glass of juice from the brightly lit table, skirting past the crowd and out the door. She would make her excuses later if anyone noted she was missing. She needed to get her feet in the snow.

# CHAPTER TWENTY-THREE

Rua picked at the flowers woven into her hair. The wedding procession had snuck around the back of the castle so as not to be seen. They waited in front of the grand doors, ready to parade in.

"That is the tenth time you've rolled your eyes," Bri said, pinning Rua with a look.

"How come you got to wear a tunic and I was given this?" she hissed in a low voice, gesturing to her figure-hugging dress. "At least Remy got a fur mantle."

Remy was already beautiful, but in her wedding dress she looked stunning. She wore a white gown with long, belled sleeves and a matching white fur mantle wrapped around her shoulders. The gold of her crown matched her golden slippers and the bouquet of gilded dried flowers in her hands. The amulet of Aelusien glowed faintly from around her neck like the last ember of a fading fire. The rest of the party wore burgundy red. Rua and Carys wore matching red gowns, while the Eagles wore burgundy tunics and stone-gray trousers. Fenrin wore a jacket the same color, bulking out his long frame.

"You look pretty," Carys chided, picking Rua's tangled hairs out of her crown of flowers.

Glowering at Carys's generous curves, she swatted the beautiful fae's hand away. She didn't want to look pretty, she wanted to look mighty, and how could people not compare them when they were wearing the same thing?

"It's time!" Talhan called from up ahead as the giant doors began to open.

The sounds of light orchestral music whirled out on the wind as Bri shoved Rua into line. First Carys and Talhan processed in. Rua was ready to move, but Bri yanked her back, the soldier threading her arm through Rua's.

"Twenty paces," Bri murmured. She didn't wear the fake smile that she was certain Carys and Talhan would plaster on their faces, but neither would the soldier ruin the performance.

Bri tugged on Rua's arm again, and then they were walking. Rua wished she could bolt down the aisle as their feet hit the crimson carpet that rolled down the entire length of the hall. Hundreds of eyes turned to her. The heat of their stares mixed with the warmth of the room, making Rua wish to retreat out into the cold again.

So many eyes.

The crowd murmured as she passed. At least her sister had permitted her to wear the Immortal Blade belted to her gown. Every single attendant gawked at the blade as she walked past. The weight of her sword on her hip made her hands loosen.

She looked up to the dais where Baba Morganna stood in her flowing red robes, that warm smile on her face. The witch who pulled down a mountain—smiling gently—it made Rua want to laugh. Beside the High Priestess stood Hale, looking regal in his charcoal jacket and trousers, a flowing burgundy cape affixed to his silver fur mantle. He looked magnificent . . . and nervous. Rua's cheeks dimpled as she stared up at her future brother. Remy was his Fated. Even so, he was anxious.

Talhan and Carys reached the dais, Talhan moving beside Hale and Carys to where Remy would stand. Bri and Rua passed the last few pews, Rua's eyes snagging on the emerald-green jacket and silver crown. Renwick stared, eyes boring into her with that piercing intensity that only he could muster. Aneryn stood beside him, beaming at

Rua. The blue witch looked her up and down with raised eyebrows and nodded in approval.

They stepped up onto the platform, Bri going to Hale's side and Rua to Remy's. It was an arbitrary division. They were all friends. Well, all friends except Rua. The Eagles and Carys were now members of the High Mountain Court as well, and even though Rua was the daughter of the last Queen and King, she didn't feel she belonged to this court at all.

A middle-aged fae sat in the front pew, blotting happy tears from her eyes. It was clear from her wavy chestnut hair and pale eyes that she was Hale's mother. Another few rugged-looking fae sat around her that Rua didn't recognize. They didn't seem like the family of a former prince.

A collective gasp pulled Rua from her thoughts as the music swelled. The crowd stood as Remy appeared in the doorframe on Fenrin's arm. The braziers flickered light against the walls, dancing to the string music, as the crowd murmured with delight, but Remy's eyes were fixed only on one person. Rua's eyes darted to Hale. She wasn't sure he was breathing. He stared at his Fated in awe, eyes welling. Rua begrudged her sister many things, but she couldn't deny how beloved she was. Remy truly looked like a goddess strolling down from the heavens to Hale.

She forced herself to look away from the magnetizing moment as Remy neared the dais. Every single well-wisher watched the Queen of the High Mountain Court . . . all except one. When Rua caught those emerald eyes, they darted down to his hands. A flicker of muscle in Renwick's cheek was the only sign he gave.

The ceremony droned on. Only Rua seemed to feel the slow drag of time as prayer after prayer, song after song, vow after vow, slogged on over the hour. She couldn't understand the bouts of tears, watching a crowd openly weep as Remy and Hale placed white bouquets of flowers on their ancestry stones. The stones would be placed at the site of their future graves in the mountainside beyond the palace. This moment and their binding, a memory that would live on with them even after their deaths.

The whole thing was bizarre and morose. It made Rua want to roll her eyes again, but she kept getting warning stares from Bri during the hour-long ceremony and she knew she couldn't afford another. She wouldn't be surprised if her guard gave her a lecture later. She shifted on her feet, wishing she could sit down. No one wanted to watch her, anyway. No one except the King of the Northern Court.

When Baba Morganna finally placed the crown on Hale's head, her father's crown, the crowd stood and cheered. Hale grabbed Remy and pulled her into an all-consuming kiss. The cheers swelled as the King and Queen of the High Mountain Court kissed passionately in front of their people. They basked in the warm reception.

The cacophony of sounds rang hollow as Rua had a horrific thought: she had been here before. She had stood here as a child as people cheered those same crowns, her parents wearing them. She frowned out over the cheering throng until Carys nudged her shin with her heel, forcing Rua to put on a fake smile. She plastered on the mirthless grin, eyes narrowing at those green eyes in the crowd. Renwick's lips pulled up slightly to the sides as he laughed at her. He rolled his eyes at the whole charade and smiled at her again. A real smile replaced her fake one. He thought it was as ridiculous as she did. The two of them smiled at each other as the rest of the world faded away. Just them and their smiles in a room full of sound.

~

The ballroom on the second floor had been transformed into a winter wonderland. White tapered candles lit the room in a romantic glow as the ten-piece orchestra performed a slow waltz. The crush of dancing people heated the room enough that the frosted doors to the balcony were thrown open. On the Winter Solstice, fae would revel through the night until the sun came peeking above the horizon, and they would sing songs and cheer the dawning of the new light.

Rua didn't know if she would make it that long. It was still several hours away.

Another two human well-wishers bustled over to her, a gray-haired couple.

"You look so much like your father," the woman crooned in Yex-shiri. Rua managed to contain her frown. She had heard she looked like her father dozens of times in the space of an hour. People thought it was a compliment for some reason, but it brought no warmth to know she looked like a man she couldn't remember.

"Thank you," Rua murmured in stilted Yexshiri, her tongue getting stuck on the Rs that rolled on the back of her mouth.

"We were overjoyed when the Queen announced she was with child with you." The woman's eyes crinkled. "It seemed like she was pregnant with you right away after your sister was born. The people joked that you demanded to be a part of that family even in the womb."

"Very good," Rua tried to say, but the words came out all garbled.

The man guffawed. "You need to practice your Yexshiri more."

"And you need to learn how to speak to royalty," Rua bit out.

A tittering, forced laugh sounded from beside her as Carys pushed into their conversation.

"Oh, the princess has an odd sense of humor, does she not?" Carys laughed as if Rua had just told the most hysterical joke she had ever heard.

The elderly couple narrowed their eyes a split second before breaking out into laughter as well. "Yes, most humorous," the man said, clutching his plump belly.

Carys looped her arms through Rua's. "I'm sure the princess would love to stay and entertain you more, but she is needed by the Heir of Saxbridge."

"Oh, yes, yes. Of course," the woman said, bowing deeply as her husband followed. "It was a pleasure, Your Highness."

"Likewise," Rua said coldly as she dipped her head to them.

Carys steered Rua away from the throng of people toward the table of decadent winter fare, framed by boughs of gold-dusted holly. The table had a spread of cuisine from every corner of Okrith, from the spiced golden dishes of the South to the tray of fresh seafood from the East. It was a medley of all of Okrith in the same way the city and castle were. Yexshire was a place for everyone. Standing beside one spiky bough was Neelo, one arm folded across their chest while the other held their book, a different one from the day before. Upon seeing Rua, Neelo closed their tome.

"Are Carys and Bri babysitting you, Your Highness?" Neelo asked, eyes darting down at Rua and over to Carys.

"So it would seem," Rua said.

"Gods, you two are as gloomy as the other." Carys sighed, turning to Rua. "Stay with Neelo, and you won't have to indulge so many simpering elderly couples."

Neelo snorted. "I do make a good repellant." Their eyes tracked up over Rua's shoulder, and their mouth tightened. "Except to one person."

"Neelo!" Talhan's voice boomed behind Rua.

"What do you want?" Neelo said, cocking their head with a hint of annoyance.

"Well, I came to save Rua from another prying couple, but since I'm here . . ." He scanned Neelo from head to toe. "Care to dance?"

"I would rather cut off my arm with that cheese knife, Tal."

Talhan laughed. "I know." He turned to Rua. "But you'll indulge me, won't you? If I have one more matronly woman put their son's or daughter's hand in mine and push us onto the dance floor, I think I'll pull my hair out."

Rua chuckled, placing her hand in Talhan's. "Fine."

No one could talk to them while they were dancing and, since she didn't bring a book, the Heir of Saxbridge's company would be stilted as well.

They circled around the dance floor, the handsome Eagle making space for them in the crowd. The music was more jolly now. The heat from the center of the dancers swirled around Rua as Talhan smiled down at her.

"Your sister and Carys have been working hard to keep me out of trouble for Remy." Rua had to shout to be heard above the loud music and throng of dancers. "I guess it's your turn."

Talhan roared a deep laugh. "They love Remy, of course they do, but they were doing it for you, Rua. To spare you from the gossips. Do you really want to have to hear stories for the rest of your life about your frowning and eye-rolling at your sister's wedding?" Rua frowned. "Yep, just like that."

"Have you come to scold me too?" Stumbling over her feet, Talhan caught her, and she fell back into the steps. She was a terrible dancer, her feet barely moving in the right direction.

"Hardly, I just wanted to dance with a companion who wasn't trying to win my hand in marriage." Talhan whipped Rua around in faster circles, the room spinning. "You don't have to love court life to be a part of it. You will find your footing here, eventually."

Rua couldn't imagine it, living here and having to bear those staring eyes and warm smiles of people who knew her parents. She didn't want to wake up each morning and see the Temple of Yexshire. She didn't want to hear Yexshiri words and be told about how much she was like her dead father. This whole city was haunted with the ghosts of forgotten stories. She wanted her own life, one she carved out for herself, one she chose.

The song ended as applause echoed throughout the room. The next song was slower. Talhan pulled Rua in closer to his body, warmth seeping from his burgundy tunic. His hand drifted down to her lower back just as the scent of cloves and snow hit Rua, and Talhan paused.

"May I cut in?" a voice sounded behind her, making her whole body go still.

"Of course, I can't be too selfish hoarding the best dancer all night." Talhan winked at Rua while she gave him a cutting look, her eyes accusing him of abandoning her.

She knew she would feel it, the impact of seeing him, when she turned around, but still it felt like a punch to her chest as she looked up into those shining eyes.

"May I have this dance?" Renwick whispered, the muscle in his cheek flickering as that memory of them smiling at each other from the ceremony played over in Rua's mind.

She already felt pulled under his spell. The impact of his stare was far greater than being tumbled in a torrent of snow.

"Yes," she murmured, placing her hand in his.

His warm fingers wrapped around her own as his other hand encircled her waist, gathering her to him. He led her in a slow waltz around the room. They did not hold to the rigid posture of the dance. No, they molded into each other, her body seeming to know exactly how to move when guided by his.

Her pulse crept up her throat. She prayed her palms didn't sweat. She'd been stealing glances at Renwick these past few days in Yexshire but to be this close to him again . . .

"I heard you learned of Bri's history," Renwick said.

The rest of the dancers moved further and further to the edge of the dance floor, giving them the floor.

"I'm guessing a blue witch told you as much."

Renwick grinned down at her. "She did."

"Why didn't Bri just tell me?"

"For the same reason you and I don't like to talk about our own family history: it pains her," Renwick said, making Rua drop her gaze. The way he said *our.*

"I thought my parents were good people," she said to her feet.

"They were good people," Renwick assured her. "Norwood was a fool. The prophecy of the Twin Eagles was a dangerous one. It threatened that Bri may take a crown from its sovereign. It was wise for your parents not to take in the Eagles. I'm sure it pained them. They were better people than any of the other crowns of Okrith."

"Not that being a good person keeps you alive," she ground out as she stared everywhere but at him.

"You think steeling their hearts with bitterness would have saved them?" Renwick asked incredulously. "You think trusting no one would have helped? Do you think they would have traded their years of happiness for another century of darkness?"

Darkness.

That was what lived inside her.

Renwick's heady scent wafted around her again as she grumbled more to herself, "Do you always smell like winter forests?"

"What?"

"That's your scent: like cloves and snow." Rua looked up to see Renwick's eyes widening as his lips pulled up slightly to the sides. Rua felt her cheeks burning. Perhaps she shouldn't have said it.

"You smell like spring in Murreneir," Renwick said, cutting off her embarrassed thoughts.

She didn't realize she even had a scent. Of course she did. But the scent of Renwick felt like a brand on her soul. She knew it without the slightest effort. It just existed there in her mind always.

"You smell like wildflowers and fresh spring rains..." His eyes dropped down to her lips. "You smell like home."

Her lips parted as she let out a jagged breath. She smelled like home to him. Home. It was a place she didn't have. But in the recesses of her mind, she knew home smelled like cloves and snowy forests.

The music started to crescendo as that revelation was laid bare. The flickering candles were too bright. The heat of all these bodies and the scent of sweat mixed with food and fires became overwhelming.

As they turned around the room, Rua felt the press of eyes upon her. Her shoulders tightened. "I wish they would all stop staring," she hissed.

Renwick's breath was hot in Rua's hair. "You can't possibly blame them. You are the most beautiful person in this ballroom."

"That is not why they look."

"You are mesmerizing, Rua. The fact you don't see it is baffling." Renwick's hand drifted a little lower on her back, pulling her hips closer to his. "But tell me, why do you think they look?"

She knew why they looked.

She forced back the pinprick of tears. The sounds were roaring in her ears now. The lights felt like a candle flame held right to her eyeball. Her chest rose and fell in short, heaving breaths as a sheen of sweat broke out on her brow. She needed to get out of this place.

"Rua?" Renwick's voice echoed from all around her, sounding muffled and far away in her mind.

Her eyes began darkening at the periphery as she realized she had stopped dancing. She felt the blood draining from her face as she looked up into those gleaming green eyes.

She remembered standing in front of the fae fire in Brufdoran...

and Balorn's promised words that she was too dark even for Renwick. She was too broken, even for the broken Northern King.

"I need to go. Excuse me," she said, hastily pulling away.

"Are you all right?" Renwick asked after her, gently.

"I am fine. I just need some fresh air . . ." Renwick made to follow her. "And a moment alone."

She didn't want him to see her like that. She needed to plunge her feet in the snow. She needed to breathe deep racks of air as tears slid silently down her cheeks. She knew it was coming, felt it rising in her as it did many nights when she woke from those haunted dreams. And she couldn't let them see it any more than they already did: that it was true. She was broken.

~

She fled up two more flights of stairs and to the balcony near the library. Rua prayed it would be vacant as she burst out into the frigid cold. An icy whorl of breath escaped her as she sighed. The balcony was empty. Diagonally down to her left was the ballroom balcony, just peeking out from the corner of the palace, enshrined in golden candlelight. No one would see her up there in the quiet darkness. She moved to the gray stone balustrade, its railing encrusted in ice. She leaned against the chest-high wall and took another deep breath as she looked out to the east. The sun would be rising soon. Longer days would be near.

From this side of the castle, the city of Yexshire was mostly obscured. Instead, she looked out over the craggy peaks of the High Mountains and thick, snow-covered forests. The forests surrounding Yexshire felt different from those in the Northern Court. They felt sharper. More spiky alpine shrubs, more dramatic peaks, thinner air. Rua realized she was still gasping, unable to catch her breath. The voice of merry laughter echoing up from the party was more haunting than any nightmare. Each laugh mocked her. Each sound called her a fraud. How could she bear the weight of another witch's smile or comment that she looked like her murdered parents?

Pulling herself up onto the railing, Rua swung her legs over the edge so they dangled in the winter air. She looked down at the drop. The foundations surrounding the castle plummeted off the cliff's side here—no need for a high wall. No one could scale that sheer crag. One of Rua's golden slippers dangled off her toes. She wanted the night air on her feet. Kicking the slipper off, she watched it freely fall into the abyss. There would be no reclaiming it. She let the other shoe fall and tumble into the darkness.

The icy bite of cold numbed her toes, and muscles she didn't know were taut loosened. Her heart no longer hammered through her chest. She was grateful that the panic ebbed but also terrified too, because when the panic went away—there was the quiet. And in the stillness of her mind, she felt that gnawing darkness inside her even more keenly. The abyss below her feet was small compared to the one inside her. Everything she threw into that pit to fill it was swallowed whole.

She needed to find Bri and ask her to train or go back to her rooms and punch her knuckles against the stone wall. She needed to do something . . . but then this feeling would return again, eventually.

Swirling her foot in the open air, she wondered what it would feel like to fall, when a sharp voice pulled her back into her body.

"Get down. Now."

Rua glanced over her shoulder to find Renwick taking up the doorframe, fists clenched at his sides. He looked at her with a mixture of anger and terror that she would choose to dangle herself over the balcony.

"I'm fine here," Rua said. "I won't fall."

"Your arms are trembling," Renwick noted, glancing down at her goose-pimpled flesh. He unbuttoned his jacket even as he spoke. "Are you coming down or am I joining you on the ledge?"

Cheeks dimpling, Rua rolled her eyes and swung her legs back over the balcony. She slid down until her bare feet touched the cold stone.

"They fell off," Rua said with a shrug, following Renwick's gaze to her feet.

"I'm sure." Renwick glided forward, wrapping his jacket around Rua, the warmth encasing her. His hands lingered on the lapel of the jacket. She smelled the wine on his breath but noted there was no acidic scent of hellebore and bloodbane. He had really given it up. It was another stark reminder that even Renwick, who had all the reason in the world to fall victim to the darkness, was able to overcome his demons. And Rua couldn't, and she didn't know why.

She realized Renwick still held the lapel of his jacket, his eyes glued to her face. When she looked up to meet his gaze, his lips parted.

"What are you thinking about?" Rua whispered, already knowing the answer.

"Do you want the polite answer or the real one?" Renwick smirked, cocking his head slightly, his lips a hair's breadth away.

"Real one. Always."

"I'm thinking about taking you against the railing." Renwick's breath skittered across her cheeks.

Rua's eyes narrowed at him, desperate to have something overtake the hollowness she felt.

"Do it, then," she said.

Renwick's eyes widened as he dropped his hold on his jacket. He retreated a step, creating space between them again. "No."

"Why not?"

"You think I don't know what you're doing?" Renwick closed his eyes and took a breath. When he opened them, the look on his face was raw and vulnerable. "You think I don't know you're punishing your-self by sleeping with me? I know, because I do the exact same thing. I poison myself with potions and you do this." He gestured between them. "That's not who I want to be to you, Rua. I don't want to be your diversion."

"What in the Gods' names do you want from me, then?" Rua shouted, her restraint finally untethered. "Because you are never will-ing to say it."

Enough of these ridiculous games.

"I want every part of you." There was no hesitation in his voice this time, nothing holding him back. "I want every beautiful dark corner of your soul."

Rua stopped breathing. He had never responded to her confession in the Lyrei Basin that she cared for him. He was half-drugged out of his mind, but still. They had managed to avoid each other after that. She assumed it was because he didn't return her doomed affections. That muscle clenched tight in her chest again. He thought her darkness was beautiful? That it wasn't a void to be filled or gotten rid of?

She swallowed the lump in her throat, shaking her head, refusing to hear it.

He took a ragged breath. "I will wait for all of you."

Rua steeled her gaze as she said, "You will be waiting forever."

Renwick's eyes swept over her again. She couldn't bear that look. He looked at her like she was already whole, and she feared if she stayed a second longer she'd start believing it too.

She darted across the balcony, pushing past Renwick, blocking the doorway. A hand on her shoulder halted her, forcing her to look into those emerald eyes one last time. Renwick held her gaze, promising the truth in his next words:

"Forever then, so long as I'm beside you."

# CHAPTER TWENTY-FOUR

R ua was about to turn the corner to her room when the sound of drunken laughter made her pause. She peered down the long, darkened hall and spotted Bri and Delta chuckling outside Bri's door. The Eagle's golden gaze looked hungrily at the Western guard. In the blink of an eye, she grabbed Delta's face and pulled her into a burning kiss. Delta didn't miss a beat, encircling Bri's waist and spinning her to the wall, arms bracketing beside her head as she pinned Bri with her muscled body. Delta broke their kiss only long enough to murmur "I missed you" across Bri's parted lips and then began fumbling for the door handle.

Smirking, Rua turned in the other direction. She would give the two flames a moment to get in the door so she didn't throw ice on their heated moment. Choosing a stairwell at random, she wound her way up narrow stone steps. As she looked out the window, she realized she was climbing up into one of the castle's towers. She stepped into the first hallway, opening into what appeared to be a sitting room. It had high vaulted ceilings and red stained glass windows. Leather chairs clustered in little seating areas, but in the far end of the room was an altar with a figure knelt before it.

Taking one look at the lone silver-haired male, Rua knew who this altar was for. She tiptoed up beside Bern, afraid to disturb him in his prayers. The altar was laden with candles, white wax frozen in pools around the wood. The candles were of various shapes and heights, but Rua knew how many there would be: twenty-eight, one for each year of her brother Raffiel's life. Behind the altar was a string held across two poles, bowing under the weight of the crimson ribbons and bouquets of dried white flowers hung across it. Behind the ribbon arbor was another tall stained glass window, peering out into the predawn gloom of the city.

Her heart began pounding again, staring at those twenty-eight candles—nine more than would be laid at her own altar if she had dropped off that ledge. A wicker basket sat beside the candles, notes and drawings filling it to the brim. Raffiel's memorial was well visited, just as he was well loved.

The knot in Rua's throat thickened. She had only ever pushed him away. She wasn't sure if she was mad at him or mad at the world or just mad at herself . . . but that anger kept her from ever getting to know him. He had tried. Raffiel visited the witch camps whenever he could, risking exposure by trekking to the northeastern High Mountains. He should have stayed put, gathering his troops and saving refugees in the mountains to the west, but for Rua, he had made the time. Her eyes welled with silent tears. And when he arrived, she would frown at him and give him the most fleeting embraces, just as she had with Remy. And now he was gone, and she couldn't take any of it back. She would never be able to tackle him into a warm hug like the Eagles did with Remy. She knew it would have made him smile. She wished he knew she loved him.

Pale blue eyes glanced to Rua, and Bern stood up. "You okay?"

"How do you do it? How do you survive it?" Rua sniffed, swallowing back her tears. "Being without him."

"I don't know how to be without him." Bern's normally cavalier expression cracked as he came to stand next to Rua. "All I know is he is gone and I'm still here, and I've chosen to make something of that, if I can."

Rua looked down at her hands. "My sister told me you are leading the community efforts, building orphanages, and aiding the shelters. The food program is a brilliant idea."

Throughout the city were collective halls that people dined in for lunch. It did not matter their level of need. Everyone gathered together to eat. The palace supplied the food, and they took turns cooking the meals. It served many purposes beyond feeding the hungry. It dampened the loneliness of those without family, it gave tasks and goals to the rudderless people who came without their own trade, and it provided food for those too exhausted from starting a new life to cook for themselves.

"The lunch halls were Renwick's idea," Bern said.

Rua darted her eyes to him. "Renwick?" Her thoughts shot back to the dining tents in the Lyrei Basin. Rua had assumed it was a function of the camp, not a tradition of the Northern Court. How could it be?

"It was his mother's idea, a tradition from her hometown of Murreneir," Bern said, "though I doubt the former Northern King would ever have let her implement such a thing in Drunehan."

"How do you know all of this?"

Bern gave Rua a half-hearted grin. "Because I have spent many a night around a card table with Renwick."

"How long have you known him?"

"All of his life. I am three years his elder." Bern's icy blue eyes crinkled as he thought back to some faraway memory. "I grew up in a gold-mining town near Silver Sands Harbor. It was far from court life but my family was rich as thieves, so we were welcomed into every kingdom in Okrith. We would go from court to court, joining in solstice celebrations and weddings. We followed the merriment wherever it went. Until the Siege of Yexshire, that is." Bern cleared his throat, rubbing the back of his neck. "I wasn't there that night. I feared Raffiel was gone, but I never found a single person who could confirm his death, and so I went looking for him. It took me many years." He smiled softly, his voice cracking. "But I found him."

"Did you know you were Fated before then?" Rua asked, chest seizing for the heartbreak she saw riddling Bern's face.

"I knew, and I didn't." His cheeks dimpled. "Raffiel was only twelve during the Siege of Yexshire. And I cared about him . . . unreasonably so." Bern laughed, even through the stabbing sorrow in his expression. "He was my best friend. When I found him again, he was nineteen, and it hit me like a punch seeing him again." Rua's eyes welled. "I think his parents knew. I think they may have been waiting until we were older to tell us. It seems like too big a weight to carry as a child."

Rua nodded stiffly, forcing back her tears again, clenching her fists so they wouldn't fall. Even a lifetime together wouldn't feel like enough. She had laughed in the fleeting face of time when it came to Raffiel; she had always assumed there would be more. That time would allow her to do better, make amends, and fix her mistakes at some point in the future. Yet here she was, thinking that she had more time still: that she could fix her broken relationship with Remy, that she could embrace her power over the Immortal Blade, that she could open her heart to Renwick. But she spat in the face of time.

"If I had grabbed the sword sooner," Rua murmured.

Bern rested a gentle hand on her shoulder, pulling her watery eyes to him. "It was not your fault, Rua. None of this was your fault," he whispered. "Raffiel knew that. He would have never wanted you to suffer that guilt."

An unwelcome tear slipped down Rua's cheek as Bern's eyes darted to the window to his right. "Come on," he said, pulling her toward the glass. They looked out over the High Mountains just as the sun peeped above the ranges. Cheering broke out from far below them as the revelers welcomed the new sun. They had survived the shortest day.

"You see that?" Bern said, tipping his head to the window as songs swelled up from below them, chants and prayers welcoming the new light.

"The sun?" Rua arched her eyebrow as she stared at the golden glow.

"It's a promise of another day, Rua," Bern said, tapping his fingers to his forehead as he spoke his Ific prayer to the God of the Sun: "The sun will keep rising and so too shall we all."

"That is all poetic nonsense." Rua crossed her arms even as her eyes remained fixed on the swelling sun, as if the most instinctive part of her couldn't tear itself away.

"Maybe." Bern chuckled. "But that poetic nonsense helps me keep putting one foot in front of the other. I ask myself what I will do with the hours of sunlight I get each day, and then I do it. That's as far as I walk into the future. Maybe one day I will think in seasons or years, but for now I think only of the sunlight of one day."

The sun rose into a golden halo, beaming its glorious light out into the mountains. Rua wondered what she would do if she allowed herself one day, just one, to release that tightness in her chest. How far could she go without that leaden weight?

She would try one simple thing first and see where to go from there.

Wrapping her arms around Bern, she pulled him into a hug. She felt his smile as he rested his chin on her shoulder. Holding him tightly, she let the tears fall down her cheeks, a dam broken by the shining rays of sunlight. Bern stroked a comforting hand down her back, holding her just as tightly with the other, and she knew he was hugging her, not just for himself, but for Raffiel as well. He carried part of Raffiel's soul within himself, his Fated's life bound together with his own. Rua imagined Raffiel's arms around her too, and she hugged Bern in the way she wished she could have hugged her elder brother before he died. Wedding or no, Bern was her elder brother now too, and she would love him like one.

"Rua!" a panicked, high voice called, bursting into the tower.

Rua whipped her head to the doorway, finding Aneryn standing there, panting and wide-eyed.

"What's wrong?" Rua asked, breaking her embrace with Bern and running over to the blue witch.

"I've had a vision. The road to the West had an avalanche, but it was man-made. I can't See," Aneryn breathed, swallowing gulps of air. "I've been so focused on casting my Sight toward Balorn that I did not See it before now."

"See what?"

"A violet shadow," Aneryn said. "I can't See Augustus Norwood any-more."

~

The pounding of Rua's fist on the door echoed down the hall. The castle was growing quiet as exhausted revelers retired to their rooms in the early dawn light, but if Augustus Norwood was on the move, all of Okrith needed to be prepared. The door finally moved, and Rua's heart stopped. Renwick opened the door in nothing but soft gray sleep pants. Her eyes roved the planes of his sculpted chest as he rubbed the sleep out of his eyes, squinting into the brightly lit hall.

"Rua?" His eyes widened, suddenly more awake at the sight of her.

She did not waste time with pleasantries and simply said, "I want to go back to Murreneir. Now."

Renwick's emerald eyes assessed her for a moment, but all he said was, "Okay. Let's go."

A heavy breath loosed from Rua's lips. She was prepared to convince him, ready to launch into a tirade about Augustus Norwood and all of the awful things he could be doing obscured from the witches' Sight. Still, it was a harebrained thing to demand to leave immediately, but he instantly agreed.

"Thank you," she said, hands trembling.

"Will you be all right to go get your things? I'll organize people to come collect them and ready the carriages." His eyes scanned her as if he were looking for an injury.

"Yes, that will be fine," she breathed, heart ratcheting up into her throat.

Renwick raised an eyebrow at her when she didn't move. "All right . . ."

Before she could give it another thought, her hands reached out, grabbing Renwick's neck. She lifted on tiptoes as she pulled his face toward hers. Her lips molded with his in a burning kiss. Renwick stayed frozen in a split second of surprise before his hands wrapped around her back and pulled her chest to his, an approving hum rumbling through him. Tingles skittered through Rua's body at that warm, tender kiss. Rua had the urge to keep going, to see where that kiss might lead them, but that would have to wait. She pulled her face away and dropped back down onto flat feet.

"I'll go get my things," she said with a coy smirk.

Emerald eyes gleamed at her. Renwick's lips parted as he nodded.

As she turned to leave, a hasty hand on the crook of her arm pulled her back, and those full lips were on hers once more. It was a fleeting kiss, but one that set her on fire.

"I'll meet you at the side entrance by the stables," Renwick said, resting his forehead on hers.

She had never before seen a smile like that on his face. It was open and genuine—real happiness that neither of them permitted themselves. It was enough. As the golden light of the morning sun beamed into the hallway, she was determined to try.

In her room, she hurriedly dumped her things in the chest that was given to her in Drunehan. Its lock was still carved with the old Northern Court crest. She should probably request a new one. She pulled up short at that thought. The lock she imagined was Renwick's new crest: the sword through the crown. She had not imagined the High Mountain crest of the crown over mountains. Her hands shook again as she felt the echoes of that kiss on her lips. She still smelled the snowy evergreen scent in her hair. It frightened her and excited her all at once— she would rather belong to the new Northern Court than to the High Mountain one.

It hadn't felt like an option before. She was always doomed to return to Yexshire and be a part of her sister's council. But now, with that kiss burning into her mind, she wondered if that could change.

She wrapped her traveling cloak tighter around her as she descended the last steps into the foyer beside the stables, the smell of hay and horse manure swirling up the stairwell. Two servants moved in front of her, hefting her black chest of clothes out the far door to the stables. As they cleared from view, she found Renwick standing in his riding clothes, an exasperated-looking Aneryn beside him, arms folded across her chest.

"You really thought you could leave without me?" she scolded Rua over her heavy, glowing blue eyes. "Me?"

"I suppose not." Rua chuckled. "We would have sent word back for the rest of you. I figured you would want to rest first. When you told me that you couldn't See Augustus Norwood, I panicked. I just . . . needed to get out of this place. I wanted to go—"

Rua didn't finish the thought, though they all seemed to know what she was about to say: home. She wanted to go home. Murreneir was the first time she felt like she was free to be herself. She felt like she belonged to the rolling powder-covered hills and breathtaking frozen lakes of sky blue and that snowy evergreen scent.

Renwick's cheeks dimpled as he watched that realization crossing her face. She wanted to stay in Murreneir. She wanted her life to be there.

Aneryn turned to the entryway table and set down two silver *druni*. They called it *a witch's goodbye.* They would see the *druni* coins and know she was gone.

A servant appeared in the archway. "Ready, Your Majesty."

Rua was grateful the stable hands were quick. Her head was pounding and her body fatigued. She was desperate to get in the carriage and sleep the whole journey north.

"Wait!" a voice shouted from up the stairwell, and Remy came barreling down. She was still in her wedding dress, Hale hot on her heels, still in his solstice regalia, though his shirt was crumpled and the top buttons of his tunic were undone. Both of them were glassy-eyed, probably both drunk and exhausted from their wedding day and the celebrations that followed.

"You were just going to leave?" Remy accused Rua. "Without even saying goodbye?"

Rua was certain that the drinks and early morning light made Remy take it harder, revealing the hurt that her sister tried to hide.

"I didn't want to interrupt your celebrations," Rua said. "We need to get back to Lyrei Basin. I'm worried about Augustus Norwood being on the move."

It was a convenient lie. Aneryn not Seeing the Norwood army could be months into the future. But it was a better excuse than telling her sister she wanted to make sure Murreneir, and not their homeland, was safe.

"That has yet to come to pass." Hale furrowed his brow at her. She was speaking about the man Hale had known as a brother, a man who had declared himself the new Eastern King by birthright, a man as evil as his father. He must have been told these visions by one of their witches too. "And the Lyrei Basin can't protect itself while you are here?" Hale asked Renwick, already knowing the answer.

The Lyrei Basin was a stronghold, not only for its positioning in the landscape and the battalion of armored soldiers, but also for the blue witch lookouts preventing any fae from getting near without the witches Seeing them.

"You could stay here, Rua. Let Renwick deal with the North. This doesn't have to fall to you." Remy's eyes were pleading even as she clenched her fists by her sides.

"I'm going, Remy," Rua said, avoiding Remy's crestfallen gaze.

"What about Bri and Talhan?" Hale watched her with wary gray eyes. He looked as tired as she felt. He probably hadn't expected his wedding night to be spent watching his wife and new sister in a shouting match . . . but if he wanted to be a part of their family, he'd have to get used to it.

"The Eagles belong here," Rua said, "with you. Their fealty is pledged to you. They should stay in the High Mountain Court."

Leaning to the side to look into the stables, Remy frowned at the two guards sitting at the back of the carriage. "Won't you at least wait for the rest of your guards before departing?" she asked.

"I am my own guard," Rua said, placing her hand on the hilt of the Immortal Blade.

"How long are you planning on staying in the North?" her sister demanded.

Rua's eyes darted from Aneryn to Renwick. Gods, could she say what she wanted to say? Could she tell her sister she wanted to stay in the North forever? Instead, she murmured, "I don't know."

Renwick took another step closer, and Remy's hands shot out. In a flash, her gold-and-silver dagger floated menacingly in the air, held aloft by her red witch magic. The amulet of Aelusien glowed crimson from around her neck.

"You stay away from my sister," she snarled as Renwick eyed the blade warily.

"Remy," Hale said quietly, placing a hand on her shoulder.

Remy's eyes widened as Rua stepped between Renwick and the blade. Rua stared into her sister's eyes, the same eyes as hers and their mother's.

"You don't know what you're talking about, Remy," Rua said in a low and lethal voice, casting out her own red magic and forcing Remy's dagger to the ground. Its loud clang against the stone floor echoed in the tense silence.

"Stay here, Rua, please. You don't belong in the North," Remy pleaded.

Rua hung her head, the secret she had been denying to herself for so long finally clawing its way up her throat. "I belong in the North. They call me *Mhenissa*."

"No—"

"I *want* to be *Mhenissa*, Remy. I want to be the Witches' Blade!" Rua shouted. The room seemed to freeze as Remy's eyes widened in horror and she shook her head.

"No," Remy whispered. Her sister couldn't seem to understand that Rua's path forward might be different from her own, that maybe her only way toward peace would be in carving her own place in the world. The people of Yexshire were already being helped. But the witches of the Northern Court were still broken and in pain. They would not trust Renwick, and she didn't know why they trusted her, but she knew it was the place she would do the most good. It was where she could make the daylight hours count for something.

Swallowing the hard lump in her throat, she said bitterly, "Thanks for being happy for me." She turned, Renwick and Aneryn moving to follow her, her foot stalling over the threshold as she stepped into a beam of sunlight.

The morning rays shining through the low window pulled her back to that moment with Bern at Raffiel's memorial. She had been so moved to make the most of this one day, and only a handful of minutes later she was already failing.

Rua gritted her teeth. "Curse the fucking Gods," she muttered under her breath and turned again before she could think about it more. She barreled into Remy, wrapping her sister into a tight hug. Remy didn't even pause, dragging her in tighter.

Pulling away just enough to see her sister's face, Rua said, "I love you, Remy. And I will see you again soon." She gave her sister one more tight squeeze and left.

Remy let her go, saying nothing more than, "I love you too, Rua. Be safe." Her cracking voice echoed after Rua into the stables.

With shaky hands, Rua climbed into the door of the awaiting carriage, Renwick and Aneryn climbing in after her. Neither of them took the opposite bench, sandwiching Rua between the two of them so that their arms all pressed together, their closeness a seeming acknowledgment of how difficult that was for her.

Renwick reached down and threaded his warm fingers through hers. The feeling of the heat from his palm eased the trembling through Rua's limbs. Gods, she had said it. She had said it out loud: she was *Mhenissa*. The Mhenbic word meant sword, protector, defender of the witches. Her sword an extension of their magic, her will and theirs enmeshed. She was the Witches' Blade.

As the carriage jolted into motion, she felt the truth of those words coursing through her, her body responding to the claiming of her Fate.

Aneryn let out a giant yawn. The exhaustion of the long day and the sleepless night of celebrating crept into her body as the adrenaline wore off.

"Mother Moon, I'm tired," Aneryn said through another yawn, resting her head down on Rua's shoulder as she had done for most of the journey to Yexshire. The rhythmic rocking of the carriage lulled her heavier into sleep.

"Me too," Rua murmured, head bobbing forward until Renwick placed a gentle hand on her forehead and guided her head to his shoulder. Rua made a sleepy hum as her eyes fluttered closed, tucking her face into his neck as his scent wrapped around her. Renwick softly chuckled as he brushed a kiss to her temple.

The carriage leveled out as they finished their rocking descent down the road from the palace and wove through the streets of Yexshire. Rua couldn't open her eyes. She did not want to look out the window, anyway. The people of Yexshire would be asleep in their beds by now. The daylight hours would be spent resting off their nightlong revels, and the feeling of her forehead pressed into the warmth of Renwick's neck was the most comfortable she had ever felt.

Before her dreams overtook her mind, she heard Aneryn's soft murmur, "I'm proud of you, Ru."

# CHAPTER TWENTY-FIVE

R enwick bolting from his seat jolted Rua and Aneryn awake. It was dark out. They had slept the entire day.

"No, no, no." His panicked voice disappeared into the cold evening air.

Smoke swallowed the castle of Brufdoran, an inferno blazing through its top-floor windows. Rua and Aneryn scrambled out of the carriage, sprinting across the snow.

"How did I not See this?" Aneryn gaped at the growing flames.

Without a second thought, Rua cast out her red witch magic, hefting up mounds of snow and hurling them through the windows. The panic made her aim poor, but enough got into the first window that the orange flames turned to black smoke. She took a breath and did it again to the second window, her mind straining harder than any muscle. It was not the weight of the snow that depleted her magic. It was the focus of keeping it steady and funneling into the right window.

"Is everyone accounted for?" Her fae ears heard Renwick from farther across the open field in front of the castle.

"Yes, thank the Gods." She knew it was Lord Omerin speaking, though she did not take her focus from the third window as she lifted again, biceps straining, hands splayed as she pushed the snow upward again. It was some relief to know that no one was inside.

"What happened?" Aneryn gasped.

"We think it was an ember from the fae fire that started it." Lord Omerin's voice sounded riddled with disbelief. "We do not know."

When the snow went through the last window, Rua took a heaving breath and finally looked to the people gathered between the house and the gardens. Dozens of people, mostly human servants, cloistered together still in their work clothes. Rua's eyes scanned wildly until they landed on Fredrik, standing beside his mother, watching Rua with awe. Good, they were all safe.

Shaking out her limbs as though she had just been lifting a heavy crate, Rua moved slowly around the castle toward the other side, watching for any more flames licking up from the windows. She reached the far side of the castle and looked up. The windows were still intact and closed, fogged with smoke, but it looked like the fire was out.

"All is well on this side," she shouted to the others gathered out of view.

A scratchy voice sounded from behind her. "All is not well, *Mhenissa*." Rua whipped her head around to see a lone blue witch.

As Rua reached for the Immortal Blade, the witch lifted her hand, pulling back her hood. Silver hair spilled from her indigo cloak, though her face seemed as young as Rua's. She recognized the acerbic witch from the forge in Raevenport. Onyx was her name.

"I am not here to hurt you, *Mhenissa*," she said, her voice rough. "I Saw the flames and knew I would be able to speak to you alone. I am here to warn you."

"Warn me about what?" Rua asked, assessing the mysterious witch. It was a long trek from Raevenport to Brufdoran to share this news.

"Rua?" Aneryn called from around the house. "You okay?"

Onyx's eyes widened, and she shook her head.

"I'm fine," Rua called. "Just checking for any last flames."

That seemed to be enough to quiet them. She knew it would only be a matter of moments before one of them came around the building to find them there.

"Balorn Vostemur is an evil man, but he is not the enemy you should be focused on," Onyx said, looking off as though she Saw it in her mind's eye. "The visions are shifting as of late, and so the blue witches have changed our minds. We will help you break Balorn's curse."

She produced a thick leather-bound book from her cloak and passed it to Rua. She traced her fingers over the Mhenbic symbols, gritting her teeth.

"You had this spell book the whole time?" Her fingers tightened around the heavy tome. She had forced herself to go to Yexshire for the promise of this book, and it had been in the North all along. "Why give this to me now?"

"Augustus Norwood has found a way to obscure the blue witch Sight. I don't know how . . . All I See is a—"

"Violet shadow," Rua whispered.

Onyx's eyes darted back to Rua. "So your witches See it too," she murmured. "And unlike the Northern King, I have no idea why I can't See Norwood's future. Whatever it is . . . it feels like death. You must go east and stop him before this new power grows."

"Why can't you See Renwick's future?" Rua cocked her head at the witch. "Why tell me this here, now? Why don't you come with us back to Murreneir?"

"I will go nowhere near the Witchslayer," Onyx snarled.

"He is a friend to the witches now," Rua said, making the witch cackle with laughter.

"If you knew how many witches he has killed," she said as her eyes darkened, "you would not dare say that to me. It is you the witches want, *Mhenissa*. You wield the Witches' Blade. You *are* the Witches' Blade. If we must allow the Northern King to live in order for you to stay, then fine."

Mouth dropping open, Rua gaped at the witch.

"How many witches has he killed?" Rua whispered, heart cracking.

The witch's eyes drifted above Rua's shoulder.

"Ask him yourself," she said, her eyes blazing before she turned and trudged away into the forest, calling over her shoulder, "Ask him about my sister."

Renwick stood in stunned silence. He looked to Rua warily as she stalked toward him.

"Who was that?" She pointed her finger toward the woods.

"Her name is Onyx Mallor," Renwick said, staring at the darkness that Onyx had disappeared into. "There are many witches like her who left the moment they were freed . . . understandably so."

"Indeed," Rua gritted out.

Those emerald eyes found hers. "I am a bad person, Rua. No amount of time or good deeds will change what I have done." He hung his head, hair slipping from the knot at the nape of his neck to frame his face. She saw the shame burning hot across his cheeks. "I'm sorry."

Were they both beyond forgiveness for all their wicked deeds?

He turned to leave, but she placed a hand on his shoulder, making him pause. "We are as wicked as each other, remember?" She forced a smile, even though she felt all his sadness. It was the thing that linked them together more than anything else: the shame of their actions, the feeling that they would never be who they wanted to be. Rua felt it in him as acutely as she felt it in herself.

Renwick's face softened. Cupping her cheek, he softly kissed her forehead. "I don't deserve your kindness."

Rua laughed gently, resting her forehead back against Renwick's lips. "Nor I yours."

"Let's go inside!" Aneryn called, trudging around the corner. "It's colder than—" She paused when she saw them. "Oh Gods, you're not kissing, are you?"

The two of them chuckled.

"No, Aneryn," Renwick said, cheeks dimpling. The look of his happiness reminded Rua, once again, to release that tightness in her chest. Threading his fingers through hers, Renwick led her back to the castle.

She wondered if she could do it—the promise she made herself to try at Raffiel's memorial. Looking back over her shoulder one more time, in the direction that Onyx had disappeared, Rua wasn't sure if she could keep that promise.

～

The moment they arrived in Lyrei Basin, they stumbled into the dining commons, abandoned for the night. Renwick and Aneryn took a
seat at the closest table, Rua across from them.

"Should we summon the green witches?" Renwick asked.

"No," Aneryn and Rua responded in unison. They were doing that
more and more.

They could eat in the morning. Rua's stomach turned to acid as she
held the ancient book of power. The Immortal Blade seemed to buzz
as if sensing the book she now held—the magic of the witches thick in
the air.

Sliding the book across the table to Aneryn, Rua said, "Open it."

The blue witch frowned and slid it back to her. "I don't read Mhenbic
as well as you."

"That didn't seem to be a problem in the Temple of Yexshire." Rua
huffed, but opened the book to the first page, anyway. "Fine."

The Mhenbic words were scrawled in thick cursive. Squinting
down at the book, she murmured the words to herself.

"Maybe don't read those words out loud," Aneryn cut in, blue eyes
flickering. "You don't want to accidentally cast any spells."

"Good point," Renwick said as he stared fixedly at his fingers. He
had been distant since the book came into their possession, seemingly
haunted by seeing Onyx Mallor again. It didn't take a blue witch's gift
of Sight to know his past plagued him.

"We don't have the Witches' Glass. We won't be casting any spells,"
Rua reminded them.

Her fingers skimmed across the Mhenbic words, page after page,
as Aneryn and Renwick watched in bated silence. A scrawling at the
bottom of the page suddenly caught her eyes, fingers snagging over the
words.

"What?" Aneryn asked, clasping her hands together on the table.

"Possession spell," Rua murmured, reading the ancient words. *"To
control those weak of mind and possess their souls."*

"Gods," Renwick breathed. "That sounds like it."

"What are the words?" Aneryn's voice wobbled. The shadows
seemed to creep closer. "How do we reverse it?"

"It says: *Touch a stone imbued with witch magic, the gem of life and power—*"

"The Witches' Glass." Aneryn's voice was so soft it was barely audible, her saucer eyes growing impossibly wide. The ancient texts of her people seemed to fill her with mounting dread.

"*Say the sacred words: Dzraa divleur.*" Rua clenched her eyes shut against the words. It meant "I possess your soul." It was what it felt like every time she thought of Balorn, like he was creeping closer to possessing her soul. She shuddered as she forced herself to keep reading. "*And to break the hold of magic upon the cursed: Dzraa diver rek mofareis.*" She looked up at her companions across the table. "*The possession of your soul is released.*"

Aneryn scrubbed her hand down her face, hanging her head. They knew the witches were cursed. They had seen the *suraash*, but the horror of their plight flamed anew. It steeled Rua's resolve, knowing beneath each of those wild faces was a soul possessed.

"I thought it would be more cryptic than that," Renwick said, staring at the book. "It seems so simple."

"That is just the translation. It is not written in common Mhenbic. The wording is old and foreign, even to me," Rua said, frowning down at the yellowing paper under her fingertips. "You would not know how to say it unless you read it here."

"Now what?" Aneryn probed, her eyes flaring with another strobe of blue glow. The blue witch was more upset than Rua had ever seen her before.

"We need to head west and confront Balorn at once. He has the Witches' Glass," Rua said. An invisible weight crushed into her chest as Balorn's smug smile flitted through her mind.

"We can't go rushing off to the West," Renwick said, rubbing his forehead. Rua's eyes tracked the movement. "It is several days' ride. We need to be prepared."

"How long will it take to be prepared?" Rua shut the book and clutched it to her chest.

"At least two days to ready the troops and gather provisions." Renwick glanced to Aneryn, eyes apologetic.

The blue witch reluctantly bobbed her chin. "Now is not the time to be hasty."

A guard strode into the tent, making them all jump. "Forgive me, Your Majesty," he said with a bow. "There is a call in the fae fire for Her Highness."

"Oh Gods," Rua groused, going through the list of people it could be.

"And you thought that book would be the scariest thing you faced tonight," Aneryn said with a laugh.

Rua scowled at her friend. "Will you take the book to Baba Airu?"

"It is late," Aneryn counseled. "We can bring it tomorrow morning."

Rua nodded, pushing back from the table and clutching the book tightly to her side. Renwick's eyes remained downcast at his hands, not saying goodbye. Rua wanted to stay and clear away the haze that seemed to cloud over him. The cursed words had rattled them all, but she knew why he took it the hardest. The curse worked on those weak of mind, and he had helped make those witches weak. She saw him piling the guilt of his actions atop himself like stones in a mighty wall.

She prayed Aneryn would have some words of comfort for Renwick, but her blue witch friend seemed equally haunted. She shouted in her mind to say something to him, anything, but instead she just turned and followed the guard out of the tent.

They twined their way through the campsite, the air not as brisk as it had been weeks before. They would have to abandon the Lyrei Basin encampment soon. The ice would thaw. Spring was on the horizon.

A wall of heat blasted into her as she pushed her way into the fae fire tent. The yellow-green flames reached higher than she had ever seen them before, as if the fire itself felt the anger emanating from the other side.

Rua braced herself as she said, "Hello?"

"What the fuck were you thinking?" It was Bri.

Rua's stomach dropped. "Hi, Bri."

"Don't you *hi* me," Bri snarled. "I'm meant to be protecting you, Rua, and you left in the middle of the night without even telling me. And now Norwood is—"

"Where is he?" Rua's eyes widened, thinking of what Aneryn had told her.

"Word was sent from Hale's spies watching the Norwood camp in the Eastern forests. The campsite is still there . . . but the numbers are halved."

"Where have the others gone?" Rua asked as she chucked her cloak on the bench behind her, sweat already beading on her brow.

"No one has seen Augustus. They trailed him out to the coast. They think he is at sea now, though we don't know where he is going."

"This is not good," Rua muttered. They already needed to find Balorn, and now Augustus was on the move.

"Yeah, no shit," Bri hissed. "We would have had an easier time figuring this out *together*, if you had stayed."

"I was worried for the Northern camps," Rua cut in.

"What a bleeding heart you are, Rua." The Eagle's voice dripped with venom. "You just wanted to get away from Yexshire."

"You don't know anything."

"Keep telling yourself that. Keep pushing everyone away." The sound of bitter laughter echoed out from the flames. "It's worked out for you so well so far."

Rua gritted her teeth, the words blasting into her as the memory of Raffiel's memorial flashed behind her clenched eyelids.

"Is that all?" She had been determined not to push everyone away, and she was already failing. Every attempt at fixing things made her backslide further into herself. Every step, she faltered.

She heard Bri's long, slow breath as the Eagle said, "Yes."

Rua thought about just turning and leaving, but it would prove every point she was trying so hard to fight. "Be safe, Bri." She forced herself to say it, even though it pained her.

She thought the Eagle might have left as she gathered her cloak and pulled it around her again. She was just about to exit the flaps of the tent when a bitter, quiet voice said, "Don't stray off any more cliffs, Ru."

∿

The sun broke through the heavy blanket of clouds as Aneryn and Rua walked side by side through the domed tents of the witches' quarter.

Rua elbowed Aneryn, asking, "What was that?"

"What was what?" Aneryn gave her a look that said she knew exactly what she was asking.

"That girl smiled at you," Rua said, never breaking her stride.

"Her name is Laris, and she's not a girl. She's the same age as you." Aneryn nudged her shoulder back into Rua.

"Tell me about this Laris?" Rua grinned.

Aneryn ducked her head in embarrassment, a giggle erupting from her lips. She seemed seventeen now, not the wise old soul that she also was. It was nice to see this side of her.

"There is nothing to tell." Aneryn tucked one of the black braids that fell across her forehead behind her rounded witch ear.

Aneryn's footsteps faltered as her hands and eyes glowed a faint blue. It was a brief flash of light, but it was enough to tell Rua that Aneryn had a vision.

"Baba Airu wants to speak with you," Aneryn said, blinking as the surrounding glow disappeared.

"How do you know that?" Rua frowned. She didn't feel like conversing with the elderly witch and discussing her Fate anymore.

"How do you think I know?" Aneryn scoffed. "I Saw you two talking."

"Maybe we were talking in two days' time." Rua shrugged.

"You were talking in two minutes' time," Aneryn countered.

"How could you possibly—"

"Will you stop asking how I know?" Aneryn cursed, exasperated. She probably had been asked the same question a million times before. "I just know! If I asked you how a thought crosses your mind, would you be able to explain it to me? Now, are you going to talk to Baba Airu or not?"

"Apparently, I don't have a choice," Rua snipped.

"You always have a choice," Aneryn replied. "The future will change if you choose not to go."

"I'll go," Rua said, shoulders drooping.

"I know." Aneryn smirked.

Rua let out a long-suffering sigh. Having a blue witch as a friend was exhausting.

"Want to dine in my tent tonight?" Rua asked. "I can't be bothered going to the dining tent."

Rua hated going into the dining tent reserved for the important fae. It was usually Renwick's councilor or other highborn fae that were in there. They all looked at Rua with distrust. She preferred eating with the witches. They looked at her like she was their friend.

"I'll see you then," Aneryn said, leaving Rua to find her way to Baba Airu's tent alone.

Rua knew the paths well by now. She knew the witches' quarter was set up like a spiral, with Baba Airu's tent at the very center—the most sacred spot in the witch's spiral.

She didn't knock as she entered, finding Baba Airu standing at her table. The High Priestess held a smoking metal bowl filled with dried herbs. Three candles were lit on the table in front of her—a white one with a blue one on either side. On the table in front of the candles was a circle of salt . . . and in the center of that circle was the silver ring from her totem bag.

Rua stood there frozen, watching as the witch wafted the smoke out over the salt circle.

"You can come in, Rua," Baba Airu said in her slow, warm tone.

Rua moved to the chair she always sat in and watched as Baba Airu put the bowl down. She muttered some words in Mhenbic, too quiet for Rua to understand. Picking up the silver ring, the High Priestess deposited it back in her totem bag around her neck.

Rua watched in surprise at the ease with which the High Priestess navigated her tent. She moved back to her rocking chair beside Rua and sat down without feeling that the chair was there first. Rua wondered how much of that was the witch's gift of Sight and how much was her being practiced at knowing where all her belongings were.

"You've been spending a lot of time in the witches' quarter of late," Baba Airu said, turning to her fire. "I'm glad for it . . . though I suspect you are more here to avoid someone."

Rua's ears burned. She wondered how much Baba Airu knew.

"I like it here. It's not as stuffy as the fae district," she said.

Baba Airu's thin lips twitched. "There was a time not so long ago when you would not have said such things," she said, rocking herself gently. "The witches have taken to you as well."

"The night of the Harvest Moon, there was a witch . . ."

"Her name is Asha," Baba Airu said. "I think the tales of your heroism in saving her may have become stretched far beyond the truth at this point. But there is little I can do to stymie the gossip. Young witches like to tell stories. I will let her tell hers."

"She called me *Mhenissa*," Rua said.

Baba Airu's lips stretched thin again as she gestured toward the Immortal Blade. "Is she wrong?"

"The honor feels like too much . . ." Rua said. Baba Airu bobbed her chin. "It will hurt them more when I leave."

"I do not think you will leave, Your Highness," Baba Airu mused. Rua bristled at her words, at her formal title. "You are meant to lead our people. The witches have chosen you."

"They can't just *choose* me," Rua snapped. It felt wrong to argue with the High Priestess, but the things she said were ridiculous.

"The Fates have chosen you too," Baba Airu said.

"No," Rua breathed before Baba Airu finished her sentence. She had feared this moment might be real. She was terrified of what the High Priestess might say next. Once the words were spoken, they could never be unheard.

"We have Seen it, Ruadora: a Dammacus leader on our throne . . . alongside her Fated."

Rua's heart stopped beating. Fated.

It couldn't be true. She balled her hands into fists in her lap as she whispered, "No."

"You cannot deny the Fates, Ruadora," Baba Airu said, her voice far too calm for the life-changing weight of what was being proclaimed. "They have woven your Fate with his long before either of you were born. It is our most powerful magic. Saying 'no' changes nothing."

"It can't be true." Rua sucked in a gasp of air. Her whole body felt weightless. "How could no one know?"

Baba Airu folded her hands in her lap. "That is a question for your King."

Rua froze. "Does he know?"

"He does."

Rua thought her eyes might go black and she would topple from her chair. She needed to get outside and into the fresh air.

"How did no one else See our Fates then?" Rua's voice was scratchy and muted. It sounded far away, even to her own ears.

"Ask him what happened to a witch named Nave Mallor," Baba Airu said. It was the first time Rua heard any bite in her voice.

Mallor. Like Onyx Mallor. She remembered the name from the witches' forge in Raevenport. The night she had given her the spell book, Onyx said to ask Renwick about her sister, and Rua had not. Shame crawled under her skin. She had wanted to avoid the answer, but she couldn't hide away from it any longer.

"Did he kill her?" Rua panted.

"He killed a lot of people to keep his secret . . . your secret," Baba Airu said.

Rua felt her throat constricting as if a hand were squeezing her airways shut. She shook her head in disbelief.

"He killed witches to keep them from telling his father that we were Fated?" Rua took a ragged breath.

Baba Airu's rocking paused. "Yes, and he killed witches so they wouldn't tell his father why they couldn't See his Fate."

"What?" Rua's whole body was trembling now. "Why couldn't they See his Fate?"

Baba Airu lifted her hand to her chest. She traced her finger around the ring in her totem bag. The silence stretched out for so long that Rua wondered if the High Priestess wouldn't answer.

When she finally spoke, Rua couldn't brace herself for what she said. "Because blue witches can't See the Fates of other blue witches."

# CHAPTER TWENTY-SIX

S he stormed through the complex of tents. Not a single guard stopped her. Her heart hammered in her throat as she struggled to take a deep breath.

*Blue witches can't See the Fates of other blue witches.*

Gods, she could barely breathe. She thought to Renwick's pointed ears. Hennen Vostemur was certainly fae. He wouldn't have knowingly married a witch. People would have known that Renwick's mother wasn't fae. How was it possible that he was a blue witch?

She thought to the note his mother had written to his little brother in that book. She had called Eadwin *mea raga*, my precious little one, in Mhenbic. Mother Moon, what was a fae Queen doing using Mhenbic sayings?

It didn't make any sense.

She threw open the heavy curtains and stormed into Renwick's office. "Is it true?"

"Rua," Renwick said, looking up, startled, from his desk. "You shouldn't be in here."

His shirt was unbuttoned as he leaned back, revealing the carved lines of his muscled chest.

Rua gave no thought to it, not with all the questions she had rising in her mind. She did not heed his warning as she stormed up to his desk. A glass vial sat at the end, just beyond his reach, and she already knew what lay inside it.

"Is it true?" Her voice rose in her chest like a roaring wave.

Renwick narrowed his green eyes at her. "Where have you just come from?"

"Baba Airu's tent," Rua snarled.

Renwick's body stilled in that telltale way, the muscle in his jaw popping out.

She slammed her hand down hard on the desk, making him jolt, finally breaking that frozen visage. "Are you part witch?"

"My mother was half blue witch, yes," he gritted out, rubbing his forehead methodically.

"Do you have visions?" Rua glared as he rubbed his head. "I thought it was headaches from your poisons." She scowled at the vial on the desk. "But you are having visions, aren't you?"

"And I would thank you to keep that quiet," he hissed. "I have worked very hard to keep that secret from those who would see me dead for it."

"Oh, I am aware of the lengths you would go," she seethed. "What happened to Nave Mallor, Renwick?"

Renwick's lips parted. "Rua."

Tears pinpricked behind her eyes, her chest caving inward, cracking under an invisible force.

"Tell me!" she shouted, eyes welling.

Renwick's gaze fell back to the bottle on the desk. "I killed her."

"Why?" Her bottom lip trembled. She already knew the answer.

"She was a strong witch. Balorn struggled to break her. She figured out why she couldn't See my Fate, and so she went looking in her mind for who my Fate was tied to. She Saw that you were still alive and . . ." Renwick rested his forearms on the desk, grimacing, never breaking his gaze from that bottle of poison. ". . . what we are to each other."

He had killed Nave Mallor to protect her from them. What Hennen and Balorn Vostemur would have done had they known a Dammacus princess was still alive in the High Mountain Court . . . they would have killed her and all the red witches around her. Renwick had been protecting her before he even knew her, protecting ... *what we are to each other.*

"You mean that we are Fated?" Rua snarled.

"Yes," he whispered.

"Why didn't you tell me?"

Renwick's eyes finally shot back to hers, wide and practically glowing. They flickered blue, she realized. Gods, how had she not seen it before? As his control slipped, the emerald turned to turquoise for a brief flash before returning to green.

"How could I tell you?" Renwick growled. He stared at the uncorked bottle on his desk, tempting him. Rua noted the bottle was still full. The pain elixir remained. But she knew from the look in his eyes that he was warring with himself whether to drink it or not. "How could I tell you that your soul is shackled to mine when you looked at me like I was a monster?"

"I don't care that you're a monster, Renwick! In that, we are the same," Rua hissed, her voice rising into a shout once more. "I care that you lied to me!"

Renwick's fingers reached out for the blue bottle at her words, but Rua was faster. She snatched the bottle off the table and brought it to her lips, sculling the bitter fluid back with a grimace.

Renwick leapt up from behind his desk. "No!"

In a split second, he was around the desk. Grabbing the empty bottle from her hand, he stared at it in horror.

"You drank it all?" Terror filled his face. "It's too much, Rua. It's nearly too much for me, and I am used to it."

Renwick bolted to the curtains and shouted at his guards, "Fetch a brown witch healer. Now!"

Rushing back to her, Renwick stood a hair's breadth in front of her, searching her eyes. "Why did you do that?"

"You are not the only one who gets to poison the pain away," she whispered. Her whole body was warming. Pleasant tingles drifted down toward her fingertips. No wonder Renwick drank this stuff.

Her eyes started to roll back as sweeping waves of warmth coursed through her.

"No!" She was snapped out of it by two strong hands grabbing either side of her face. Renwick's eyes blazed at her. "You have to fight it, Rua. It will pull you under too quickly." His voice dropped into a worried whisper as he pressed his forehead to hers. "Stay awake, please."

That delicious tingling warmth spread down her body. Her lips parted and her eyes closed. Renwick jolted her back, shaking her head as his fingers clenched her face tighter.

"Fight it, Rua. I can't lose you," he pleaded as her eyes rolled back again, lost in the undertow. "Fight. You are strong."

"I'm not strong," she murmured, the potion loosening her tongue. She released a pleasant hum but was jolted again and opened her eyes. "It feels like everything breaks me, but I have been through nothing compared to you."

"You really think you've been through nothing? Except having your whole family killed at a young age, being displaced by war, being ignored and resented your whole childhood, being abducted and nearly killed . . ." The normally frozen face of the Northern King was now riddled with anger and fear as if he would battle back the darkness for her. "Shall I go on?"

Her heart thundered in her chest even as that warming sensation made her limbs feel heavy. "It is nothing compared to your suffering," she said, lifting a limp hand to his cheek.

"You say that only to deny that what you feel is equally real."

"I should be able to control the sword better," Rua panted, her chest rising and falling faster even as sleep summoned her. "I should be able to control *myself* better. I don't know why I can't handle it."

"Maybe if you were ever allowed to fucking feel something, all of this wouldn't have hit you so hard," he growled.

"Says a Vostemur," she huffed.

"I. Am. Not. My. Father," Renwick gritted out.

Rua's heart plummeted into her stomach as she shook her head. "No." She didn't mean it like that. She didn't know why her tongue betrayed her with those words. But she didn't have time to contemplate it as her legs buckled. She thought he would let her fall for what she said, but just before she hit the ground, he lashed out and caught her.

"Stay awake, Rua. Please!" Renwick's panicked voice sounded far away. The periphery of her vision blackened until all she saw was that fearful look on his face.

"I'm here," she heard a soft female voice say as footsteps rushed over to her.

Her eyes fluttered closed.

~

The smell of cloves and freshly fallen snow amongst evergreen trees wrapped around her. She felt the crisp winter air, even in the warmth of her bed. But it wasn't her bed. The sheets felt softer. The pillows felt different, and that scent was not the bergamot and tea aroma of her own tent.

The pounding in her head made her want to close her eyes again, an invisible vise squeezing her skull. Her throat was dry and rough as she swallowed. She blinked her eyes open. Beside the bed sat Renwick in a crushed velvet chair. His crumpled clothes and tousled hair denoted he had been in the chair for a long time. But his eyes were clear and bright as he stared at her, his lips slowly pulling up into a smile.

"You're alive." He swept his hair off his face.

"I'm not so easily killed," Rua whispered, sizing up the scratch marks down his face. She didn't remember doing it, but as she opened her mouth to speak, Renwick cut her off.

"I deserved it," he murmured. "I deserved it and a lot more, Rua. I should have told you the first moment I saw you, I just . . ." His eyes desolately searched hers. "I couldn't bear you hating me for it."

Rua didn't reply. She begrudgingly understood, but she did not forgive him.

"Do you have visions?" she asked instead.

Renwick snapped his head up as if smacked. "No one has asked me about it before."

"No one that survived," Rua said, and instantly regretted it, as Ren-

301

wick hid his crestfallen expression behind his steely armor again. "I can't imagine what it would be like growing up knowing you were part witch in a court that tortured and enslaved them."

"Could you imagine what they would have done to me if they had known?" he whispered in a hollow, haunted voice.

Rua shuddered. "They would have wanted to see how far they could push you, like they did the others."

Renwick bobbed his head, swallowing. "I don't have visions as clear as someone like Aneryn; they're just little flashes in my mind. I push them down as tightly as I can."

"Does it hurt? Pushing the visions away?"

Those emerald eyes found hers. "Yes."

She took a deep, jagged breath. He pushed them down so tightly. She couldn't imagine what it would feel like to deny her own magic. It was its own kind of torture.

"Do you ever glow?"

"Once," he said, hanging his head in his hands again, his muscles coiled like he was readying for battle. "When I was eighteen. I went to a brown witch apothecary in Murreneir. I thought I was going to die and she gave me the potion . . . poison," he corrected, dragging his hands down his face. He looked so raw in that moment, so unlike the rigid posture and fine clothes he normally disguised himself in.

"You've been drinking it since you were eighteen?" Unwelcome tears began welling in Rua's eyes at the thought. He had spent nearly a decade of his life poisoning away his visions, living in fear of being discovered by his father.

"Most of my visions are feelings, things I just somehow come to know, like I know that Thador is riding back from Drunehan, though he has not told me it is so." He licked his bottom lip and pressed his lips together as if debating whether to say his next words or not. "I've had one clear recurring vision in all of my life."

"Of what?" she asked, her heart stuttering as those piercing eyes found hers again.

"You."

She knew he would say it, but it still made the whole world stop, as if she were free-falling through time. The walls of the tent bowed and shook as a rogue gale swept across the campsite. The shaking of the fabric was the only sound.

"I Saw you in the mountains," he said, looking up to the ceiling, clenching his jaw between sharp breaths, as if he could push his feelings down into his gut as easily as he did his visions. "You were hiding behind a hut, chin on your knees, crying." His voice broke. "And I knew then who you were, what you were to me."

Rua didn't know which moment it was. Her whole life she had spent hiding to shed her tears alone. She couldn't let the witches see it, see her weakness, a stone they placed on her that she still carried. As she scanned Renwick's drooped shoulders and cracking expression, those cursed tears kept springing to her eyes, and she looked up to the ceiling, just as he had. It was a trick she had learned that helped keep the tears from falling. She wondered if he had learned it too. In that moment, looking at the Northern King, Rua didn't feel like they were royalty; she felt like they were two lonely people who had always struggled to hide themselves from the people who were meant to love them.

"We have met before, though, haven't we?" Rua whispered, keeping her eyes glued to the roof. She searched her mind for the memory, but it was not there. She thought of smoke and screams and pain, but she couldn't be certain they were her real memories or just the terrifying thoughts of what it must have been like. "You were there that night, when Hennen tried to kill us all?"

"I was." His voice trembled. "I saw a witch grabbed you and fled. She practically flung you from the flames. I got Raffiel out, covered for him while he scaled a window ledge. I tried to make it look like I was fighting his own guards. I've been playing both sides for a long time."

"Why would you help us before you knew who I was to you?"

His lip trembled as his voice cracked. "Because I never wanted anyone to die." Their eyes dropped to each other's and a thick tear slid down Renwick's cheek. "I may be a monster for all the things I have done to survive these many years, but I am not my father."

The sight of his tear made the dam behind Rua's eyes release, and the flood came thick and fast, tears streaming down her cheeks. He had been helping her family before he even knew they were Fated. It wasn't some magical bond that had made him do the right thing. It had been his will all along. Something about that thought made Rua release a shuddering sob. Renwick moved from the chair as if possessed by the sound. He cupped Rua's face and pressed his forehead to hers.

"I am sorry," he whispered as she reached up and brushed her salty lips over his. "I am so sorry for all the pain I have caused you."

"No," she said, reaching her hand up and bracketing his hard jawline. "You are not a bad person, Renwick." He tried to pull away, but she pulled his forehead back to hers, holding him there, forcing him to hear her confession. "I know you don't believe it, but it's true. You did terrible things, and you did courageous things, and I don't know what that all adds up to and I don't fucking care. I'm not counting marks against your soul. I'm not counting at all." The tears fell heavier, covering both of their cheeks as she said the words to him she had so despairingly needed to hear herself. "I see you, all of your dark corners, just as you see mine. And I love you."

His face crumpled as his lips collided with hers. How desperately they both needed it—to love someone, to be loved, to permit themselves the truth that had been raging inside of them. Her arms wrapped around him tighter, pulling him onto the bed, needing to feel his chest pressed against hers. He propped himself up by one straining arm as he smothered the blankets between them, kissing her like it might be his only chance.

"Your Majesty," a hurried voice called from beyond the tent wall.

Renwick broke their kiss with a growl. "What?"

"Baba Airu has agreed to meet with you," the messenger said.

Rua's swollen lips parted as she took a shallow breath and looked up at Renwick. "You should go."

"No," he snarled, making her smile and brush another kiss to his lips.

"I need to bathe and eat some breakfast anyway," she murmured against his mouth. "Go."

He paused, sniffing as the tears on his cheeks dried, seemingly debating whether he should leave her after such a life-altering confession.

"I promise I'm not fleeing Lyrei Basin anytime soon," Rua said with a half-smile, wiping his lingering tear with her thumb. She saw it on his face—how much those words meant to him—the child who was abandoned by his mother.

He looked at her like she was the golden dawn. "I would tear down the sky for you," he promised, leaving her with one last kiss.

# CHAPTER TWENTY-SEVEN

Raga snorted happily as Rua fed the horse another apple. Renwick was still meeting with Baba Airu. After she bathed, Rua couldn't bear to pace around the King's tent, waiting for him to return. It all felt too delicate. Their promises and confessions still felt paper thin, and she didn't know how to carry on until she felt those words fulfilled in every part of her soul.

"I know he's not going to take it back," she murmured to Raga as the horse sniffed her face. She rubbed a hand down her neck in solid, sweeping strokes—just how the mare seemed to like it. "I know that," she repeated, trying to keep her limbs from trembling.

She had barely been able to stomach a piece of bread. Renwick Vostemur, King of the Northern Court, was her Fated. Not only that, but he was part blue witch. No one had ever known she even had a Fated. . . and she had been glad for it. But now, knowing the truth validated every betrayed feeling she had ever had for him. He had been secretly helping her family since before he even knew they were Fated. He was not the monster everyone thought he was. All the pieces were coming together in her mind, and it made her want to laugh and cry and scream all at once.

A hawk screeched overhead, and she knew another one of Renwick's visions had come true. The clopping of hooves sounded behind her, and she glanced over her shoulder to see Thador riding into the stables.

"Your Highness," he said with a dip of his chin. He paused before dismounting his horse and passing the reins to a stable hand. Striding over to her, he crossed his arms. "You look like you're about to burst out of your skin."

"I am," she whispered to keep her voice from wobbling. She felt like she needed to scream until it shredded her lungs or punch something until her knuckles bled—anything to relieve the rising tide in her.

"So, you know then." The giant fae leaned against the stable gate as he laughed. His riding clothes were caked in thick snow. A scarf tied tightly at his neck accompanied his fur hat and woolen gloves.

"Know what?" Rua hedged, eyeing him.

Thador guffawed. "That you are his Fated."

Her stomach dropped. "You knew?"

"He didn't tell me, if that's what you're wondering," Thador said, turning to lean his forearms against the stable gate, looking weary from being out in the cold for so long. "But it doesn't take a blue witch to see the two of you together. He is a different person when he looks at you . . . and you him."

Rua clenched and unclenched her hands, shaking out her limbs as if getting ready to spar. "Why would the fates choose us to be together?" she groaned. Her thoughts whirled. It felt shocking and inevitable all at once, and she couldn't contain all the disparate emotions battling in her mind.

"Maybe they knew you were both haunted by death and the guilt of your decisions," Thador mused. "Maybe they paired you together because you saw each other beyond the crowns and titles."

Another unanswered question sprung into her mind. "Is that why they call me *Mhenissa*? Because I am his Fated?"

"You have earned that title all on your own, Princess." They heard Ehiris call from the skies. "Though I know the witches are glad that you are tied to him. They believe you will make him a better ruler . . . I believe so too."

"Do you know"—she eyed him sideways—"about who he is?"

"We've never talked about it. Not even once." Thador's dark eyes flitted to her for the briefest moment and then back to the horses. "I saw his eyes glow the day I met him. It was the last time he ever cried."

Rua's chest tightened and she understood the power of the tears he had shed just moments earlier in the tent. She absently scratched Raga behind the ear. "How long have you been his guard?"

"Gods, I've lost track," he said, loosening the scarf knotted at his neck. "Over twelve years."

She thought to when was the last time he cried, knowing it must have been the death of his mother and brother. Their deaths were made all the more painful knowing his mother fled without him. It shattered her heart, that feeling of being unwanted. It was something she had never grieved for herself.

"I'm glad he has you now," Thador said, as if reading her train of thought. "He needs to let these things out somehow. He needs to cry and grieve. I'm glad he has someone to lean on other than me."

The lumbering ogre seemed different in this light, his soft words just as gruff, his stature just as mighty. But the tenderness to his words made her ache.

"I'm glad he has you too," she whispered.

"I serve you too now, you know," he said in that brusque voice that seemed like he was grumbling even when his words were kind. He glanced over to her, giving her a smirk.

Rua blinked at him. It was true—she was the Fated of his King. Her throat tightened under an invisible grip as a realization struck her: she would one day be Queen.

Thador's grin turned foxlike as the understanding crossed her face. It already felt like too much to be someone's Fated, let alone a King. It seemed no matter how hard she tried to outrun her destiny, the life of a royal fae was inevitable. How was she meant to lead a kingdom? She couldn't even take care of herself.

Raga's ears shifted, pointing to the open stable doorway as Rua's stomach roiled. She didn't turn, couldn't move, already knowing who was there. She realized it was because he was her Fated, some magical link between them that she felt pulsing in the air like the magic of her sword.

Thador snorted at the terrified look on her face and whispered to her, "It's going to be okay," before turning and greeting Renwick with a loud, "You managed to keep alive while I was gone, I see."

Rua didn't turn to look at them, staring fixedly at Raga. She thought the contents of her lean meal might come spilling back up. Her destiny was waiting behind her, and it made her whole body tremble.

"How is Drunehan?" Renwick asked, his voice straining in what Rua assumed was the force of Thador's hug.

A smile pulled on her lips. The two of them were gruff and rigid in equal measure, but she loved that Thador hugged his King when no one was watching . . . no one except Rua. She was permitted to peek behind their guise now that she wasn't going anywhere. She tried to take a deep breath, but her lungs rebelled. Curse the Moon, she wasn't going anywhere. She couldn't understand why it struck such fear into her. If she wanted to leave, she knew Renwick would let her go . . . but it wasn't the forces of the world she feared; it was her own will that terrified her. She wanted to be here with him. She wanted things so fiercely she scarcely knew existed in her . . . and finally wanting something—someone—was the most frightening feeling of all.

"Rest well," Renwick said, making Rua realize she hadn't listened to any of Thador's updates from the former capital city. "We leave for the West in two days' time. Prepare yourself for what's coming."

Those ominous words hung in the air. Her worries suddenly felt small. She feared for a future not guaranteed. They still had to battle Balorn, find the Witches' Glass, and break the curse on the *suraash*. If they could survive all of that, surely she would be able to survive the thing she feared now—happiness.

Renwick ambled over to the gate as Raga shifted around Rua to greet him. Clearly, the mare was partial to the King. Renwick reached up and rubbed a hand down her cheek as Rua stared at her hands.

"Baba Airu was contacted by the Raevenport witches," he said, the surprise of his statement pulling Rua's eyes to him.

The sight of him blasted through her—the sharp cheekbones and shining emerald eyes, the alabaster skin and full lips. It was as if she had never seen him before, as if her soul finally recognized him. But his words were enough to break through to her. "What did the witches say?"

"They want to reunite with their coven in exchange for the blue witch fortress," Renwick said, lips parting as he stared at Rua's mouth.

"The Temple of Hunasht?" Her brow furrowed. "They want to live in those haunted halls?"

"They want to tear it down and build a new forge there." Renwick shifted closer to her. "I, of course, have given them my blessing to do with their temple as they wish. It should have never belonged to the fae, anyway."

"That's incredible," Rua murmured. "Though I don't blame them for wanting to leave Raevenport." She chuckled lightly, seeing Renwick's smile from the corner of her eye.

"I think we both know what gave them the strength to return," he said, his magnetizing gaze pulling on her again. "It was you, Rua."

His admiration rolled through her, but she shook her head, summoning the strength to reach up and touch his face. "It was us, Renwick."

His eyes closed at the sound of his name, as if savoring her words. He turned his face into her hand, his lips brushing her palm. "This is real, isn't it?" he whispered into her skin. "Why do I keep feeling like at any second it will all be taken back?" His brow creased. "I don't deserve—"

"Stop," Rua said, pressing her fingers to his lips. Her fears melted from her like the snow in the springtime sun, knowing Renwick's feelings churned through him just as acutely as her own.

Renwick's eyes widened as she stretched up on her toes and brushed her lips to his. She held for a moment, waiting for his lips to respond, but he held perfectly still. Dropping back to her heels, she searched his face. She saw it all—joy, sorrow, awe, terror—all the things battling within her own chest. And she suddenly knew, even in this, she was not alone.

She saw the second that frozen facade broke, the ice fissuring and then splintering apart as he grabbed her by the back of her neck and pulled her mouth to his. Every kiss was a promise—that this was real— it was new and raw and terrifying, but it was real. His arms wrapped around her, pulling her against his hard chest as he kissed her. A groan erupted from him as she snaked her fingers up into his hair.

Raga's stomping hoof was enough to pull them apart for air.

"Come back to my room with me," Renwick panted, hands clenching the sides of her cloak.

A smile stretched across Rua's face as she nodded, finally knowing how she wanted to greet that rising tide of emotions in her.

～

The soft glow of midday light filtered into the King's bedchamber. Rua barely had a moment to take in the room before Renwick's hand slipped around to cup the back of her neck. He traced his lips over her mouth in a soft, yielding kiss.

He pulled back, eyes darkening. "Permit me something," he said, his lips only a breath away. "Let me make love to you."

Rua moved her head away in surprise, and he released his hold on her. She didn't know what she was expecting, she understood sating carnal pleasures, but lovemaking felt far scarier. "I . . ."

"I promise I'll have my way with you a million more times after, if you desire." He laughed, even though his eyes watched every emotion dance across her face. "But let me make love to you, please." He begged with such an urgency it made her legs weaken.

"I don't know how." Rua's eyes dropped to her hands. She knew how to exist outside this tent. She knew how to cut away at people before they came too close. But this . . . this . . . she did not know how to do this.

Renwick threaded his fingers through hers and lifted her hand to his lips.

"Shall I show you?" he murmured into the back of her hand.

He released her hand back down and waited for a response. Rua knew he longed for this moment, but she also knew he would not judge her for saying no. That did not scare her. The thing that frightened her most of all was how badly she wanted it too.

She looked up into those green eyes, summoning every ounce of bravery. "I trust you."

His light eyebrows lifted and his lips parted, as the shock and sorrow and desire all streaked through that handsome face in rapid succession.

He moved to her in one slow step. Cupping her cheeks, he kissed her. A sweet, soft caress. This kiss was something she had never known but needed desperately. She kissed him back, lips tingling as they moved over him, inhaling the smell of snow and cloves with each breath.

Renwick's deft hands moved to the buttons of her dress, slowly baring her chest to the cool air. The heat from his own body greeted her exposed skin as he slid the garment down.

Stepping back from her, his eyes roved her naked body. Her cheeks heated.

"You are so incredibly beautiful," he whispered.

Rua dropped her gaze, clasping her hands together, trying to bear the weight of his stare.

"You think I jest?" His voice was a feral snarl. He moved back to her, grasping her jaw so that she would meet his eyes. "Not a single female holds a candle to you, Rua, not one. Not in your beauty or your strength or your cunning. I do not exaggerate, love."

*Love.* She felt that word skitter down her bare skin.

Renwick moved around to the back of her, his fingers moving in featherlight touches up and down. The sensation made every tiny hair lift over her body.

His hand wrapped around her stomach, pulling her back into his hard, wide chest. His nose dipped into her wavy brown hair, breathing in her scent. That hand on her belly circled her flesh in soft strokes as Renwick skimmed his teeth up her neck and to her ear.

"Do you want me to touch you?" he murmured.

Rua panted out a breath at the feeling of his lips. "Yes."

That slow circling hand drifted lower, tickling through the hairs between her legs as it moved closer to the apex of her thighs. Her body trembled, and Renwick held her tighter to him.

The first contact of his finger down the center of her made her gasp in a little breath. Renwick smiled into her neck as he lavished it with kisses. He slid that finger up and down, spreading her liquid heat over that sensitive button between her legs.

Rua moaned, her head falling back over Renwick's shoulder.

He kissed her cheek, moving back to her ear to whisper, "Let's see how many of those delicious little noises I can elicit from you tonight."

He nibbled the shell of her pointed ear. The feeling seemed to send a bolt of lightning straight down to where his fingers moved over her. Rua's chest felt heavy as she took another quick breath.

Renwick's other hand snaked around to palm her breast. His fingers twirled her hardened nipple, pulling another moan from her lungs. That arm tightened around Rua until Renwick held her entire body weight as that finger moved lower and dipped inside her.

She gasped as that finger explored her hot, wet core. Flickers of trembling rhapsody shot through her. Her fingertips and toes curled as he added a second finger. That building feeling was too much as she climbed higher and higher to that euphoric cliff.

She began to panic, grasping for purchase on Renwick's arms. It was too much.

"You're safe, Rua." Renwick's soft voice held her to this world. "Let go."

Her core tightened at his words, and then she was falling. A rumbling filled Renwick's chest as her moan turned into a rapturous cry. Her body spasmed as her muscles clenched around his fingers. He kept moving them, wringing out every little sound until she went limp in his arms.

Unsheathing his fingers from inside her, Renwick moved his hand in gentle massaging brushes up her side, as though calming a wild animal.

He released her back to the ground, and she turned into him, resting her forehead against his chest. He kissed the crown of her head as she breathed deeply, stroking down her spine.

Though the desperation was slightly sated, that desire still coursed through her veins. She lifted her fingers and unknotted the neck of his shirt.

Renwick's lips pulled up as she opened the neckline of his shirt to the light dusting of chest hair beneath. Renwick lifted his arms as Rua pulled the shirt up over his head and threw it to the ground.

She marveled at his chest once more. The veins of his arms pulsed out from thick corded muscles that carved into his pale skin. She trailed her fingers down his chest, knowing that though it seemed immaculate, his body hid the scars of all his father had done to him. It pained her to think of it—this King who thought himself a monster was really an avenging God.

Rua moved her fingers down to the button of his trousers, his hardness straining to be freed. Undoing each button slowly, she hooked her thumbs into his undershorts and trousers and pushed them down together. Renwick's eyes never left Rua's as he stepped out of them and kicked them away.

Her lips parted as she looked over him—the sight of his thick, hard length made her pause. She remembered that night in the forest and the days afterward that it took for that soreness to ebb. Her eyes dropped away from him, but Renwick saw it all.

He lifted his hand, gently cradling the back of her neck as he said, "Stay with me tonight. Let's just sleep, Rua." His lips whispered across her mouth. "Just please, stay with me."

That plea broke her. He did not care about how much she would give him. He just wanted her to be near. Rua could stare down evil men and drive a killing blow with her blade, but this . . . this was the thing she didn't know how to do: letting someone love her.

But she couldn't deny her feelings any longer, not with this beautiful male standing raw and open in front of her. She wanted him and she would claim him.

Summoning her courage, she looked back up into those emerald eyes. "I do not want to just sleep."

Renwick's cheeks dimpled. "What do you want?"

"I want you. All of you." His face broke for a moment at her words, like she had cracked his chest open and his soul was straining out for her.

His mouth collided with hers in a claiming kiss. Rua's hands flew up around his muscled back, pulling him against her. She felt him hard against her belly. Their lips stayed connected as they shuffled back to the bed, Renwick's hand clenching the back of her neck as he guided her down onto the pillow.

He trailed kisses down her collarbone and to her breast, where he sucked her nipple into his mouth. Rua arched into him with another throaty moan.

"So many glorious little sounds you make," he murmured as his mouth drifted down her belly. "I wonder what sound you will make when I do this."

Before she knew what was happening, his hot tongue slid over her wet folds, making her cry out. Rua gripped the sheets beside her as his mouth moved over her core. That fiery, damp friction made her pant, her voice ratcheting up an octave. Gods, she climbed toward that cliff again.

Renwick released her, leaving her panting and breathless as he trailed his mouth back up her body. As his head hovered over her, his tip nudged at the slick wetness between her legs.

Rua's mouth opened as she took another drag of air. That blazing look alone was pushing her higher.

Renwick's eyes stared down at her in awe as he rested himself at her entrance. "If you feel anything other than ecstasy," he rasped, "please, Gods, tell me."

He waited until Rua nodded and then pushed into her. He moved at a slow pace, his mouth opening further the deeper he dove. Her body opened to him, her steaming core stretching to accommodate him further. It felt nothing like that night in the forest, nothing at all. It made every muscle in her body tingle, every cell honing in to the fullness inside her.

Each inch made her heart climb higher up her throat until her legs were trembling.

Renwick's chest heaved, stilling as he sheathed himself fully inside of her. He waited, watching her face with worried restraint. Rua was certain it would break him if he thought he had hurt her again.

Rua reached up and cupped his cheek. He turned his face into her touch, kissing the inside of her wrist.

"It's you," she whispered, her heart cracking open. "It's us. You're really here."

"I'm here." Renwick shuddered as he began to move. "I'm yours."

He slid out of her with deliberate slowness, almost to the tip, and then pushed back into her again. The sensation of those taunting thrusts left Rua aching with want.

She moved her hands down to his hard backside, demanding his hips move. Renwick grinned down at her as he moved in rolling pumps into her, making her body feel lighter with each movement, like she was floating above the bed. Bolts of lightning shot through her veins as he moved faster, eliciting a low moan.

"Does it feel good to have me inside of you?" Renwick growled, lowering himself to nibble her neck.

"Yes," she panted. "Gods, yes."

He moved faster, each thrust making another wild sound escape her throat, her body possessed with desire.

The muscles in Renwick's arms tightened as he climbed closer to his release.

He stilled, leaving Rua breathless, his brow slick with sweat. His eyes flickered turquoise and he clenched them shut.

It made Rua ache that he would hide any part of himself from her even now. She breathed, tracing her fingers across his jaw and up his temple.

Lifting her head, she murmured across his lips, "Look at me."

Hair fell around his face as he hung his head, arms shaking with restraint. His chest heaved but he didn't obey, a decade of fear and hiding giving him pause. But he needed to know who he was to her. Not Witchslayer. Not King. As she fused her body with his, she branded his name upon her heart.

"Renwick, Fated," she whispered. "Look at me."

His eyes flew open, flaring the most brilliant aquamarine. She stared at him in wonder. Even with him buried deep inside her, she was still mystified that this feeling between them was real. A lifetime passed between one breath and the next, two souls turning into one.

"I love you," he vowed, confirming every racing thought in her mind. He thrust into her, claiming her body as he claimed her with his words.

"I love you," Rua cried out, moving her hips to match his pace until the whole bed shook.

His lips collided with hers, swallowing her moans of pleasure. Her heart exploded from her chest, higher and higher, the endless building maddening and euphoric all at once. She grabbed his muscled backside, fusing them together as her groans became feral. Rua writhed beneath him as those deep, driving thrusts pushed her over the edge. Renwick barked out her name as he followed her over the cliff. They toppled over and over, muscles clenching and spasming as release tore through them together.

The climax echoed through Rua's body, so all encompassing, so earth-shattering. It was the first moment in her life that she felt completely certain: she was the Fated of Renwick Vostemur, the Northern King.

~

The sun was high in the sky when Rua lifted her head off the soft feather pillow. She blinked her eyes open, scanning the room for a pitcher of water. She propped herself up on her elbow as she spotted one sitting on the table across the room. As she moved to shuffle off the bed, a hand snaked around her stomach and hauled her back against a warm, hard chest.

"Stay," Renwick whispered in a sleep-addled voice.

A smile tugged up the corners of Rua's lips. "I was just going to get a glass of water."

"Use your magic to bring it to you," Renwick murmured into her hair.

The red witches taught them to only use their magic for things it would be too hard to do without it. It was considered wasteful to use magic on such simple things when it could be used for helping the community. But Rua rarely used her red magic anymore. It wasn't good to let that magic stagnate, either.

She pulled up on that coil of buzzing magic deep in her belly, the vibrations pulling out to her fingertips and her eyes as she focused on the pitcher of water. She lifted her hand, and the pitcher tipped gently over, pouring water into the glass next to it. She curled her fingers inward, and the glass floated over to her. She snatched it out of the air and took a long sip before turning and passing it to Renwick.

He smirked and took the glass from her.

"You are magnificent," he said.

Rua felt the blush creeping up to her delicately pointed ears as she lay back down. Renwick set the glass on his bedside table and leaned on his elbow, looking over her. He bent his head just enough to brush a soft, languid kiss over her lips. Already, Rua felt that warm buzzing in her core that she knew didn't come from magic.

She reached for Renwick's neck and pulled him back to her, his smile pressing against her lips as he chuckled, "You are voracious, aren't you?"

"Yes," Rua said against his lips, eliciting a growl from him as he opened his mouth to her, deepening her caress.

Renwick broke off the kiss, his eyes already filling with heat again. They hadn't slept more than a couple of hours. It was like years of pent-up desire had been unleashed on them all at once. Rua wasn't sure how long this constant yearning would be inside her, how long she would be desperate for his touch.

Renwick nudged her with his nose, leaning his forehead against hers. "Are you sore?"

"A little," Rua confessed. Her body was tired, and she was sore, but not in the painful way it had been before. It felt like when she trained in a new combat technique, unused muscles flaring back to life. It made her body echo with the pleasure from the night before. It made her want more of it.

"Maybe we should get breakfast," Renwick said, even as his hands traced down her bare sides to settle on her hips. He looked up to the

ceiling, the beams of sunlight coming in around the chimney. "Or perhaps it's time for lunch."

"I am not hungry for food," Rua pouted, wrapping her arms around
his neck and pulling his chest back against hers.

"Gods." Renwick's eyes blazed at her. "If you keep looking at me like
that, I don't think we will ever leave this tent."

"Good."

Renwick gave a wicked smile as he bent to kiss her neck. He trailed
leisurely kisses along the underside of her jaw as she threaded her fingers through his hair.

Rua hummed a sweet sound as she rolled onto her side, Renwick
curling around her back in the same position they slept in for those
brief hours that morning. He ran his hand over the swell of her breasts,
circling her peaked nipple, and down to her hips.

Rua stretched back to stroke him as he let out a groan. She had
memorized the feel of his perfect body, things she knew nothing about
the night before. There was an odd sense of pride in her for what she
had done. She had overcome that fear. She had let him in. And it seemed
she would be rewarded for it endlessly.

Renwick's hand strayed from her hip, dipping down between her
legs as he moved his torso flush against her back. He was ready, pressed
against her backside as his fingers rubbed her up and down.

She let out a soft moan. His fingers had already figured out how
to elicit that sound from her so easily. He spent all night testing each
movement, listening for her sounds of pleasure, honing in to what
she liked, and now he understood how badly she wanted his touch.
He knew the exact moment she craved more as he dipped his fingers
into her.

Rua arched her head back as Renwick nibbled her ear. His hot breath
heightened the tingling between her legs. Bucking his hips, Renwick
held her firm against him as he smirked into her hair. His other hand
reached up to her breast, finding the hardened peak of her nipple and
rolling it between his fingers.

Rua let out a deep groan that bellowed up from her throat. She
reached back and stroked him again, eliciting a growl of pleasure that

rumbled through his chest. She grinned as she replaced that smugness with heat.

"So eager," he gritted out, even as he moved himself against her hand. "You are making it very hard to ravish you."

"Ravish me later," she breathed, positioning him between her legs. "I need you now."

Her body was desperate for that connection. She didn't think that desperation would ever ebb. It was the physical manifestation of their wholeness. She was certain of it, of who they were to each other when he was moving inside of her.

Renwick groaned as he pushed himself into her hot, wet core. His hand kept circling that bundle of nerves as his other hand pinned her backside against him. He moved in her slowly at first, so slowly. She knew a time would come when they would have quick passionate bursts of frenzied lovemaking, but not today. This meant something more to him, and he seemed determined to take his time with her. She knew he wouldn't be able to bear messing it up again. Neither of them could. They needed this togetherness more than Rua ever could have understood.

She let him inside in every way, and he let her see all of him too.

Renwick moved in slow, rolling thrusts into her, growling as he buried himself fully inside of her. He stilled, his chest heaving against Rua's back.

Rua twisted to meet those shining eyes. He looked at her like she might be a mirage, like he couldn't believe it. She saw it in his eyes as he shook his head at her.

"I love you," he whispered, pain lacing in his voice. He could say it a million times and it would never feel like enough. She knew instinctively the fear he felt because it mirrored her own. It was something good, finally, and it was terrifying that it might be taken away.

Rua moved before he finished speaking. Pulling herself over, she turned to him, needing to see his face. She did not want to have him in that position, not with that look in his eyes, like he was terrified this wasn't real.

She pushed his chest back down onto the bed as she straddled his hips. His lips parted as he looked up at her. Positioning him at her entrance, she slowly lowered herself, watching his eyes gutter as she sheathed him inside of her.

It wasn't until they were fully joined that she reached a hand to his face. Her thumb skimmed the fresh stubble along his jawline.

"I love you too," she whispered.

Renwick's mouth went slack as his eyes flared. Rua looked at him in a silent promise. He did not have to fear her anymore. She would not take this away from him. She was here. This was real.

Rua lifted her hips in a testing roll. She wasn't sure how to move. Renwick's hands came up to her hips as he guided her up and down on him. Her mouth fell open as she found her rhythm.

They were locked in each other's gazes as she moved faster. She felt him ratcheting up as he lifted his hips to thrust into her. The sensation created spots in her vision. But she knew he would wait for her, and for some reason, that nagged at her. He didn't always need to be in control. She was here for him. He could let go of who he felt like he had to be with her, if only with her. She moved herself quicker as his fingertips pressed harder into her flesh.

"Rua, I—"

"It's okay," she panted, moving her hips faster to meet each thrust. "Let go."

At her command, he groaned, his movements turning jerky as he released into her. She rode him until his last panting breaths and then rolled off. But he was right there, crawling down her body, tracing kisses with his mouth and tongue. His heavy panting breaths tickled across her skin as he made his way down to the apex of her thighs.

The first lick of his tongue had her seeing stars. Her hands fisted into the bedsheets, trying to anchor her body against the sensation. Her toes curled as she arched backward. Renwick let out an approving hum that vibrated into her core as his tongue swept over her. Crying out, she was certain it could be heard from several tents away. Renwick's tongue moved faster, lashing her up and down, and Rua screamed as her climax ripped through her.

Each one felt bigger than the last as she tumbled over the edge. Skitters of lightning ecstasy tore through her body, shattering her into a million pieces and pulling her back together again. Renwick's mouth finally released her, and he traced kisses back up her hips, collapsing his face into her belly. She massaged her fingers through his hair.

"Now we can get some breakfast," she murmured, her voice rough.

Renwick laughed into her soft flesh.

A pointed cough from outside the tent's curtain had them both stilling.

"Your Majesty?" a voice called.

Rua's face reddened. Someone had been waiting for them to finish. It was too much of a coincidence. Gods, how long had they been listening?

"What?" Renwick shouted back without taking his cheek off Rua's skin.

"Aneryn is waiting outside for the princess . . . ," the voice said.

Rua sighed. Of course it would be her. She had told Aneryn that they would dine together the night before.

Renwick let out a long exhale as he buried his face in her warm flesh, kissing her skin one more time.

"Tell her she will be out in a few minutes," Renwick said.

"Yes, Your Majesty," the voice replied.

"Oh Gods," Rua groused. "I don't want to have to face her."

Renwick laughed, the vibrations radiating out through her center.

"I could tell you she won't suspect anything . . . ," he murmured, "but we both know that's a lie."

"Do I tell her?" Rua wondered.

Renwick propped his chin up on her stomach and looked up at her. "That is up to you," he said. "I would like to shout it from the rooftops."

Rua grinned down at him as she traced the lines of his face. "There are no rooftops to stand on in the Lyrei Basin, only tents."

"I'm sure I can work something out." He winked at her. She loved this playful side of him, so loose, so himself. It was a side only she got to see.

Rua took another slow breath. "Okay, wish me luck."

Renwick moved off her so she could go to the washing bowl in the corner. This beautiful, delicate thing was just between them, standing there in that tent. But she knew when she stepped out of his room, everything would change.

# CHAPTER TWENTY-EIGHT

The snow-laden branches bowed above them in the twilight as they rode in the open sleigh. The rest of the camp had given them a wide berth that day. Rumors of their coupling must have spread like wildfire. Even Aneryn took one look at Rua and had suddenly found herself too busy with some mysterious work to catch up. Rua snickered at the memory of the blue witch's expression. She was giving them time to be together before the army marched westward to confront Balorn.

"I bet it is even more beautiful here in spring," she whispered, looking up at the trees. She imagined them in full bloom, filled with songbirds, the lakeside teeming with life.

A soft smirk played on Renwick's lips. "Does that mean you're staying in the North?"

She realized she hadn't said it out loud to him—that she wanted this to be her home.

"It does," she murmured, breathing in the fresh pine-scented air.

Flurries of snow danced around them as the horses pulled them up the hillside and into the forested slopes of the basin. The canopy protected them from the heavier gusts as they rounded to the far side of the ice lake. The glowing lights of the campsite disappeared around the bend. Rua tucked her head into Renwick's shoulder, the warmth of his skin heating her face. She knew exactly how that skin would feel under her lips. She leaned up and planted a slow kiss to his pulse, making the King smile. She trailed kisses up toward his ear, nibbling the lobe in a way that made him choke out a cough.

He chuckled. "That is not why I brought you up here, but I can't say that I mind."

"Why did you bring me here?" Rua looked up through an opening in the canopy of evergreens, stars flickering to life in the twilight.

Renwick smiled. "Patience."

Rua pressed her lips to his ear again and whispered, "I have none of that."

She moved her hand to his thigh, stroking up the corded muscle, her hand finding him already straining against his trousers.

"Rua." Renwick's warning was cut short by a hiss as Rua unbuttoned his trousers, freeing him into the air. She mischievously chuckled at the sound. "Wicked thing."

Heat rose in her core, that constant desire strumming through her unendingly.

She stroked him up and down, eliciting a groan from him as the sleigh slowed. He pulled the horses to a halt and threw the reins down to their feet, launching himself at her in a desperate way that made her squeal with delight. She loved how easily she could snap the leash on his restraint.

In a blur of movement, he grabbed her face with both hands, his lips meeting hers in an all-consuming kiss. She moaned into his mouth as his tongue slid in. He pressed her back into the bench seat as she reached for him. Renwick's hand roved from her face over her leathers toward that hot, pulsing button between her legs. She bucked into his hand from beneath her trousers as he grinned against her lips. His hand dipped into her waistband until it was sliding down her wet center. Rua mewled louder, the sound echoing into the forest all around them. As Renwick dipped his fingers inside of her, she threw her head back, breaking their kiss to moan to the stars. Every nerve in her body homed into her aching, wet core and those fingers massaging her. She stroked Renwick again as he touched her, them both panting as they pulled each other higher and higher to that glorious precipice.

In one sharp breath, Rua looked at Renwick with molten heat in her eyes, and he seemed to know exactly what she was going to say. He made quick work of unbuttoning her trousers, hauling the leathers down to her boots as she lifted her ass into the air. She shucked her boots until she was bare from the waist down and straddled Renwick. His hands bracketed her sides as she positioned herself over him. Heavy pants came from her open mouth as she slowly slid herself down onto his hard shaft. She shuddered as he stretched her until she had him fully sheathed inside her. The feeling made her body achy and light as the promise of a climax built.

Rolling her hips, she held Renwick's hooded gaze. She slid back down on him again, a little quicker, her breathing ratcheting up until she couldn't control her speed anymore. Her wildness took over as she began to ride him faster, Renwick lifting his hips to meet her, bouncing her up with every thrust. The frenzy consumed her as he chased her mounting climax higher and higher. Her breathy moans turned to screams as with one final pump, her release came crashing through her. Renwick kept moving, drawing her out more and more, one orgasm colliding into the next until he groaned and followed her over the edge.

They stayed like that for several breaths, foreheads pressed together, muscles still twitching, until their pulses slowed and Renwick smiled. They both laughed, that mischievous lover's laugh of two people so in love they didn't care about anything other than being joined together. This was the kind of reckless she wanted to be.

"Now, what did you want to show me?" Rua asked, delighting in Renwick's stunning smile that so few got to see.

"Everything," he said, his swollen lips tenderly meeting hers.

She cupped his face, brushing her hand down his cheek. "I love you," she whispered.

"I love you more." He smiled.

Rua shook her head. "Impossible."

She couldn't begin to tell him all the ways that he had saved her. She knew she had rescued him in just as many ways. They were flawed and healing, but at least together it was okay. At least here with him, she was allowed to reveal whatever feelings whispered from her soul.

"Where are we going?" she murmured against his lips.

Renwick brushed her wavy hair absently off her face. "To see the stars."

~

She had never seen anything like it. Glowing colorful lights stretched up toward the horizon. The triangular beams shone white light, edges bleeding into all the colors of the rainbow: greens and pinks and blues. They had found a quiet spot on the steep ridge in between the two lookout towers to watch the dancing lights. Renwick wrapped his warm arms around Rua, holding her back against him as they watched the display of winter colors. Breaths steaming into the darkening night, Rua leaned her head against Renwick's shoulder, a sated smile on her face.

Pointing a finger up toward the brightest shining star, Rua murmured, "I have never seen Alces so bright."

She remembered many nights looking up to the guiding star as a child, wishing she could run away. She dreamed of following that star to another city in her books, dreamed of the life she could live if not for her name and title.

"That is Arctus Orientales; my people call it the Winter Snake," Renwick said, pointing to a scattering of stars to their left. Rua wondered if that was why they had a snake on the Northern crest. A snake suited Hennen Vostemur. She was glad that Renwick had taken the creature off his crest in favor of a simple sword and crown. She turned to look at the new crest embroidered across the folds of his cloak in silver thread. He must have commissioned it the moment she selected it that night in his tent. She traced the sword as Renwick placed a kiss on the top of her head.

Moving her fingers to the stars around his crest, she said, "And these are the stars on Remy's wrist?"

Her sister's identity had been confirmed by the Northern King from the freckles on her wrist, an exact match of a constellation in the Northern Court skies. Rua frowned at the four stars. It shouldn't matter to her that her sister bore the same constellation on her wrist.

"Gavialis Minor," Renwick said, pointing to the skies. Above the guiding star was a collection of five stars, brightly twinkling.

Rua narrowed her eyes and glanced back to Renwick's cloak as a smile played across his lips. She traced her fingers across his cloak again. "Those don't match."

"I changed them," he said softly.

Rua scanned the skies. "To what?"

A booming explosion sounded across the ridge.

Shouts rang out across Lyrei Basin. Rua spotted the cloud of purple smoke silhouetted against the glowing winter lights. The violet shadow crept its way toward them, mesmerizing in its strangeness.

"We need to get back to the camp," Rua breathed as more alarmed shouts erupted from the lookouts.

"Your Majesty!" a frantic voice called from the closest tower.

They bolted toward it, finding a blue witch pointing down the steep ridge below the tower. *"Suraash."*

"Shit." Rua's eyes widened at Renwick. "I left the blade in the sleigh."

She had only brought her dagger from Bri out of habit, not even on its belt. She had slipped it into her cloak in case she wanted to use it to cut some winter plums from the trees. She hadn't thought she would need the Immortal Blade to go for a walk through the snow.

She cursed herself. She had brought that sword with her everywhere, but she was too swept up with the attentions of her Fated and had forgotten her responsibility.

"Run back to the sleigh," Renwick said. "Take the horses, it'll be faster. Warn the camp."

"And leave you here to fight them alone?" Rua asked incredulously. "You are the King. If anything, it is you who shouldn't be putting your neck on the line."

"And you are the future Queen," Renwick said.

Rua gaped at him. "If that was your proposal, it was terrible."

Renwick huffed a laugh, grabbing her cloak in his fist and hauling her to him. "Go get your sword and come back," he said, his mouth colliding with hers in a scalding kiss. "I'd rather you fight by my side, anyway."

Rua flashed him a quick grin, that kiss making her feel invincible, as she turned and ran back in the direction of the sleigh. Renwick shouted orders, bolting between the watchtowers.

"I can't See anything! My vision is completely clouded," a witch yelled down to him as Rua dashed through the forest.

She suspected it had something to do with the lavender haze filling the skies. It smelled fruity and floral, like the scent of perfume, with a hint of bitterness she couldn't place. It was strange and familiar all at once.

As she reached the sleigh, the smoke filtered down, hanging around her like a thick fog. Her limbs felt lighter as she breathed in the heady scent. She wanted to close her eyes and take long drags of the sweet air. What was this magic? It felt like she had drunk a whole bottle of wine. She beseeched herself to keep her wits as she buckled her belt, the Immortal Blade hanging heavy on her hip once more.

The shouts resounding from all around pulled her out of her stupor long enough to look up. Three hooded figures emerged from the smog. Thick woolen scarves were pulled up to their bottom eyelids, covering their noses and mouths. Rua scrambled for her sword with clumsy fingers as the first figure charged, the other two right behind her.

Her hand missed, *missed*, the hilt of her sword as the first figure crashed into her, bowling her back into the sleigh. The figure's cloak slipped back, revealing the carved symbol of the *suraash*. Rua shoved away the witch's clawing hands as she felt the nails of another sink into her calf. She threw out her red witch magic, trying to push them off her, but her power was barely an ember. It felt like when she tried to cast in a warded room; the smoke must be dampening her witch powers somehow.

She shouted a pained cry as the one straddling her punched her in the ear. The high ringing seemed to snap her back to her senses, her eyes clearing from their glaze. Thrusting her hand into her cloak, Rua yanked out her dagger and plunged it into the witch's neck. The *suraash*'s eyes widened in horror as blood rained down. The heady smoke threatened to pull Rua under again, but a voice deep from inside screamed to keep fighting. She freed one leg from the witches, kicking the other hard in the face as she shoved the dying witch off her and darted out the other side of the sleigh.

The wound in her calf throbbed with every stride, but she ran with all her might through the trees, the two remaining witches hot on her heels. She cleared through the forest, the air becoming more crisp as the winds whipped away the lingering smoke. She took another steadying breath, unsheathing the Immortal Blade as the *suraash* charged after her.

Trying and failing to steady herself, she sliced her shaking arms through the air. It took her three hacks of the blade to halt the first witch, as the other barreled toward her.

Rua cursed the Gods as another ten *suraash* broke through the trees, baying like a pack of wolves on a hunt. Another three witches came running to her left, boxing her in against the shoreline of the ice lake. Her magic was not working fast enough. Sheathing her blade and muttering curses, she turned and ran out onto the ice.

She slipped over almost instantly, knees cracking against the frozen surface. She got to her feet again just as the first witch slammed into her, and they went skidding across the slick lake. With hungry, wild grunts, the witch tore at Rua's face. As the pack of witches thundered onto the ice, the lake groaned, fissures cracking beneath their weight. Rua felt the echoes under her back as the ice bowed. The lake was thinnest here at this end. She did not know if it would hold them all.

Another crackle rang out from under them as Rua screamed, "Stop! Stop!" but it was too late. As the horde of witches descended on her, a creaking groan rent the air and the ice broke, the frigid waters swallowing them whole.

The cold hit her like a punch to the chest, and she fought every urge in her body not to gasp under the water. The surrounding witches yanked and clawed at her even as they plummeted downward. Rua flailed, desperately trying to fight the heavy weight of her cloak, boots, and sword. She kicked upward with all her might, bleary eyes searching above her in the darkness for the hole from which they fell.

Witches writhed and spasmed, some already floating lifeless around her, suspended in the icy waters like constellations in a blackened sky. No one fought her now. Even the cursed *suraash* halted their bloodlust in a desperate bid for survival. Rua kicked off her boots and unclasped her cloak. She debated abandoning her sword and dagger, but she couldn't let them go. She shoved harder upward until her head hit the thick layer of ice above. Her lungs strained desperately as her mind denied them their yearning to breathe in. Thrusting her dagger up into the ice, her vision began clouding. A crack finally fissured the ice, barely enough to get her fingers through. She pressed her lips to the hole and took a hungry drag of sweet air. The rising panic in her wavered to the cold. Even with the breath, she needed to get out of the ice quickly. Splashing echoed as she peered over the body that plummeted into the water: Renwick.

His eyes scanned desperately for her. There was the entry point. Taking one more sip through the hole in the ice, she swam across the lake's thick crust, battling the weight of her sword with every kick of her legs. She reached the opening, face breaking the surface as she gasped in the cold air.

Renwick let out a panicked sob. "Thank the fucking Gods."

Rua threw her sword and dagger onto the ice as Renwick slid up onto his stomach and then into a crouch, testing the sturdiness before he dragged Rua onto the ice.

He bent over her, eyes scanning her frantically for injures that she couldn't feel. Her whole body numbed, even as it trembled violently.

"Hang on," Renwick pleaded, cupping her face with icy fingers. "We've got to get you back to the camp."

Rua's eyes fluttered shut as Renwick pulled her limp body up.

"No! No, stay with me," he begged her as Rua forced her eyes open again.

"How quaint." A voice called from across the ice.

Renwick lifted his head as he clutched Rua to him. His eyes narrowed at the figure beyond her.

"You," he said as the darkness claimed her.

# CHAPTER TWENTY-NINE

oooseflesh rippled across her exposed skin. The heat of the fire
couldn't warm her. Rua was faintly aware of her clothes, a
satin slip and nothing more, but the surface under her wasn't
a warm, soft bed.

She wheezed, eyes flying open. She was strapped to a hardwood
table by thick belts, her hands bound and tied by a rope under the table.
She flailed desperately, but as she yanked one hand, the rope burned,
pulling against her opposite wrist.

"Rua," a voice called.

Tilting her head backward, she looked to her right and saw Renwick shackled to the stone wall. His shirt was stripped off but he still
wore his crumpled trousers from when they fell through the ice.

Gods, Rua remembered it now.

His hair and clothes seemed dried. Urgently scanning him for injuries, she saw no bruises marring his skin.

"Where are we?" she murmured, looking down at the black silk slip
she wore with horror—the same nightdress that the *suraash* wore in
the Temple of Hunasht. The room that had become their makeshift
dungeon looked like it was a kitchen. Open shelves filled with glass
jars of preserves and bottles of vinegars lined the far wall. The smell

of pepper and rosemary hung in the air. The shackles Renwick wore looked like they were brought with their captors, bolted to the rings in the stone used to cure meats, not hold prisoners.

"Your guess is as good as mine," Renwick said. "Judging by the Western crest"—Renwick nodded to the crest hanging on the wooden beam above the open doorway—"I'd say we're either in the Western Court or close to it."

"How is that possible?" Rua stared around the room, looking for more clues. "The West is several days' ride away."

"You've been out for a while," Renwick said. "I think they have been drugging us. I came to hours ago when we were still in a carriage; they knocked me out again . . . It's not just Balorn, Rua, they have—"

"You're awake, Princess?" a smooth voice sounded from the doorway, and Rua craned her neck to see Balorn leaning against the frame.

"You," she hissed at him.

He smoothed his auburn hair out of his face, standing with a casual courtier's grace as if they were meeting for a summer fete and she was not bound to a table.

"You're not going to say 'Release me this instant,' are you?" He chuckled, sidling over to her and running a warm, rough hand up her bare calf and pausing on her thigh. "Although, I'm sure I can make you beg."

The chains from behind her rattled as a deep growl rumbled from Renwick's chest. Balorn looked up to his nephew, sliding his hand up Rua's side, skirting over her hip, belly, breast and up to her mouth, swiping his thumb across her bottom lip as Renwick snarled again.

"She really is your Fated, isn't she?" His dark forest-green eyes crinkled in delight.

Renwick's voice was a menacing hiss. "Don't. Touch. Her."

"Oh, I think I will." Balorn smiled, eyes skimming her body as he pulled the dagger from his hip. "Such beautiful, smooth skin."

"Don't!" Renwick shouted as Balorn ran the blade across Rua's thigh. She felt the blade push against her, but it did not slice open her flesh.

"Fascinating," Balorn murmured, changing the grip on the dagger and thrusting it down to stab into her leg. Renwick's screams echoed in the small room, but the dagger froze as if Rua's skin were made of steel. "Even separated from the Immortal Blade, it still protects you."

"It is bound to my blood." Rua spat, saliva trailing down Balorn's pristine white sleeve.

Striking out faster than she could see, Balorn smacked the back of his hand across her face. Her cheek stung, and her eyes welled as he guffawed.

"Hands still work." He grinned, turning toward the mantel. He grabbed an unlit candle from the candelabra and held it to the crackling fire. "But hands are boring."

Stalking back to Rua, he grabbed her pointer finger. She thrashed against his grip, straining to curl her finger under, but the ropes binding her wrist chafed her with every flail, ripping her skin. Balorn held the flame to the tip of Rua's finger, and she screamed as the white-hot fire flayed her flesh.

"Stop! Balorn, stop!" Renwick roared as his chains rattled.

"Fire," Balorn mused, removing the candle from Rua's skin at last. "My favorite."

Throbbing pain bolted up her arm as her fingertip pulsed. Balorn stooped to one knee. Bringing his face to her hand, he pulled her burned finger into his mouth and licked it with his tongue.

"Better?" He smiled up at her like a coy lover.

"You are a demon cursed by the Gods," Rua snarled at him, her whole body trembling.

Balorn smirked. "You think your Fated is so much better than me? He was my apprentice once." He lifted his gaze and cocked his head at Renwick. "How many witches have you killed? What is the tally on your soul?"

"Too many." Renwick's chest heaved from battling against his restraints.

"You were always terrible at drawing out the pain though."

"Yes," was all Renwick replied with a wary nod.

"Were they all mercy killings? Ha!" Balorn chortled, walking over to Renwick. "After all this time. I thought you were just inept with the blade, but you killed them quickly on purpose, didn't you, little Witch-slayer?"

"Don't call me that," Renwick gritted out. As Balorn gained one more step, Renwick lashed out, grabbing the chains and lifting his foot to kick Balorn hard in the gut. Balorn tumbled backward across the floor.

Dusting himself off and rising, he said, "I knew I should have dangled you." He shook his head as if it were a joke they would all laugh about later. "You seem to forget I have your Fated strapped to a table."

"How did you know what she was?" Renwick breathed.

Balorn quirked his eyebrow. "It would take the will of the Gods to make someone love you, Witchslayer."

Rua strained against the belts. Balorn could hack away at Renwick's flesh in a million different ways, but he knew the best way to torture his nephew. Rua knew those words would break him more than any blade. She clenched her fists as she writhed. Renwick grew up with these people telling him how unlovable and unworthy he was, the same isolation as Rua, but in a crueler form.

"He has earned my love," Rua growled, pulling Balorn's attention back to her. She had to say it, had to let Renwick know his uncle's words weren't true. If they weren't going to survive this day, Renwick would not die with any doubt.

Balorn rubbed his thumb over her burned finger. "Does it hurt, my dear?" He flashed his white teeth. "Do you think your toes would hurt more?"

Moving toward the edge of the table, he dripped candle wax down her skin as he went.

Rua saw the cloud of smoke before a figure turned the corner.

"You can play your games when we reach Valtene, Balorn," the voice said. The blond-haired young fae puffed on a roll of paper.

Rua gawked at his rounded jaw, upturned nose, and black, soulless eyes.

"You died," she whispered, her mind flashing back to when Hale stabbed him through the chest.

"You think I'm Belenus, don't you?" he mused. "We got mistaken for each other a lot. That will happen less now that your sister's Fated killed him."

Augustus Norwood.

He was the spitting image of his brother. Rua tried to think of any distinction between the two and came up lacking. She noted the way he said "your sister's Fated" even though he grew up thinking Hale was his older brother.

He stalked into the room, the cloud of smoke trailing behind him. He was tall and lean, a matching frame to how Rua remembered King Norwood. Taking a long drag of his cigarette, he blew the smoke into Rua's face. She tried to turn away, but his hand lashed out and he gripped her cheeks between his thumb and fingers.

"You'll want this. Trust me." His voice was quiet and hollow as he stared at her. "Even after that swim in the ice lakes, you still stink of Renwick."

Where Balorn was smarmy and charming, Augustus was nothing but cold. He blew another puff of smoke into her face, the sweet, heady aroma pulling at her. It wasn't the smell of a regular cigar. It reminded her of . . .

"The violet smoke," she whispered as the hammering in her chest ebbed. Her limbs felt loose and languid, and the throbbing in her fingertip seemed far away.

"This is a less potent concoction," Augustus whispered in her ear. As he bent, Rua saw his chest through the gaping neckline of his pewter tunic. On a golden chain around his neck was a glowing blue stone.

Bile crept up her throat. She instantly knew what it was. It beckoned to her in the same strumming song of power as the Immortal Blade.

The Witches' Glass.

"What do you want from us, Augustus?" Renwick's voice interrupted her horror.

Rua tried to hide her shock at the revelation as Augustus whirled to her Fated.

"I want to take back my birthright," he said with a chilling arrogance that only a spoiled fae could muster. "And I will punish all the courts who allied with that bastard Hale over the rightful heir to the Eastern throne, starting with the South."

"You would raze the Southern Court?"

"Not all wars are won at the tip of a blade, *Princess.*" Augustus eyed her, his voice dripping with disdain. "The South is a mess, the slightest nudge and they will crumble." He pulled his cigarette from his lips and examined it before taking another drag. "Balorn can have the North and West for aiding me."

"You think the West will bow to him?" Rua snarled, glancing at Balorn leaning casually against the wall, captivated by their conversation.

"They already have," Balorn said, his grin widening. "It is done. The Queen is dead."

Rua's mouth fell open. The relaxing of her muscles tugged her down toward sleep, but the shock of his confession kept her conscious. The Western Queen was dead? The West bowed to Balorn now? The questions spun in her mind, thick and fast. How? When? And then Rua thought of Remy. If they had attacked the North and the West at the same time, did they attack Yexshire too?

"And where does the High Mountain Court fall into your plans?" Rua hedged, fearing the answer.

"Leave them to their ruins. Let your sister keep her little amulet. It will do nothing to help her," Augustus snarled, adjusting the collar of his tunic to hide the stone he wore underneath. "I will enjoy watching Hale as time destroys his family. Let them starve, cut off from the aid they so desperately need to rebuild." The paper burned to its stub, and Augustus flicked it into the fire. "Pity you won't be there to watch them destroy themselves. You should have accepted Balorn's offer when it was still available to you."

"You are a fool," Rua said. "You cannot trust Balorn or the monsters he makes."

"The Eastern King knows more about making monsters than me," Balorn crooned, eyes dropping knowingly to his chest. "Don't you, Augustus?"

Augustus pulled another cigarette from his pocket, lighting it on a candle. Purple smoke haloed his head as his pupils dilated more.

"The blue witches were merely a test, proof that it could be done," Augustus said, leaning into Rua and blowing a violet cloud of smoke across her face. "Don't fret, Princess. Sleep now."

That golden pleasure coursed through her veins. She heard Renwick faintly shouting her name. Far away, too far. She was floating now. The warmth spread over her as if slipping into a bath, the floral scent reminding her of someone. An image flashed into her mind, and she was certain for the first time who it was: her mother. She smiled to the former Queen of the High Mountain Court as the violet smoke pulled her under.

～

The burning of her wrists pulled Rua from her drugged slumber. She was no longer on a table. The muscles in her armpits strained as the wagon jostled. Her hands were tied out on either side of her slumped head as she sat crumpled on the hard wooden slats. At least they hadn't tied her standing, she thought. Her arms might have pulled out of the sockets.

Heavy eyelids reluctantly fluttered open as she surveyed the covered wagon. They immediately snagged on Renwick, tied up across from her. His eyes shone in the dimness of the tent. He still remained in only trousers, though Rua noted they were new ones. It wasn't until she saw her bare skin that she realized she was still in nothing but the satin nightdress. The cold stabbed through her all at once, and she shuddered. New bruises mottled Renwick's face and chest. They had beaten him bloody while she had been out. They held each other's gazes for a long moment just breathing and staring. The lump in Rua's throat tightened.

"We should be reaching Valtene soon," Renwick said, his voice scratchy even as he tried to be hopeful. "They will bring us to shelter. You will be warm again."

Rua shook her head.

"Balorn has affections for you, Rua." Renwick seemed to debate saying his words. "You could play into them. He would feed you and clothe you . . . You could survive this."

"No." Rua strained against her bindings, not caring that it aggravated her raw skin. She leaned her chest forward, coming halfway into the carriage before her arms relented. "I will never do that. I don't care if I have your blessing. I would rather die."

Renwick hung his head, his disappointment palpable. He wanted her to save herself that badly. Gods, she wished she could touch him. She yearned to lean her head against his chest and cry.

"We may survive this," Renwick said desolately. "They haven't killed us yet."

"Do you think they went after the camp?" Rua wondered at the rest of the Lyrei Basin. She thought to Aneryn, her teeth clenching as she worried for her friend. "Or just came to grab us?"

"I was awake when they dragged us away," Renwick said. "It seemed like they stopped when they captured us. Gods, I pray they did. Augustus and his soldiers . . . They have these burning targets they volley into the air and archers shoot them down, exploding them over their victims."

"The purple smoke," Rua murmured. "It's like a sleep potion. Like a drug." Rua wondered if the pounding headache hammering at her temples was from Augustus's smoke or from the days of no food or drink. "But it stops witch magic . . . how?"

Tunneling down into her stores of magic, Rua felt no red power in her gut. She looked to the metal beams bolted to the wagon. Sure enough, they were etched with Mhenbic wardings. Augustus didn't need to blow his poisonous smoke to keep her magic at bay. The wardings would control her magic well enough while they traveled. She looked around the wagon, but there was nothing there. She couldn't see her sword or dagger. An aching loss, like a living thing, gnawed at her gut. The Immortal Blade was a part of her. Just as Renwick felt like part of her soul outside her body, so too did the blade. She thought it was a curse for so long, but it was a gift, a blessing.

"I have an idea about the magic of the smoke, but it's not good," Renwick said, lifting his gaze back to Rua's. "I think Augustus has found a violet witch."

Eyes widening, Rua gaped. "But all the violet witches died almost a century ago. The Eastern coven is gone."

"Perhaps some went underground, into hiding," Renwick contemplated. "Or maybe Augustus just figured out how to use their magic spells without them. Maybe he's using other types of witches to cast their spells."

Rua pursed her lips. It was not unheard of, witches having the powers of other covens. Certain spells were easy enough for almost any witch to cast, like protection spells or cleansing rituals. Baba Morganna had the Sight of the blue witches and the animation powers of the red witches. But for a witch to know how to summon violet witch magic without ever knowing one? That seemed unlikely. The witches kept spell books and sacred symbols, archiving the traditions of their magic, but their culture was mostly oral history. The core of their magic was taught from other elder witches, not read from a book.

"Why would the violet witches serve Augustus?" Rua asked, leaning back against the wagon as they bumped over the uneven terrain. Her thighs and backside were going numb from sitting on the unyielding wood floor.

"The violet witches have always served the Norwoods," Renwick said. "Perhaps they felt called out of hiding by the announcement of the competition for the throne."

Her lips and the tip of her nose chilled more with every breath. She thanked the Gods that her matted hair blanketed her back and warmed her slender fae ears.

"The witches would do all this just for the threat of a new King or Queen?" Rua wondered. "They showed no allegiance to the Norwoods before now?" She gasped, the memory flooding back into her as she stared up at her Fated. "Augustus has the Witches' Glass."

"I thought that could only work for the blue witches."

"The spell book said the stone imbued with witch magic would bless or curse any witch who touched it . . ." Rua grimaced as the wagon rocked again. "Or maybe it is the *suraash* who created the purple smoke."

Shaking his head, Renwick pursed his lips. "I don't know. It seems like violet witch magic to me."

She rolled her ankle, hoping to stave off the pins and needles creeping up her legs. "I thought the violet witches just made perfumes."

"They were more powerful than that. They made magical scents, yes, but also incenses and powders that when burned and inhaled had different magical properties: healing, strength, courage, for example."

"Shit." That sounded exactly like what it was. "Augustus seems hooked on the stuff."

Renwick clenched his jaw. "He does," he said tightly. "It is why one puff could knock you out while he can smoke a whole stick. He's built up a tolerance to the magic . . . I know the feeling."

"I didn't mean that," Rua said quietly, looking at the shamed expression on Renwick's face. She hadn't meant to hurt him.

"I gave it up, Rua," he whispered, looking forlornly into her eyes. "I gave it up for the future I dreamed of us having together. The thought of you and me . . . has kept me going for longer than you know."

"We are still alive, Renwick," Rua soothed, the sound of his name on her lips making him take a sharp inhale of breath, fighting against tears that were welling in both of their eyes. This might be the end of them. She wasn't sure why it hadn't been ended already. "Why keep us alive?"

"I have an idea, but you're not going to like it," Renwick said, frowning. "They're either luring the people who will rescue us into a trap, or they're luring them away from their own cities to attack there."

"Remy wouldn't leave Yexshire unprotected . . ."

"Wouldn't she?" Renwick assessed her. "Your sister loves you, Rua. She would burn Okrith to the ground to find you."

"She will leave some soldiers, at least . . . surely," Rua added, suddenly not so convinced. Her sister would come for her, she knew it. She only prayed that Remy reached them before a trap was laid or before Augustus's plans for Yexshire could be realized. "You think they truly assassinated the Western Queen?"

Renwick released a slow breath. "I do."

"Gods," Rua muttered. "So Abalina Thorne is the regent now?"

"Unless they killed her too." Renwick grimaced as the wagon jerked around a corner and his torso swayed.

Rua shook her head at the floor, tears welling again. She had thought when Hennen Vostemur died the world would get better, but it had only descended into more chaos. The High Mountain Court was just beginning to rebuild, the East had no sovereign aside from a deranged spoiled boy, the North was divided, half its blue witches in a hidden forge, and now the Western Queen had been killed. The Southern Court was the only one seemingly unscathed, partying in debauched revelry as the world descended into turmoil. Augustus seemed to have a plan for the South, too. He seemed ten steps ahead of them. How? When had he managed to concoct this plan, and with what aid? The Vostemur-Norwood alliance lived on through Balorn and Augustus.

The battle for their courts felt even more insurmountable now than it did before the Battle of Drunehan. Rua's chest cracked as she let out a shuddering sob.

"Rua," Renwick whispered in that soft, comforting tone that only made her tears fall faster.

She looked up to him, her Fated, with watery eyes. "If we're not going to make it—"

"Don't say that," Renwick bit out, but Rua shook her head as hot tears slipped down her cold cheeks.

"If we're not going to make it—"

"We will," Renwick growled.

"I need you to know . . . I love you." Her lips trembled as she spoke, leaning forward from her bindings, her body straining toward his. "I love every part of you, *mea raga fede.*"

Renwick jerked forward at that. *My precious Fated one.* Yanking on his binding, he lurched his head forward, still just a hair's breadth from her face. "I love you, every part of you in this life and the next, my Fated, my Queen."

She wanted to throw her arms around him but only their mouths reached, her lips sliding against his in a hot, desperate kiss. Possibly their last. She thanked the Gods that at least she could touch him, her soul needing to breathe in his life force and taste his skin one last time. Her tears fell onto his cheek. Her arms screamed at her, but she did not care. She needed this last kiss. The "I love yous" whispered across their lips felt like more powerful magic than any sword. It was the kind of spark that existed beyond time, like she finally felt the thread that the Fates wove into the world. This was the magic the oracles prophesied. This was Fate, a real living ember that would exist in the world long after their deaths. The world would still feel their love even then.

The wagon jolted to a sharp halt, and they slammed apart, falling backward. A scream rang out, and then a chorus of shouting.

A loud clanking sounded at the wagon door as the sound of swords clashing echoed all around them. Someone was breaking the lock. With one final blow, the wagon doors creaked open.

A little head popped up to the wagon, braided hair and obsidian skin. Nymphlike eyes peered back at them as the flickering blue hands pulled open the wagon door.

"You two always leave me behind." Aneryn smirked at them even as she hastened into the wagon. The second she stepped over the threshold, her blue glow disappeared, the witch wardings forcing away her magic. She didn't even seem to notice as she unsheathed the dagger on her belt and cut through Rua's bindings first. Arms sagging with relief, Rua scrambled to pull the rope off her bloody, raw wrists.

Rua looked out at the melee. Soldiers in shining new Northern crests battled against soldiers wearing Eastern and old Northern insignia. But it was not the fae warriors who caught Rua's eye. Dozens of blue cloaks whorled through the battle, brandishing swords, daggers, bows and arrows: the blue witches. She spotted the flash of Onyx Mallor's silver hair. Rua knew in that moment that the blue witches had not come for Renwick—they had come for *Mhenissa*. They had come for her.

# CHAPTER THIRTY

Ahawk screeched overhead. She knew that bird. Thador was here with their army. Rua stumbled as she got her footing, her legs tingling with numbness. She got a good look at their surroundings for the first time. A line of twenty wagons disappeared around the bend. The carved-out road dipped downhill to her right through a marshland of tall grasses. To her left was a rocky forest of leafless trees. More soldiers wearing the new shining Northern armor came barreling down the hill, Thador at the front, sword in hand.

But out of each wagon poured more guards of the East, and from around the bend . . . They scrambled across the ground like a pack of wild dogs aiming for the Raevenport blue witches—more *suraash.*

The surrounding chaos grew with shouts of terror as the *suraash* entered the fray. More and more surged around the bend with no end in sight. With no steel or armor, they were still formidable opponents on the battlefield through sheer ferocity alone.

Aneryn scrambled off the wagon, her blue magic circling her hands and beaming from her eyes again. Renwick jumped down, landing on surprisingly steady feet. Rua was relieved that he didn't seem badly injured, or maybe it was pure adrenaline keeping him going. Renwick's firm hands grabbed Rua's waist and placed her down on the rocky road. The uneven stones bit into her bare feet. It was as cold as ice, but only small scatterings of leftover snow remained on the hard ground.

"You two need to get out of here," Aneryn ordered. "You have no weapons and you're practically naked—"

Rua bowled into Aneryn, knocking the air out of her friend as she grabbed her in a tight hug.

"You saved us," Rua whispered.

"The witches will always come for you, *Mhenissa*," Aneryn said, giving Rua one last squeeze before pulling away, tears streaking her cheeks, and Rua finally saw the fear in her eyes.

"What?" Rua asked, swiping away Aneryn's tears.

"I don't See us winning this battle," she whimpered through more welling tears.

Those tears were a punch to Rua's chest. She surveyed the battle downhill, witches fighting witches, soldiers fighting soldiers. The odds were five to one. Balorn and Augustus had brought a whole battalion with them.

A lone Eastern soldier reached them from the front of the caravan, sword drawn. Renwick turned on him—barefoot and empty-handed, he sparred with the soldier like they were equally matched. Aneryn screamed as Renwick took a hit to the side but it was a strategic blow, getting him close enough into the soldier's body to eliminate the threat of the sword. He punched the guard in the throat, and with a choking gasp, the guard dropped his sword hand, giving easy access for Renwick to snatch it and turn the blade on the soldier. He moved with precision, striking the killing blow with ease. Rua watched as her Fated turned into a lethal and calculated warrior. Blood poured from the soldier's wound, slashed across his neck, the hot liquid steaming in the frigid cold. Aneryn took a shuddering breath, snapping Rua's attention away from her shirtless Fated and his bloody sword.

"Where is the Immortal Blade?" Rua grabbed Aneryn by the shoulders and shook her out of her stupor. "We can change the tide of this battle with it."

"Balorn has it," Aneryn panted. "He's in the front carriage."

Rua leaned past their wagon, looking down the road to the black carriage at the front of the caravan. She narrowed her eyes, scanning the terrain for signs of him, feeling for the Immortal Blade with her magic. A blond figure bolted through the fray, racing to the edge of the marshes and into the trees, three guards at his heels.

"Shit," Rua gritted out. "Augustus is getting away. He has the Witches' Glass."

"I'll go after him," Renwick said, taking a step downhill before Rua caught his arm.

She was about to argue with him when Thador and four other Northern soldiers reached them. Without hesitation, Thador grabbed the dagger off his belt and handed it to Rua with a nod. She tipped her head in thanks. Another two blue witches fled from the marshes up to them, retreating to higher ground. Onyx Mallor heaved heavy breaths, holding a bloody dagger, her face splattered in the viscous scarlet liquid. Their gazes locked, and Rua saw the emotions colliding behind Onyx's eyes. The blue witch had come to the aid of the people who had killed her sister, the future too dire to stay out of the fray. The sticky truth of their choices never seemed to be black and white. Onyx touched her fingers to her forehead at Rua, and the other witch followed in a begrudging sign of respect. Screams rent the air all around them, along with the baying howls of the *suraash*. Rua needed the Immortal Blade— to end this—but they also needed the Witches' Glass. They needed to split up.

Renwick gripped Rua's chin, pulling her gaze back to his mesmerizing eyes. "I would tell you to hide and wait for me to return." His voice was edged with sorrow as he glanced over Rua's shoulder to the three witches behind her. "But I know you will protect your people."

Rua nodded, grasping the hilt of the dagger tighter. "I will protect our people," she pledged, as if taking her royal vow. If they were not going to survive this battle, she was not going to be cut down cowering under a wagon.

Renwick's lips collided with hers as he pulled her into a desperate, blistering kiss.

"Go kill Norwood," Rua said as Renwick pulled away. "And get the Witches' Glass. You remember the words of the spell?"

Renwick nodded. He could end this curse and the battle would be won.

A flash of movement uphill caught her eye. Balorn and two *suraash* bolted up into the trees. The light caught the ruby glint of the Immortal Blade.

"Go get your blade," Renwick replied, taking one last breath beside her as if he were warring with himself to stay. But she needed her sword to turn the tide of this battle as much as they needed the Witches' Glass. They had to stop Augustus Norwood before his plans for Okrith were actualized.

"I will see you in the next life, *mea raga fede*," Rua said again, and dashed uphill to follow Balorn, Aneryn, Onyx, and the other blue witch following her. Renwick and his soldiers rushed down into the marshes to chase Augustus. Armored or not, Renwick was one of the best fighters Rua had ever seen. They would need him against Augustus's horde.

Rua's feet hit the thick layer of fallen leaves with relief. Her thighs barked their displeasure as she hustled uphill, but the movement warmed her exposed skin as the slip bounced up and down her legs. In that moment, she did not care if everyone could see her naked form, though she wished she had something to tie back her hair and a vest to hold in her breasts. They would get in the way, but it did not matter. She needed to catch Balorn. There would be no one to laugh at her ridiculous attire if they were all dead.

They reached the ridgeline at the top of the hill and paused, breathing. Her eyes scanned the valley below, but she couldn't see Balorn.

"They are hiding behind that rock," Aneryn whispered through heavy breaths, pointing to a giant limestone boulder surrounded by smaller lichen-covered stones.

Rua looked to the two other witches, lifting a finger to her lips in a request to stay silent.

Aneryn grabbed Rua's elbow and whispered in her ear, "He's going to feign a punch, making you fall against the rock. Don't dodge the hit."

Aneryn took another steadying breath. "Ignore the witches, focus on Balorn."

"Do I win?" Rua tried to smirk, but it felt forced. Half of her mind was swirling through every scenario of Renwick being killed. The battle in the marshes could consume him and his soldiers. If they made it through the battlefield, Augustus could have too much of a lead on them. If they didn't catch Augustus and break the curse, the horde of *suraash* would kill them all. Rua tried to push the thoughts of Renwick bloody on the cold forest floor from her mind, but they consumed her.

"It depends on how well you focus," Aneryn snarled, as if knowing exactly where Rua's mind wandered. "And how well you heed my warnings. Balorn is stalling you on purpose. We can't afford to delay," the blue witch added, shoving Rua forward, her footsteps crunching loudly in the surrounding quiet.

Balorn stepped out from behind the boulder, flashing Rua that ever-charming grin of his. He looked at her as if he didn't hear the clanging of swords and gurgled screams echoing over the hillside. Rua clenched her hand around Thador's dagger as she warily approached.

"You look like the Goddess of Death, my dear." Balorn's cheeks dimpled. "How stunning you would have been by my side. I fear Augustus won't let me keep you now though."

"It's over, Balorn," Rua fumed, shaking her head. "Give me the blade."

"It has only just begun, *Princess*," Balorn snickered. "The witches have Seen it. It does not matter one bit whether you or I survive this day. Okrith is already on its path. The courts will implode. Every kingdom will fall."

"No." Rua lashed out for him then, swiping with her dagger, as Balorn unsheathed the Immortal Blade.

Her stomach turned to acid seeing him wield her sword. No magic aided Balorn, but knowing her enemy used it had her seething with rage. She had half a mind to grab it by the sharp edge just to feel the sword's power again.

The *suraash* emerged from behind the boulder, screeching as they launched themselves at the waiting blue witches. Rua turned to follow them as they slammed into Onyx, the blue witch slashing at her fellow witches as they clawed at her wildly. Rua barely had a moment to register what she had done as a fist smashed into her jaw, bowling her backward. She went down hard, elbow and hip cracking into unforgiving stone.

The toe of a boot collided with her hand, kicking the dagger from it as it scattered into the leaves. Aneryn screamed as she and the other witch tried to fend off a *suraash* together, the Forgotten One easily taking on the two of them as Onyx battled the second. There would be no backup. Another kick to her face elicited a sickening pop as Rua's head twisted, her nose breaking. Her vision clouded with white spots as her eyes watered.

Rua scrambled backward as Balorn's boot stomped down on the satin of her dress, holding her in place. He pointed the Immortal Blade at her throat.

"How fitting that you would die by your own blade." He chuckled, pushing so the steel grazed Rua's neck. "You are truly pathetic without its magic, aren't you, my dear?"

Blood trickled from Rua's nose, trailing down across her pointed ear and into her matted hair. The metallic tang poured down the back of her throat as she tried not to choke on her own blood.

"You think the witches are so below you, Balorn, that you forget something," Rua choked out, chest heaving.

"What?" Balorn grinned, eyes gleaming.

Rua reached her splayed hand out to the side. "I have witch blood in my veins." The discarded dagger levitated into the air, its hilt flying into her hand in the blink of an eye. Balorn's eyes widened before she drove the blade deep into his calf. A scream bellowed out of him as Rua rolled out of the Immortal Blade's reach. She scrambled up to her feet, Balorn hobbling after her, practically hopping on one foot. She wasn't swift enough. His hand snatched her hair, yanking her back against him.

"I was going to kill you quickly, Princess, but now I think I will take my time." His tongue licked the trail of blood up her ear as Rua tried to drive her dagger into him again, but he easily dodged it. Ripping her hair, he pulled her to the ground, the leaves slipping out from under her feet. Balorn dropped on top of Rua with enough force to knock the wind out of her, straddling her, his heft pinning her to the ground.

He opened his mouth to speak when a whistle sounded in the wind. Balorn fell backward, tumbling into the leaves, an arrow protruding from his throat. Rua gaped at the arrow tied with crimson fletching.

Tilting her head uphill, she saw the archer clad in shining black leathers, bow still held aloft, a golden circlet holding back the cascade of flowing black curls. The warrior Queen's eyes filled with vengeance as she watched Balorn gurgle his last breaths.

Her sister. Remy.

~

Blood burbled from Balorn's gaping mouth, his wide eyes scanning the sky. His trembling hands grasped the arrow deep in his throat, but he did not tug it free. He held out his other hand like he was waving someone down.

"No!" Onyx screamed, pulling Rua's gaze to her.

The *suraash* scrambling on top of her rolled away, grabbing the blue witch's dagger.

In the blink of an eye, the witch shouted *"midon brik dzuurus,"* piercing the dagger into her chest. The witch collapsed into spasms in the fallen leaves, cracking her head on the granite as she fell until her body froze at last.

Balorn's chest heaved as he wrenched free the arrow in his throat. Rua gawked as color came back to his pale cheeks, his blue lips pink once more. He brushed the hair off his face and sat up with a smile.

Acid burned her throat. There were hundreds more cursed witches ready to trade their lives for his.

Rua kicked the Immortal Blade from his reach, crouching to grab it from the frozen ground. The whirring in her ears began the second she touched the blade, her veins filling with white gold as the air seemed to bend around her, hair blowing back on an invisible wind.

Rua pointed the sword at Balorn.

Wiping blood from his lips, Balorn huffed a laugh. "You can keep trying to kill me, love. They'll keep bringing me back."

An arrow whizzed through the air in response. Remy watched her arrow strike through the chest of the second *suraash* still struggling against Aneryn. The cursed witch dropped like a stone. There were more witches willing to sacrifice their lives for Balorn over the hill, but the screams that echoed over to them told Rua the battle still raged.

They needed to go help the others. They couldn't delay.

"The *midon brik* only works if there is a thread of life, Balorn," Rua hissed, lifting the tip of the Immortal Blade to him in menace as she remembered Raffiel's lifeless face. No witch could have reached him in time, even if there had been one willing to sacrifice themselves. "There will be no thread if I cleave your head from your body."

Balorn smirked. "This is not how the witches have Seen me die."

Rua blinked at his utter confidence. The shuffling to her left pulled her eyes to where Aneryn stood, the Raevenport witches beside her. All three glowed blue from their eyes, blue flames circling their hands. The three stared him down as if they were the Fates coming to claim his soul.

"Futures change, Balorn," Aneryn said, casting her menacing blue gaze to the fae who had destroyed her coven and her family.

"May you know no peace in the afterlife," Onyx cursed, her blue hands trembling. They had lost so much because of this man.

"No," Balorn breathed, that smug charm wiping away into sheer terror. "This is not my Fate. This is not . . ."

"Goodbye, Balorn," Aneryn said, nodding to Rua.

Rua moved at her friend's command, a conduit for their vengeance, the Witches' Blade. The sword glinted as it cleaved Balorn's head from his body, blood spraying.

They all stared in silent disbelief.

The clanging of swords pulled them back from the sweet reprieve. Remy looked out from her vantage point at the crest of the hill, cursing at what she saw.

"Let's go," she said, nocking another arrow.

Rua began to hustle up after her sister when Aneryn shouted. "Wait! Here." She took off her cloak and passed it to Rua. Nodding in thanks, Rua wrapped the warm cloak around her, the clasp holding the indigo fabric over most of her cold, exposed body.

When they reached the top of the hill, the road was filled with soldiers, skirmishes breaking out around each of the wagons. The swampland beyond was filled with a swarm of *suraash* and more Eastern soldiers. Their soldiers were badly outnumbered. Both Balorn and Augustus had brought the full force of their armies, whereas Remy and Thador had to leave their armies behind to protect their homelands.

Rua's eyes landed on the group of four warriors fighting off a dozen soldiers. Hale, Carys, and the Eagles moved in a lethal dance, their backs to each other, making an impenetrable ring around a group of injured witches and soldiers. They protected their fallen comrades with a practiced ease, each charging soldier easily cut down by one of their blades. A pack of *suraash* charged up the hillside toward them. Rua's chest seized, lifting her sword, but a wagon flew into the air and landed on them, rolling down into the swamp.

Hale looked up at the Queen beside Rua and winked. Rua turned to see the amulet of Aelusien glowing around Remy's neck.

"What?" Remy looked sideways at Rua.

"I . . . You're just vicious, that's all." Rua laughed with surprise.

"You thought I just wanted to sit around and embroider cushions together?" Remy smirked, making Rua snort. This sister she could get to know more of. This person felt like her family. Remy nodded to Rua as if she felt the same way, as if they were finally seeing each other for the first time. "Let's end this."

Rua gripped the Immortal Blade tighter, and they charged downhill.

The dance of two sisters, Remy moved the wagons into barricades while Rua sliced down soldiers with her sword. The blood of their people sang in their veins as the two Queens wielded their magical talismans. It was no longer a wounded song; it was power personified.

They charged down onto the road, Remy loosing arrows as Rua

attacked the Eastern soldiers, focusing first to where the blue witches battled them back in the swamps. The rotten stench of the bog swirled in the air, mixing with the scent of loamy soil and freshly spilled blood.

A pained cry called out over the din. Rua was so tuned into the sound, she heard it ringing in her ears. Looking out to the forest's edge, she saw Renwick stumbling back into the swampy skirmish. Bloodied and distraught, he hefted the immense weight of a body across his shoulders. Rua knew who it was the instant she heard the frantic screeches of a hawk circling above them.

Cutting wildly through the air, Rua hacked a path for him through the press of bodies. Renwick hustled up the hillside to their awaiting comrades. Fear rose in Rua's throat as she watched her Fated limp up the hillside, legs barely able to make it to the road. They reached Talhan first, the Eagle grabbing Thador from Renwick's shoulders and guiding him to the ground. Renwick feverishly looked around, searching for an exemption from the death of his friend. Those emerald eyes landed on Rua, and they softened in a brief second of relief.

"Archers!" Renwick shouted to them. "In the woods."

Just as his warning reached them, an arrow flew from the far tree line, striking down one of their soldiers in the bog. Another arrow came whooshing out from the shadowed trees. Remy's magic managed to deflect the arrow before it struck another person. The arrows added to the chaos as the angry horde of *suraash* were turning the tides even more against them. Rua cast out her magic, feeling for the location of those archers, trying to hack them down blind as she had in the Temple of Hunasht. But the days of traveling through the cold with no food had tempered her powers. Her arms ached from holding aloft her sword alone. Blood still oozed down her face from her broken nose.

"Get to the others," Remy said, seeing Rua swaying on her feet. Too tired to protest, the adrenaline waning to utter fatigue, Rua blinked absently to her sister for a moment.

A shout snapped her out of it. Talhan let out a pained bark, an arrow protruding from his thigh.

Shit.

Rua dashed, her bare feet cutting across the jagged rock.

"Get behind the wagon!" she screamed, slicing down the last of the soldiers. The arrows were coming thick and fast, swarming the skies as the remaining Eastern soldiers retreated into the woods.

The onslaught of arrows was relentless. A shriek lodged in her throat as she watched Hale dart out from undercover to grab people to safety. Three arrows struck him in rapid succession, knocking him back with each blow, but he simply ripped them out and carried on. He wore the *Shil-de* ring, Rua remembered. He couldn't be killed.

Chest tightening, she found Renwick running through the chaos. He moved with incredible speed, dodging each arrow with seeming foresight. Rua's eyes widened as she gaped at her Fated. He Saw the arrows, he must have. He was using his blue witch magic.

Her comrades switched formation from fighting in a circle to dragging the wounded bodies behind one of the upturned wagons. Rua ran down to the space between them and the flying artillery, an arrow slamming straight into her chest like a punch.

"Rua!" Bri shouted as Rua ripped the arrow from her cloak and another struck her in the arm.

"I'm fine, the arrows can't hurt me," she yelled. "Keep going."

A mop of blond hair caught her eye, the figure now recognizable as he stood to his full height. Fenrin's eyes and hands glowed with bronze light, bottles of elixirs strapped in a belt diagonally across his chest. He was healing the fallen even while they were under fire.

Renwick grabbed Rua's arm, snapping her from her stupor and yanking her down to hide with them behind the wagon. He lifted his thumb up to her nose, though he did not touch it.

"I'm okay," she breathed, looking at his wounded leg seeping blood.

"I'm okay," Renwick echoed, panting.

"Did you get the Witches' Glass?"

Renwick's face broke as he shook his head.

The wagon at their backs rocked from the wave of *suraash* scrambling against it.

"If we can't save them, then we have to kill them," Rua said, making to rise before Renwick put his hand on her shoulder and pushed her back down. "We won't survive this otherwise."

"There's too many." His chest heaved. "If you attack them, you will die."

Rua's eyes flew wide. "You have Seen it?"

Those emerald eyes flickered blue as they watched her warily. "I have."

She yanked him into a tight embrace, breathing in his scent, tears springing to her eyes. At least she would die in his arms.

"Gods," Renwick gasped, looking down at Rua's hip.

The Immortal Blade beamed with glowing red light under his palm. Renwick pulled back, his eyes filled with blue magic as his flaming blue fingers touched the ruby pommel.

"A stone imbued with witch magic," he murmured, light strobing off his hands.

Time froze as Rua watched the buzzing magic of her sword hum into his fingertips. The curse said *a stone imbued with witch magic*—it did not say which stone.

As the screaming witches surged closer, Renwick squeezed his eyes shut and whispered, "*Dzraa divleur rek mofareis.*"

Then there was nothing but silence.

The arrows ceased, giving way to a stark stillness. A pile of *suraash* lay lifeless, while others were slowly coming to, as if waking from a dream. They cowered and cried, no longer raging beasts but fearful, broken souls. They were not monsters, only weapons wielded by a true evil.

As the dust settled, Baba Airu strode through the clearing, placing a gentle hand on the forehead of the nearest *suraash*. The witch surrendered to her Baba's touch, her trembling ceasing. Another *suraash* reached up to the High Priestess as one by one they lifted their hands to her in supplication.

Rua and Renwick looked around with wide, shocked eyes. They had survived the battle . . . they had broken the curse.

Baba Airu turned to Rua, a soft smile playing on her face as another *suraash* reached up to take her hand. Her arms faintly glowed blue as she held the witch's hand, until the witch's quaking spasms ceased. Rua had never seen such magic. It looked as if she were absorbing the lingering effects of the curse into her own body.

As she rose to step toward Baba Airu, Rua's voice was tinted with surprise. "You came."

"My people needed me," Baba Airu said, her voice so steady and calm, as if trying to pull the panic from the air. Her head tipped toward the ground. "As do yours."

Rua scanned out around her at the piles of pale, lifeless bodies, her eyes landing on Thador again.

Ragged breaths hoisted Thador's chest, his face draining of color, the mirror of Balorn's dying face a moment before.

A pained gasp rang out beside them as Aneryn approached and stooped beside the giant warrior. Thador raised a trembling hand up to her cheek, his eyes looking back to each and every blue witch around him. He marked each one with his gaze.

"Don't you dare save me. Any of you," he said, his lips pulling to one side as the sound of blood rattled in his chest. "Your lives are worth more than mine."

"No," Aneryn whispered, heavy tears sliding down her cheeks.

"You'll take care of Ehiris for me?" he whispered to Aneryn.

She nodded, biting her wobbling lip between her teeth as his eyes began to glaze.

"No, no, no," Bri shouted, the sound of slapping coming from behind them. "Tal, come on."

Rua whirled. Bri crouched over her twin propped against a rock. Talhan's face was gaunt and drawn. A thin trail of blood leaked from his lips. Rua scanned the warrior wildly for more injuries as his sister peeled open his fighting leathers, revealing a stab wound to the chest. Rua's whole body froze. It looked like the size of a throwing knife, viciously deep, blood dripping down his paling chest. Bri desperately pressed her bloodied, shaking hands to the wound. How had he kept fighting for so long? He ripped the arrow from his outer thigh, chest rising and falling rapidly.

Fenrin raced to Talhan, uncorking a bottle with his teeth and pouring his brown witch potions into the stab wound at the center of Talhan's chest.

"It is too late, Fen," Talhan wheezed. "Save it for the others."

"Come on, Tal," Fenrin gritted out, shoving away the warrior's trembling hands. "I can save you."

Fenrin's glowing brown fingers pressed his potion into Talhan's chest, urging his fae healing to quicken. The brown witch magic worked on their potions and elixirs, not on the bodies themselves. Fenrin pushed more of his power into his magical potions, even as he was applying them. Sweat broke out across his brow, his biceps straining as he pushed into Talhan's chest.

Bri's body shook violently, silent sobs racking through the normally stoic, even-keeled warrior. Distraught and panicked, she darted her golden eyes to the witches, landing on Renwick, staring into his glowing blue eyes.

"Is he going to be okay?" she whispered, clenching her fists so tightly her knuckles turned white.

"I can't say," Renwick breathed, lost in his vision.

"What do you mean you can't say?" Bri hissed.

"I have Seen two futures," Renwick said, moving over to Talhan and crouching beside him. The warrior's golden eyes blinked at Renwick as if he were a stranger. "Do you want to know what I have Seen?"

Renwick leaned in and whispered into Talhan's ear. The Eagle's chest spasmed as he nodded, a faint smile pulling at his lips.

"Did you know?" Renwick asked.

Talhan took another shaky breath. "I had hoped."

Renwick peered at Talhan, a silent conversation seemingly passing between them. Talhan grimaced, lifting his hand to Renwick and shaking it. A deal sealed. A promise, though Rua did not know what.

Talhan's cheeks pinked up again, the brown witch magic beginning to course through his veins. The group waiting with bated breath around them let out a collective sigh. He was gravely injured, but for the first moment, there was a glimmer of hope that he would survive.

Renwick stood from beside the Eagle and turned back to Aneryn and Thador. Lifeless eyes stared up at the circling hawk in the sky.

Thador was gone. Renwick's face broke, that calm mask slipping away to utter devastation. He fell to his knees beside his friend. Rua instantly dropped beside him, uncaring as the rock sliced into her legs. She grabbed Renwick, pulling him into her as he sobbed into her shoulder. For a long time in his life, Thador had been his only friend in a court of evil fae.

Rua clung to her Fated, promising vengeance even as her own tears fell. They would find Augustus Norwood. They would halt his terrible plans. One friend was saved from the brink of death, another lost over its edge, an edge they had all come so close to. The solemn silence hung heavy around them as they stared out at all the fallen, the only sound the forlorn calls of a hawk from the sky.

# CHAPTER THIRTY-ONE

It was the middle of the night as they crowded around the tavern table in Valtene. A fire roared to life at the end of the long room. Empty trays lined the wooden table, only a few nuts and roasted potatoes left amongst the feast they had just eaten. Empty pitchers of wine dotted down the table. The crew had drunk the tavern dry. They laughed and chatted in the crazed way of people who had survived near death. Talhan had demanded to be part of the festivities, propped in a chair with heavy blankets and pillows Hale had stolen from a room above. Talhan now slept even as they roared and cackled, their laughter loud enough for the Gods to hear. It was what they did when someone they loved died.

This fae celebration of life felt so foreign to Rua. Remy, too, seemed confused by it all. The witches mourned their dead in solemn prayers and muttered chants over lit candles. Seemingly more subdued than the rest of the crew, Fenrin had already retired to his lodgings. Aneryn was nearly asleep, leaning heavily against Bri's shoulder.

Their group had occupied every spare room at every inn and tavern in Valtene. The High Mountain faction would rest and recover before the journey back to Yexshire. They would wait until the western road was cleared. Talhan was still not well enough for a long, jostling carriage ride anyway.

Rua still feared there would be Balorn loyalists in the town, but news of his death would spread. They had frantically made a fae fire when they reached the town. Bern reported that Yexshire was safe; so was the Lyrei Basin according to Berecraft. Neelo said there was no sign of Augustus in the South. But the Western Court was quiet. Not a single reply came from Swifthill despite their many efforts to reach them. Rua feared what that would mean for the Western Court. They had sent a rider from Valtene to the capital to see if it was true. Had the Western Queen been killed? The lack of response made Rua fear the worst.

Hale threw his hand of cards down onto the table as Renwick chuckled.

"How do you do that?" Hale groused.

"I would say it's luck," Renwick said with a drunken grin, "but we both know it's skill."

The High Mountain King had procured a pack of cards from somewhere in the town. Rua knew what the gesture meant. Renwick had lost his friend that day.

Remy leaned into Rua. "You and that sword were magnificent together."

Baba Airu was right. It was witch magic tethered to the blade. Wielding it with anger and fear had made her rash and violent. No better than Balorn, but . . . she looked at Renwick and then to Aneryn, Bri, and Tal. Now she felt something slower and steadier warming her veins. It pulsed there always, a well she could dip into. There would be more anger and fear and pain, she was certain of it, but she would make that warmth, that love, count for more. That was the power she would use to be *Mhenissa*.

"Just as you and that amulet are," Rua replied.

"The talismans of our people." Remy touched the red amulet around her neck. "I suppose the Immortal Blade belongs in the North now."

"It does not matter which color magic it was forged with," Rua said.

She had spent her whole life separating the covens in her mind, but they were all witches. She wondered if any witch had ever tried to use another coven's talismans to cast their own spells before. They had always been so proudly divided, it probably had never been attempted. "It is witch magic. It was always meant to protect the witches, whichever court it resides in."

Remy just hummed a low, sad sound.

"I am still of High Mountain blood. I still have red witch magic." Rua turned to her sister. "It does not matter where I live. I am still your family."

Remy's brown eyes glanced to her, face softening as she wrapped her arm around Rua.

"I'm glad you're my family, Ru." The sound of her nickname made Rua smile.

"Even if I'm a surly grump all the time?"

Remy laughed. "Yes, even then."

Renwick stood from the benches, stretching his neck and rolling his shoulders.

"I'm going to bed," he said in a quiet voice. "Good night."

Rua made to move, but Renwick gave her a look. "Enjoy this time with your family," he said with a half-smile. Rua watched as he stalked out the door, heading to the inn down the road.

She felt the pain radiating off him like a living thing. She knew he couldn't take the happy distractions anymore. He needed to go mourn his friend. Her chest cracked open at that. He was so used to walking away, always suffering alone, just as she had always done.

Remy followed Rua's gaze to the darkened doorway. "Go."

"I'll see you in the morning," Rua said, looking out to the others, her eyes snagging on Aneryn sleeping on Bri's shoulder.

Remy snorted. "I will get your friend to bed."

"Good night," Rua said to the table, and they all turned their glassy, drunken eyes to her and waved.

Rua moved down the streets dusted in powdered white. She shuddered, thinking of the Witches' Glass still around the neck of Augustus Norwood. What could that magic stone do now that the *suraash* were free from their curse? How had he accessed the ancient violet witch magic? She had thought Balorn's death would be the end of her troubles, but it felt as if they were just beginning. An image flashed in her mind of Remy on that hillside, backlit in hazy light, holding her bow. It bolstered her knowing that from now on, whatever she was faced with, they would face it together.

Her ankle wobbled, nearly stumbling on an empty bottle discarded in the middle of the street. She had been so lost in her thoughts, she hadn't spotted them. On the stoop to her left sat two drunk old men, passing another bottle between them. They were the only residents of Valtene still awake at this hour.

They chuckled, looking at the sword on her hip. They must not have known who she was. How strange she must look to them—how little they knew.

Dropping her gaze, she intended to move past when one called, "Playing swordsman?" Rua braced for it, that raging storm building inside her, but the Immortal Blade sat silent in its scabbard. "You're a little girl."

Their mouths dropped agape as she looked at them. "And?" Her lips twisted upward into a grin that struck more fear into them than the sword she wielded. As their eyes widened, she released a deep belly laugh that erupted from her, morphing into a witch's cackle. There were a dozen ways she could kill them and all she wanted to do was laugh at the absurdity of it all. She was a girl, a fae, a royal, and a warrior . . . and to these men she had nothing to prove.

They scrambled up the stoop and into the darkened doorway. Chuckles still vibrated from her chest as she moved down the lane. When she spotted the lamp outside the inn, still flickering as she passed the rows of darkened shops, her sniggering ceased. Her Fated had left to mourn. It was a strange duality, her joy and sorrow, how strange it felt to know that both feelings existed within her at the same time—both real and honest—both lighting different parts of her soul all at once.

She snuck into the shadowed entryway and tiptoed up the stairs, moving silently down the hall to Renwick's room. The door was unlocked.

She crept into the quiet darkness, finding Renwick sitting at the edge of the large bed, head in his hands, shoulders slumped. Walking slowly over, she sat beside him as she listened to his sharp breaths. She rested her warm hand on his back, and his sobs grew. Her heart ached for him. He had lost another brother.

"I'm sorry," he sniffed, wiping his eyes with the back of his hands.

Rua grasped his fingers. "Never be sorry for this, never," she whispered, begging that he trust her. "I want it all, Renwick, every dark corner of your soul."

He looked up at her with welling eyes, hearing back the words he had promised to her.

"We keep desperately throwing things into that chasm, knowing it will never fill and we will lose ourselves trying to fill it. Let it rise to meet us instead. We won't hide these things away anymore, not from each other," she vowed. "I will lean on you, if you will lean on me."

Tipping his head down, Renwick leaned his forehead against hers. Rua wiped his tears with her thumbs as he planted a salty kiss to her lips.

"I will lean on you," he promised, his lips against her mouth.

Rua kissed him back harder in response, his hands reaching up and fisting in her hair with desperation. She wrapped her arms around his neck as he turned and pinned her into the soft mattress. She knew how badly they both needed to feel that promise fulfilled. It did not fix the darkness. It did not take away the sorrow. But they would deny it no longer. Let it exist. No more hiding their pain. They had each other now.

~

Rua leaned back against Renwick's chest as they sat on the snowy rooftop of the inn. They had climbed up through the skylight and now sat wrapped in a heavy wool blanket, watching the sunrise. Renwick wrapped his arms tighter around her, his lips skimming her ear as he smiled. The stars still twinkled in the sky as the horizon brightened to a faint golden glow.

Rua wondered if her sister and friends still slept at the tables of the Wyxshire Wood tavern. The tavern servants would be certainly shocked to find the King and Queen of the High Mountain Court asleep on their tables come morning. It seemed to be the way of Remy and her court, never sleeping in their fancy beds. Rua supposed she was a part of that too. Now that she was Renwick's Fated, she was a member of the Northern Court as well. She had two homes. She had more people. They would all embrace her, she knew, if only she let them.

"What did you have to show me before the sun came up?" Rua murmured, sleepily surveying the quiet streets. In the town stables, the soft whinnying of horses greeted them.

"I didn't finish showing you the stars," Renwick said, running his hand down her bare arm, warm in their wrapped blanket. "We got interrupted last time."

Rua thought to the explosions of violet smoke, to the pack of wild witches, and the freezing plunge into the ice lake. "That's one way of putting it."

Renwick huffed. It seemed so easy to make him smile now. Balorn was dead, and Augustus's army was in tatters. The war with the Norwood Prince was not over, but the battle had been won. He would need time to regroup, and they would have time to hunt him down. Bri and Carys had already volunteered to find Augustus. They would leave that morning, for it was already the new day. The soft yellow light on the horizon promised to banish the stars for another cycle.

Renwick pointed up toward the constellations to the far left. Rua followed his finger to the six stars forming a circle low on the horizon. "Callix Occidentalis, they call it the Sapphire Ring. It haloes directly above the new Palace of Murreneir."

Rua thought of his cloak, the one that had been torn from him during the ambush only a handful of days before. The remnants of that day and the days in Balorn's captivity still marred their skin. They were broken and gleeful at the same time, heartbroken for their losses and joyful that they had survived. All those scattered feelings coalesced into one.

Rua traced the circle of stars in the air, thinking to his new crest—the ring around the sword and crown. A beautiful new crest. It suited him perfectly, elegant, regal, precise.

Heavy lashes slanted down to her as Renwick reached up with his thumb and stroked her bottom lip. She leaned back to look him in the eyes. His cheeks dimpled as he stared at her.

"I'm glad you chose the Sapphire Ring," Rua murmured, mesmerized by those emerald eyes. "It is like a crown atop our palace." Renwick's face split into a wide grin. "What?"

"I just like when you say 'our,'" he said, his hand dropping from her face. "I chose it for another reason too."

"Oh?" Rua furrowed her brow at him.

Rua's lips parted as he fumbled in his pocket. She watched the King in awe as he produced a ring. Rua gaped down at the diamond circled by six sapphires.

"This was my mother's ring," Renwick said, his voice shaking despite his smile, as if he weren't sure of what Rua would say. "It was in my pocket when we were attacked, and I thought it was gone but . . . Aneryn found it in Balorn's belongings and . . . I'm rambling." Renwick cringed, and as he nervously smiled at her, Rua's mind went completely blank. "Ruadora Clodia Dammacus." Rua blanched at her full name, making Renwick chuckle. "You shine brighter than every star in the sky. You are brave, cunning, and caring . . . though you would never admit it," he huffed. "You have saved my people, and even more so, you have saved me. I have loved you with all my soul from the moment I first Saw you in my mind's eye."

He stared down at her like he Saw all the way back to that first memory of her.

"Are you asking me something?" Rua prompted as his mind wandered away.

Renwick laughed at himself. He had forgotten the most important part. "Will you marry me?"

Rua was certain she was bursting, like her joy might explode out of her, as she said, "Yes."

Renwick was instantly cupping the back of her neck as he pulled her into a burning kiss. Rua threaded her hands through his hair, holding him just as tightly to her.

Breaking their kiss with the widest grin, Renwick slid the ring on her finger. The heavy weight of the diamond made the ring tip to the side.

"I'll fix that." He laughed.

Rua kissed him again. "Don't bother." She grinned. "I intend to employ a team of green witches to cook us the finest meals in Okrith. My fingers will be so plump the ring will never come off."

"Excellent." Renwick wrapped his arms around her as they looked out over Valtene. Rua rested her head against his hard chest. By the time the ice melted, they would be ready to move into their new castle. They would soon be hiring carpenters and decorators to outfit their home. The gold Hennen once hoarded would line every pocket in the Northern Court, from the masons to the weavers to the blacksmiths.

Their happy moment was cut short by the sound of whispered, snarling voices. Rua glanced down to the quiet streets below. The Twin Eagles were awake, looking disheveled and scowling at each other. Talhan swayed, moving with a deep limp. Rua was surprised he could stand at all.

"You would leave just for her?" Talhan asked as Bri stormed toward the stables.

"She's not just some girl, Tal," Bri growled back. "She wouldn't ask for help if she didn't need it. I will still be back east in time for the games. Go back to the tavern; you're too injured to be out here."

"And what about the hunt for Augustus? Isn't that more important?" Talhan grabbed Bri's arm, making her whirl.

Rua didn't breathe as she looked down at them. This didn't seem like a conversation they should interrupt. Renwick's silence indicated he agreed.

"Once you heal, you and Carys will find Augustus, no problem," Bri said. "The West is in shambles. They need help."

"Then we can send help!" Talhan shouted. "Why does it have to be you?"

"Because Delta asked me to come, and she wouldn't ask unless she really meant it."

"You don't need to do this. You don't owe the West anything," Talhan snarled. "We swore we would never go back to Swifthill."

"Things change, Tal," Bri said. Talhan looked at her like she had smacked him in the face.

"Yes," he said, looking her up and down. "They certainly do. Mother and Father will be so proud."

Bri rocked backward, and for a moment, Rua thought the female Eagle would strike her brother, but she didn't.

"You're a real piece of shit, you know that?" Bri growled, adjusting the shoulders on her pack. "Tell the others I said goodbye."

"No."

"Fine," she spat, stalking into the stables.

Talhan's limp worsened as he thundered off back toward the tavern.

Rua blinked at the space where the two had stood. It felt jarring to see the Eagles fighting. Renwick's warm hand squeezed her side.

"The life of a royal fae," Renwick murmured into her hair. "Celebrating and fighting and making decisions that affect the whole continent within the span of an hour. Painting with every color all at once."

Turning to her Fated, Rua cupped his cheek. "I need to go say goodbye before she leaves."

Renwick kissed her forehead. "I know."

"I love you," Rua said, brushing her lips to his again, deeply breathing his scent.

Renwick used his thumb to twist the heavy diamond ring upright again. "I love you too, my Fated."

# CHAPTER THIRTY-TWO

The sky filled with streaks of pink and gold light as she stepped into the silent street. The town of Valtene still slept. Rua was about to move toward the stables when something to her left caught her eye. Near the end of the road where the town faded into the forest, a tall figure stood. From his height alone, Rua knew who it was.

She had intended to catch Bri before she left, but instead found herself winding her way toward Fenrin. He stood in the middle of the street, staring up at a derelict shop. The main houses faded into ramshackle dwellings as she neared. It looked like the town had been attacked or invaded more than once over the years. The Northern skirmishes were evident from the caved-in ceilings and charred windowsills.

As she reached Fenrin, Rua saw the splintering sign: Doledir Apothecary. The windows were smashed and the door broken in. Drifts of snow scattered the floors, and the shelves were stripped bare of any goods.

Fenrin was so lost in his thoughts, wringing his hat in his hands, he didn't acknowledge her until she spoke.

"Did you know them?" she whispered.

He didn't look at her as he responded. "Yes."

She stood beside him for a long moment before asking, "Do you want to go inside?"

He shook his head, his straw-blond hair falling into his eyes. "Do you ever wonder if you've made your family proud? If your ancestors are watching?"

Her eyes darted to him as he finally glanced down at her. Simply nodding, he gave her a sad smile.

"They would be proud of you," Rua murmured. "I'm sure of it. You saved Talhan's life today and many others."

"Renwick saved him," Fenrin said, a tinge of bitterness in his voice. The towering giant beside her seemed unwilling to see himself the way the rest of them did. Rua knew the feeling all too well.

She huffed a laugh. "You think whatever Renwick whispered in his ear would have done anything without your magic healing his wound?" She grinned up at the brown witch. "You think his whispers stopped the bleeding?"

Fenrin's lips pulled up into a begrudging smirk. "I would say you sound a lot like your sister right now, but I know you wouldn't like it."

Rua shrugged, looking up at the golden sun peeking above the trees. "There are far worse people I could be compared to."

That made him chuckle. Something in her eased at the sound. She was determined to wring it out of him, and she didn't know why. Maybe she felt drawn to the familiarity of his pain.

The clop of horse hooves sounded down the road, and Rua looked up to see Bri riding toward them.

"Stealing horses?" Rua asked, the lingering smell of hay wafting toward her as she crossed her arms.

"Delta contacted me through the fae fire," Bri said, glancing toward the brown witch. "You okay, Fen?"

Rua snorted. Even as she absconded in the early dawn light, the Eagle checked on her friend. The brown witch nodded.

"How far to Swifthill?" he asked, putting his woolen cap back on his head.

The warm sun heated her face, banishing the chill. A promise of spring was on the horizon this morning, still far in the future but assuring its arrival.

Bri shifted, getting comfortable in the saddle. "Three days." The mare she chose seemed docile—not the warhorses she usually rode. "I am needed there," she added tightly, as though bracing for another battle.

"I know," Rua said. "I'm not here to stop you. Although, I am remembering you shouting at me through a fae fire for leaving without telling you."

"I'm a terrible hypocrite, Ru. You should know by now to listen to my advice, not follow my actions." Bri gave her a wink.

"Swifthill—how bad is it?" Fenrin said into the quiet. Rua considered him, wondering if he had family in the capital of the Western Court too.

"It's bad," Bri replied, pulling out gloves from her saddlebag and shoving her fingers into them. She clenched her hand, stretching the leather. "Augustus has the witch hunters in his pocket. He is offering a bounty on the heads of the Western fae royals and their courtiers. I suppose they are fae hunters now."

"No," Rua gasped. The Western Court had been rife with witch hunters since the Siege of Yexshire.

"The Western Queen has left them unchecked for too long, and now look what it has done," Fenrin growled. "Those witch hunters are their own breed of fae, vicious as anything."

Rua remembered the prophecy of the Eagles, tilting her head up at Bri. "Are you planning on taking the throne?"

Bri and Fenrin both erupted into laughter, as if her question were a brilliant joke.

"Gods no," the Eagle said. "I hate the West. But Abalina Thorne is struggling to fight off her own people, and for some reason those same people support me, believe I should be their ruler. I need to help Abalina prove them wrong."

Rua's eyebrows shot up as she guffawed. "You're helping the Western Queen so you can exempt yourself from future responsibility to her court?"

"Exactly." Bri scanned the rows of decrepit townhouses, years of war evident in every shard of broken glass. "We need to end this. The West has suffered enough . . . and then I will be off to the Eastern Court, where I intend to win myself my own crown." Bri winked at her. "*That* is the true meaning of the prophecy."

Rua remembered the prophecy told to her on Remy's birthday: *The Eagles are born—Briata will seize the crown from its sovereign.* It made sense that it would be the crown of the Eastern Court now. Even with all of Norwood's calculations, he did not know the Eagles would vie for his own crown.

"Sounds simple when you put it like that. Save a kingdom. Win a crown." Rua laughed, squinting into the morning beams of light. "You will make a good ruler, Bri."

Bri looked pointedly at the ring on Rua's finger. "As will you."

Rua moved aside, Bri's horse chuffing.

"Stay safe, Bri," Fenrin said, stepping out of the way as he took one more forlorn glance at the Doledir Apothecary. "Thank you for helping the West."

Bri bobbed her head at Fenrin.

"I will miss you," Rua added as Bri's horse shuffled a step.

"I'll miss you too, Ru." Bri smiled down at her, eyes twinkling. "Though I'm looking forward to getting out of this bloody snow."

"If the North hosted a Spring Equinox celebration . . . ," Rua asked, awkwardly clasping her hands. "Would you come?" It was a sudden thought. Rua wasn't even sure she could make such a decision, but they would have to host a celebration in the North at some point or another. It was the first time she had ever asked someone to visit her. It was the first time she wanted to try. She'd shove her awkwardness and fear aside to keep whatever friendship they had built going.

"Count me in," Bri said as her golden eyes flitted to the woods ahead.

Rua glanced beyond the horse to see Renwick backlit by the pre-dawn light, watching at the steps of the inn, waiting for her.

"Say goodbye to the others for me?" Bri asked Fenrin as he stroked her horse's neck.

"I will." Fenrin nodded.

"I'm sorry about Tal," Rua added.

"He'll be fine." Bri rubbed the back of her neck. "He'll get over it, eventually. We'll laugh it off or it'll come to blows; either way it'll resolve itself."

"Is that what it means to be a sister?" Rua grinned.

Bri chuckled. "You see, Ru? You and Remy are already great at it."

Rua gave Bri one last smile, leaving the Eagle to ride off toward the woods. Fenrin turned and strode through the broken-down doorway of the apothecary, deciding to venture into its depths after all. Rua watched him for a moment, another reminder of all they had lost. She thought she was alone in her darkness, but it was all around her. So many of her friends were displaced, strangers to their people, hurt and broken. No one had made it through the last fourteen years unscathed. But they had found each other. They were no longer alone. And for the first time, Rua was determined to hold on to them as fiercely as she hoped they would hold on to her.

Renwick's posture straightened slightly as she approached, even though his back was turned, basking in the dawning light. She threaded her arm through his, steering him back to the inn as the sun hit their faces.

"Let's get to bed." She yawned.

Renwick kissed the top of her head. "I like the way you're thinking."

"To sleep," Rua insisted as they trudged up the snowy steps.

"Mm-hmm." Renwick smirked, seeming to know her exact train of thought.

She threaded her fingers through his, a playful smile pulling up her lips. She had promised herself she would make the most of the daylight hours, after all.

Stopping Renwick on the stoop, she traced a finger up his jawline. "We are holding a Spring Equinox celebration, by the way."

Renwick grinned, leaning in to brush his lips against hers. Tingles echoed through her body as he whispered, "Anything for you, my Queen."

Rua smiled against his mouth, clasping her hands around his neck. She would give herself over to this happiness. The fear of losing it would no longer hold her back. However long it lasted, she would make it count for something. She felt the darkness and the joy. One did not deny the other. She could hold it all.

# ACKNOWLEDGMENTS

To my #Booktok fam, thank you for being the most incredible, kind, and uplifting community! Your support and encouragement helped make this book happen and I love getting to connect with so many amazing people while also making goofy, ridiculous videos! And thank you to everyone in the High Mountaineers reader group. It is an absolute joy connecting with you!

Thank you to my gorgeous family for all of your love and support. To my husband, thank you for encouraging me and helping puzzle our days together to make it work for our family. We've been on so many adventures around the world together and I'm so grateful for your support on this new one! And thank you to my silly, smart, brave kids—I hope you always remember that no one decides how bright you shine but you.

Thank you to my mom for being my hype person, helping me ship my signed bookplates, and for always encouraging my stories. Thank you to my dad for your willingness to listen to me panic-call you for advice and always cheering me on.

Thank you to Bianca Bordianu from Moonpress designs for this stunning cover. I've loved working on this series with you.

Thank you to Aria J. for the editing services and for rescuing me

ACKNOWLEDGMENTS

when I was in a pinch! It was fantastic working with you! And thank you to Kelli from KDL editing for the proofing!

To my amazing team of alpha and beta readers, thank you for helping make this book the best it could be!

Thank you to Norma from Norma's Nook Proofreading! You are equal parts proofreader and therapist and I so appreciate you!

Thank you to Kristen Timofeev for the design for the Map of Okrith!

Thank you for reading Rua's story! The journey continues in *The Rogue Crown*, The Five Crowns of Okrith Book Three. Turn the page for a sneak peek!

Don't miss any of the adventure—Read all of the Okrith Novellas for FREE by signing up to A.K. Mulford's newsletter!

*www.akmulford.com*

# THE ROGUE CROWN

The pleasant hum of liquor buzzed through her limbs as Bri wound her way down the narrow paths. Her hand skimmed over the curving walls as she ducked under clotheslines.

Her mind focused on the information she had just learned. Someone in the palace knew more than they were saying. She was becoming increasingly convinced that it was an inside job. No one was beyond suspicion.

Shouts rang out from up ahead. "Stop, thief!"

Bri rolled her eyes. Of course.

The buildings were different, the food unfamiliar, but these seedy parts of a city were always the same. She turned the corner just in time to see a cloaked figure racing down the path. One snarling, muscled fae chased after them. The thief darted down a side road, one Bri knew led back the way she came.

With a smirk, she turned around, putting her plans for sleep on hold for another hour. Maybe this thief knew about the recent events in the castle. Her grin widened. It didn't matter—she loved the chase.

Leaping over piles of refuse, she barreled toward the other end of the alley. Judging by the brief glimpse of the thief, they were an entire head shorter than her, with heavy, thundering footsteps. She estimated the time it would take them to run the long way round. They were headed toward the markets. Smart. The perfect place to get lost amongst the labyrinth of stalls. First, they would have to make it down the road up ahead, and those fae chasing after the cloaked figure looked like they were gaining on them. If Bri judged it just right, the thief would be stumbling out the other side . . .

Now.

She collided with the figure, knocking them back. The cloak didn't slip from the thief's face as they yanked a hand axe from their belt, their other hand clutching a large coin purse.

A fae lay behind the thief, clutching his stomach and groaning. Despite being smaller than Bri, they had already incapacitated him before she'd caught up.

Bri smirked. "Impressive."

"Get out of my way," a feminine voice snarled.

Bri's brows lifted, expecting an entirely different sounding person. The thief turned toward the noise of feet echoing off the cobblestones.

"What did you steal?" Bri asked, her hand drifting toward her amber dagger.

"Something that shouldn't have belonged to them in the first place," the voice hissed. Whoever this thief was, they had a deep, resonant tone—warm, yet raspy. It made Bri squint as if trying to see through the shadowed hood.

Bri toed the fallen male with her boot. "I'm glad they deserved it."

"Indeed."

*Indeed.* Not the tone she'd expect from a thief.

Five more lumbering fae turned the corner. They were muscular and stout, with menacing faces that fit perfectly in these parts. They were either the lackeys of potions dealers or brothel guards. Armed to the teeth, all five looked like they knew how to fight.

"Fighting or running?" Bri asked, watching as the fae horde charged them.

The cloaked figure was already turning. "Running," the thief said, bolting down the alleyway.

Bri dashed after the swishing cloak. "Good idea."

"I don't need your help," the thief growled. "Just stay out of my way."

Bri ignored their warning, darting through the narrow bottleneck of rounded houses and following them into the markets. They dove into the maze of darkened stalls. Shop owners had closed up for the night. Empty tables stretched out as far as the eye could see, covered in abandoned bare baskets and empty crates. Heavy blankets strung from ropes partitioned the stalls.

Bri kicked over a table behind her, then another, forcing the fae chasing them to leap over or go around. She followed the shadowed figure under two heavy walls of blankets. The thief panted heavy breaths, their speed dwindling, making it easier to keep up. They wouldn't outrun the fae chasing them.

"Turn right," the thief called, ducking under another curtain.

Bri's arms wheeled as she popped up from behind the curtain, nearly colliding with a thick wood pole that held up the thatched roof. That would slow the fae down. The thief and Bri careened through the stalls, setting a distance between them and their assailants. Bri spotted another square of blankets—a makeshift changing room, perhaps—and made a quick decision.

She snatched the back of the winded thief's cloak and yanked them into the changing room.

"Wh—"

"Shh," Bri whispered.

Their chests rose and fell against each other in the inky blackness. Even with her fae sight and the bright moon beyond the curtains, she couldn't see the cloaked figure a hair's breadth away.

Her heartbeat pulsed in her ears as she listened for the heavy footfall of the fae chasing them. Their footsteps faltered.

"Where did she go?" one snarled.

"She stole the night's earnings, that fucking bitch," another growled.

The sound of their boots grew closer. The pursuers kicked over a table that skidded across the earthen floor. One brushed against the wall of the pair's hiding spot and the thief sucked in a shallow breath, tensing. Bri gripped the hilt of her dagger, her muscles coiled like an asp ready to strike. This thief seemed like a good enough fighter. They could probably take on five of the fae if they had to.

"Show your face, Airev," another shouted.

*Airev.* It was a Mhenbic word, though Bri didn't know what it meant. She barely spoke the witches' native tongue, and that word eluded her.

"Footprints this way," another voice shouted far in the distance. "Let's go."

383

The fae took off through the markets. Bri waited until her straining ears couldn't hear them anymore and she finally let out a sigh.

"What a bunch of idiots," the thief muttered, brushing their cloak against Bri to step out into the open air again. Airev sat, leaning against the upturned table.

"They seemed like they could hold their own in a fight," Bri said, leaning around the giant beam holding up the market roof. "But clearly not the smartest bunch."

"Maybe they think footprints only last for an hour," the thief mused. Bri chuckled, stooping to sit on the dusty, cold earth. "Give them five minutes to get a bit further, and then you can head on your way."

"Do you want to tell me what that was all about?"

"Not particularly."

Bri huffed. "Why do they call you Airev?"

Airev turned their axe over in their hand. It was a simple weapon— the short handle barely long enough to grip with a curving long blade that hooked at the end. It wasn't as bejeweled as Bri's daggers, but it looked like it could inflict some serious damage.

"Some people profit from the fear of others," Airev said, tossing the coin purse in their hands. "I steal it and give back to those brave enough to stand up to those beasts."

Bri cocked her head, assessing them. "A worthy pastime, I suppose."

"And what are you doing out here?"

"I've come to Swifthill to investigate the murder of the Queen."

"I know why you're in Swifthill, Briata Catullus. Why are you in back taverns of Southside?"

Bri scowled, realizing she'd let her glamour slip. The alcohol mixed with the adrenaline of the chase made her forget she was meant to appear as a human.

A thin braid spilled from the thief's hood, its ends adorned with golden rings. The thief swept the braid back into the recesses of their hood, but it was too late.

"I should have known from your sour tone," Bri huffed, "and that scent. The same one clinging to the halls."

The thief went still. "What?"

"You smell like jasmine and rose oil and wear gold in your hair. You speak like royalty," Bri said, reaching a hand out and tugging back the thief's hood. "But that's because you are, aren't you, Princess?

# ABOUT THE AUTHOR

A.K. Mulford is a bestselling fantasy author and former wildlife biologist who swapped rehabilitating monkeys for writing novels. She/They are inspired to create diverse stories that transport readers to new realms, making them fall in love with fantasy for the first time or all over again. She now lives in New Zealand with her husband and two young human primates, creating lovable fantasy characters and making ridiculous TikToks (@akmulfordauthor)